Disney Fairies

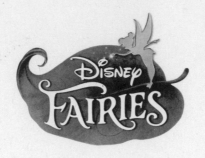

Tinker Bell's Secret

By Haruhi Kato

TOKYOPOP

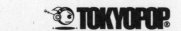

HAMBURG // HONG KONG // LOS ANGELES // TOKYO

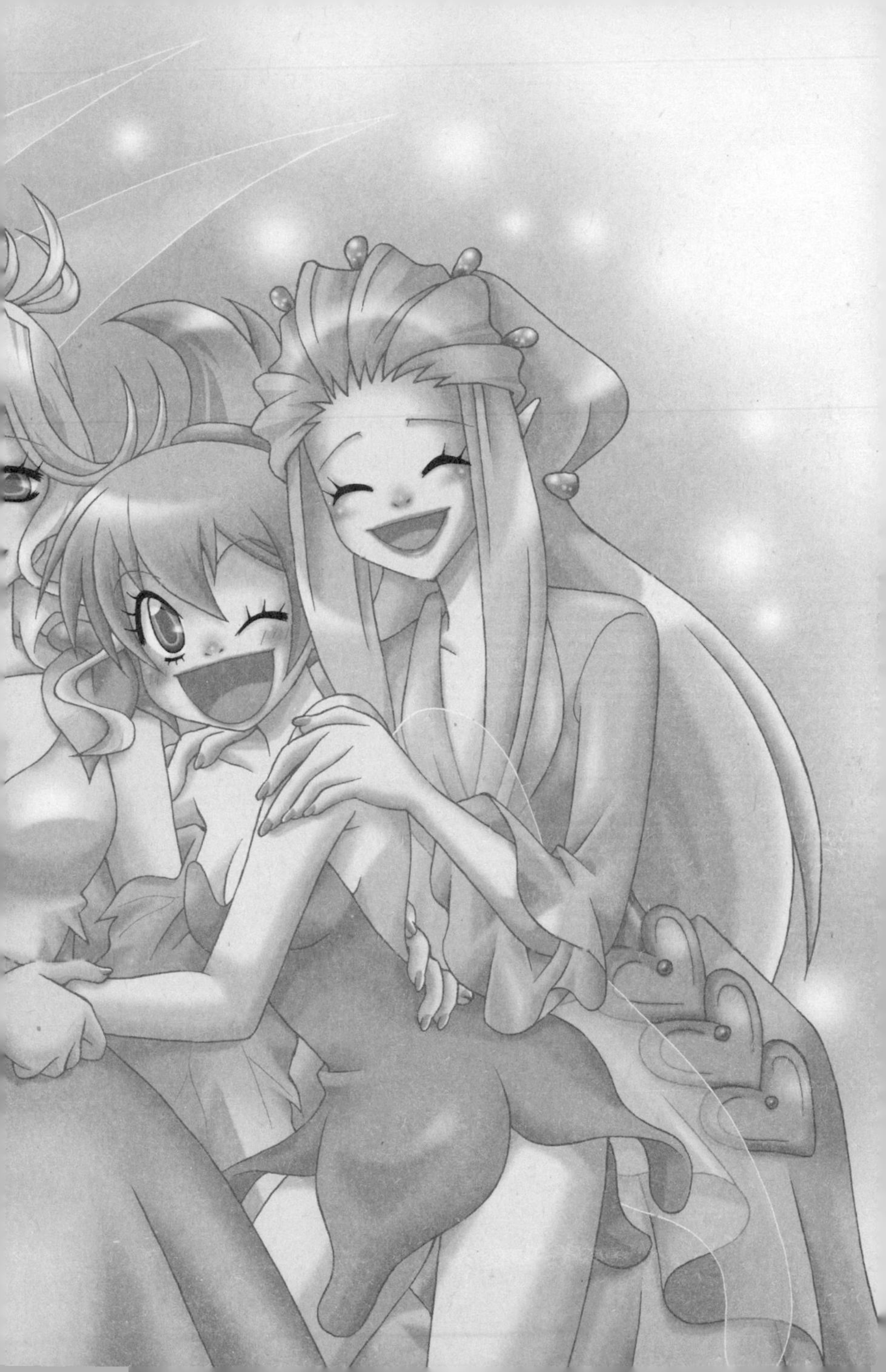

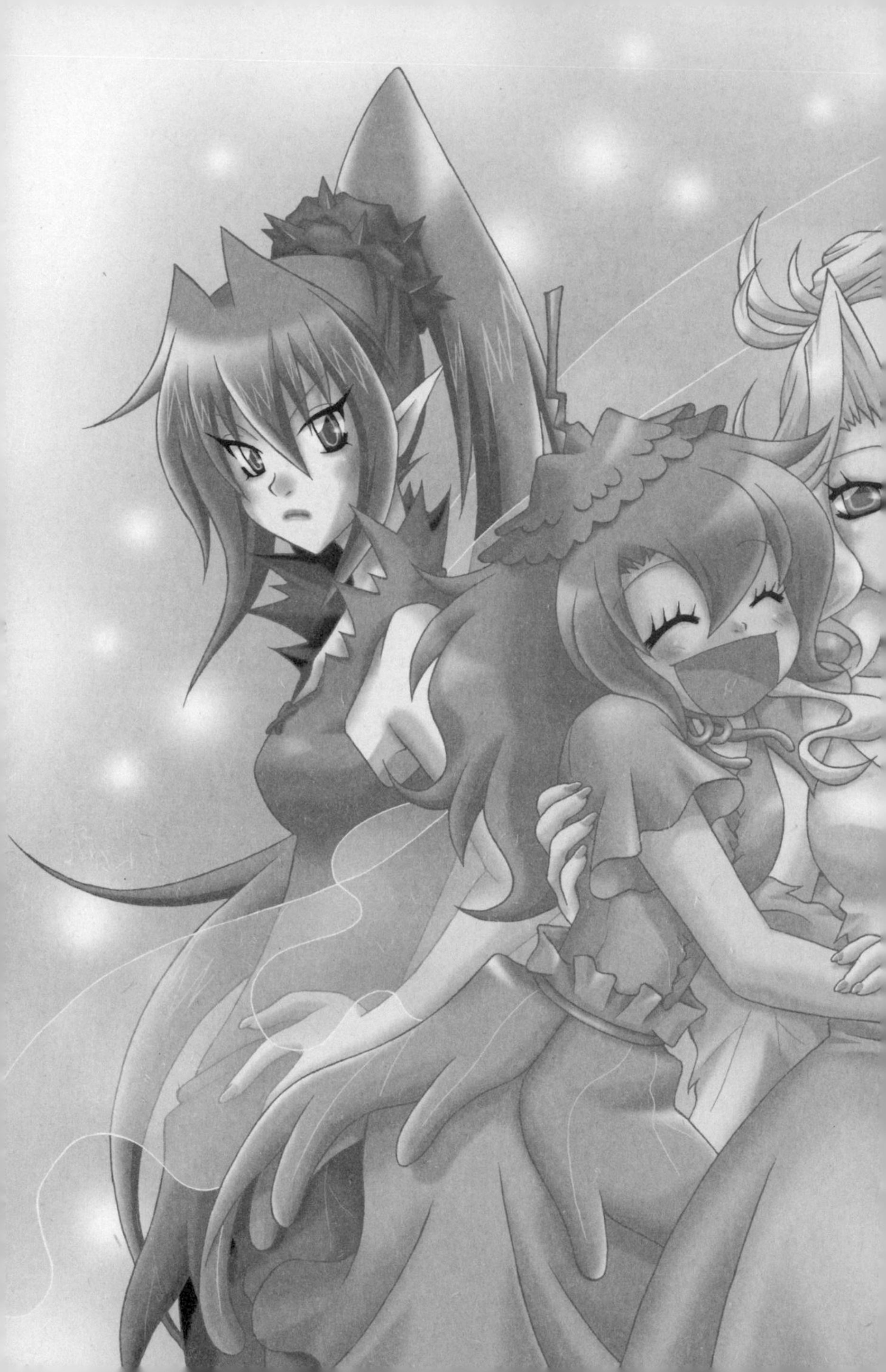

THE FAIRIES OF PIXIE HOLLOW

HAVE YOU HEARD OF NEVER LAND?
ALL YOU NEED TO DO TO GET THERE IS FIND
THE SECOND STAR TO THE RIGHT AND HEAD STRAIGHT
ON TILL MORNING. NEVER LAND IS A MAGICAL
ISLAND WHERE MERMAIDS PLAY AND NO
ONE EVER GROWS OLD. WHY DON'T
I SHOW YOU AROUND?

LISTEN CAREFULLY. CAN YOU HEAR SOMETHING,
FAR OFF IN THE DISTANCE, THAT SOUNDS LIKE A
BELL? IF YOU FOLLOW THAT SOUND, YOU'LL ARRIVE
IN PIXIE HOLLOW, A VALLEY INHABITED BY FAIRIES.
THIS IS THE MOST IMPORTANT, SECRET PLACE ON
NEVER LAND. HERE YOU'LL FIND A HUGE MAPLE TREE,
KNOWN AS THE HOME TREE, HUNDREDS OF FAIRIES,
AND MALE FAIRIES KNOWN AS SPARROW MEN. THERE
ARE FAIRIES WHO CAN MANIPULATE WATER, THOSE
WHO CAN ZIP ALONG WITH THE WINDS, AND YET
OTHERS WHO CAN SPEAK TO ANIMALS. ALL
OF THE FAIRIES WHO LIVE HERE HAVE
THEIR OWN TALENT UNIQUE TO THEM.

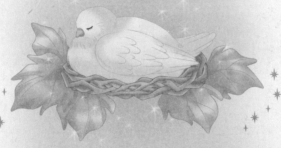

NOT FAR FROM THE HOME TREE IS MOTHER DOVE,
A SNOW WHITE DOVE THAT MAKES HER NEST ON THE
BRANCH OF A HAWTHORN TREE, AND IS THE MOST MYSTICAL
BEING LIVING ON NEVER LAND. THE FAIRY DUST THE FAIRIES
USE THAT GIVES THEM THEIR GLOW AND GRANTS THEM THE
ABILITY TO FLY IS MADE FROM MOTHER DOVE'S FEATHERS.
SITTING ATOP OF HER EGGS, SHE WATCHES OVER THE
FAIRIES AND, IN EXCHANGE, THEY CARE FOR HER.
AS LONG AS HER EGGS ARE SAFE AND SOUND,
NO ONE ON NEVER LAND WILL AGE. ONLY
ONCE HAVE MOTHER DOVE'S EGGS BROKEN,
BUT THAT'S A STORY I'LL SAVE FOR ANOTHER
TIME. TODAY, I'D LIKE TO TELL YOU ABOUT
THE FAIRY KNOWN AS TINKER BELL...

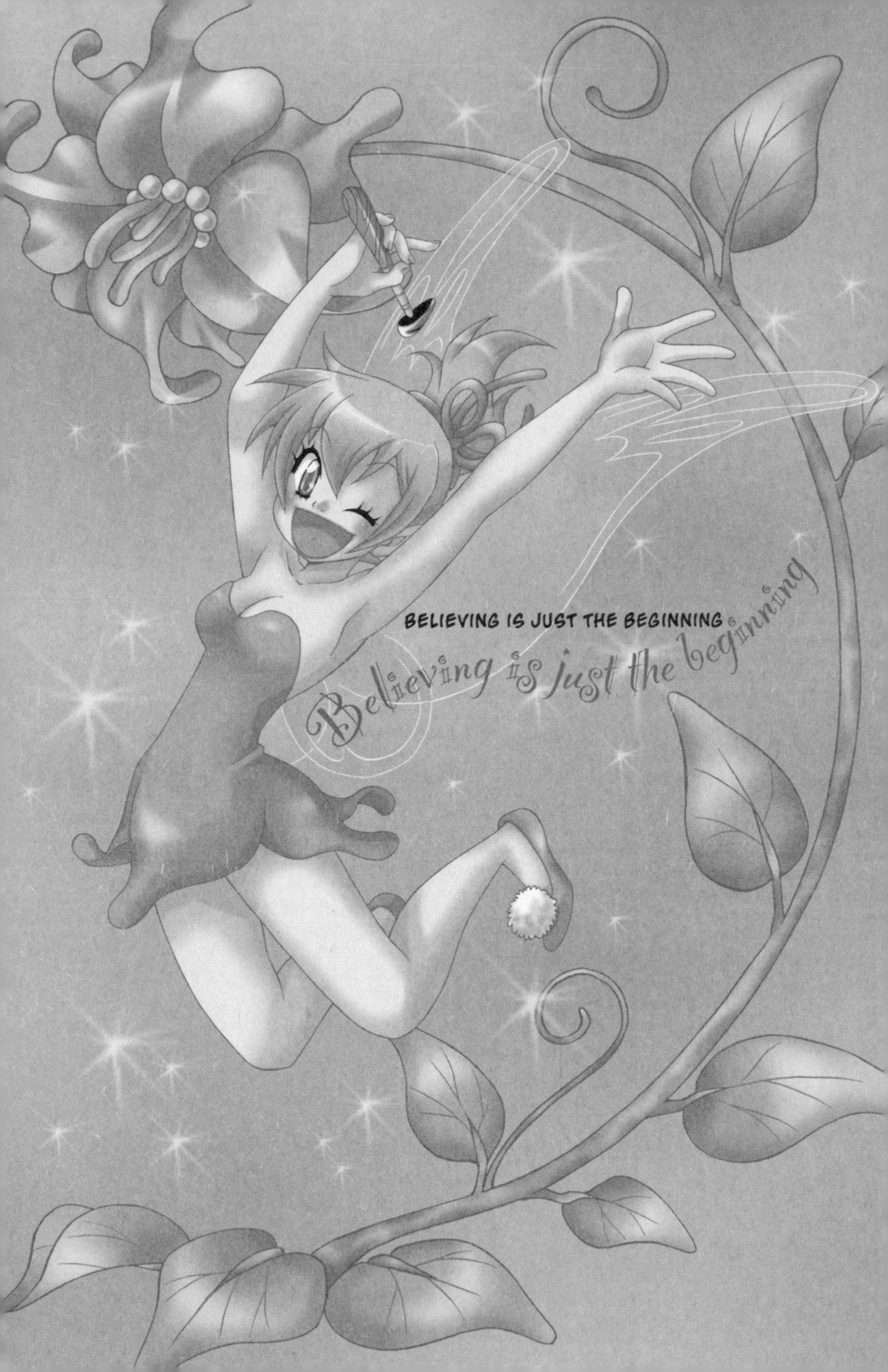
BELIEVING IS JUST THE BEGINNING
Believing is just the beginning

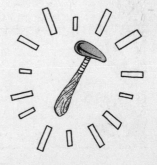

READ THIS WAY

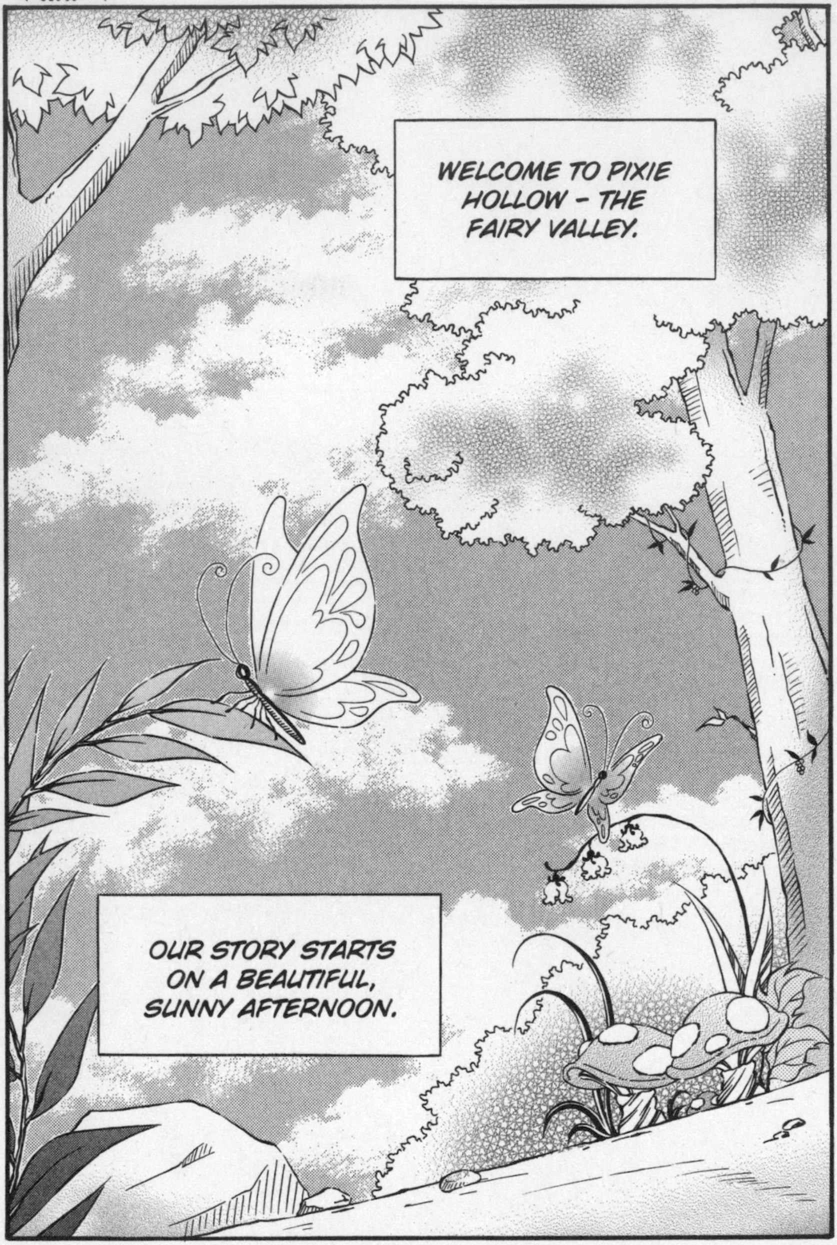

WELCOME TO PIXIE HOLLOW - THE FAIRY VALLEY.
OUR STORY STARTS ON A BEAUTIFUL, SUNNY AFTERNOON.

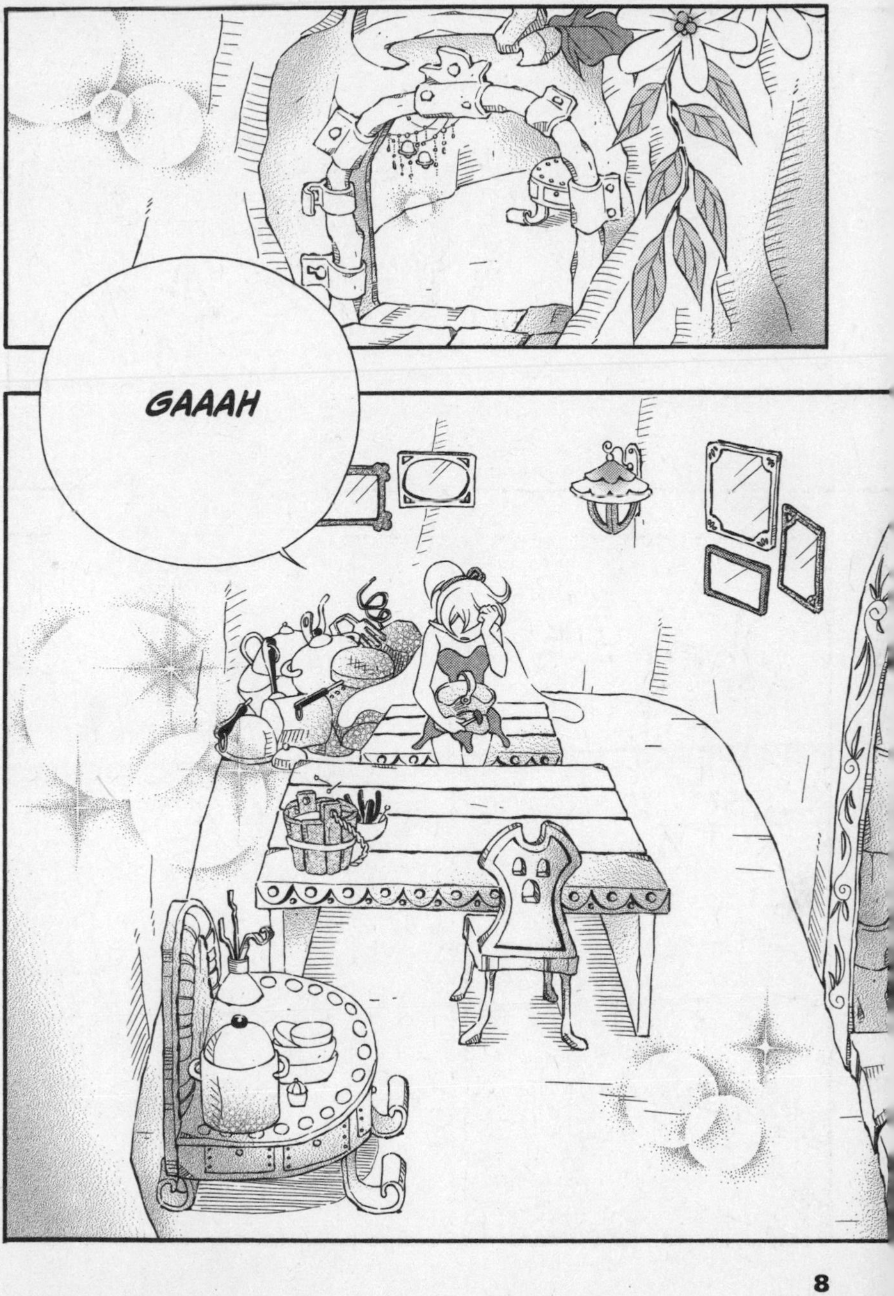
GAAAH

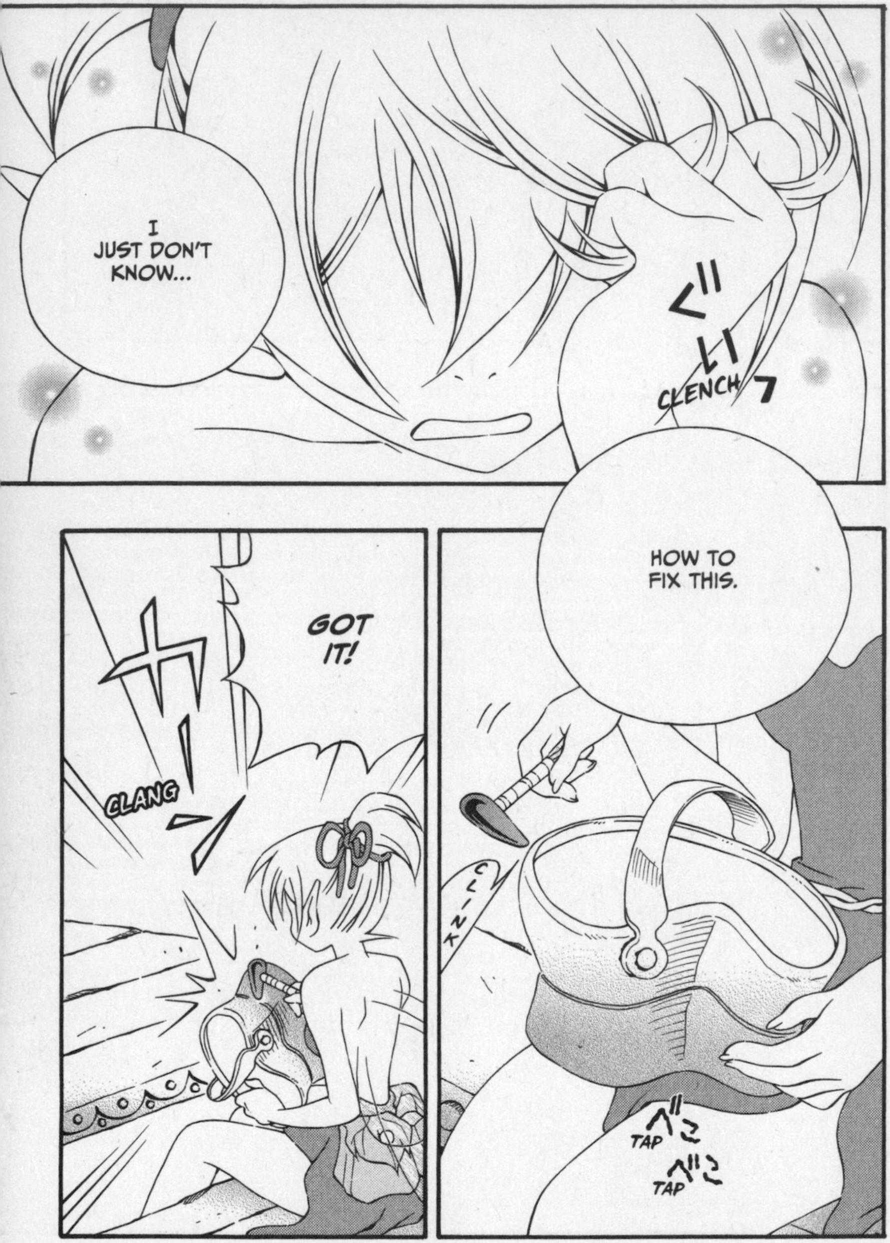
I JUST DON'T KNOW...
CLENCH
HOW TO FIX THIS.
CLINK
TAP
TAP
GOT IT!
CLANG

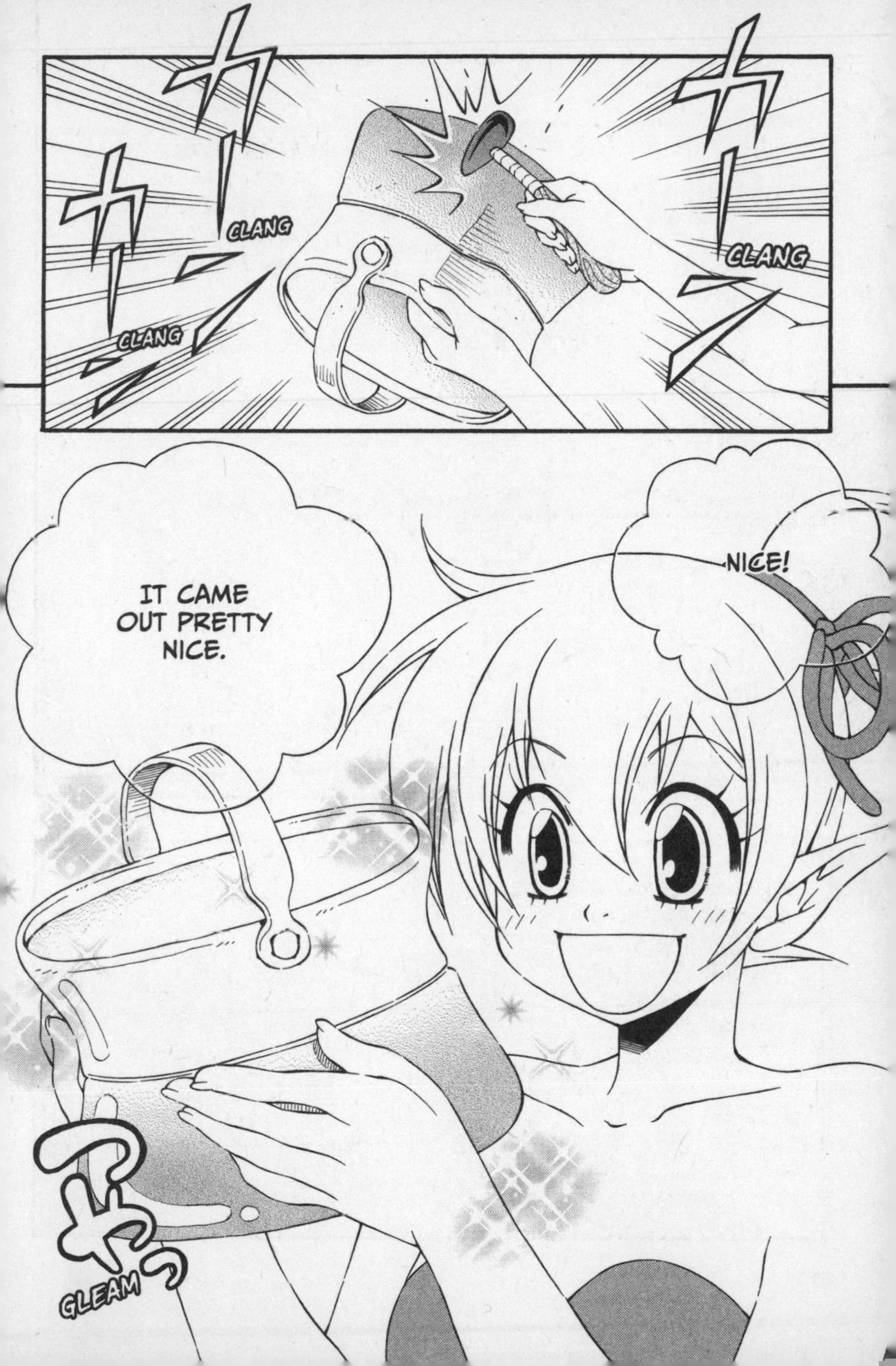
CLANG
CLANG
CLANG
NICE!
IT CAME OUT PRETTY NICE.
GLEAM

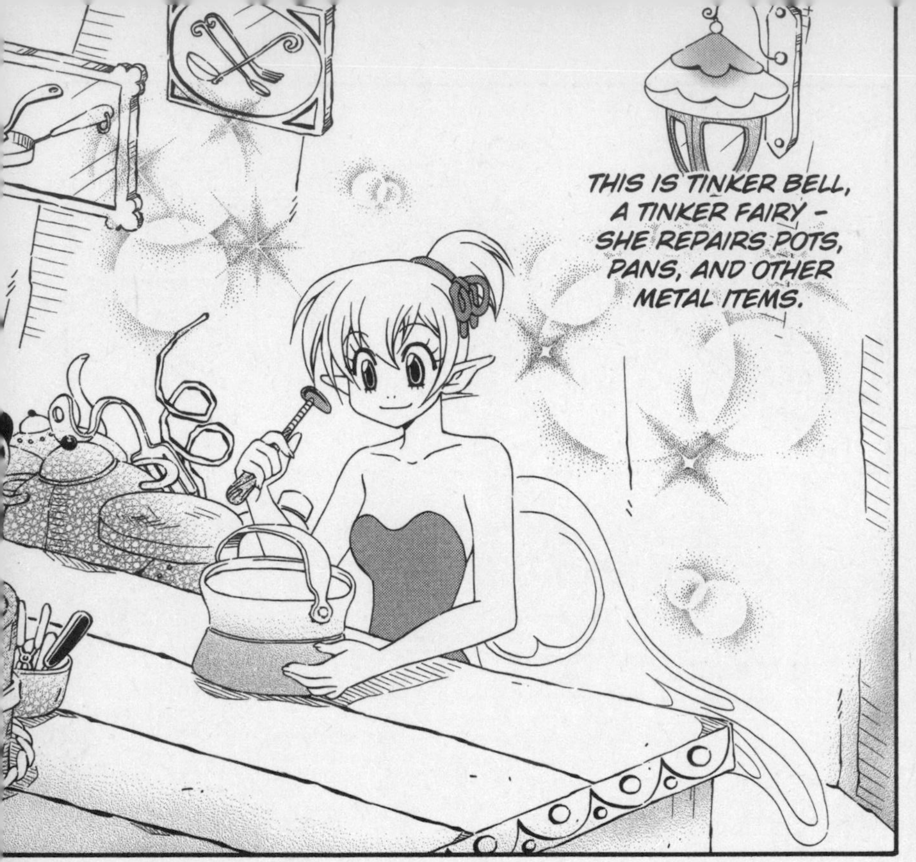
THIS IS TINKER BELL, A TINKER FAIRY - SHE REPAIRS POTS, PANS, AND OTHER METAL ITEMS.

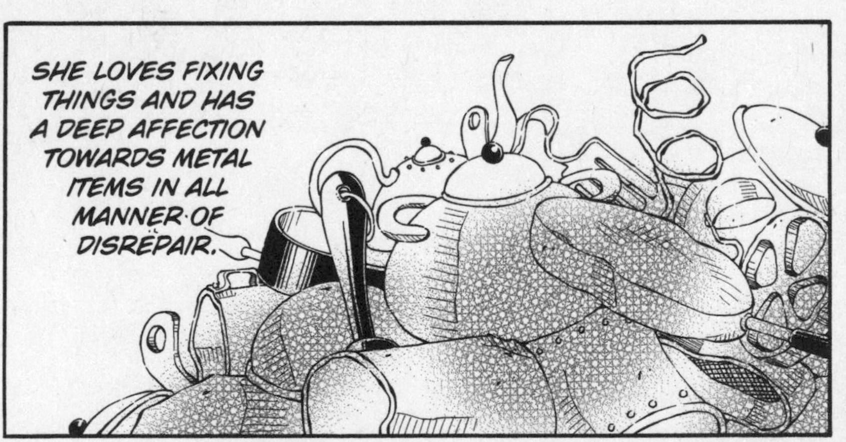
SHE LOVES FIXING THINGS AND HAS A DEEP AFFECTION TOWARDS METAL ITEMS IN ALL MANNER OF DISREPAIR.

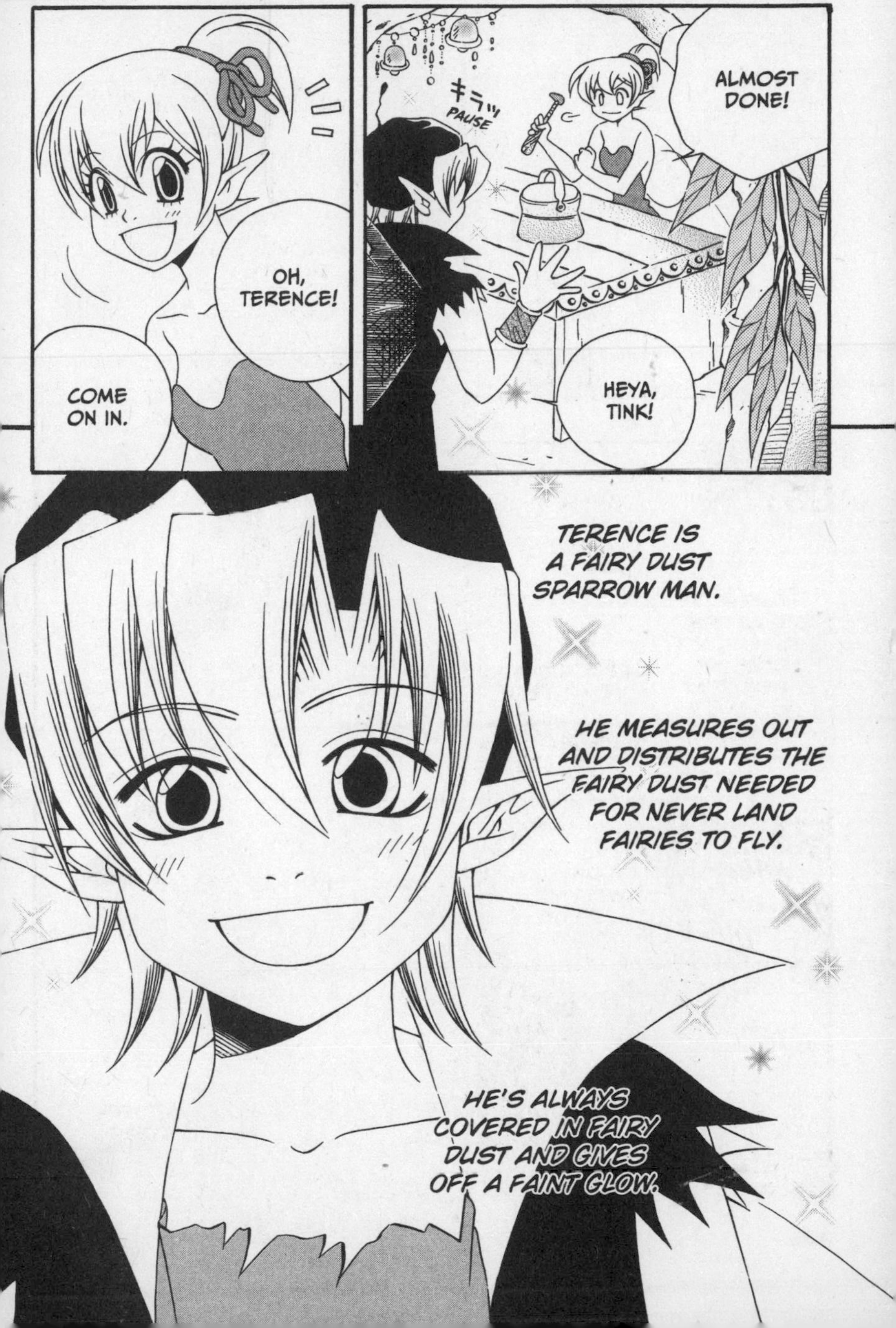
ALMOST DONE!
キラッ
PAUSE
HEYA, TINK!
OH, TERENCE!
COME ON IN.
TERENCE IS A FAIRY DUST SPARROW MAN.
HE MEASURES OUT AND DISTRIBUTES THE FAIRY DUST NEEDED FOR NEVER LAND FAIRIES TO FLY.
HE'S ALWAYS COVERED IN FAIRY DUST AND GIVES OFF A FAINT GLOW.

READ THIS WAY

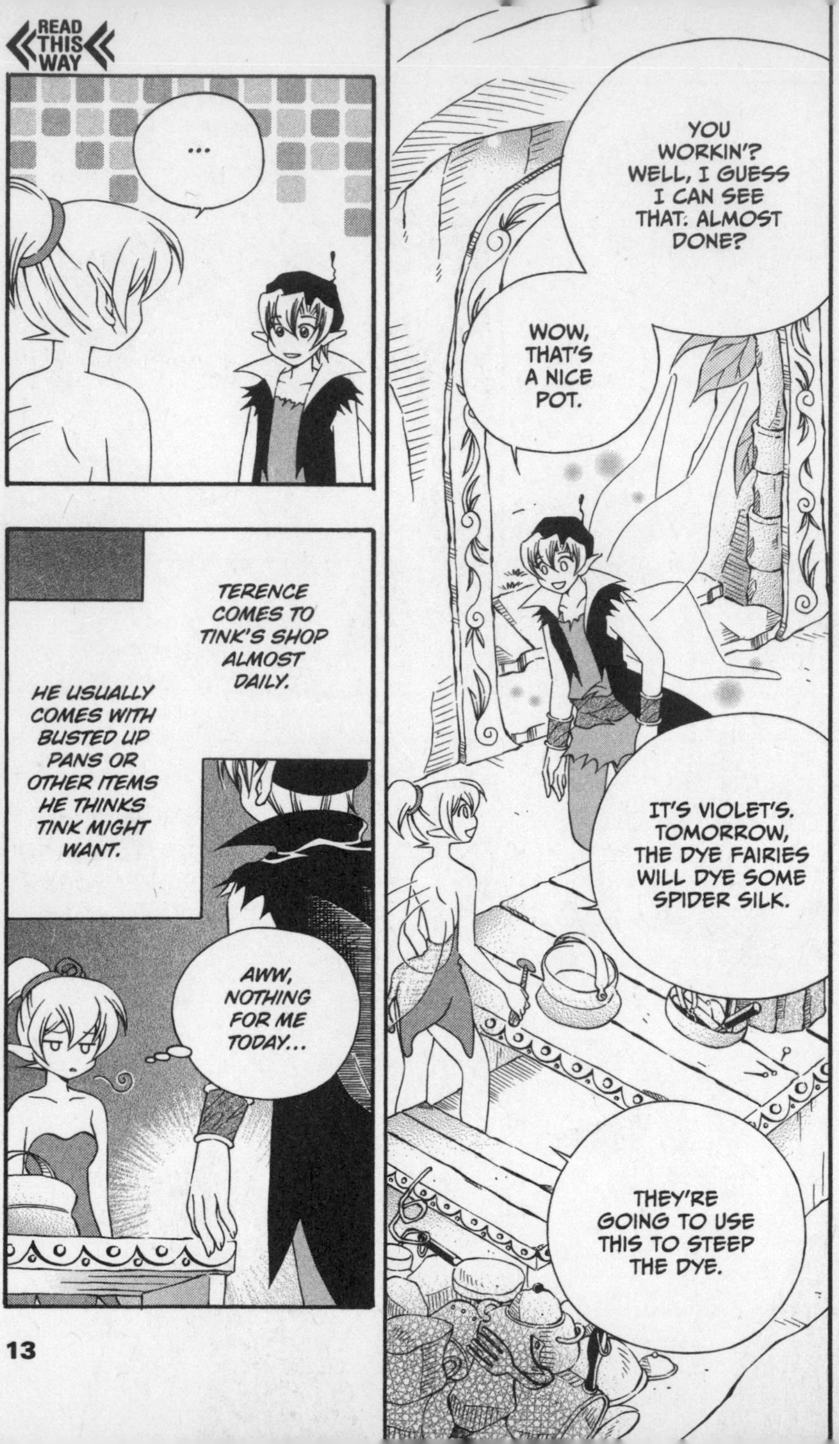
YOU WORKIN'? WELL, I GUESS I CAN SEE THAT. ALMOST DONE?
WOW, THAT'S A NICE POT.
IT'S VIOLET'S. TOMORROW, THE DYE FAIRIES WILL DYE SOME SPIDER SILK.
THEY'RE GOING TO USE THIS TO STEEP THE DYE.
...
TERENCE COMES TO TINK'S SHOP ALMOST DAILY.
HE USUALLY COMES WITH BUSTED UP PANS OR OTHER ITEMS HE THINKS TINK MIGHT WANT.
AWW, NOTHING FOR ME TODAY...

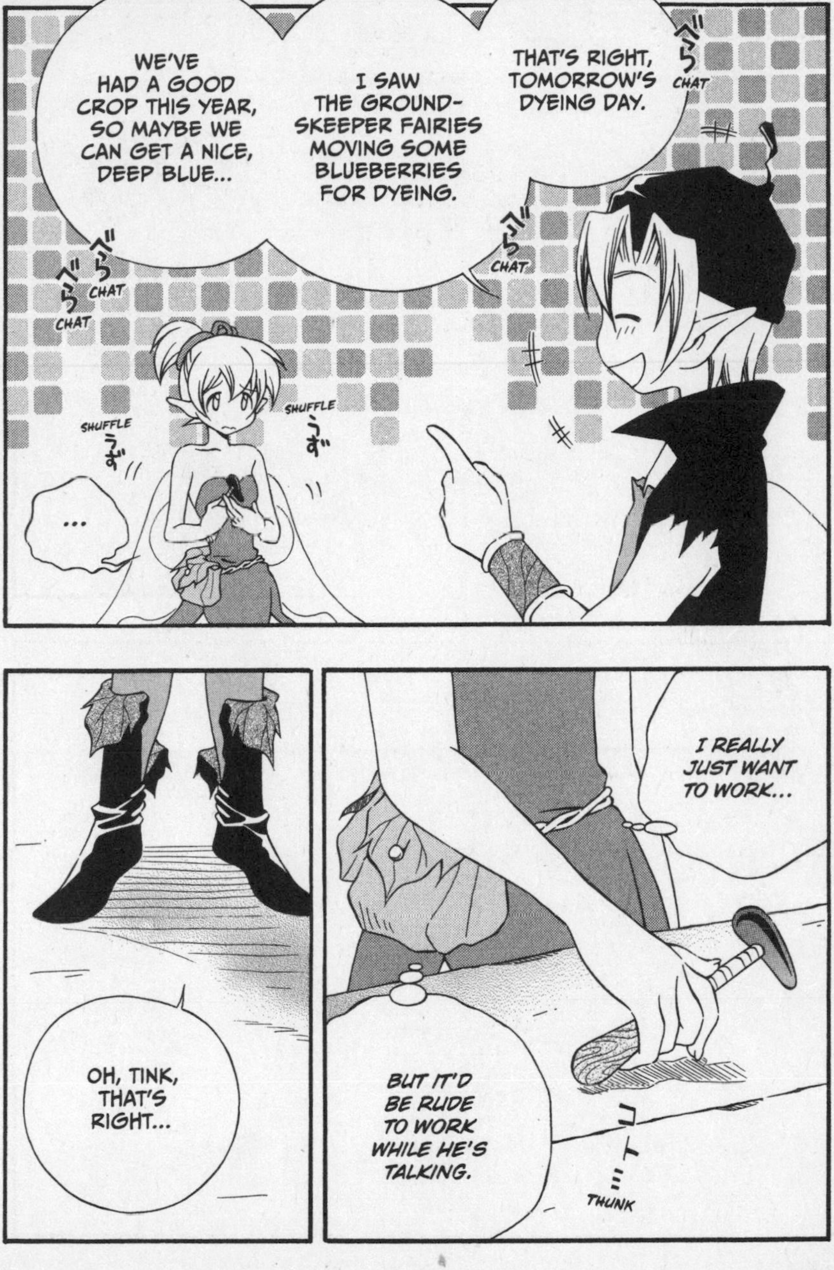

CHAT
THAT'S RIGHT, TOMORROW'S DYEING DAY.
I SAW THE GROUND-SKEEPER FAIRIES MOVING SOME BLUEBERRIES FOR DYEING.
CHAT
WE'VE HAD A GOOD CROP THIS YEAR, SO MAYBE WE CAN GET A NICE, DEEP BLUE...
CHAT
CHAT
SHUFFLE
SHUFFLE
...
I REALLY JUST WANT TO WORK...
BUT IT'D BE RUDE TO WORK WHILE HE'S TALKING.
THUNK
OH, TINK, THAT'S RIGHT...

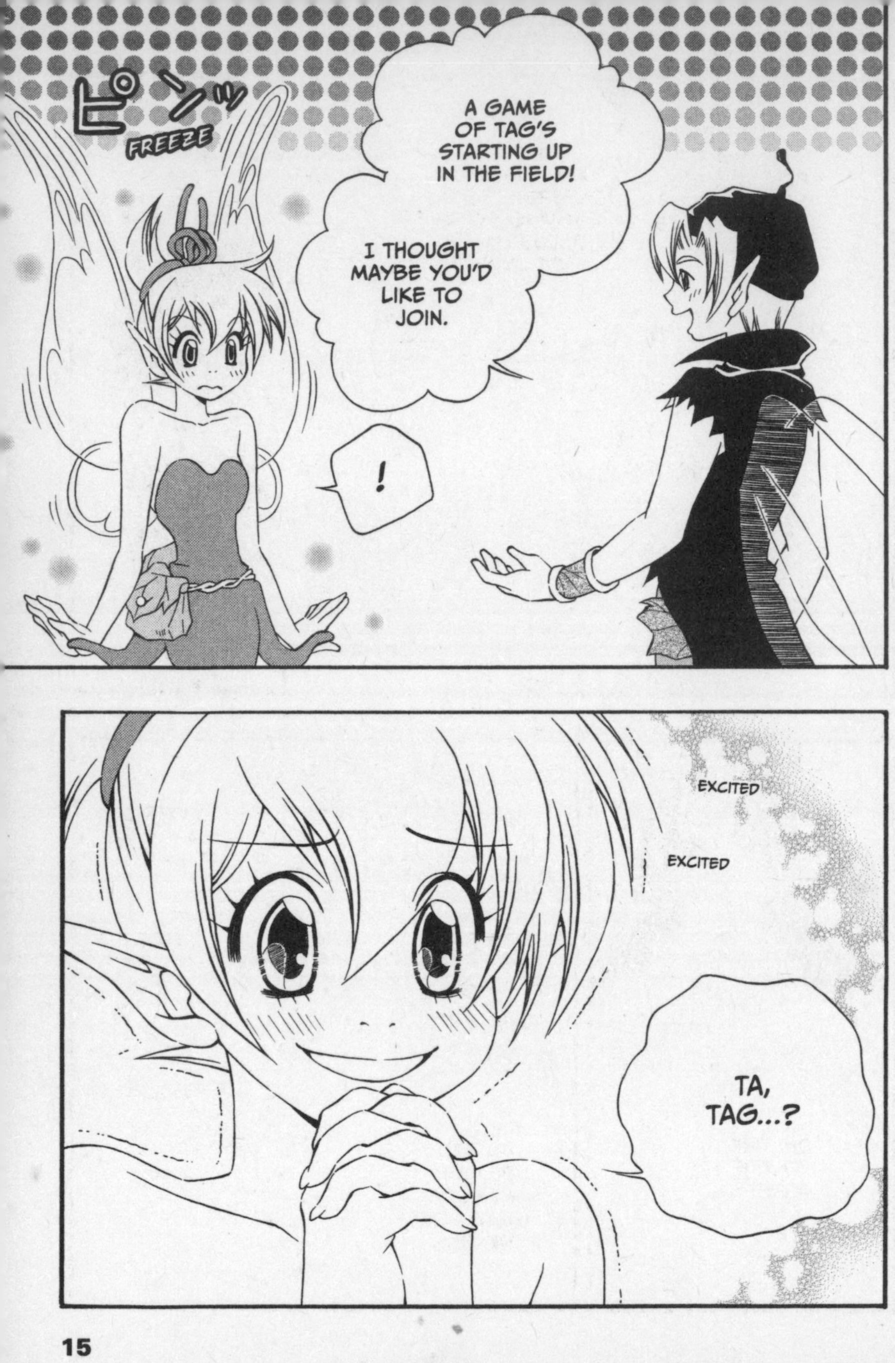
A GAME OF TAG'S STARTING UP IN THE FIELD!
I THOUGHT MAYBE YOU'D LIKE TO JOIN.
ピンッ
FREEZE
!
EXCITED
EXCITED
TA, TAG...?

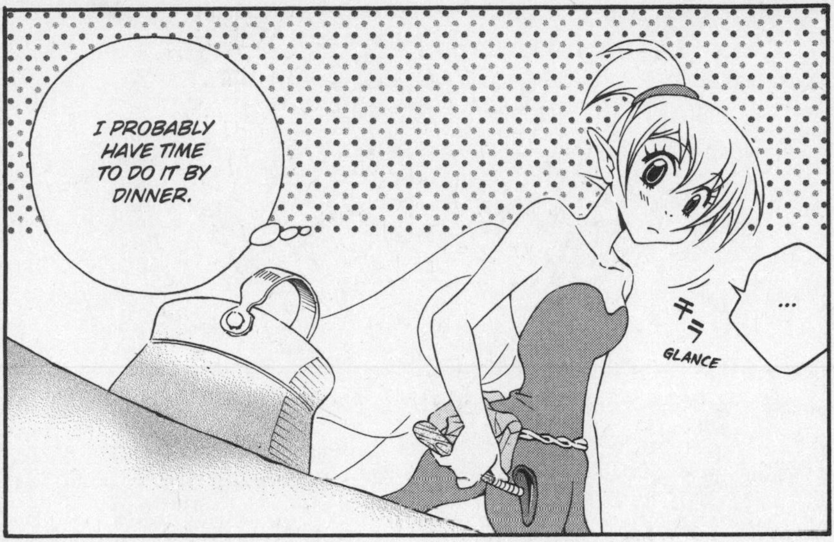
...
チラ
GLANCE
I PROBABLY HAVE TIME TO DO IT BY DINNER.

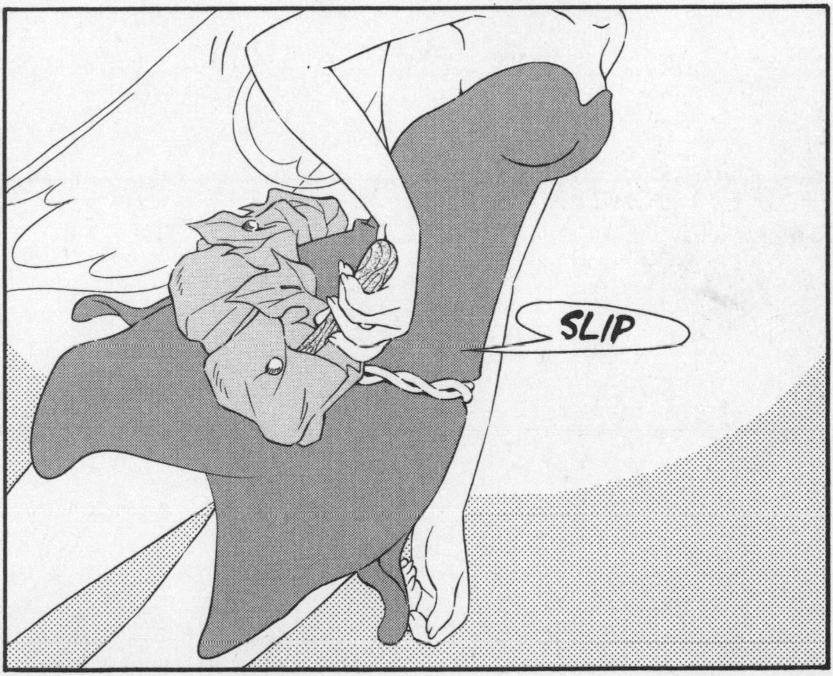
SLIP

READ THIS WAY

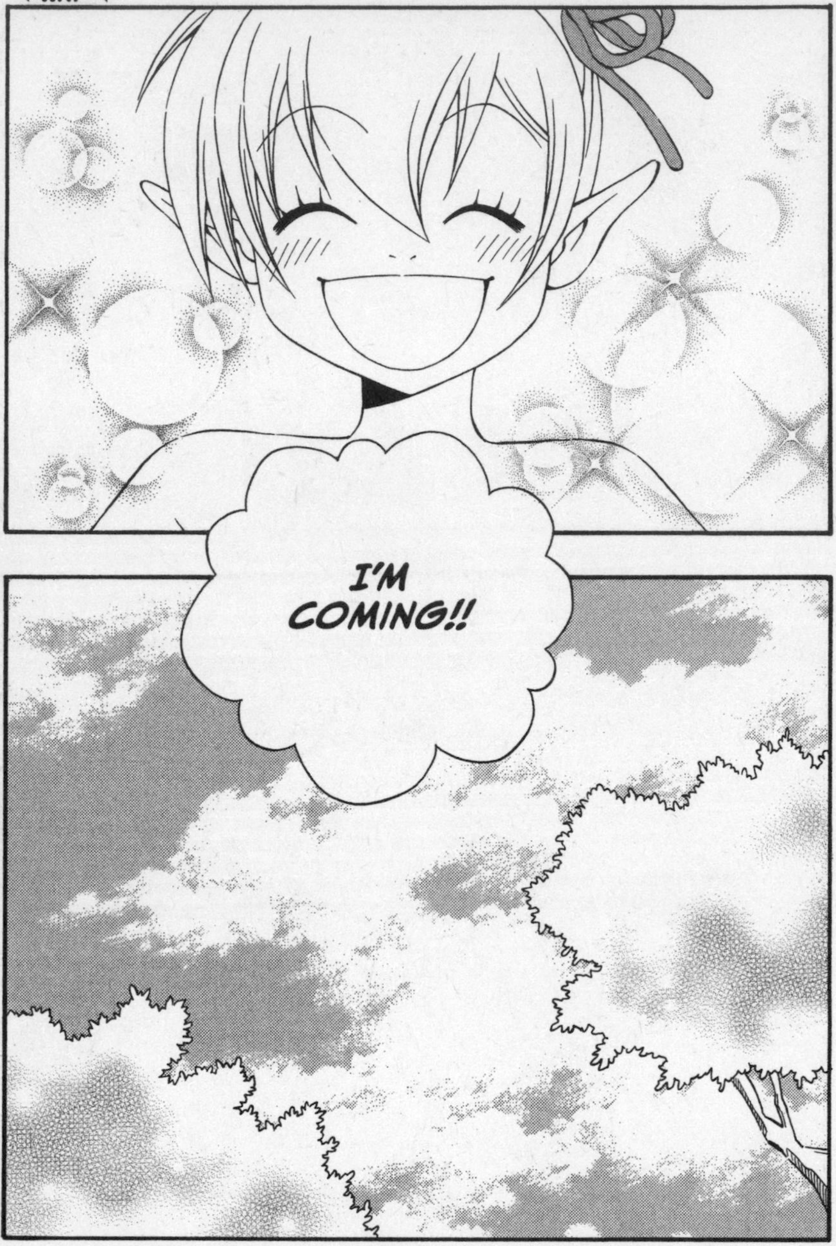
I'M COMING!!

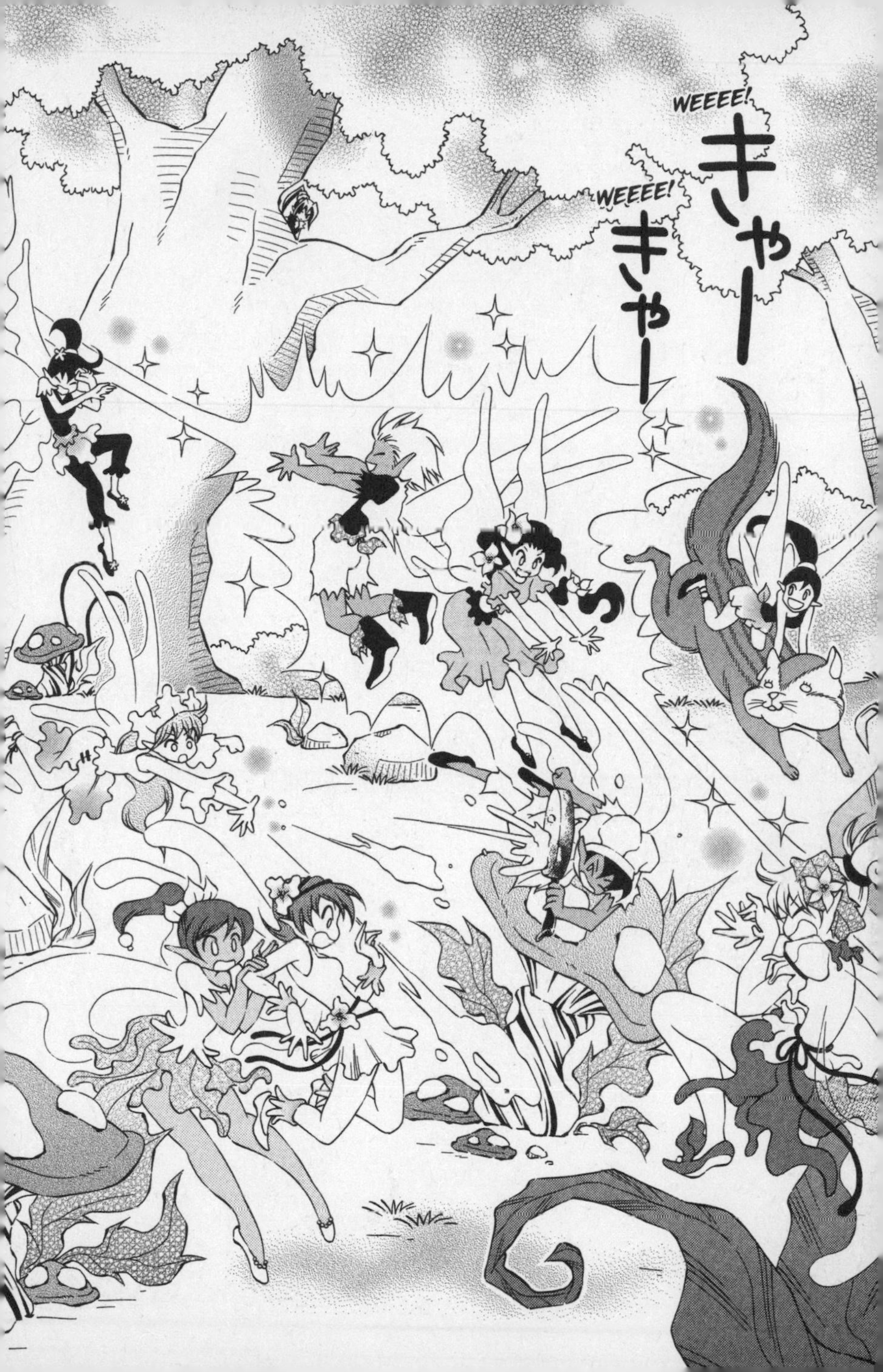
キャー
WEEEE!
キャー
WEEEE!

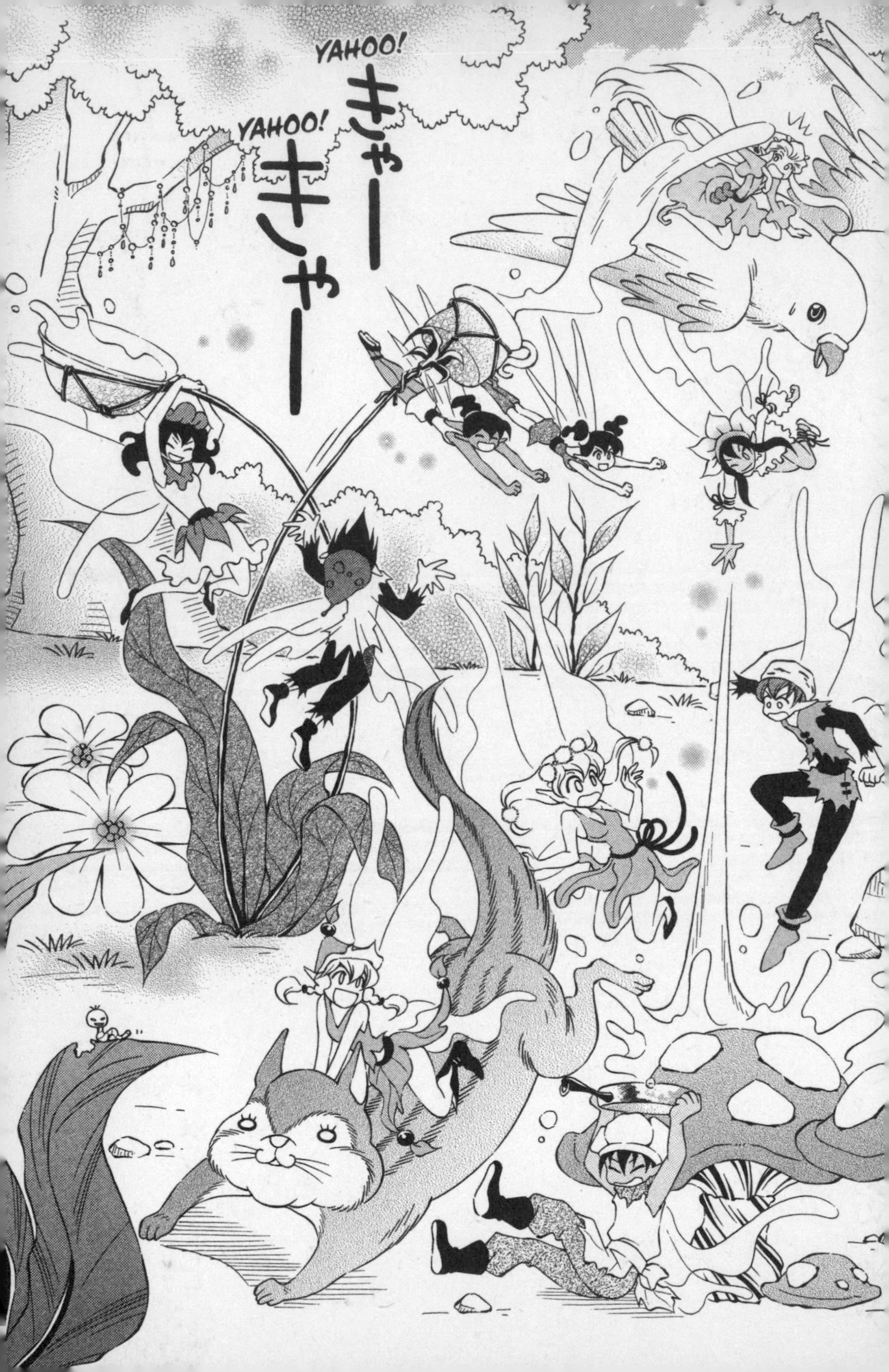

YAHOO!
きゃー
YAHOO!
きゃー

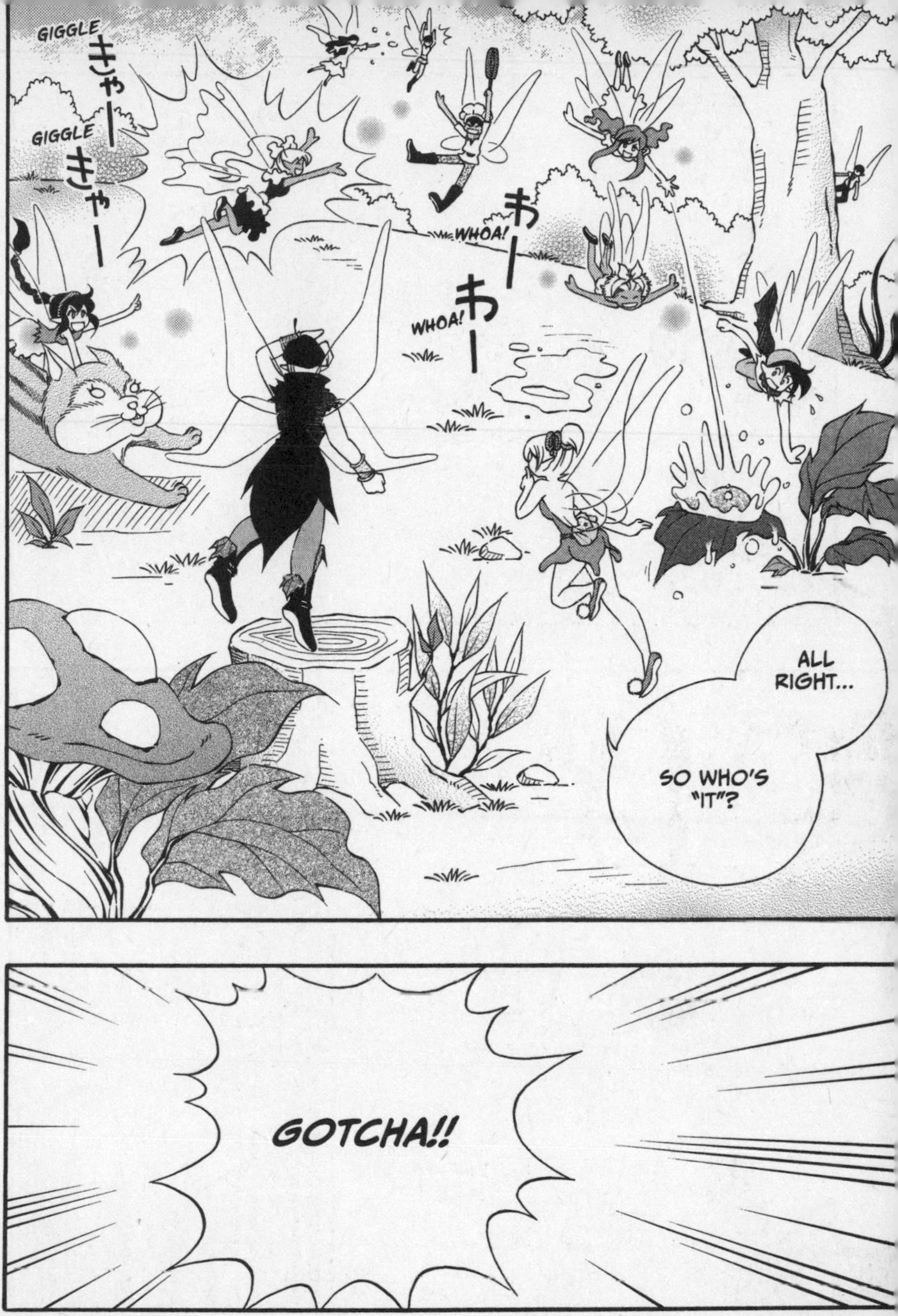
WHOA!
おー
WHOA!
おー
GIGGLE
きゃー
GIGGLE
きゃー
ALL RIGHT...
SO WHO'S "IT"?
GOTCHA!!

READ THIS WAY

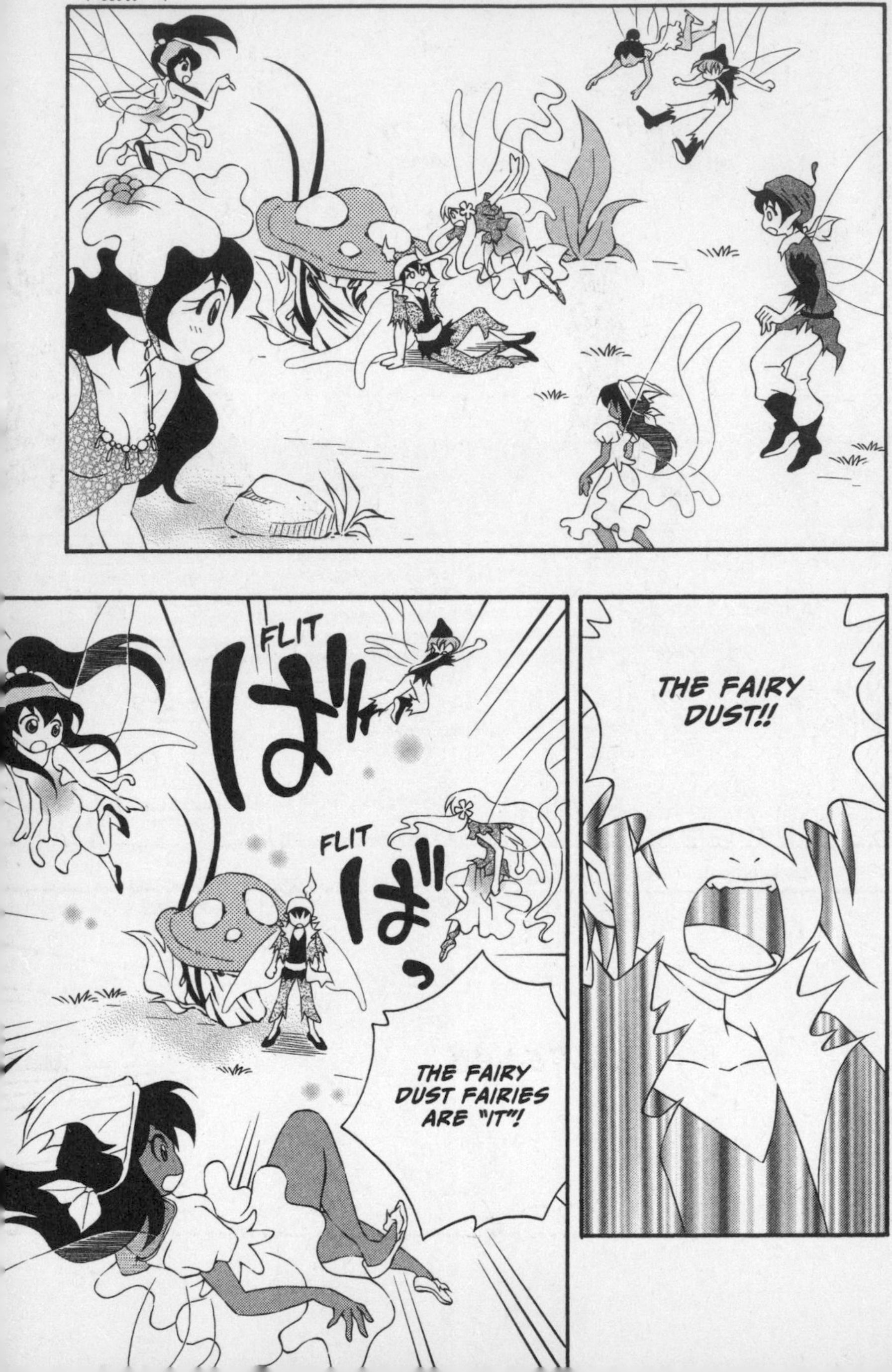
THE FAIRY DUST!!
FLIT
ばッ
FLIT
ばっ
THE FAIRY DUST FAIRIES ARE "IT"!

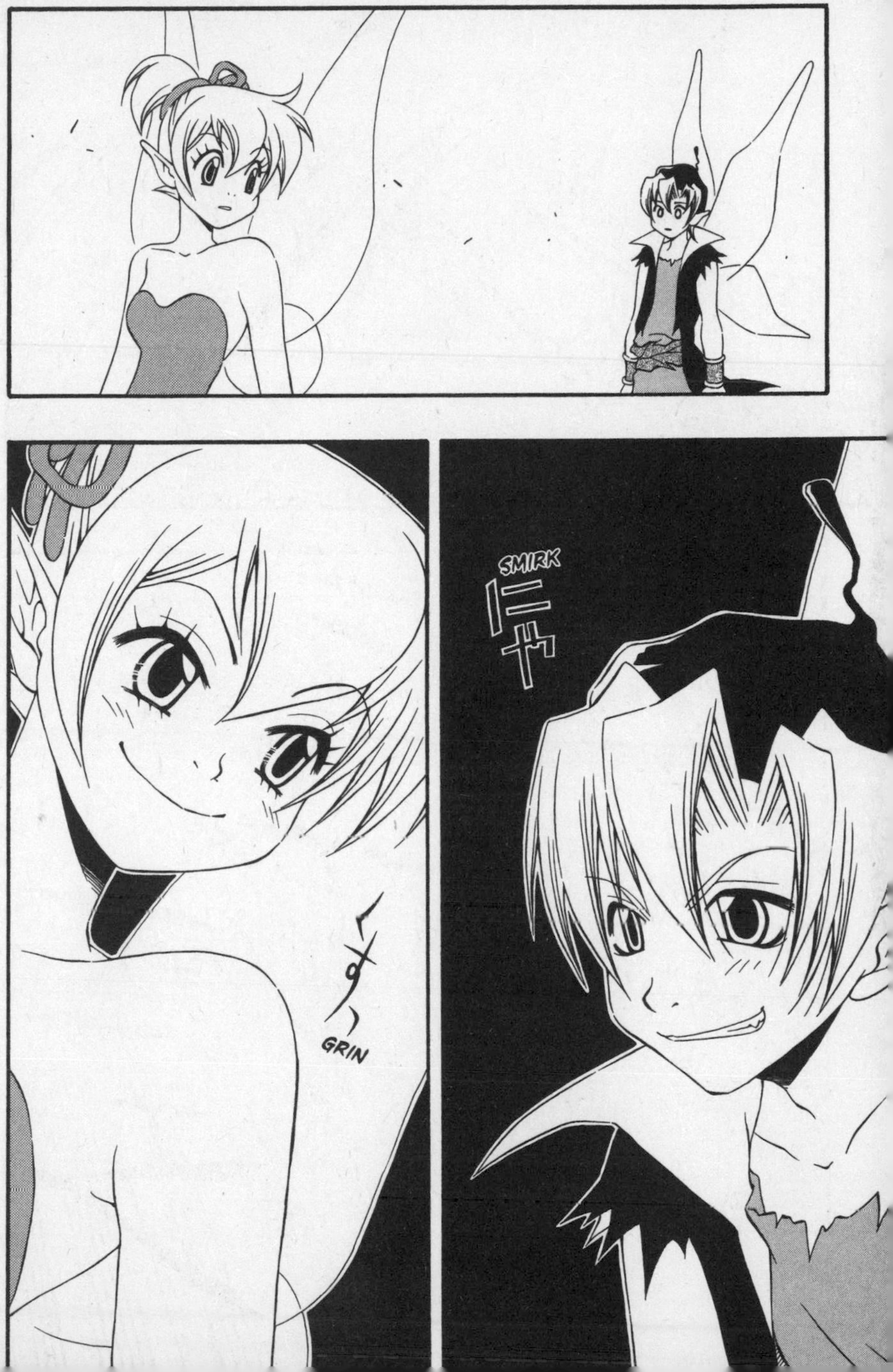
SMIRK
ニヤ
くすっ
GRIN

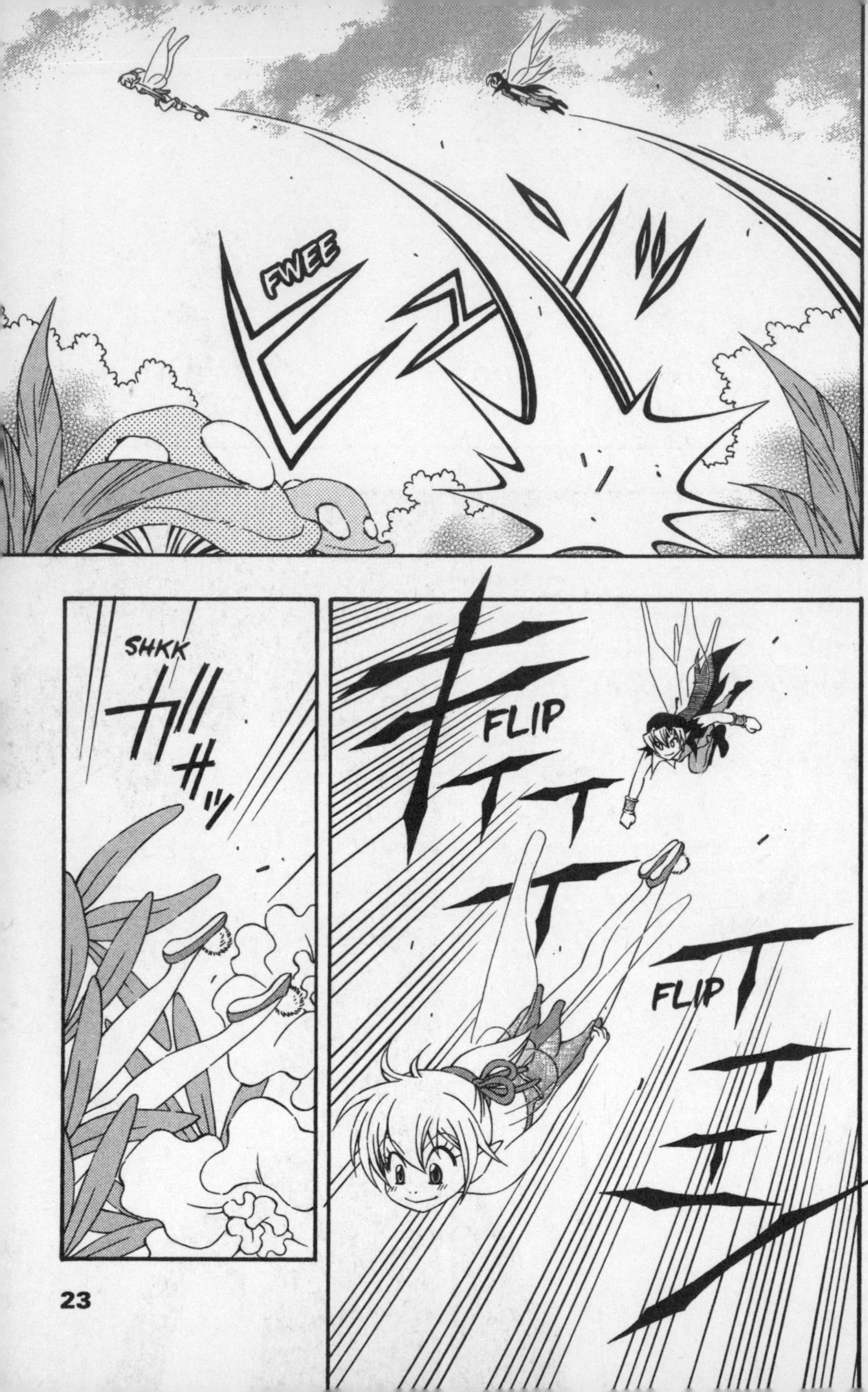
FWEE
FLIP
FLIP
SHKK

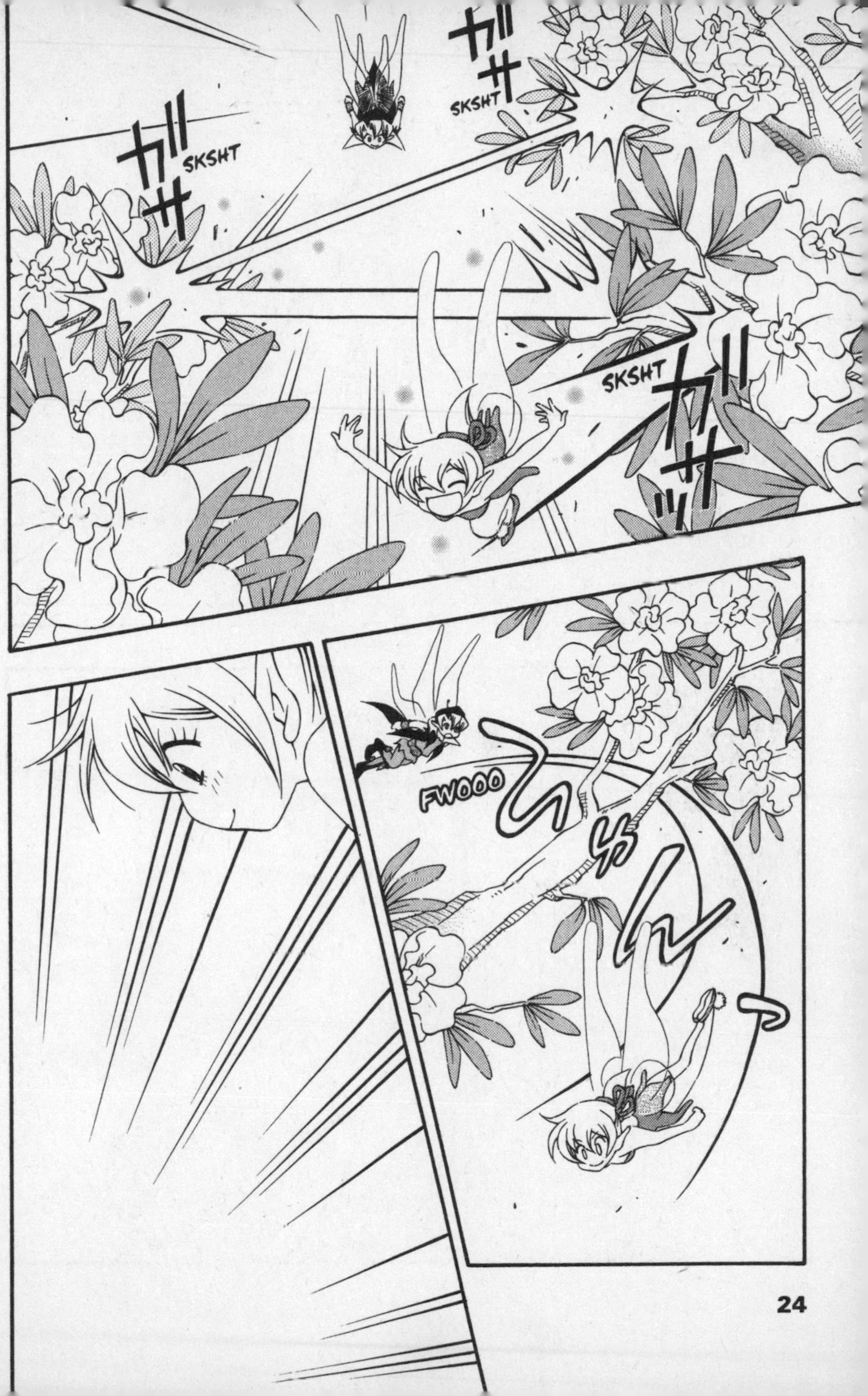
ガサ
SKSHT
ガサ
SKSHT
SKSHT
ガサッ
FWOOO
ひゅんっ

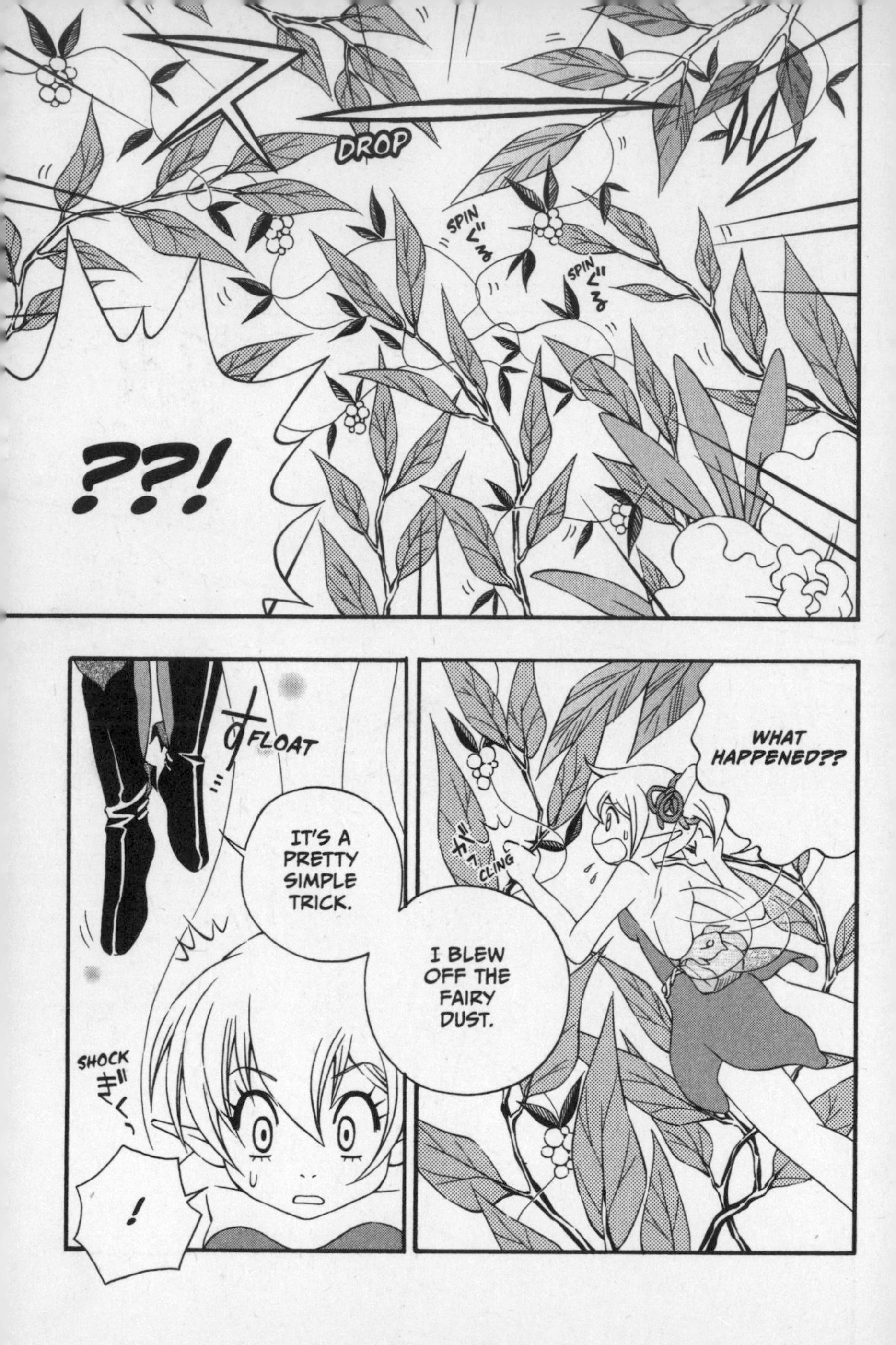
DROP
SPIN
SPIN
??!
WHAT HAPPENED??
CLING
FLOAT
IT'S A PRETTY SIMPLE TRICK.
I BLEW OFF THE FAIRY DUST.
SHOCK
!

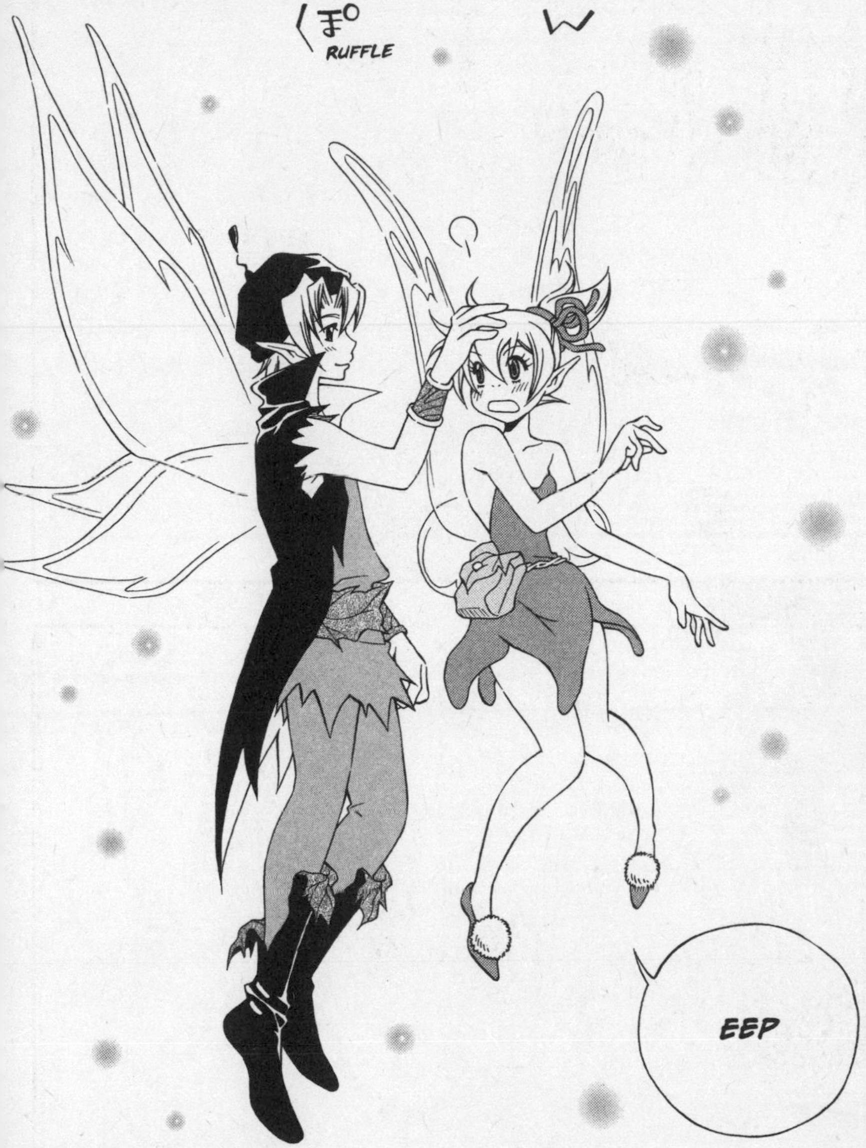
RUFFLE
EEP

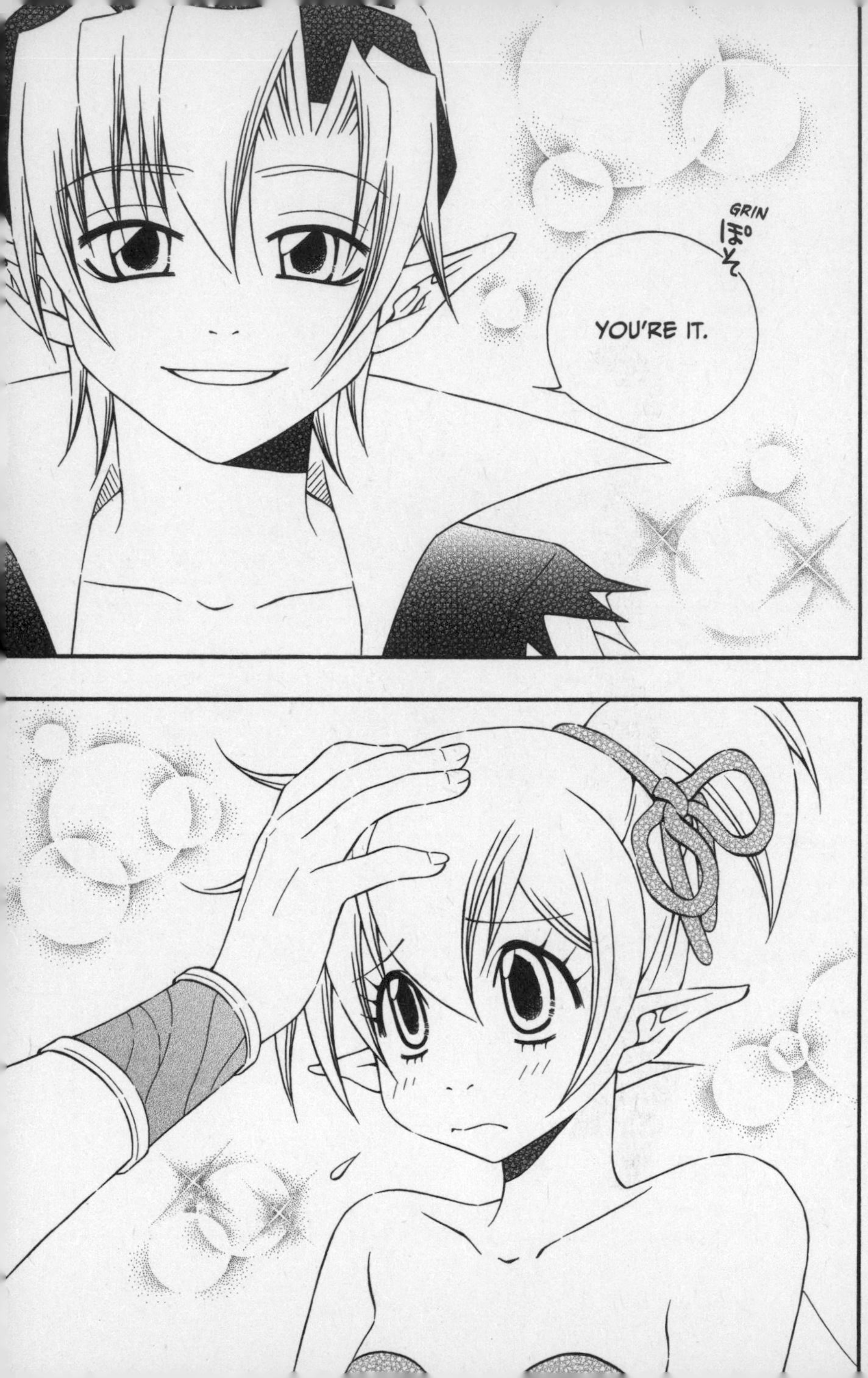
GRIN
ぽそ
YOU'RE IT.

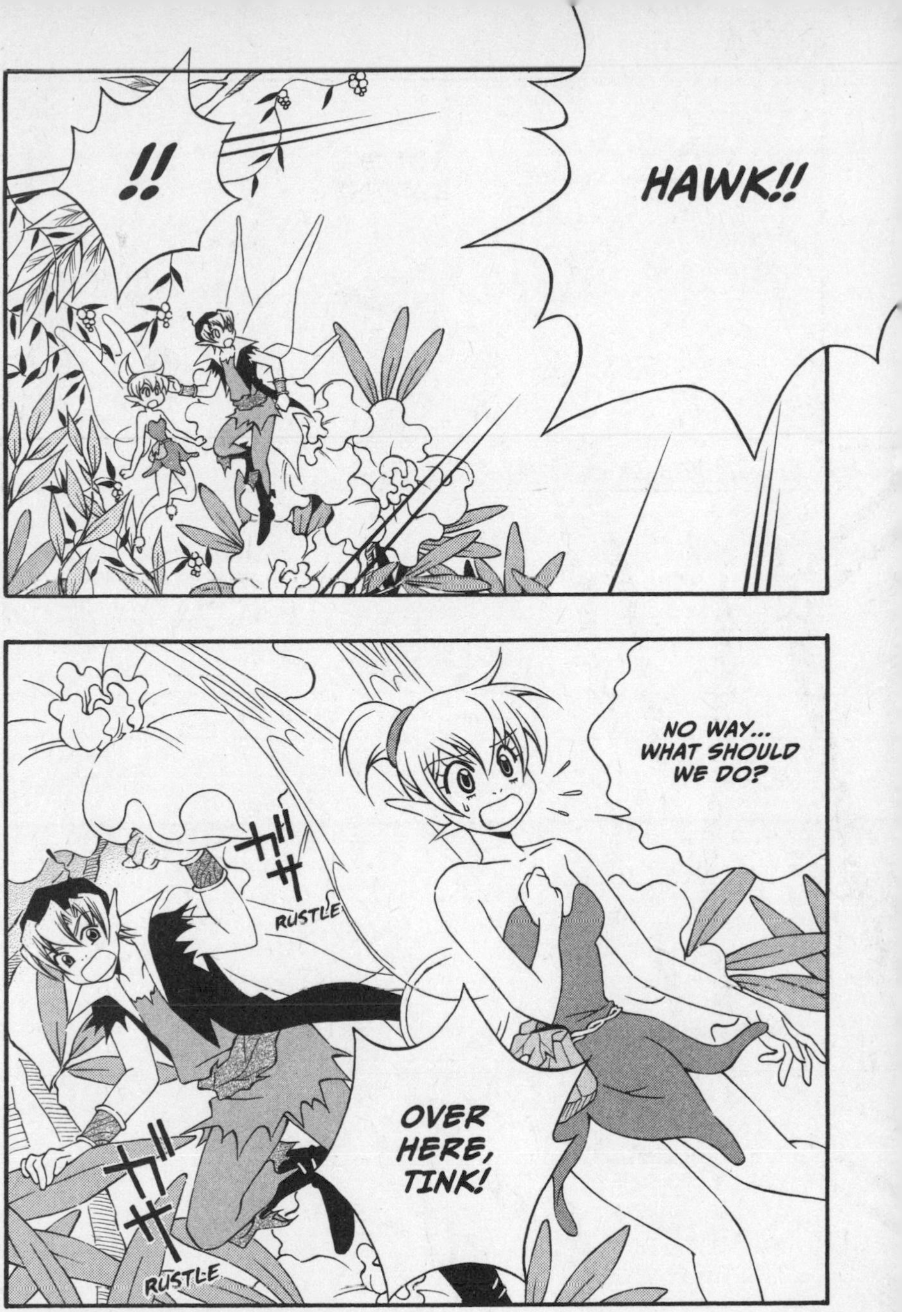
HAWK!!
!!
NO WAY... WHAT SHOULD WE DO?
ガサ
RUSTLE
OVER HERE, TINK!
ガサ
RUSTLE

READ THIS WAY

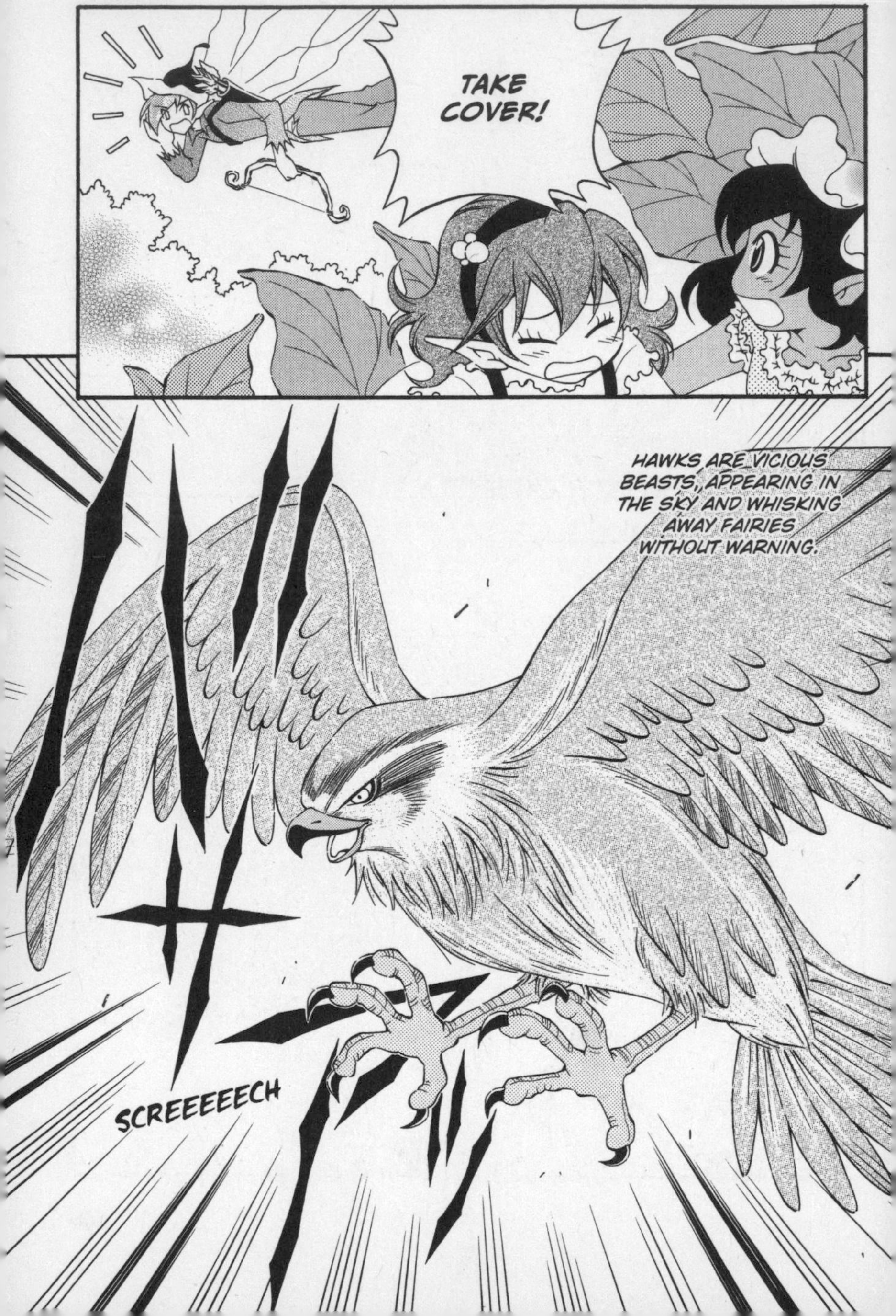
TAKE COVER!
HAWKS ARE VICIOUS BEASTS, APPEARING IN THE SKY AND WHISKING AWAY FAIRIES WITHOUT WARNING.
SCREEEEEECH

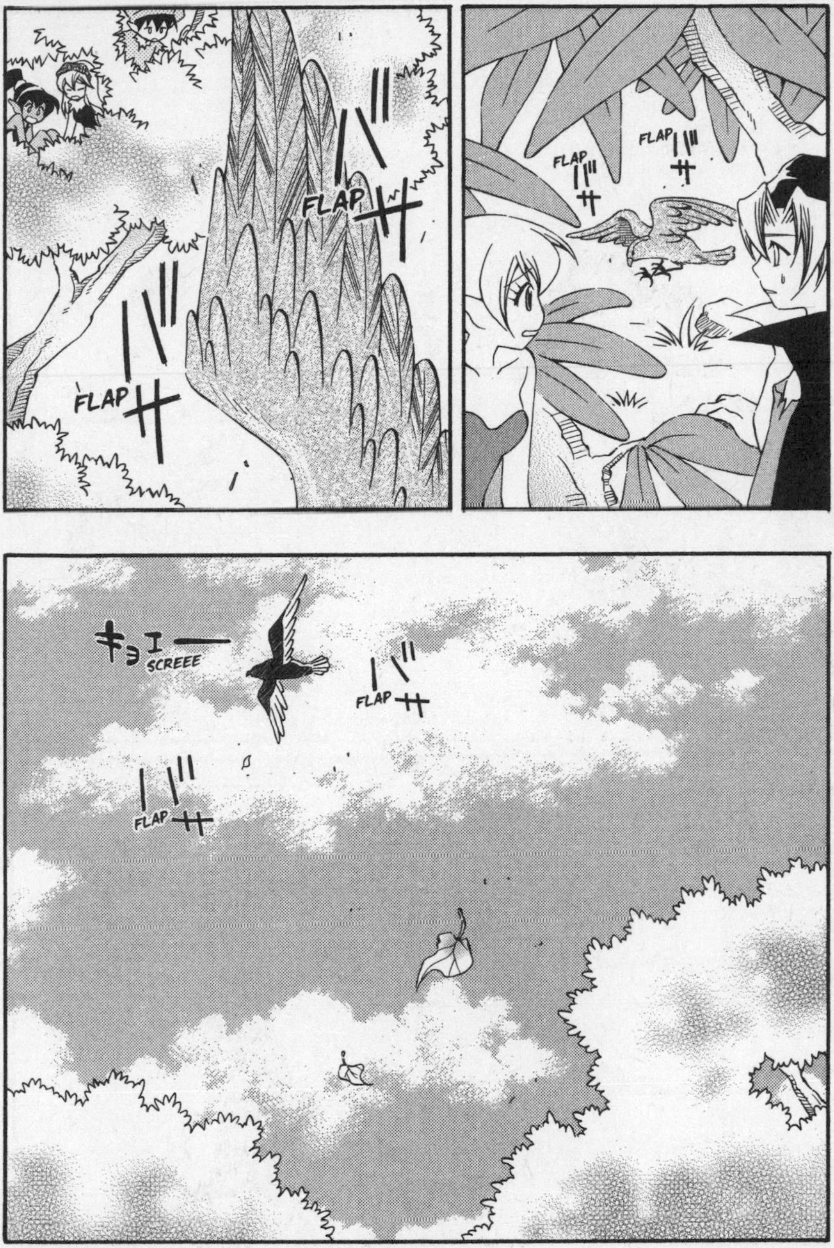
FLAP
バサ
FLAP
バサ
FLAP
バサ
FLAP
バサ
バサ
FLAP
キョエー
SCREEE
バサ
FLAP

READ THIS WAY

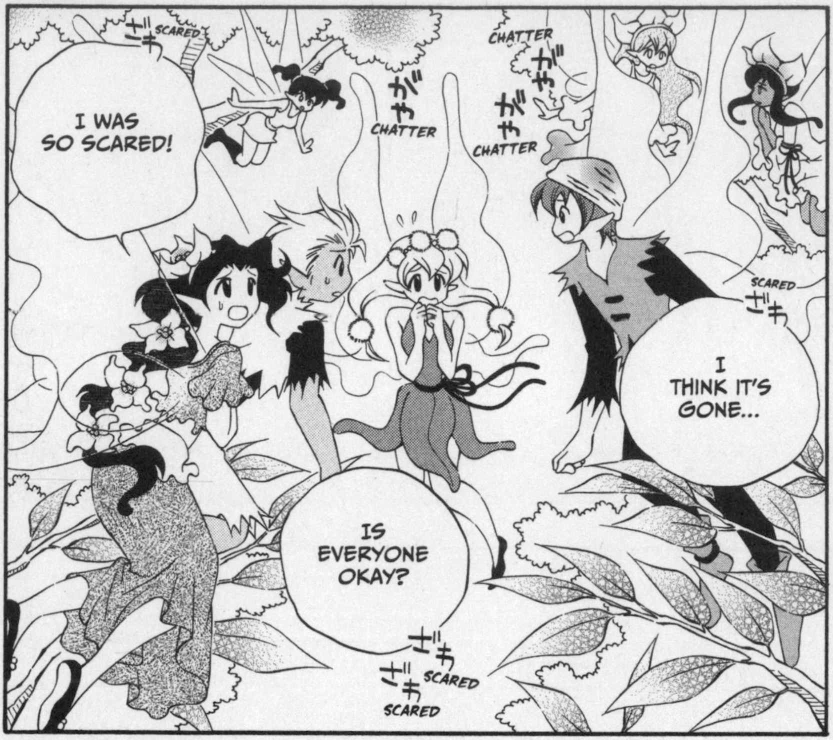
CHATTER
CHATTER
CHATTER
SCARED
I THINK IT'S GONE...
I WAS SO SCARED!
SCARED
IS EVERYONE OKAY?
SCARED
SCARED

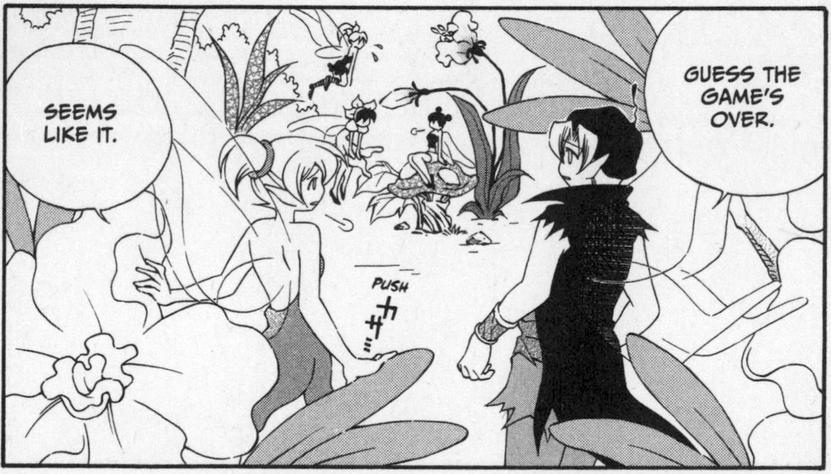
GUESS THE GAME'S OVER.
SEEMS LIKE IT.
PUSH

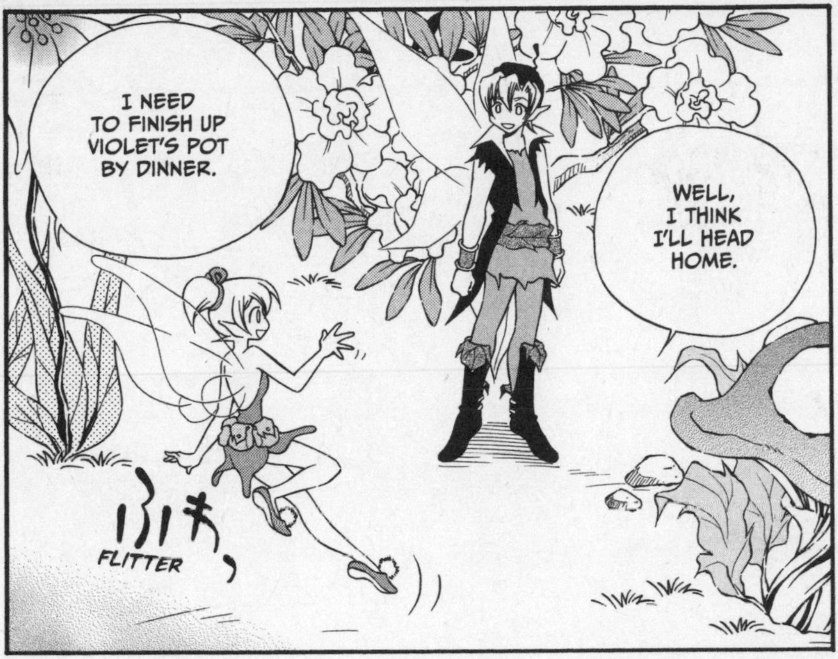
WELL, I THINK I'LL HEAD HOME.
I NEED TO FINISH UP VIOLET'S POT BY DINNER.
FLITTER

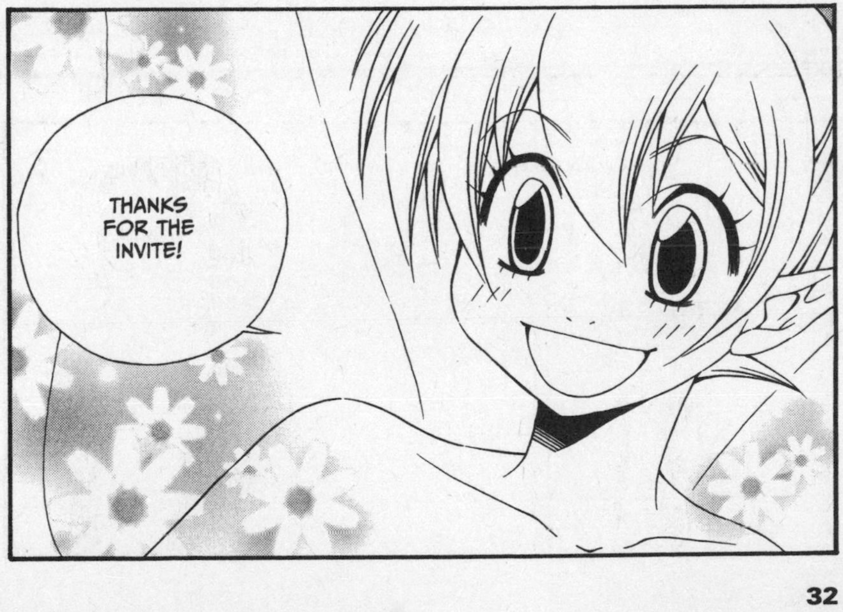
THANKS FOR THE INVITE!

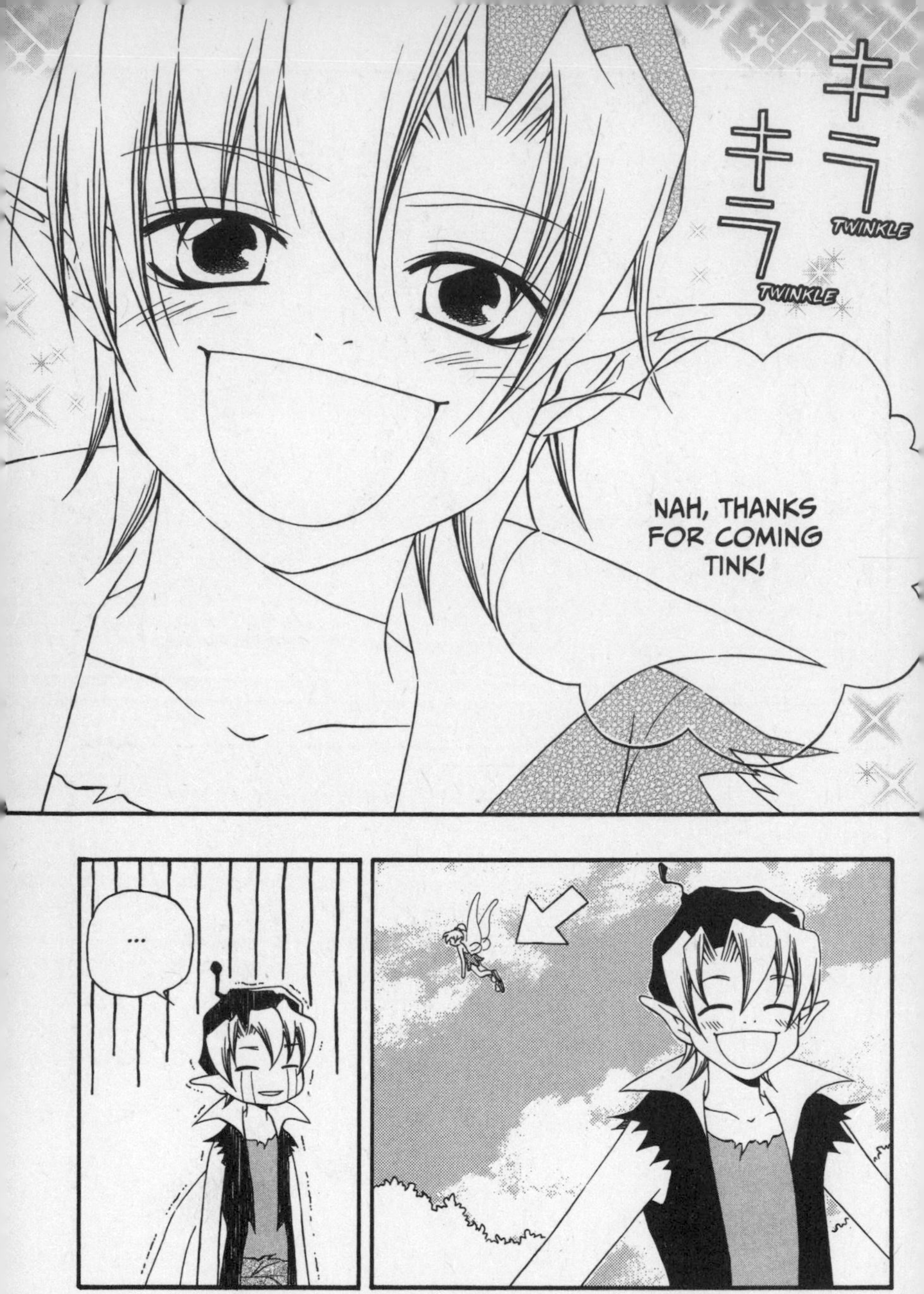
キラキラ
TWINKLE
TWINKLE
NAH, THANKS FOR COMING TINK!
...

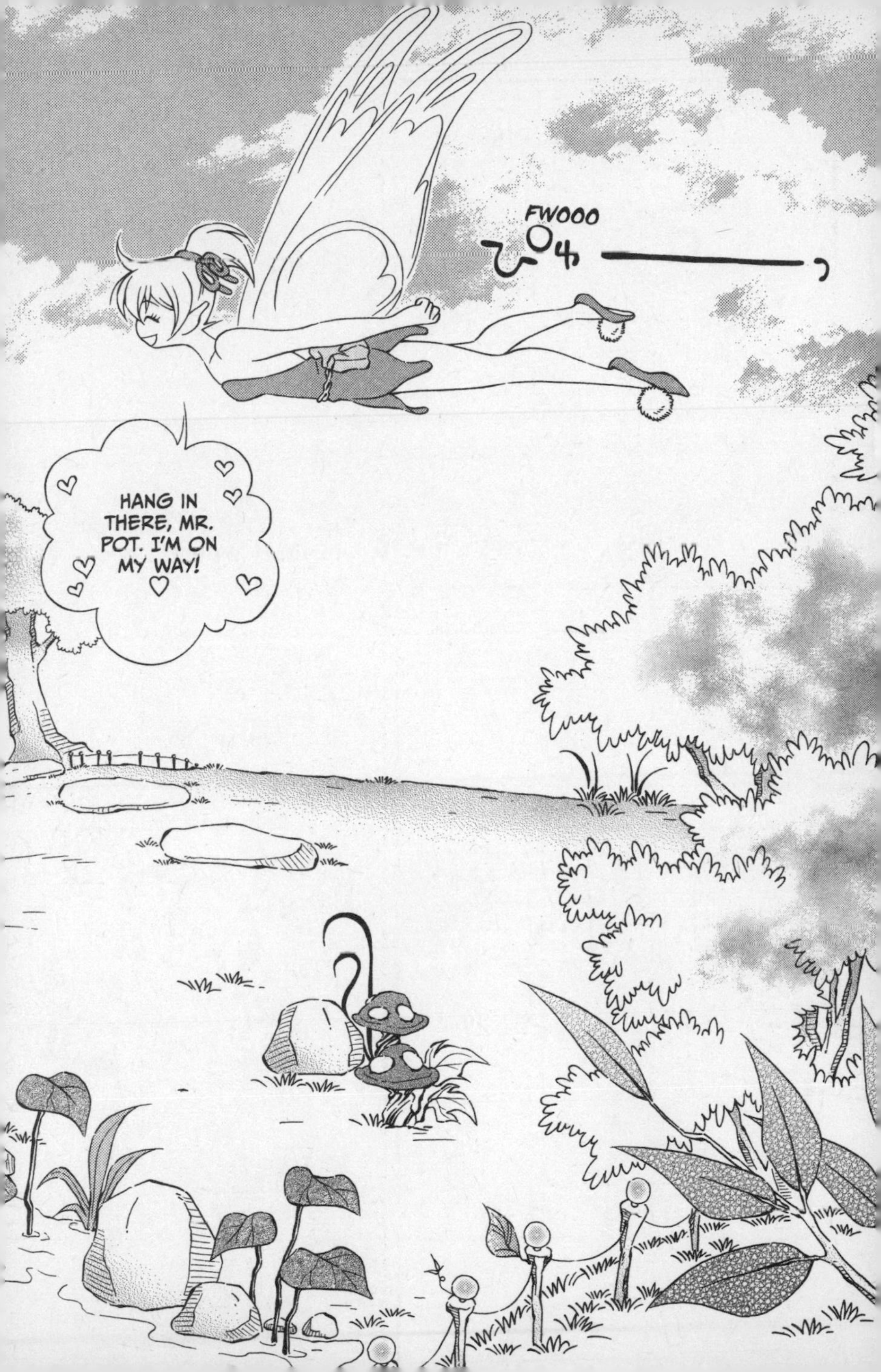
FWOOO
ぴゅ——っ
HANG IN THERE, MR. POT. I'M ON MY WAY!

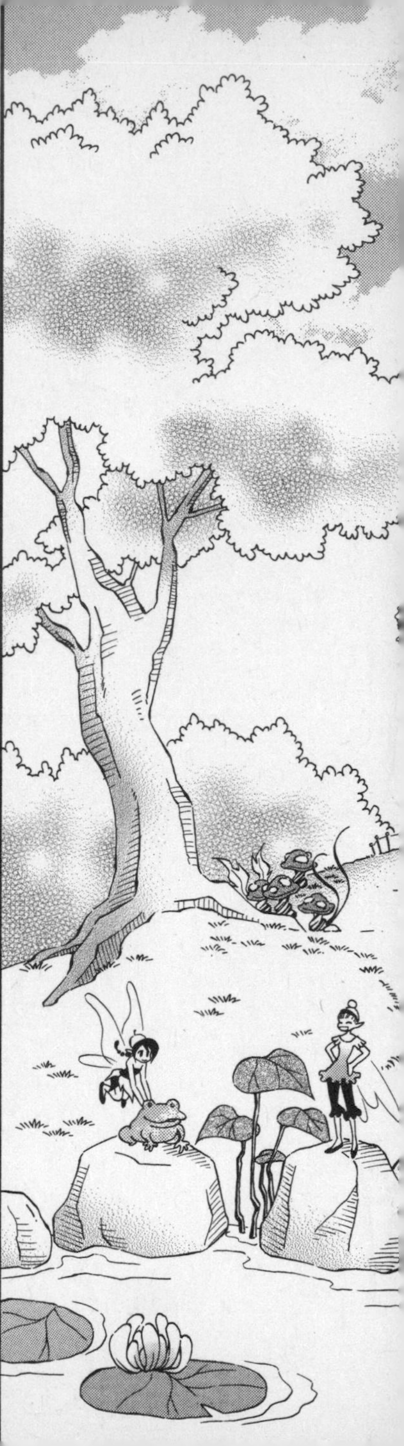

READ THIS WAY

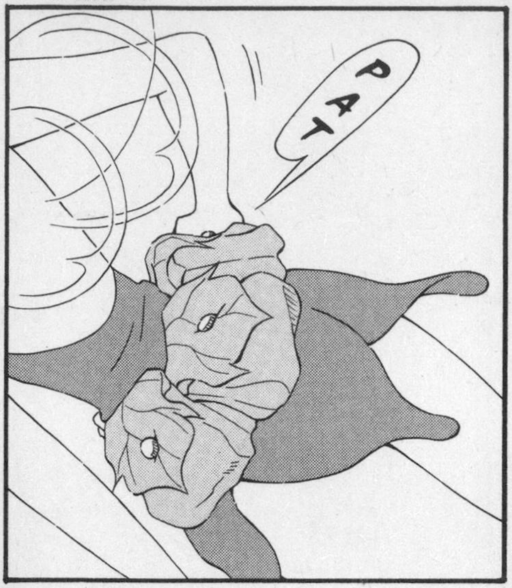
PAT

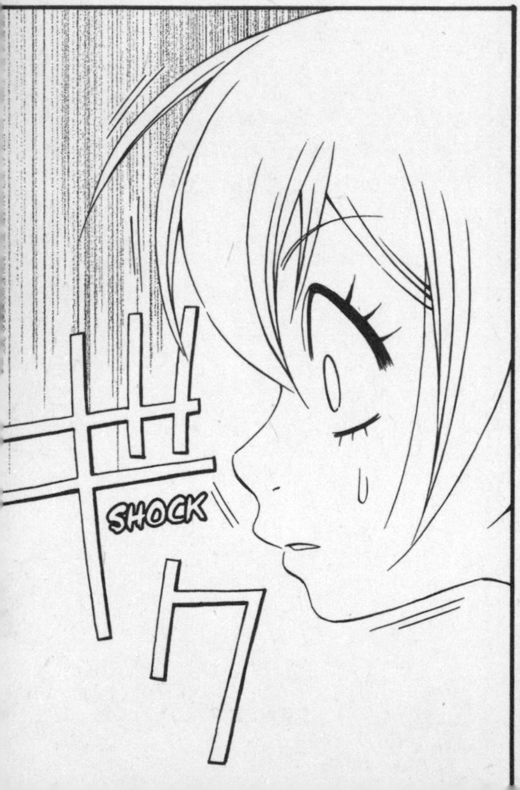
SHOCK

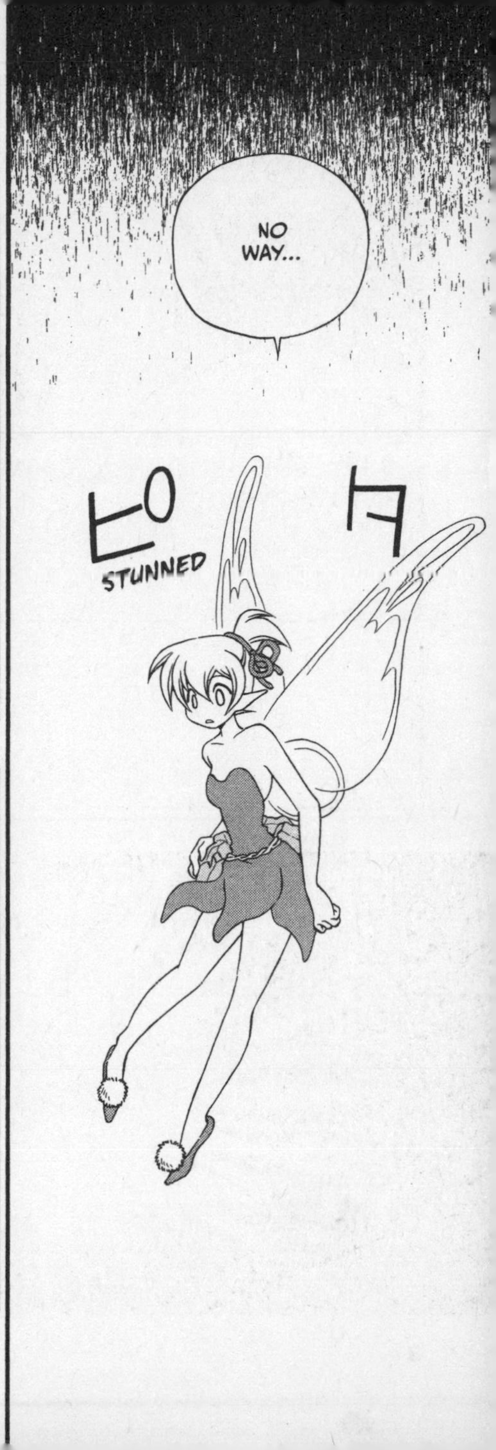
NO WAY...
ピタ
STUNNED

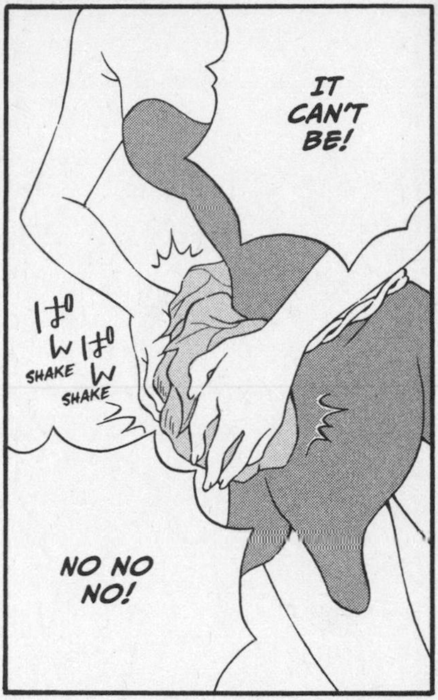
IT CAN'T BE!
ぱんぱん
SHAKE SHAKE
NO NO NO!

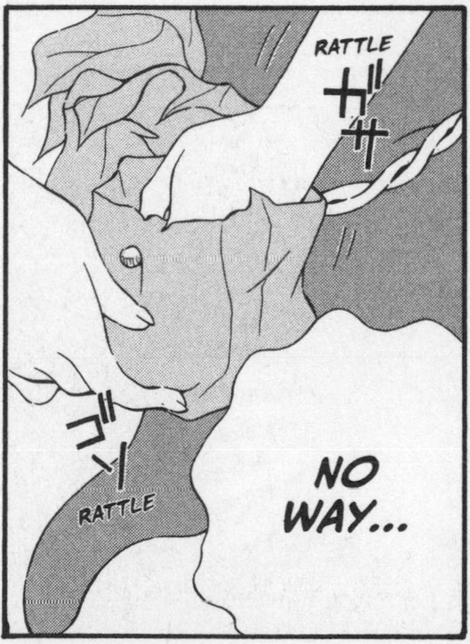
ガサ
RATTLE
ゴソ
RATTLE
NO WAY...

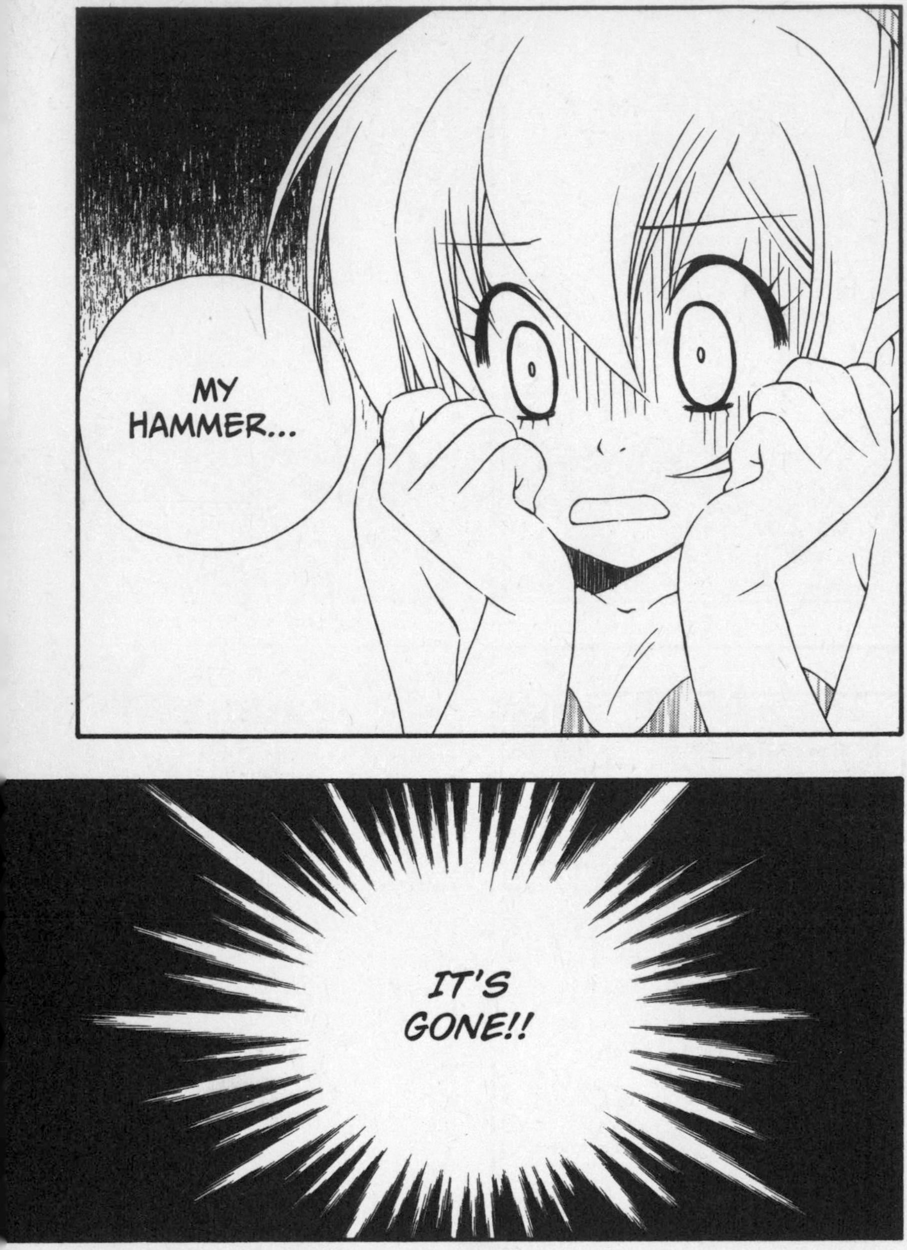
MY HAMMER...
IT'S GONE!!

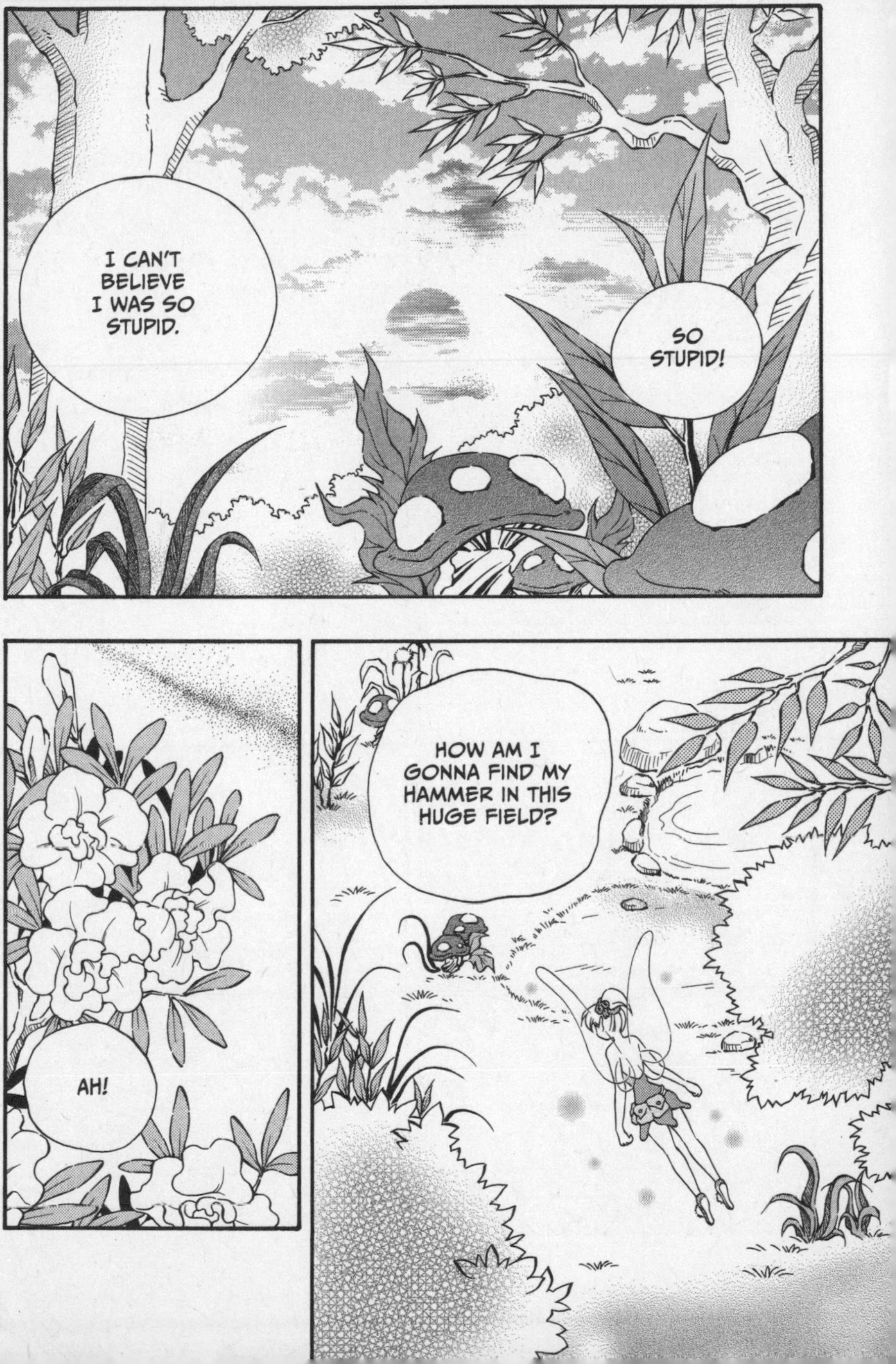
I CAN'T BELIEVE I WAS SO STUPID.
SO STUPID!
HOW AM I GONNA FIND MY HAMMER IN THIS HUGE FIELD?
AH!

READ THIS WAY

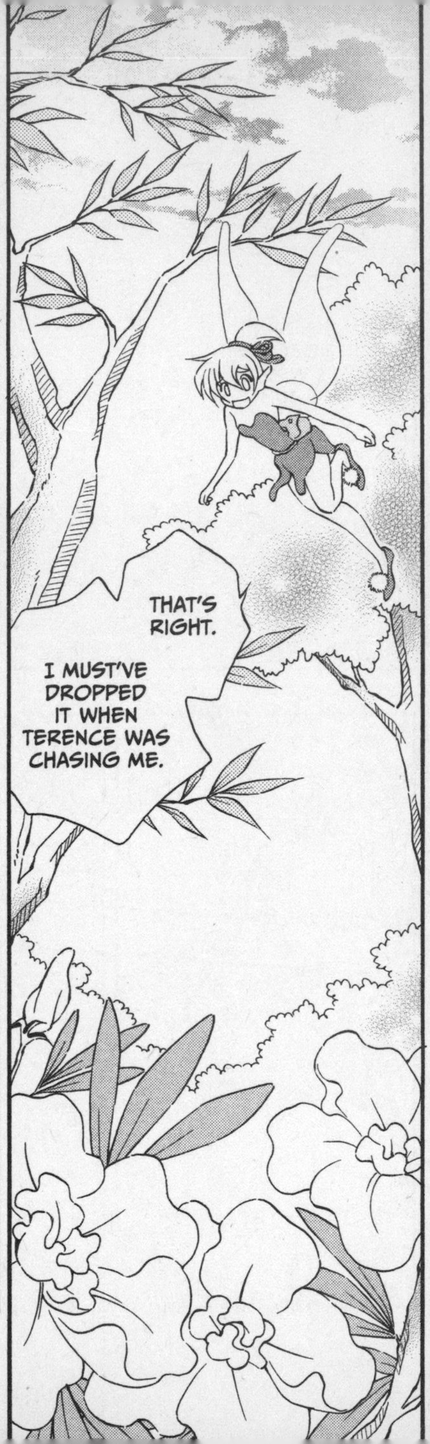
THAT'S RIGHT.
I MUST'VE DROPPED IT WHEN TERENCE WAS CHASING ME.

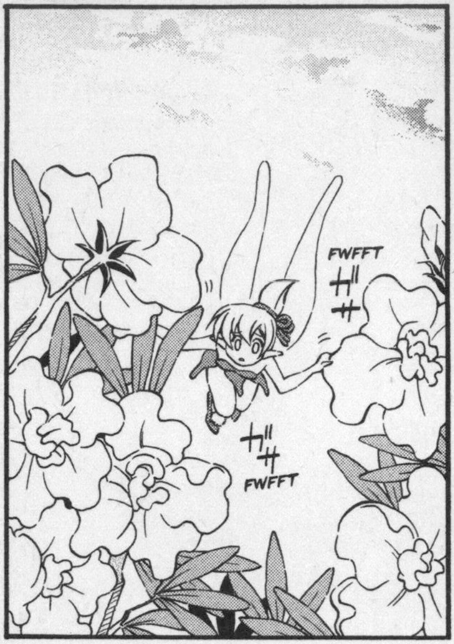
FWFFT
FWFFT

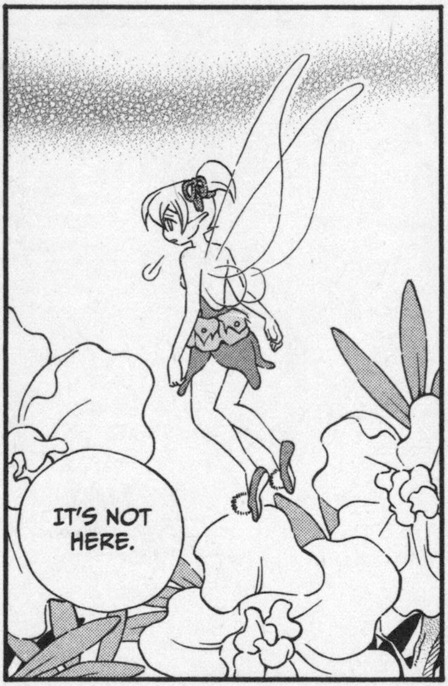
IT'S NOT HERE.

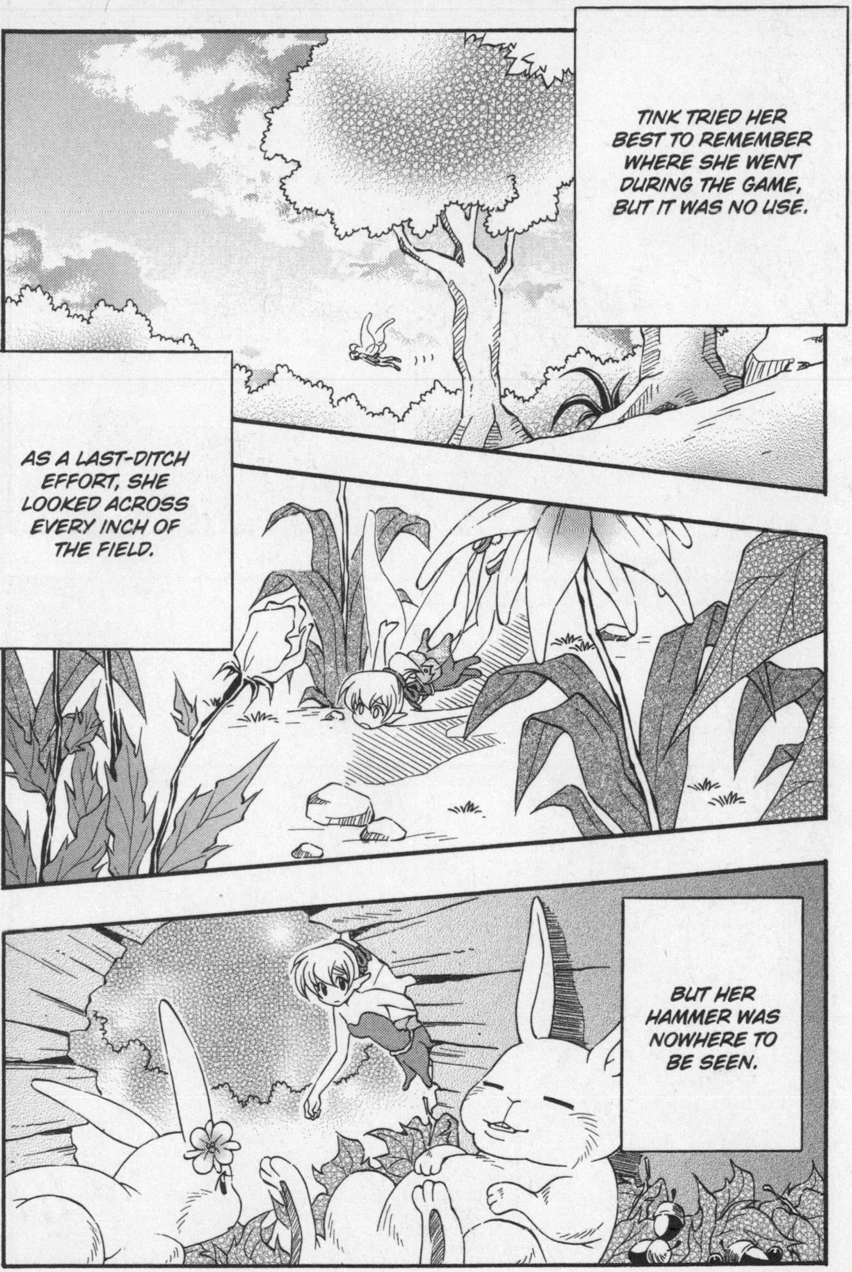
TINK TRIED HER BEST TO REMEMBER WHERE SHE WENT DURING THE GAME, BUT IT WAS NO USE.
AS A LAST-DITCH EFFORT, SHE LOOKED ACROSS EVERY INCH OF THE FIELD.
BUT HER HAMMER WAS NOWHERE TO BE SEEN.

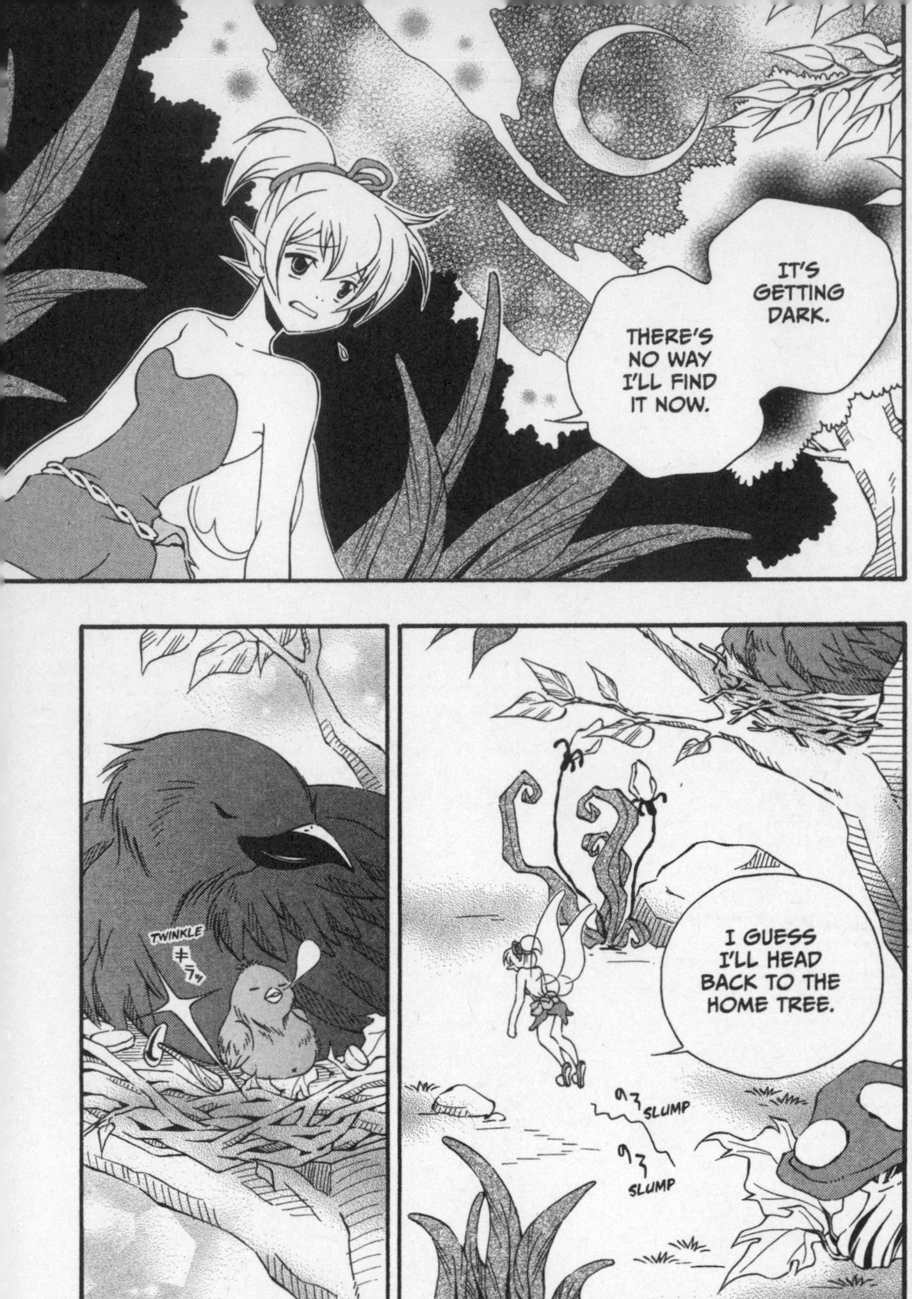
IT'S GETTING DARK.
THERE'S NO WAY I'LL FIND IT NOW.
I GUESS I'LL HEAD BACK TO THE HOME TREE.
SLUMP
SLUMP
TWINKLE
キラッ

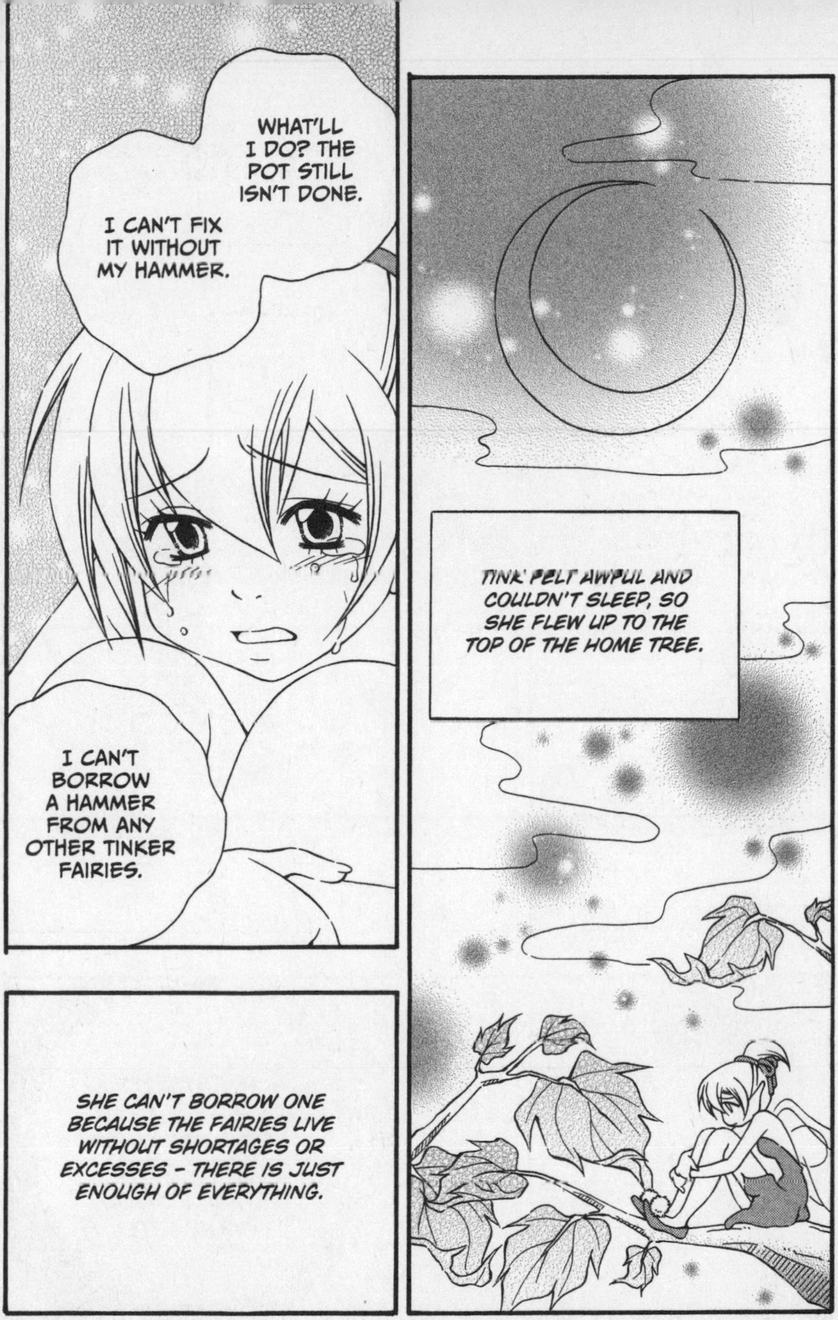
TINK FELT AWFUL AND COULDN'T SLEEP, SO SHE FLEW UP TO THE TOP OF THE HOME TREE.
WHAT'LL I DO? THE POT STILL ISN'T DONE.
I CAN'T FIX IT WITHOUT MY HAMMER.
I CAN'T BORROW A HAMMER FROM ANY OTHER TINKER FAIRIES.
SHE CAN'T BORROW ONE BECAUSE THE FAIRIES LIVE WITHOUT SHORTAGES OR EXCESSES - THERE IS JUST ENOUGH OF EVERYTHING.

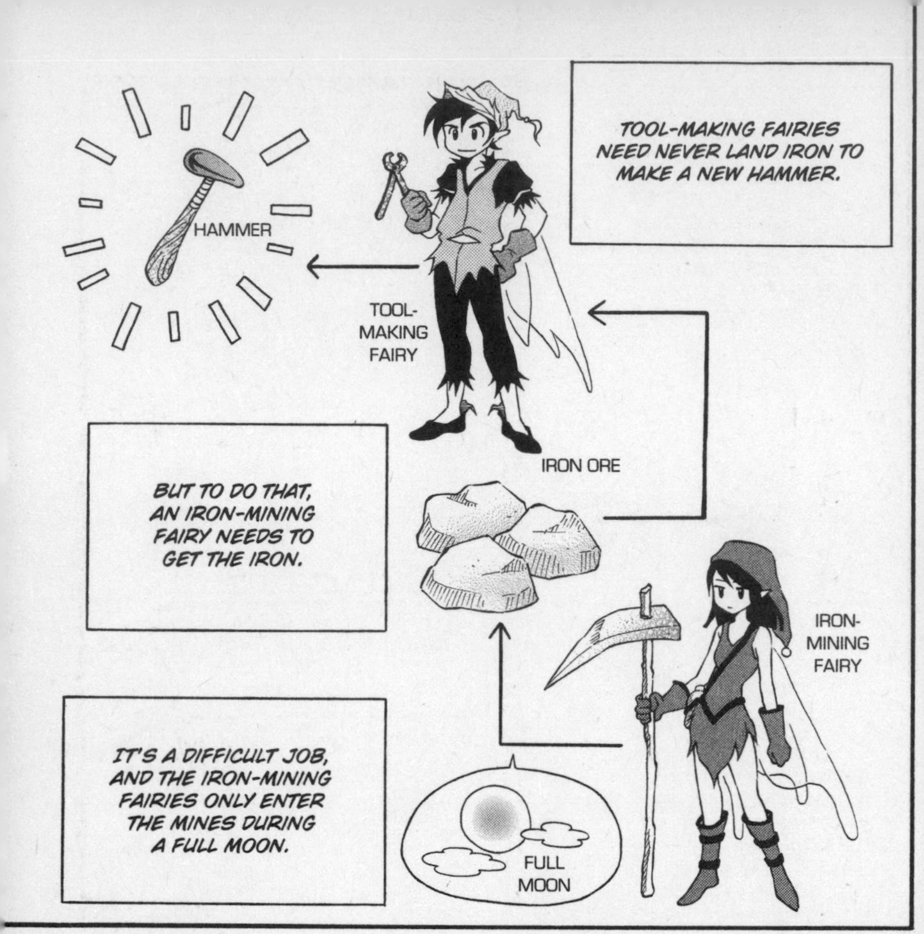
TOOL-MAKING FAIRIES NEED NEVER LAND IRON TO MAKE A NEW HAMMER.
HAMMER
TOOL-MAKING FAIRY
BUT TO DO THAT, AN IRON-MINING FAIRY NEEDS TO GET THE IRON.
IRON ORE
IRON-MINING FAIRY
IT'S A DIFFICULT JOB, AND THE IRON-MINING FAIRIES ONLY ENTER THE MINES DURING A FULL MOON.
FULL MOON

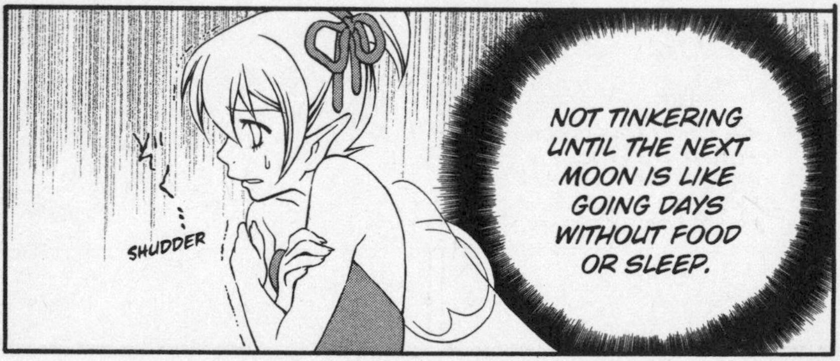
NOT TINKERING UNTIL THE NEXT MOON IS LIKE GOING DAYS WITHOUT FOOD OR SLEEP.
SHUDDER

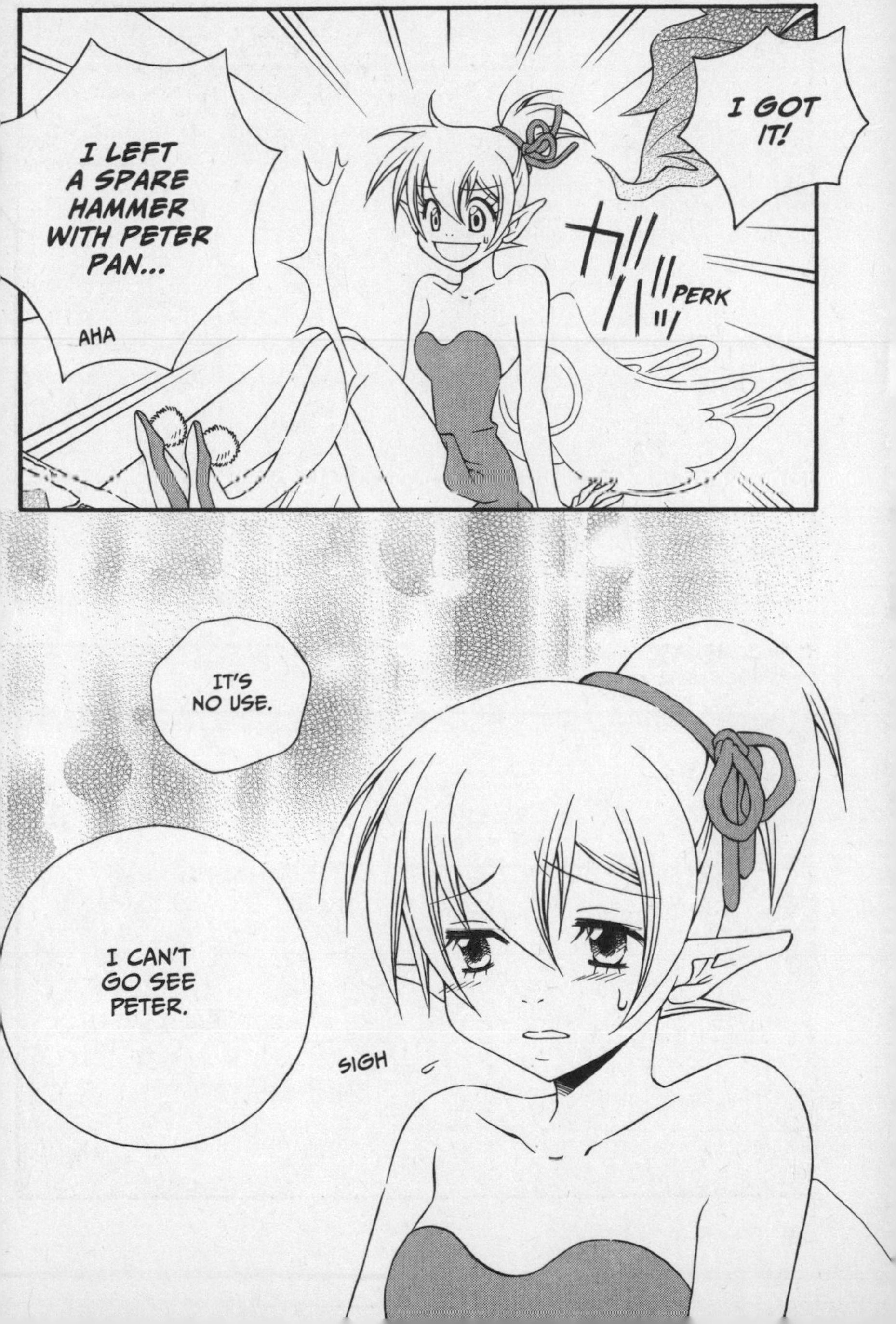
I GOT IT!
PERK
I LEFT A SPARE HAMMER WITH PETER PAN...
AHA
IT'S NO USE.
I CAN'T GO SEE PETER.
SIGH

READ THIS WAY

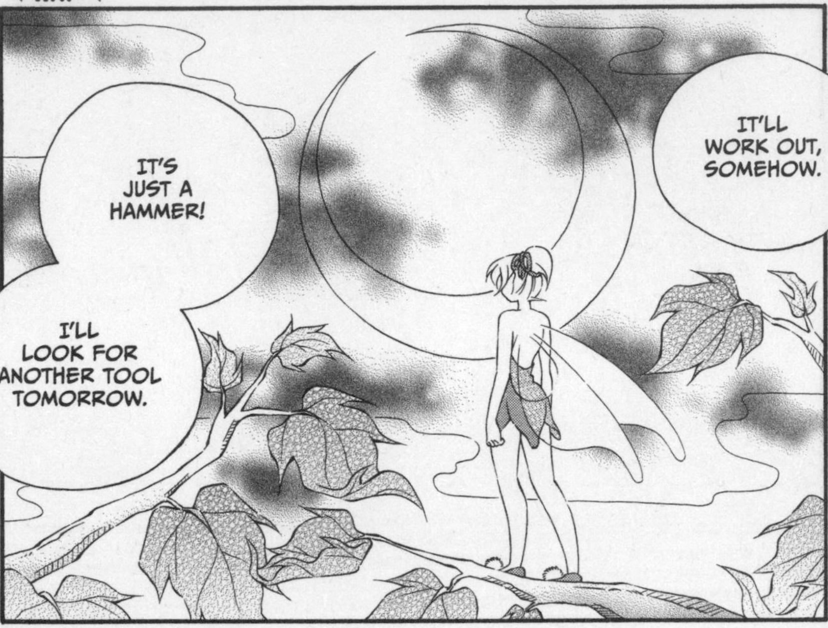
IT'LL WORK OUT, SOMEHOW.
IT'S JUST A HAMMER!
I'LL LOOK FOR ANOTHER TOOL TOMORROW.

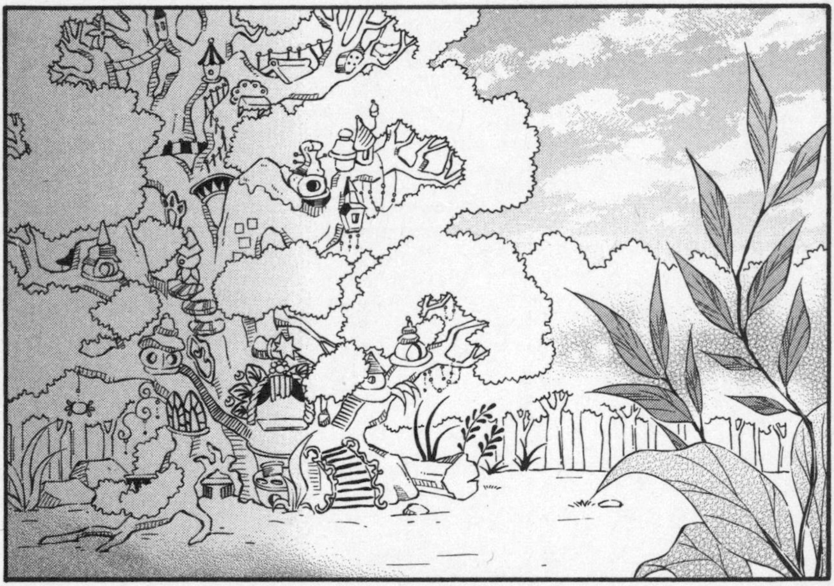

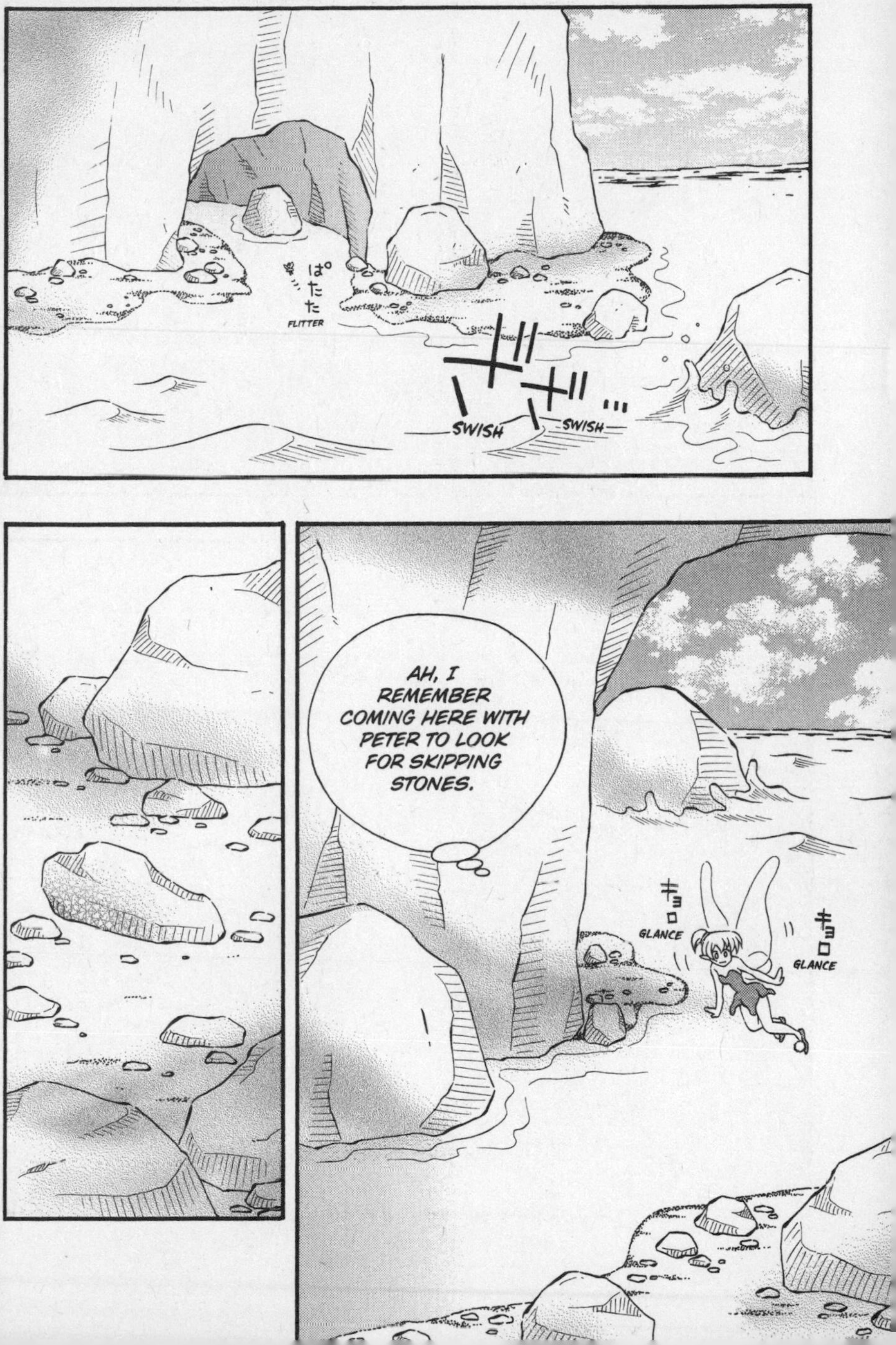
ぱたた
FLITTER
SWISH
SWISH
AH, I REMEMBER COMING HERE WITH PETER TO LOOK FOR SKIPPING STONES.
キョロ
GLANCE
キョロ
GLANCE

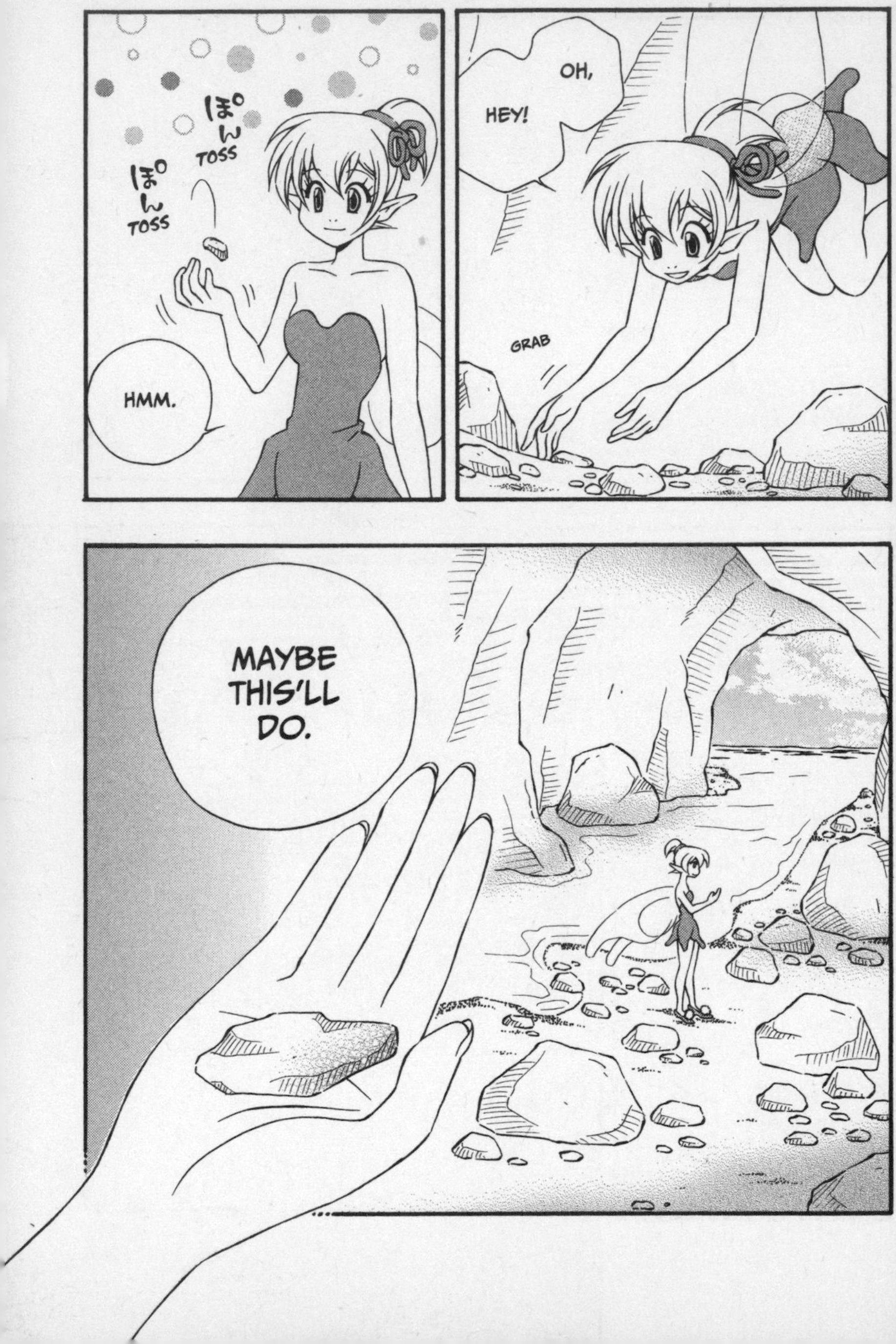
OH,
HEY!
GRAB
ぽん
TOSS
ぽん
TOSS
HMM.
MAYBE THIS'LL DO.

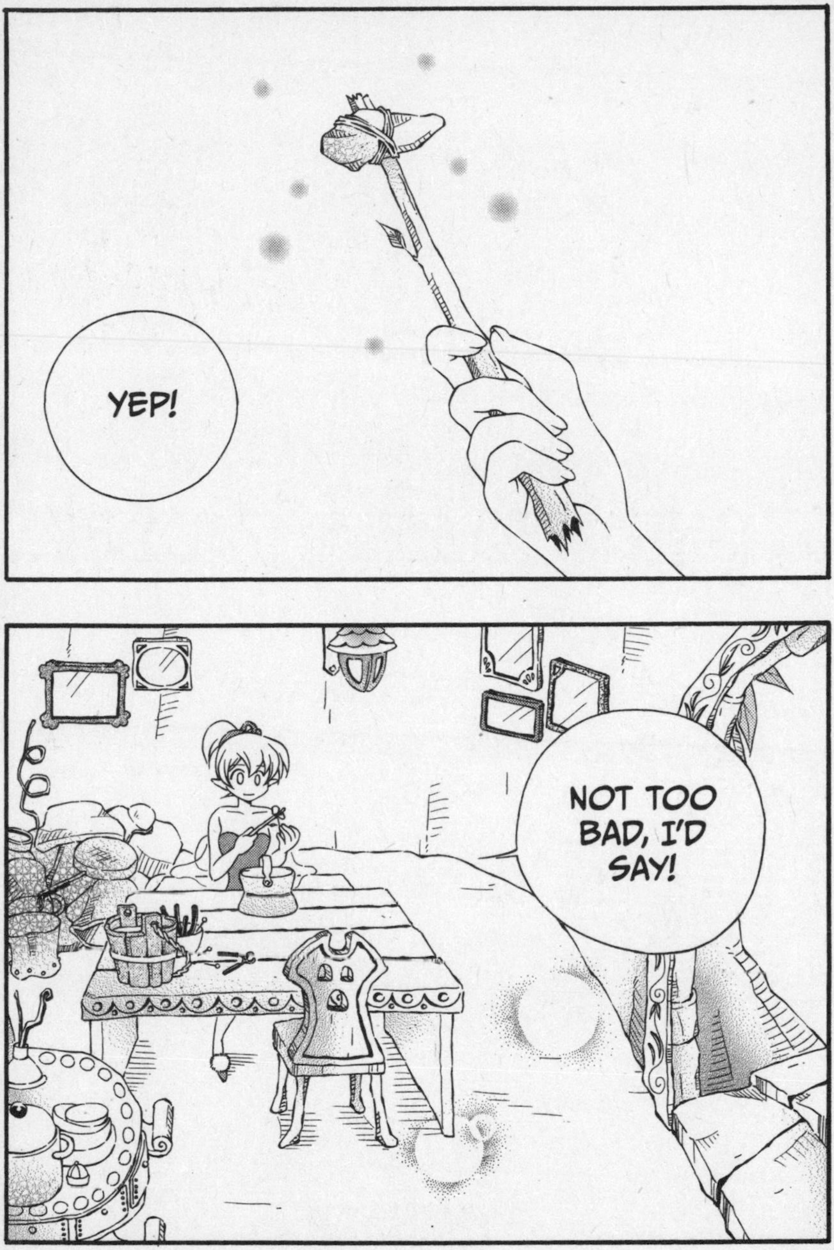
YEP!
NOT TOO BAD, I'D SAY!

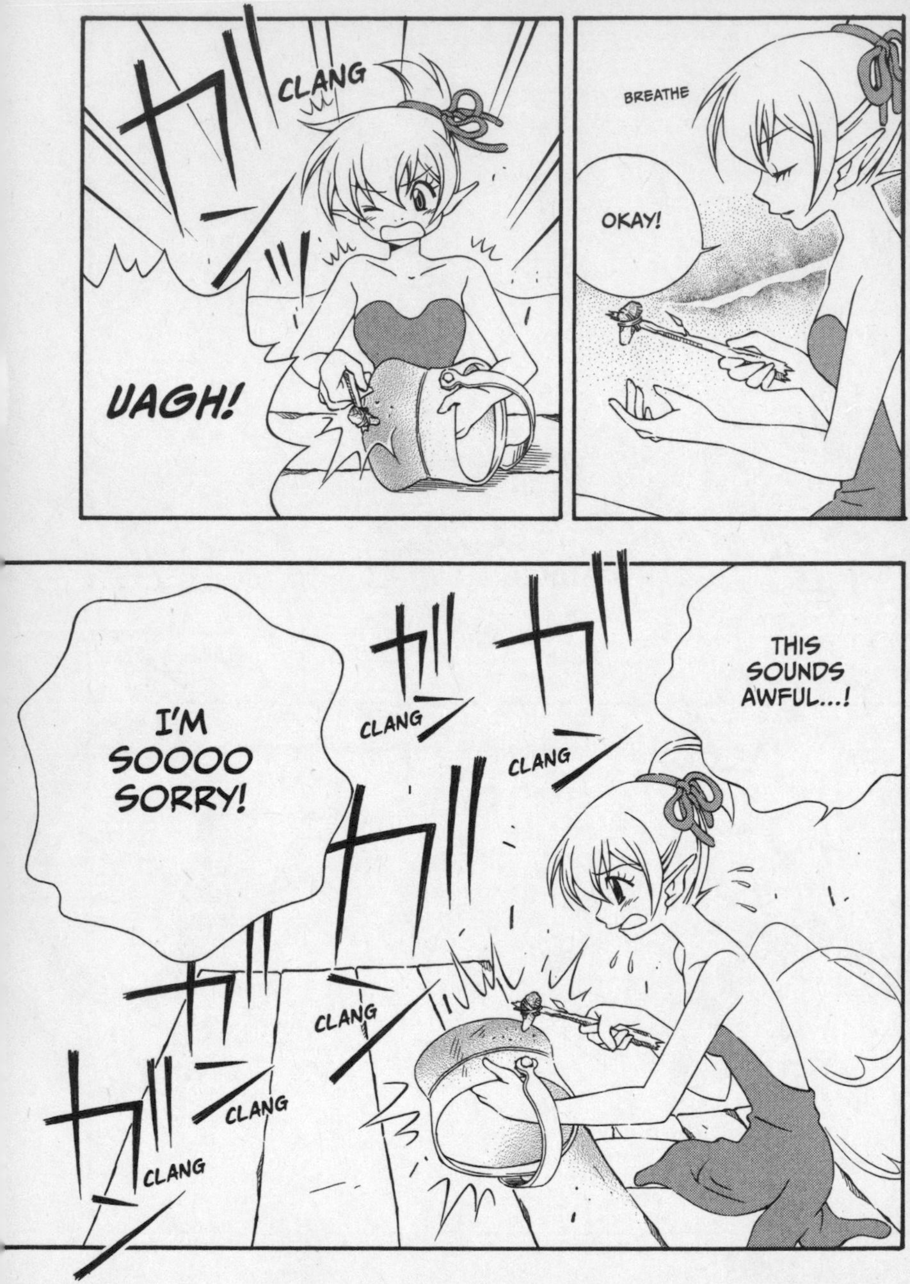
BREATHE
OKAY!
CLANG
UAGH!
THIS SOUNDS AWFUL...!
CLANG
CLANG
I'M SOOOO SORRY!
CLANG
CLANG
CLANG

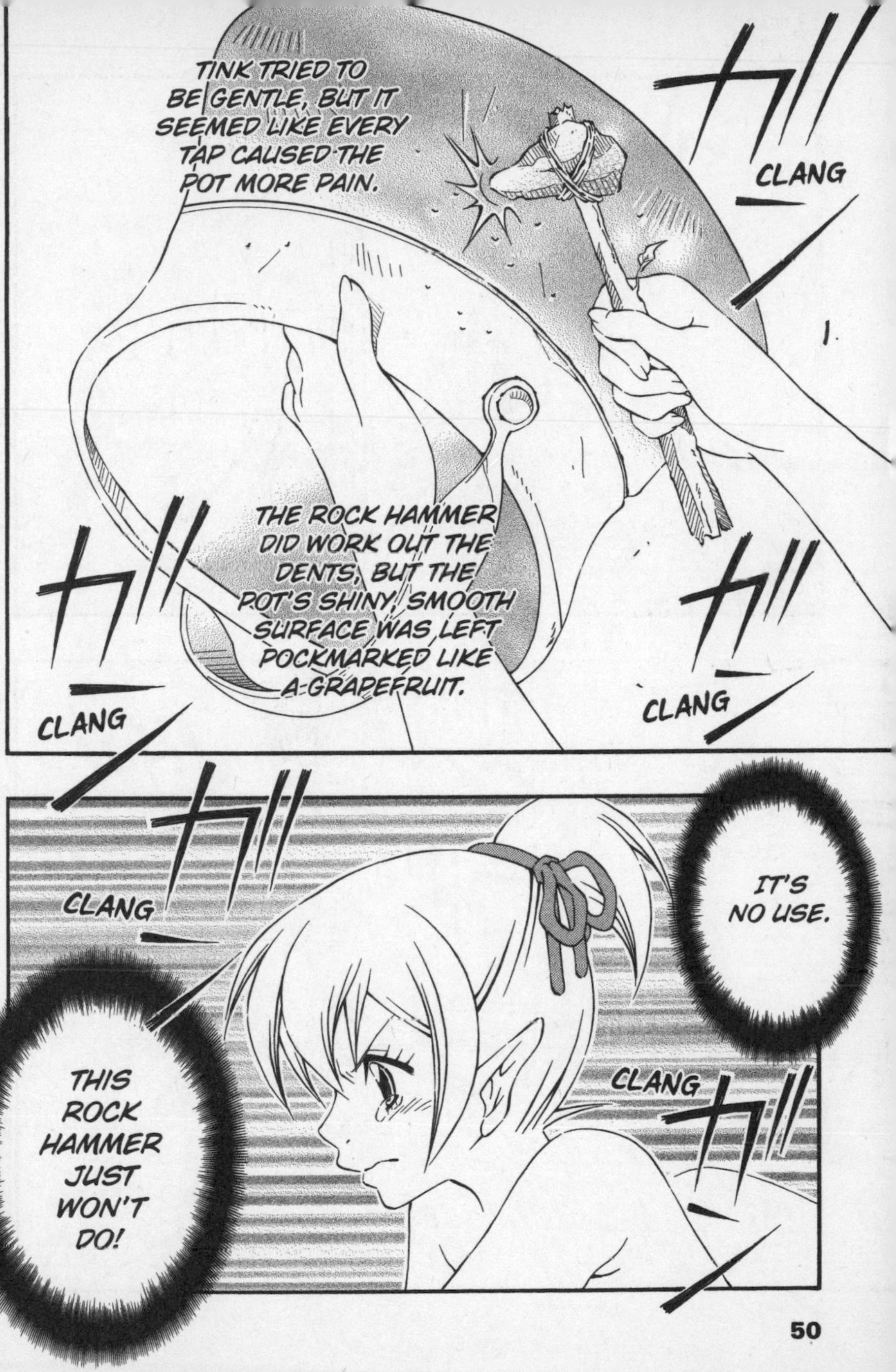
CLANG
TINK TRIED TO BE GENTLE, BUT IT SEEMED LIKE EVERY TAP CAUSED THE POT MORE PAIN.
THE ROCK HAMMER DID WORK OUT THE DENTS, BUT THE POT'S SHINY, SMOOTH SURFACE WAS LEFT POCKMARKED LIKE A GRAPEFRUIT.
CLANG
CLANG
IT'S NO USE.
CLANG
CLANG
THIS ROCK HAMMER JUST WON'T DO!

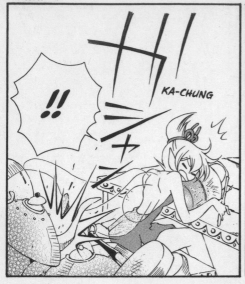

!!

KA-CHUNG

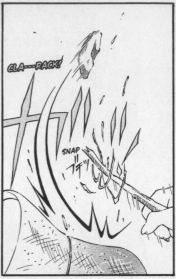

CLA---RACK!

SNAP

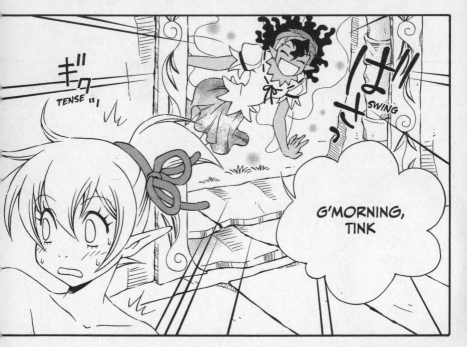

TENSE

SWING

G'MORNING,
TINK

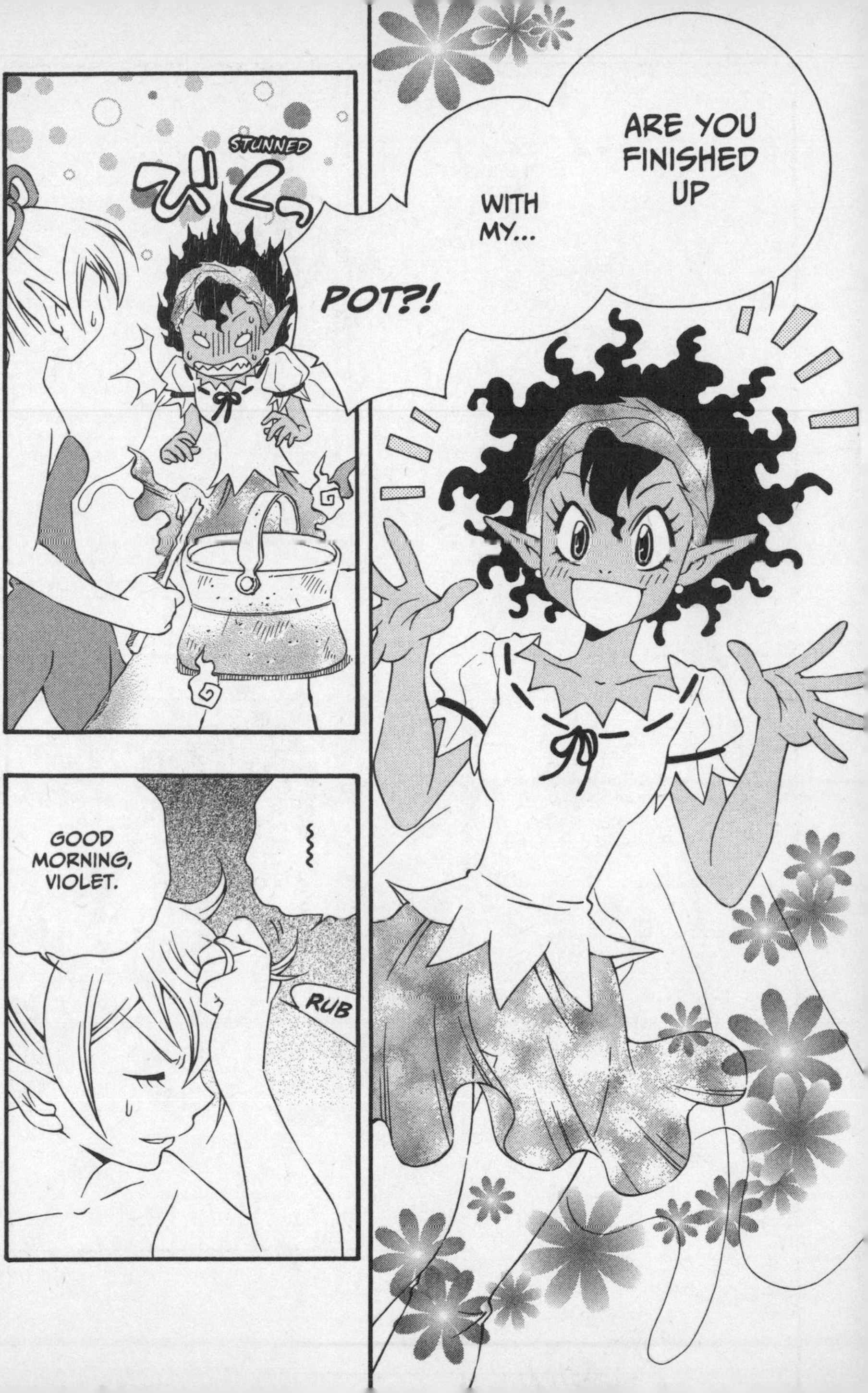

ARE YOU FINISHED UP
WITH MY...
POT?!
STUNNED
びくっ
GOOD MORNING, VIOLET.
RUB

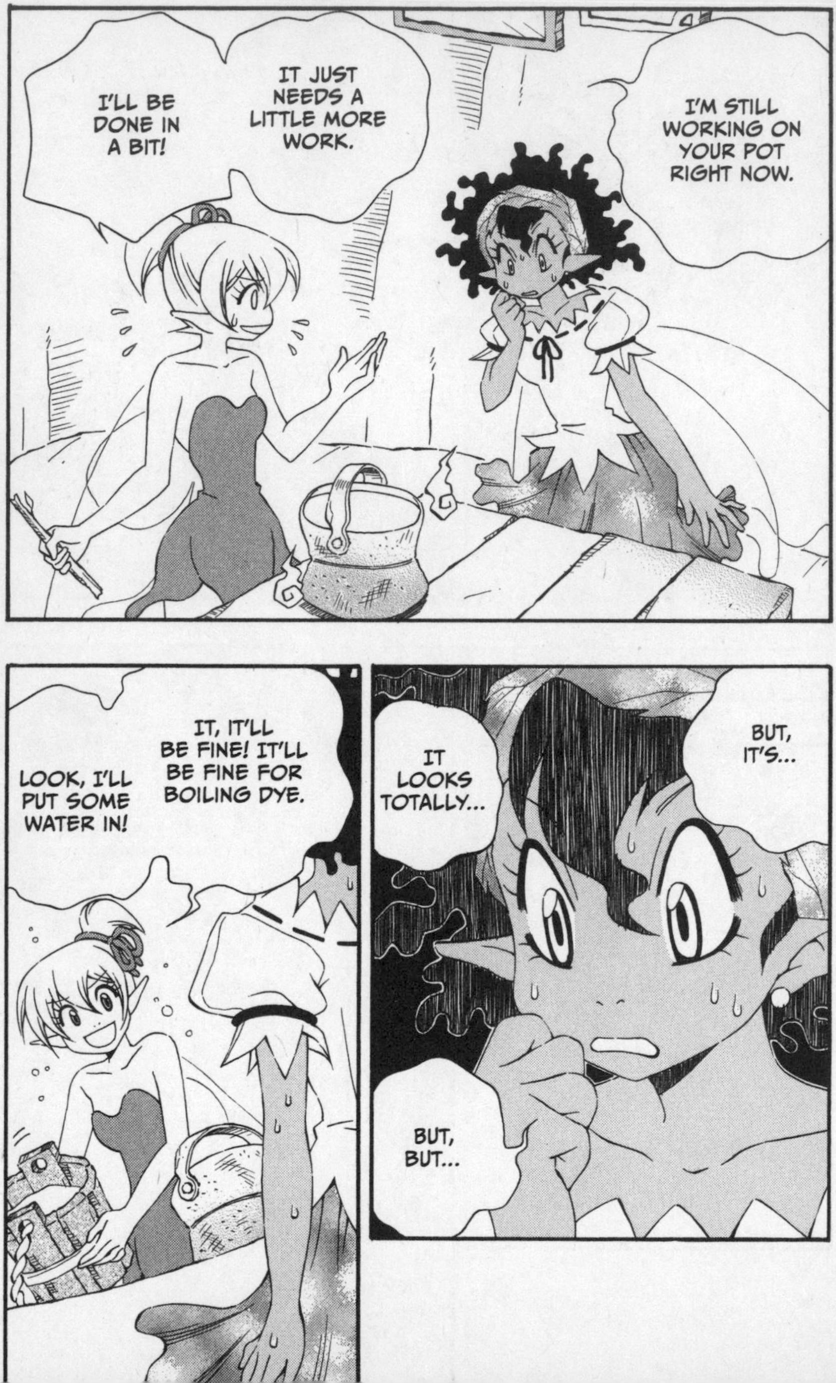
I'M STILL WORKING ON YOUR POT RIGHT NOW.
IT JUST NEEDS A LITTLE MORE WORK.
I'LL BE DONE IN A BIT!
BUT, IT'S...
IT LOOKS TOTALLY...
BUT, BUT...
IT, IT'LL BE FINE! IT'LL BE FINE FOR BOILING DYE.
LOOK, I'LL PUT SOME WATER IN!

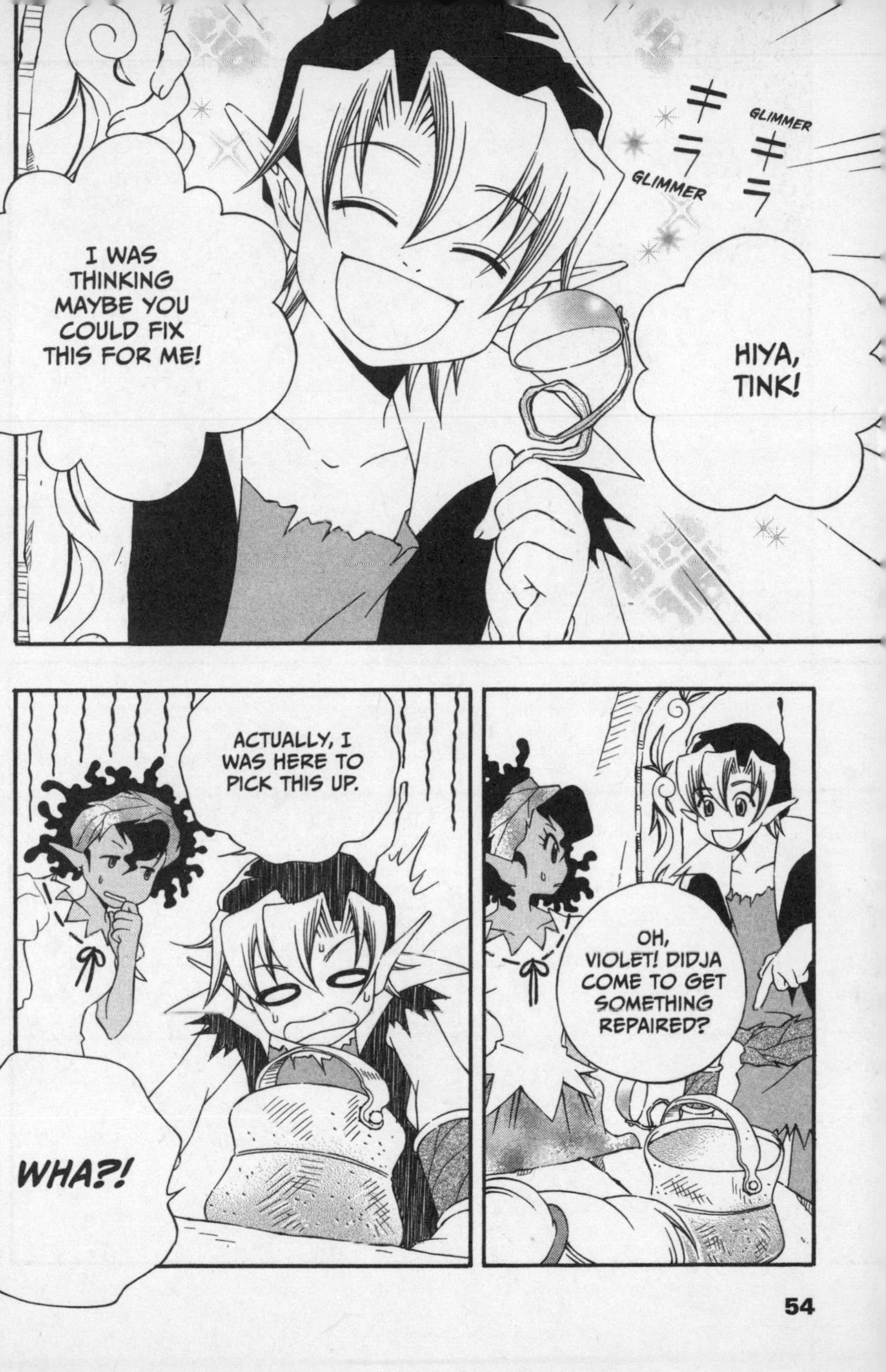
キラキラ
GLIMMER
GLIMMER
HIYA, TINK!
I WAS THINKING MAYBE YOU COULD FIX THIS FOR ME!
OH, VIOLET! DIDJA COME TO GET SOMETHING REPAIRED?
ACTUALLY, I WAS HERE TO PICK THIS UP.
WHA?!

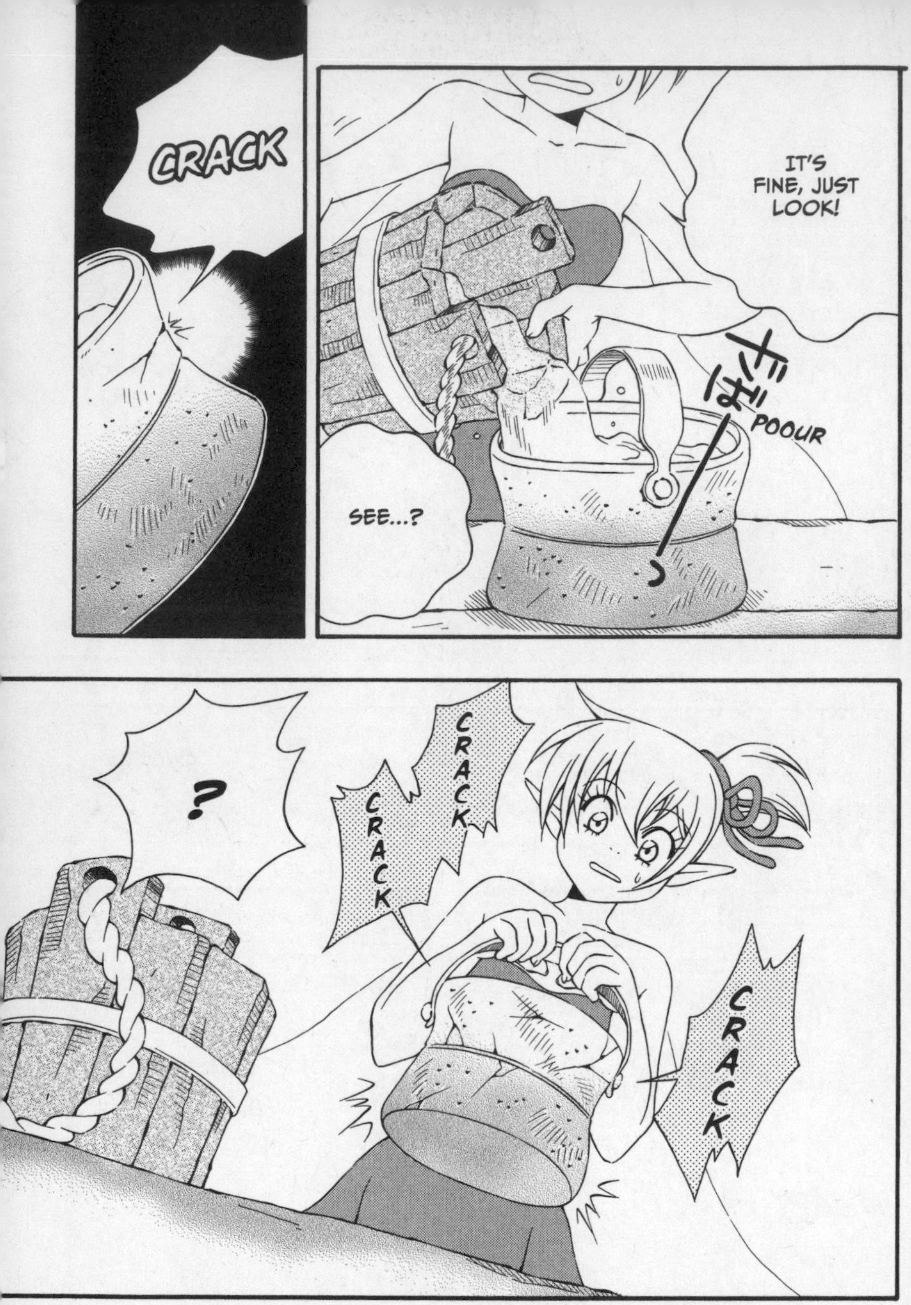
IT'S FINE, JUST LOOK!
POOUR
SEE...?
CRACK
CRACK
CRACK
CRACK
?

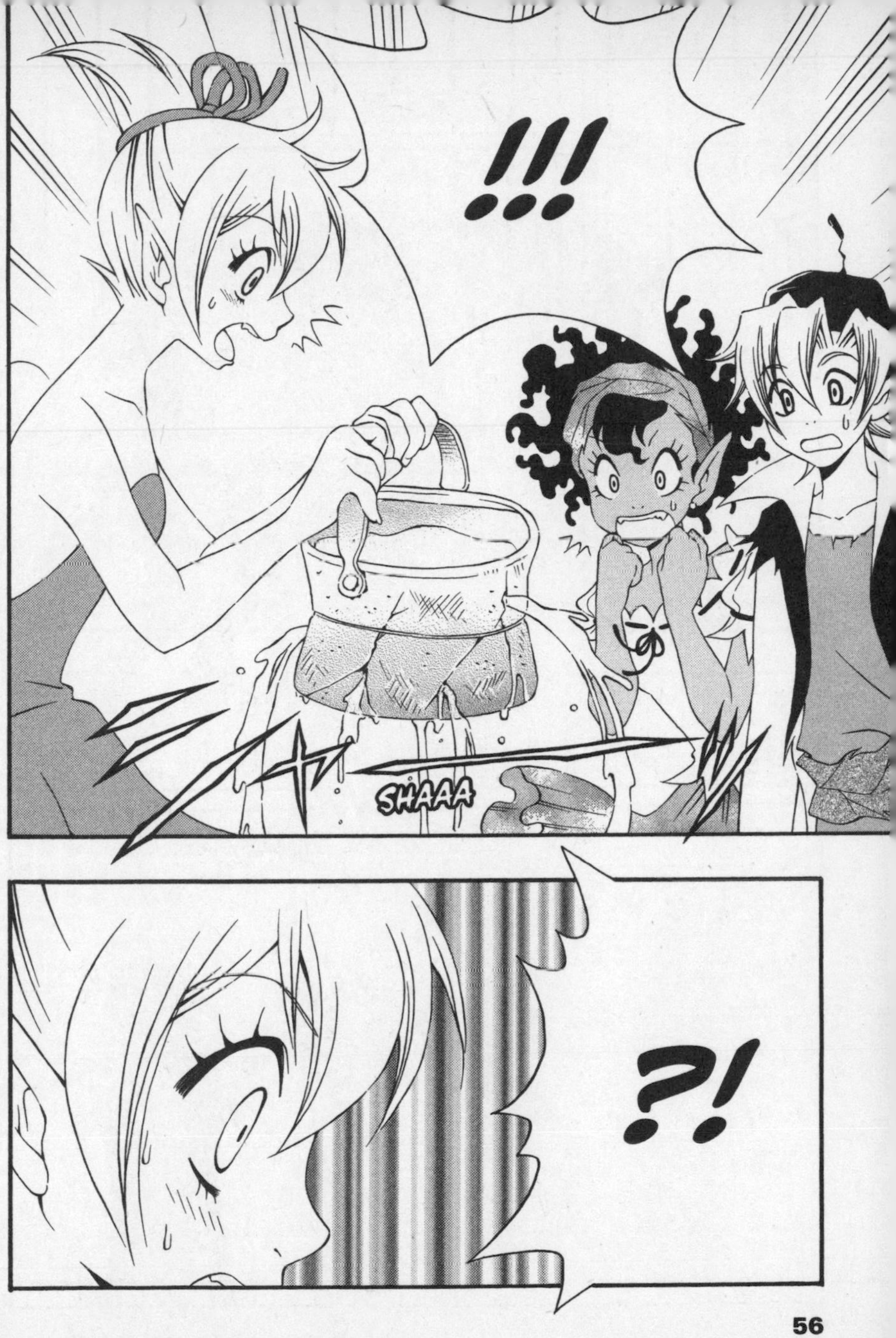
!!!
SHAAA
?!

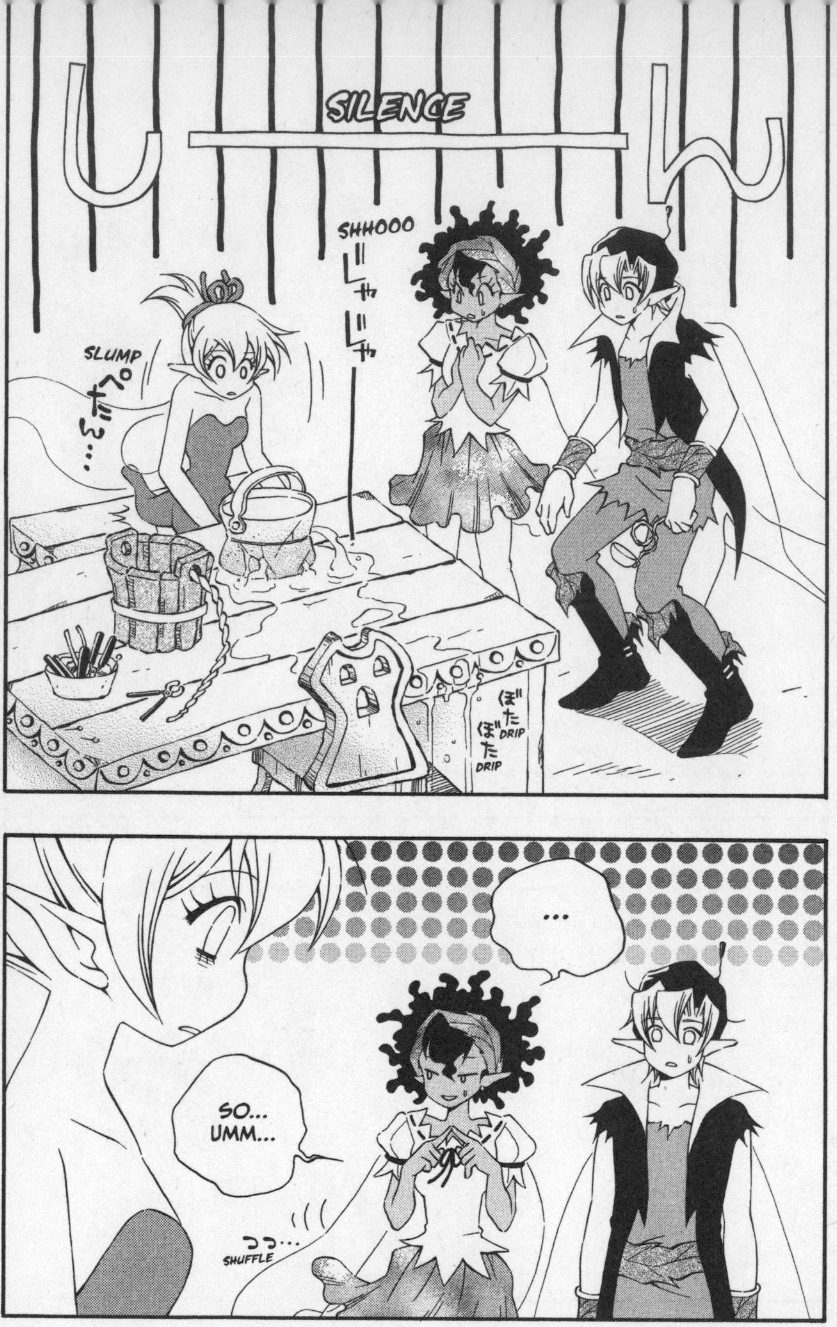
SILENCE
SHHOOO
じゃじゃ
SLUMP
ぺたん…
ぽた ぽた
DRIP DRIP
...
SO... UMM...
つつ…
SHUFFLE

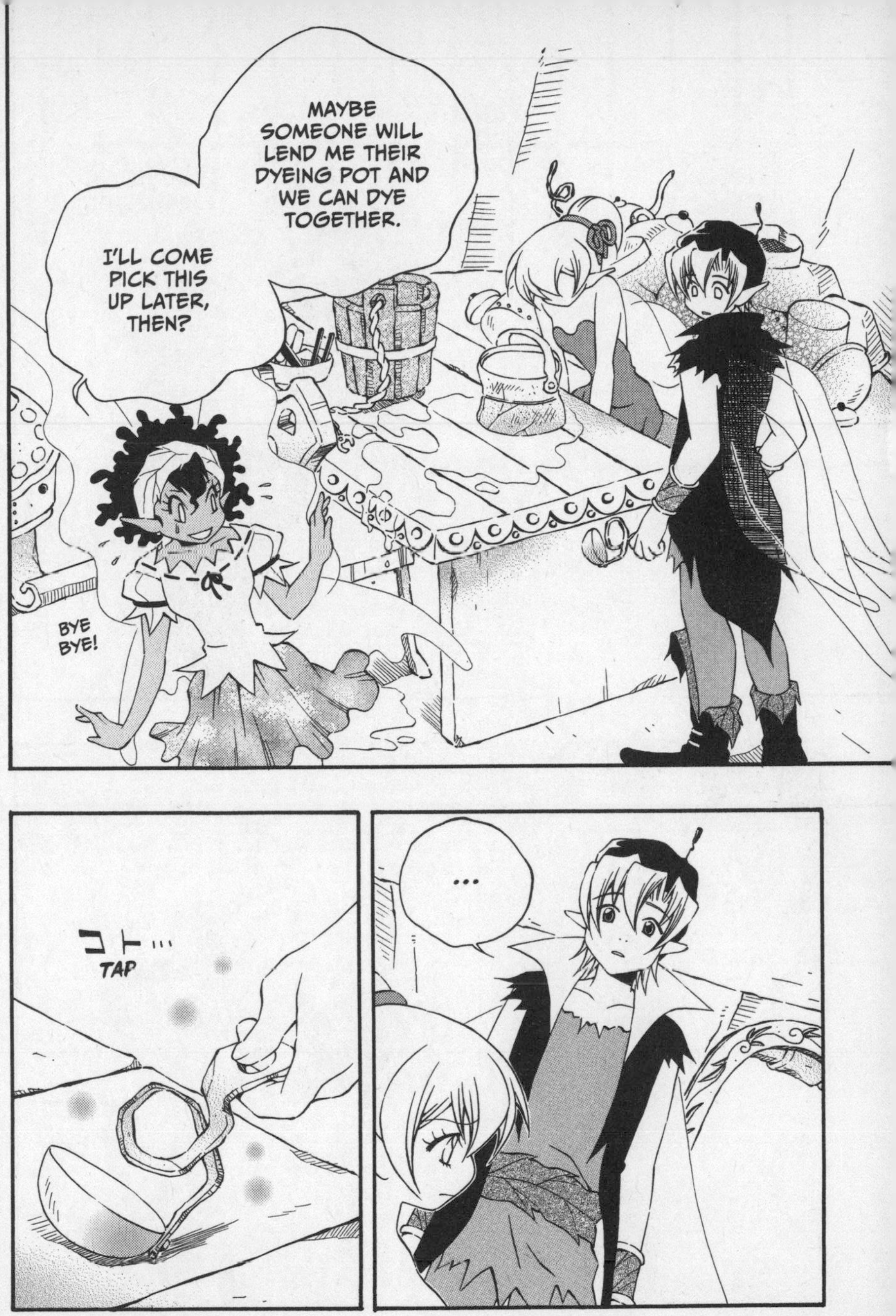
MAYBE SOMEONE WILL LEND ME THEIR DYEING POT AND WE CAN DYE TOGETHER.
I'LL COME PICK THIS UP LATER, THEN?
BYE BYE!
...
コト…
TAP

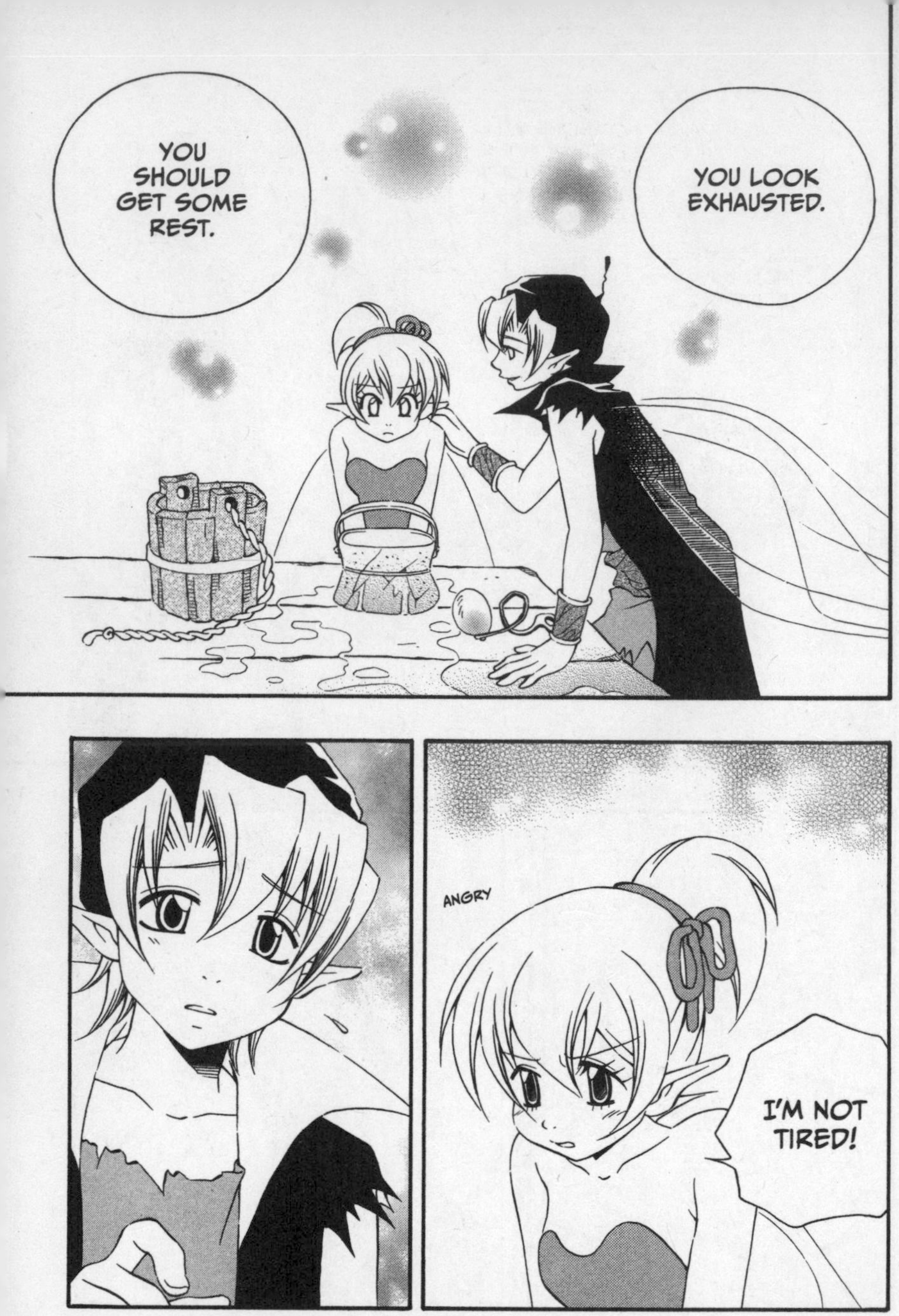
YOU LOOK EXHAUSTED.
YOU SHOULD GET SOME REST.
ANGRY
I'M NOT TIRED!

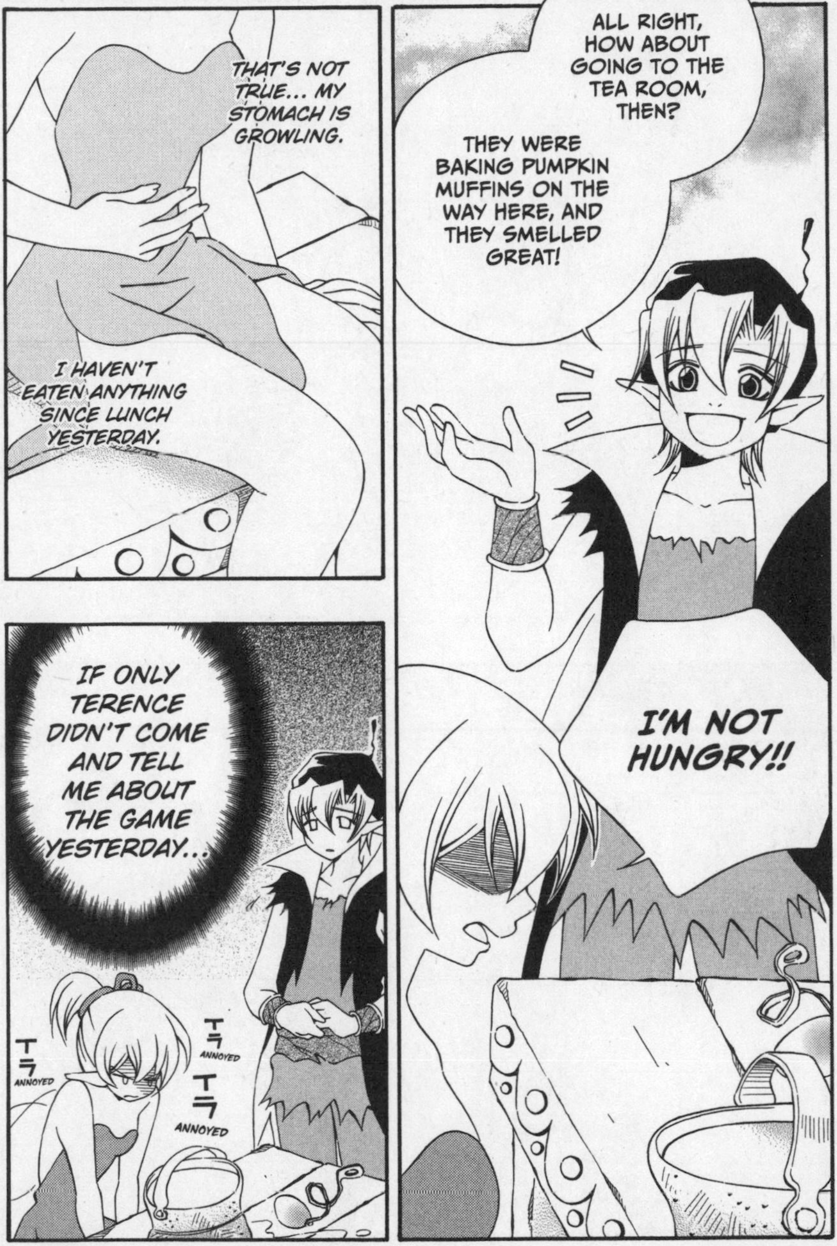
ALL RIGHT, HOW ABOUT GOING TO THE TEA ROOM, THEN?
THEY WERE BAKING PUMPKIN MUFFINS ON THE WAY HERE, AND THEY SMELLED GREAT!
I'M NOT HUNGRY!!
THAT'S NOT TRUE... MY STOMACH IS GROWLING.
I HAVEN'T EATEN ANYTHING SINCE LUNCH YESTERDAY.
IF ONLY TERENCE DIDN'T COME AND TELL ME ABOUT THE GAME YESTERDAY...
ANNOYED
ANNOYED
ANNOYED

READ THIS WAY

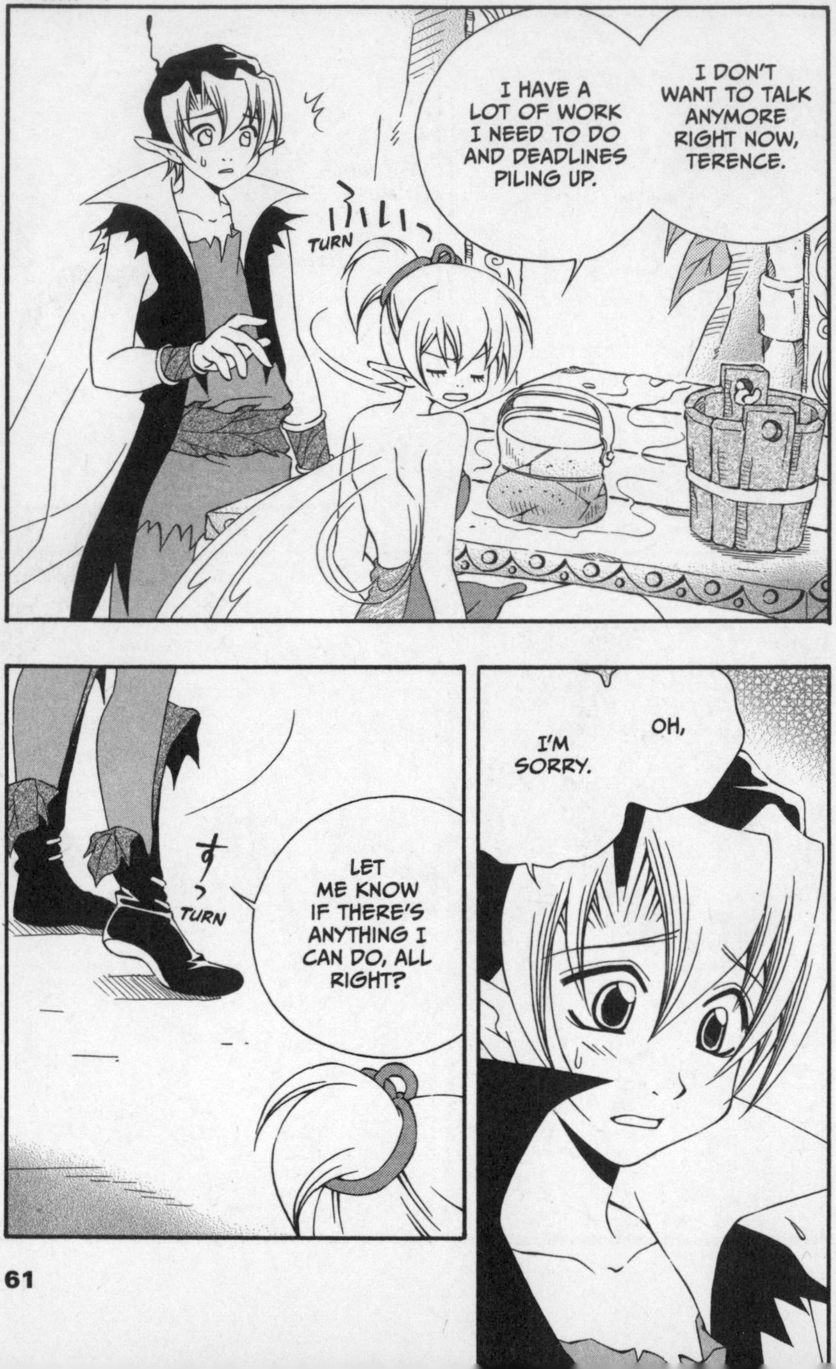

I DON'T WANT TO TALK ANYMORE RIGHT NOW, TERENCE.
I HAVE A LOT OF WORK I NEED TO DO AND DEADLINES PILING UP.
ふいっ
TURN
OH,
I'M SORRY.
LET ME KNOW IF THERE'S ANYTHING I CAN DO, ALL RIGHT?
すっ
TURN

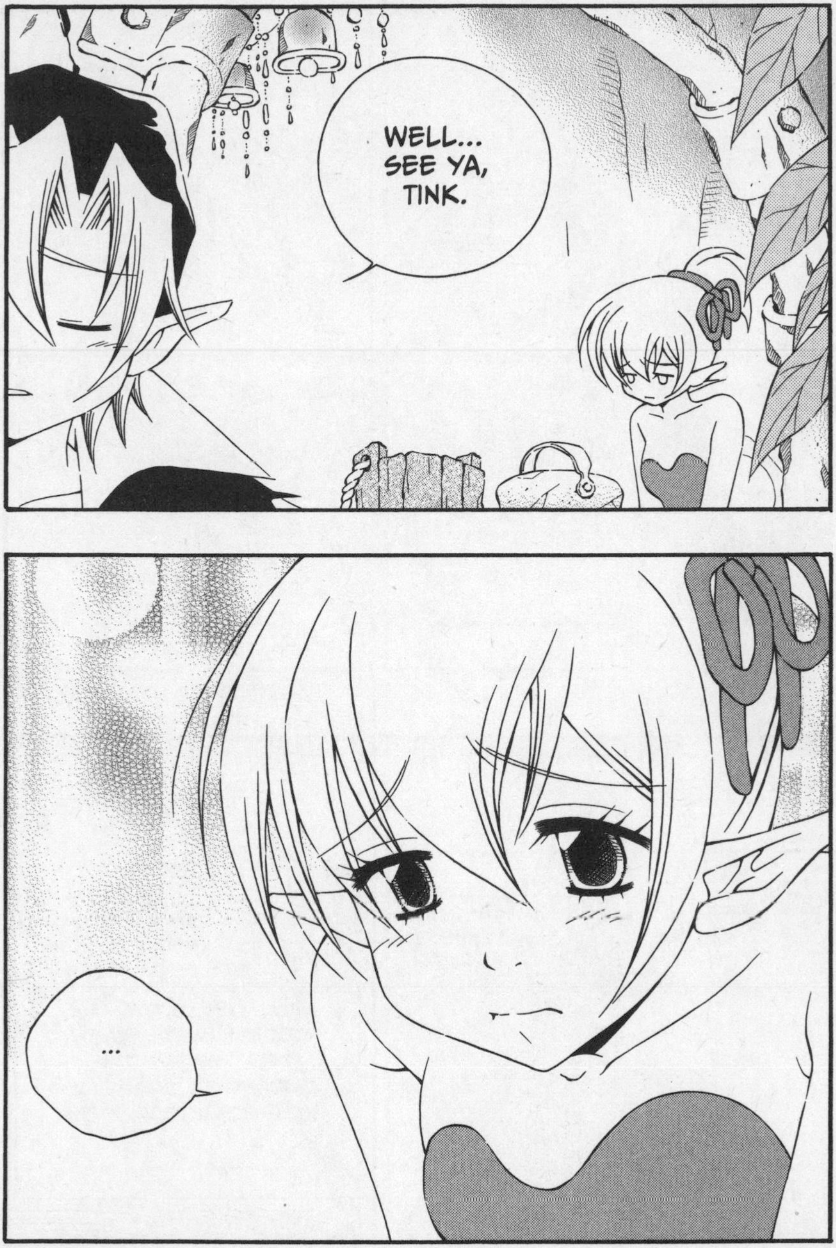
WELL... SEE YA, TINK.
...

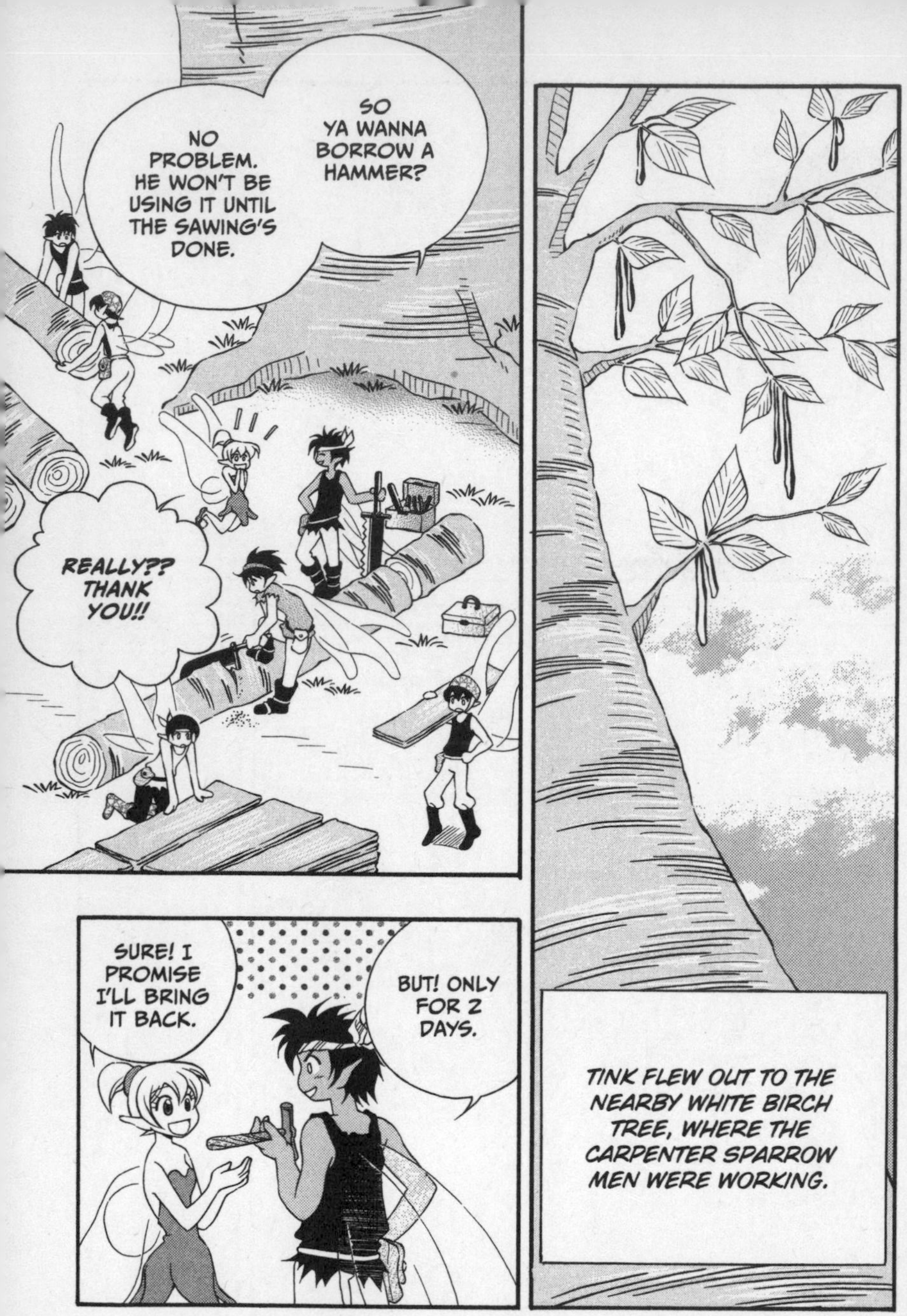
TINK FLEW OUT TO THE NEARBY WHITE BIRCH TREE, WHERE THE CARPENTER SPARROW MEN WERE WORKING.
SO YA WANNA BORROW A HAMMER?
NO PROBLEM. HE WON'T BE USING IT UNTIL THE SAWING'S DONE.
REALLY?? THANK YOU!!
BUT! ONLY FOR 2 DAYS.
SURE! I PROMISE I'LL BRING IT BACK.

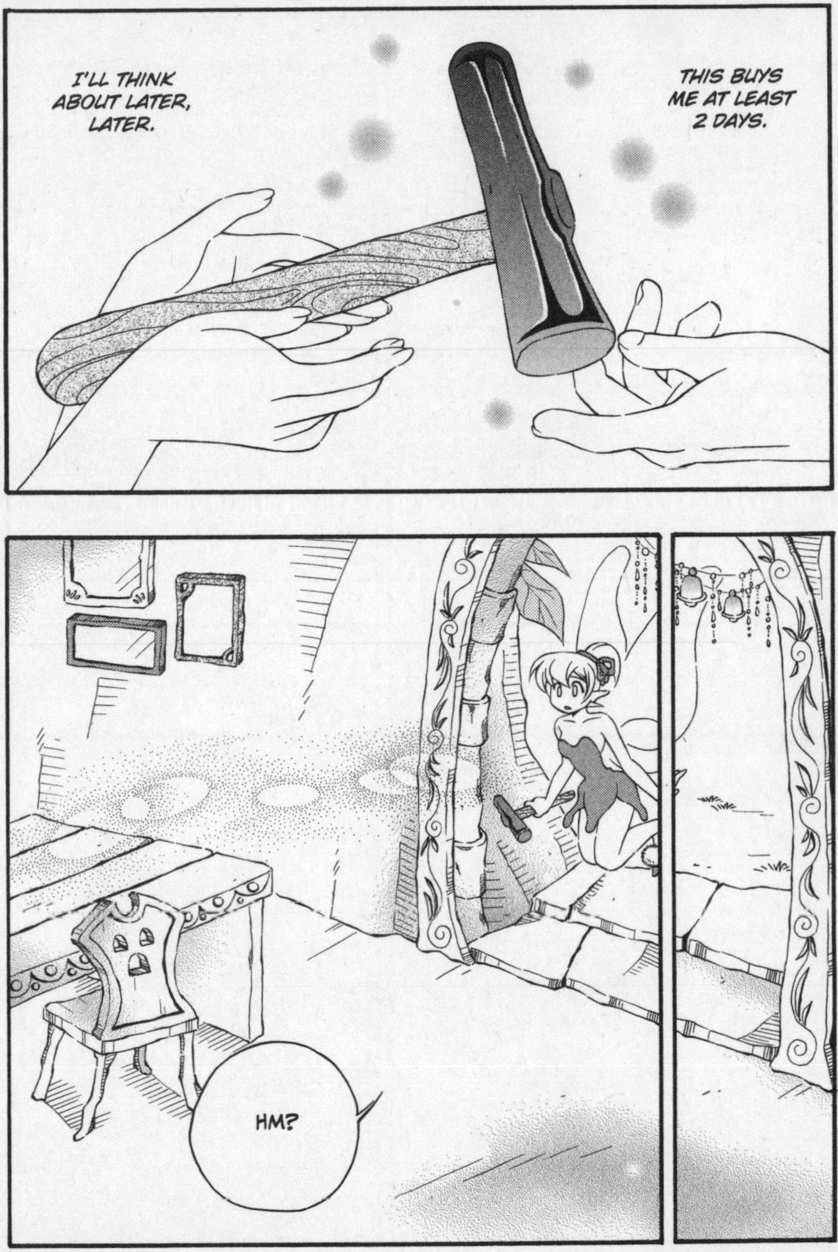
THIS BUYS ME AT LEAST 2 DAYS.
I'LL THINK ABOUT LATER, LATER.
HM?

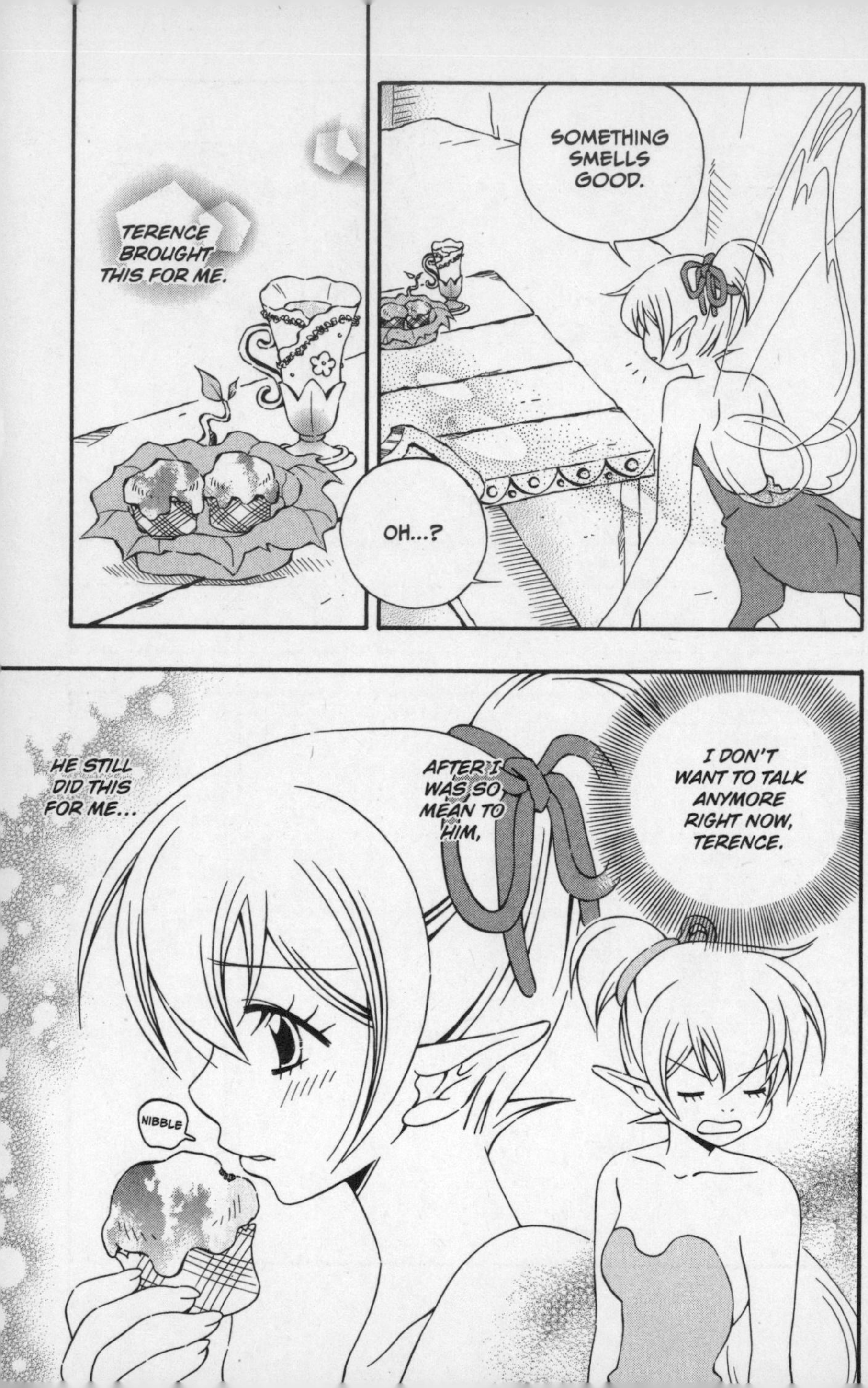
SOMETHING SMELLS GOOD.
OH...?
TERENCE BROUGHT THIS FOR ME.
I DON'T WANT TO TALK ANYMORE RIGHT NOW, TERENCE.
AFTER I WAS SO MEAN TO HIM,
HE STILL DID THIS FOR ME...
NIBBLE

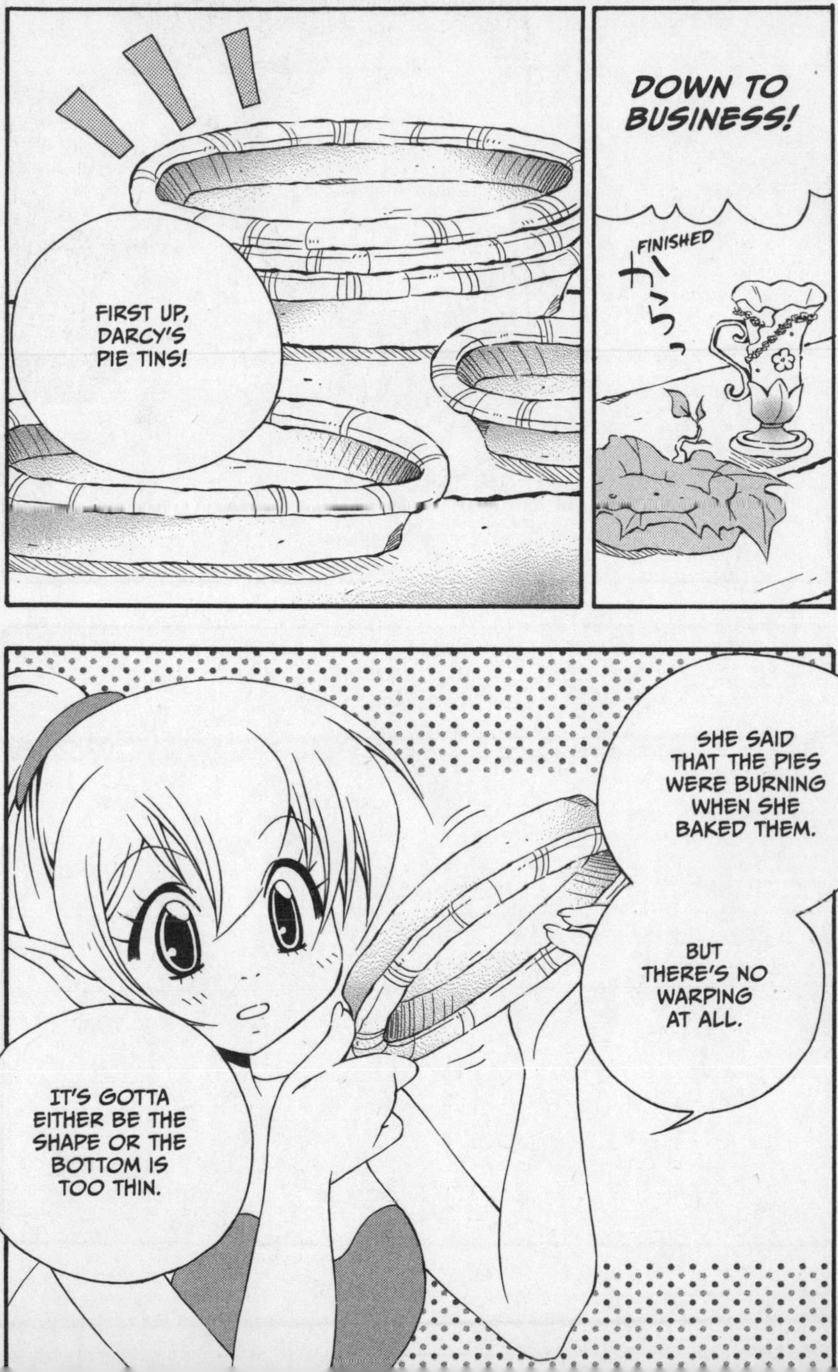
DOWN TO BUSINESS!
FINISHED
FIRST UP, DARCY'S PIE TINS!
SHE SAID THAT THE PIES WERE BURNING WHEN SHE BAKED THEM.
BUT THERE'S NO WARPING AT ALL.
IT'S GOTTA EITHER BE THE SHAPE OR THE BOTTOM IS TOO THIN.

READ THIS WAY

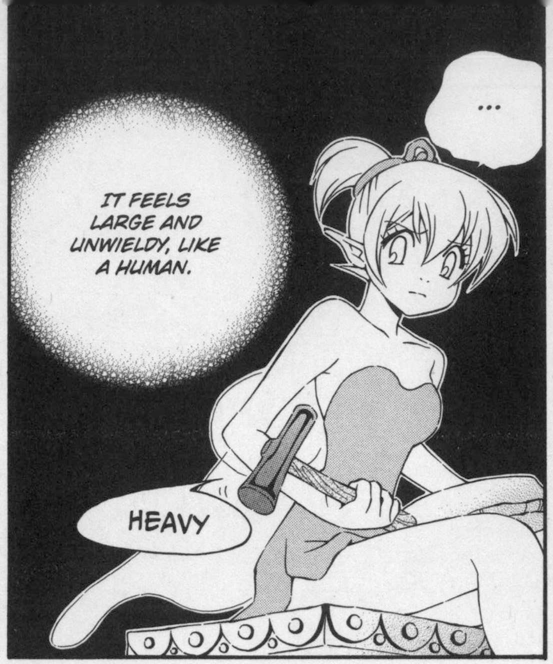
...
IT FEELS LARGE AND UNWIELDY, LIKE A HUMAN.
HEAVY

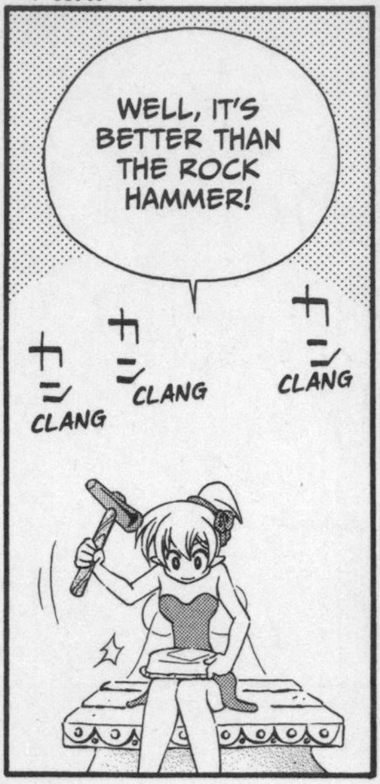
WELL, IT'S BETTER THAN THE ROCK HAMMER!
カン CLANG
カン CLANG
カン CLANG

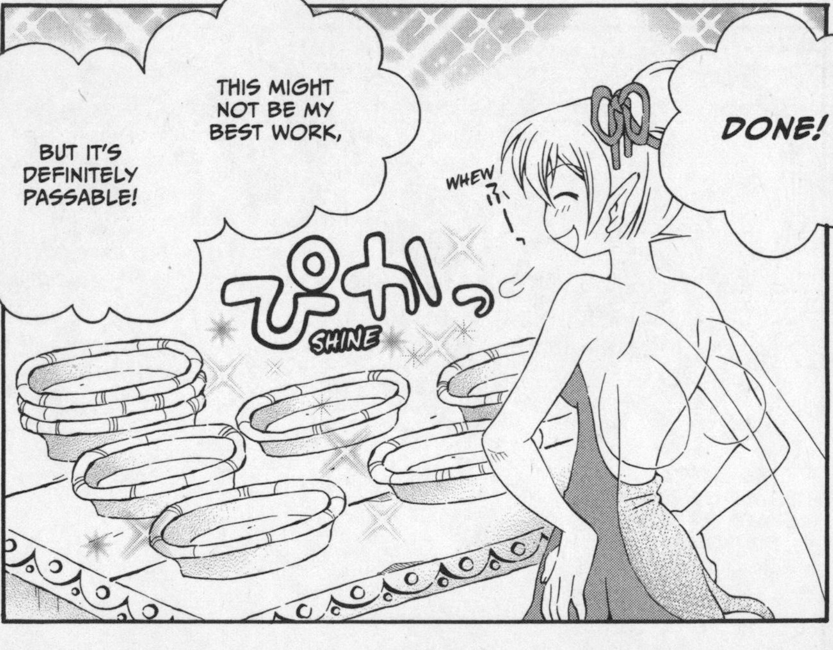
DONE!
THIS MIGHT NOT BE MY BEST WORK,
BUT IT'S DEFINITELY PASSABLE!
WHEW ふー
ぴかっ SHINE

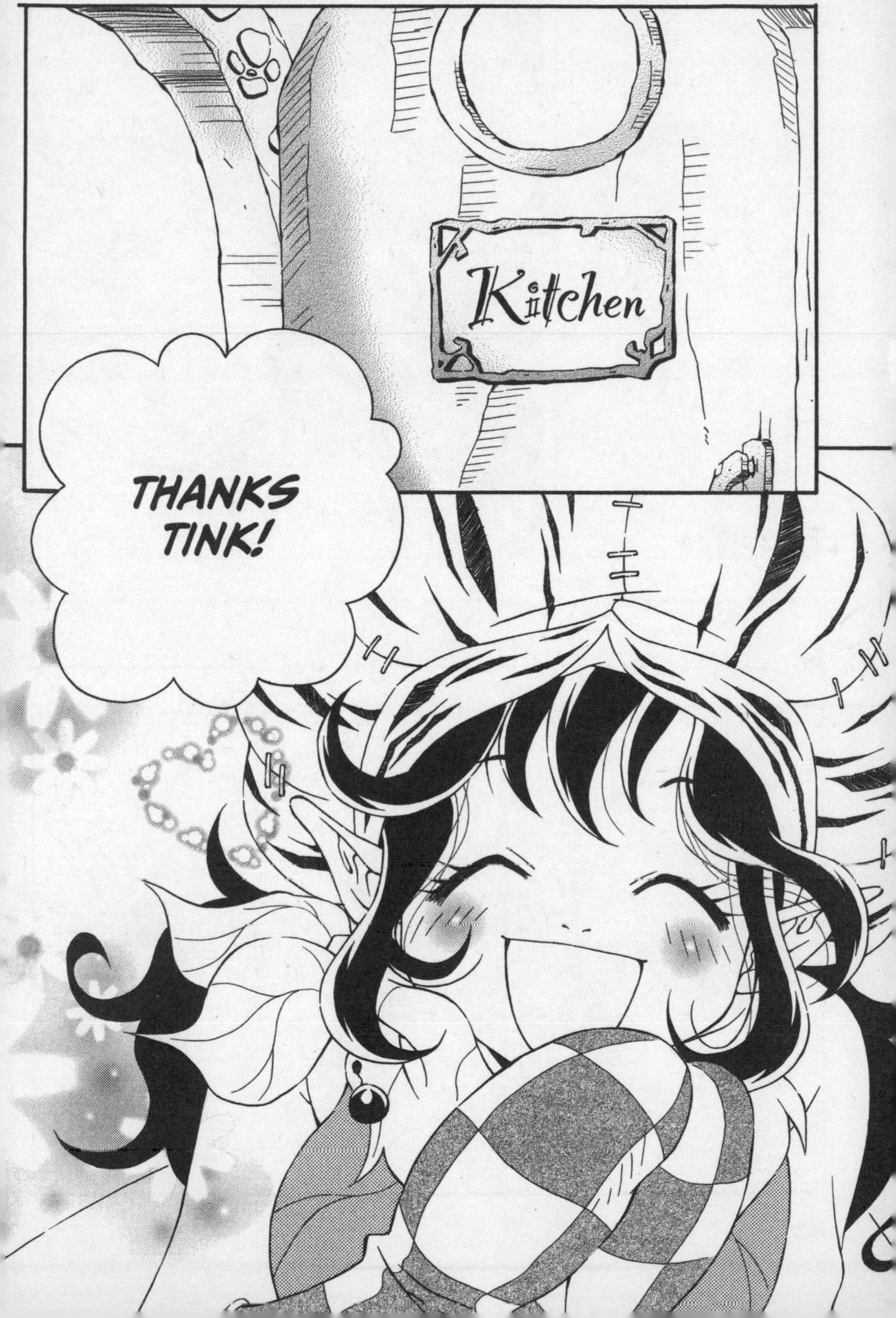
Kitchen
THANKS TINK!

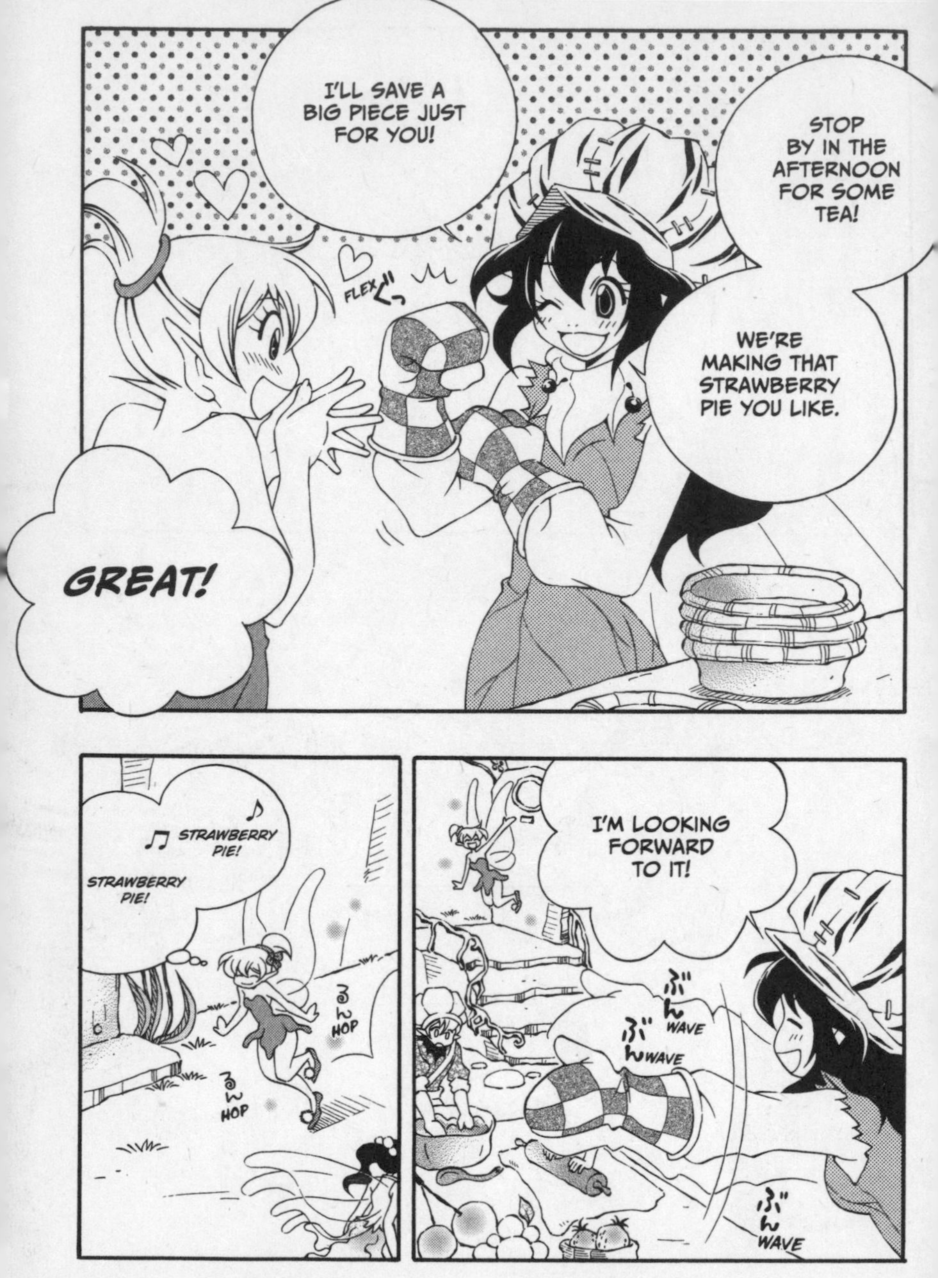
STOP BY IN THE AFTERNOON FOR SOME TEA!
WE'RE MAKING THAT STRAWBERRY PIE YOU LIKE.
I'LL SAVE A BIG PIECE JUST FOR YOU!
ぐっ FLEX
GREAT!
I'M LOOKING FORWARD TO IT!
ぶん WAVE
ぶん WAVE
ぶん WAVE
STRAWBERRY PIE!
STRAWBERRY PIE!
るん HOP
るん HOP

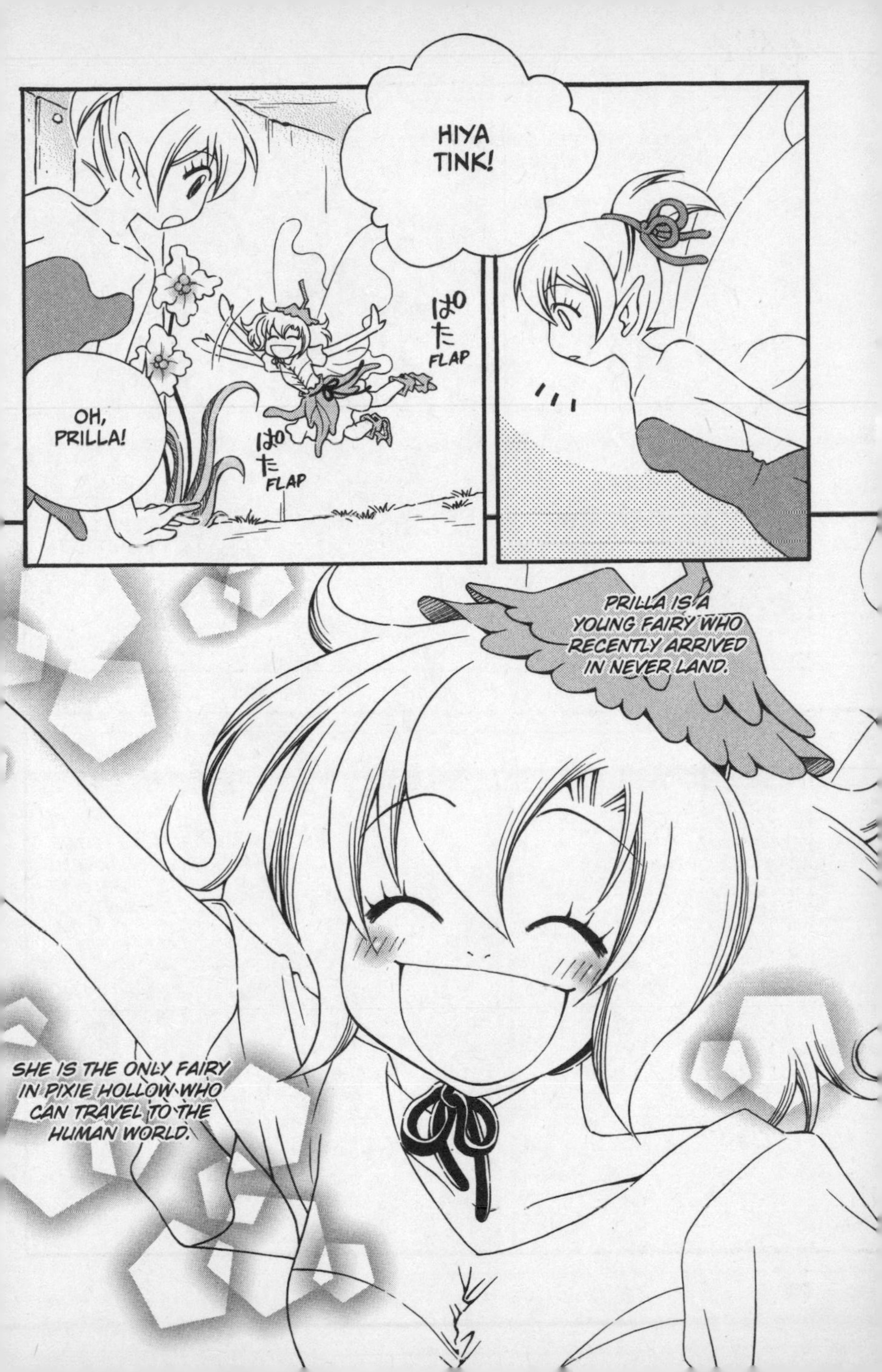
HIYA TINK!
ぱた FLAP
ぱた FLAP
OH, PRILLA!
PRILLA IS A YOUNG FAIRY WHO RECENTLY ARRIVED IN NEVER LAND.
SHE IS THE ONLY FAIRY IN PIXIE HOLLOW WHO CAN TRAVEL TO THE HUMAN WORLD.

READ THIS WAY

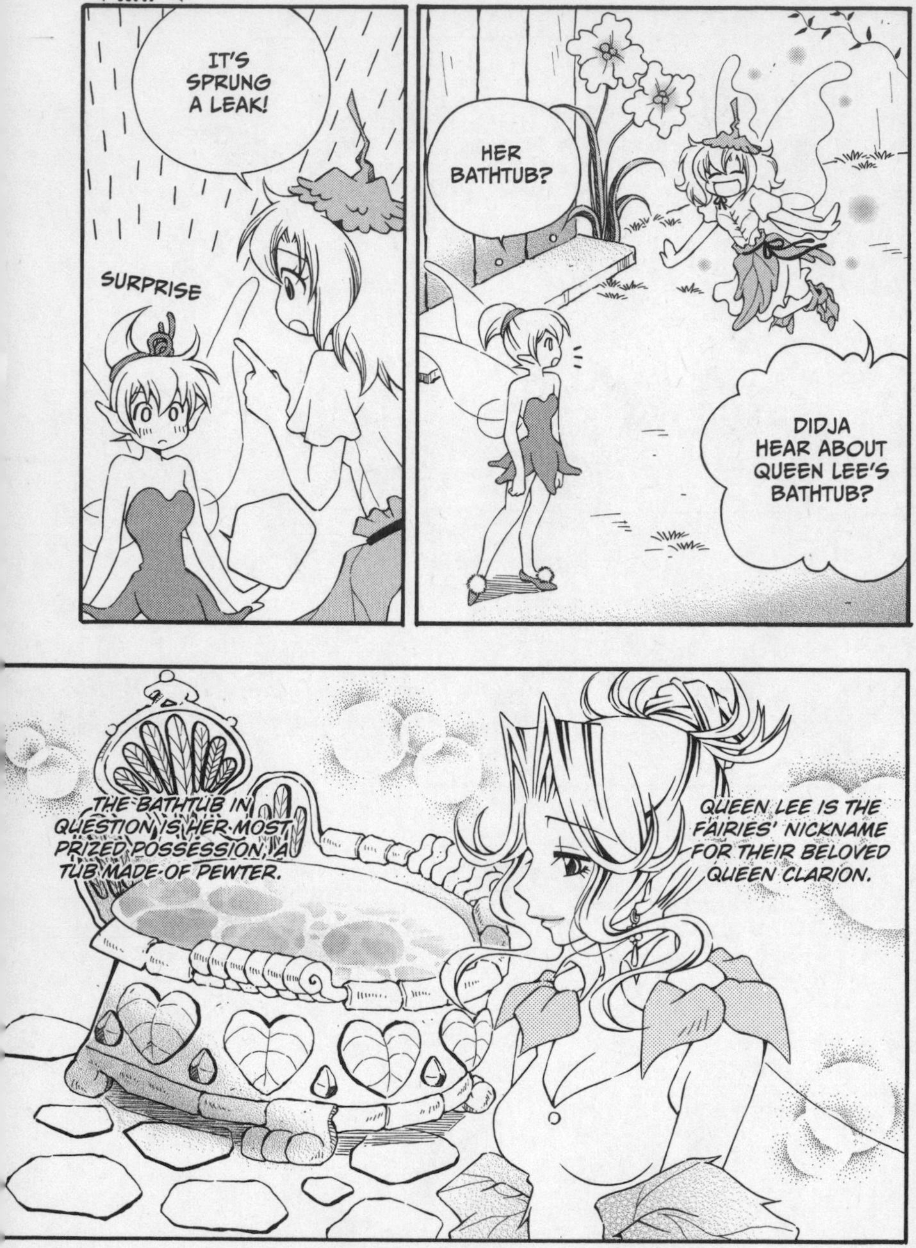
DIDJA HEAR ABOUT QUEEN LEE'S BATHTUB?
HER BATHTUB?
IT'S SPRUNG A LEAK!
SURPRISE
QUEEN LEE IS THE FAIRIES' NICKNAME FOR THEIR BELOVED QUEEN CLARION.
THE BATHTUB IN QUESTION IS HER MOST PRIZED POSSESSION, A TUB MADE OF PEWTER.

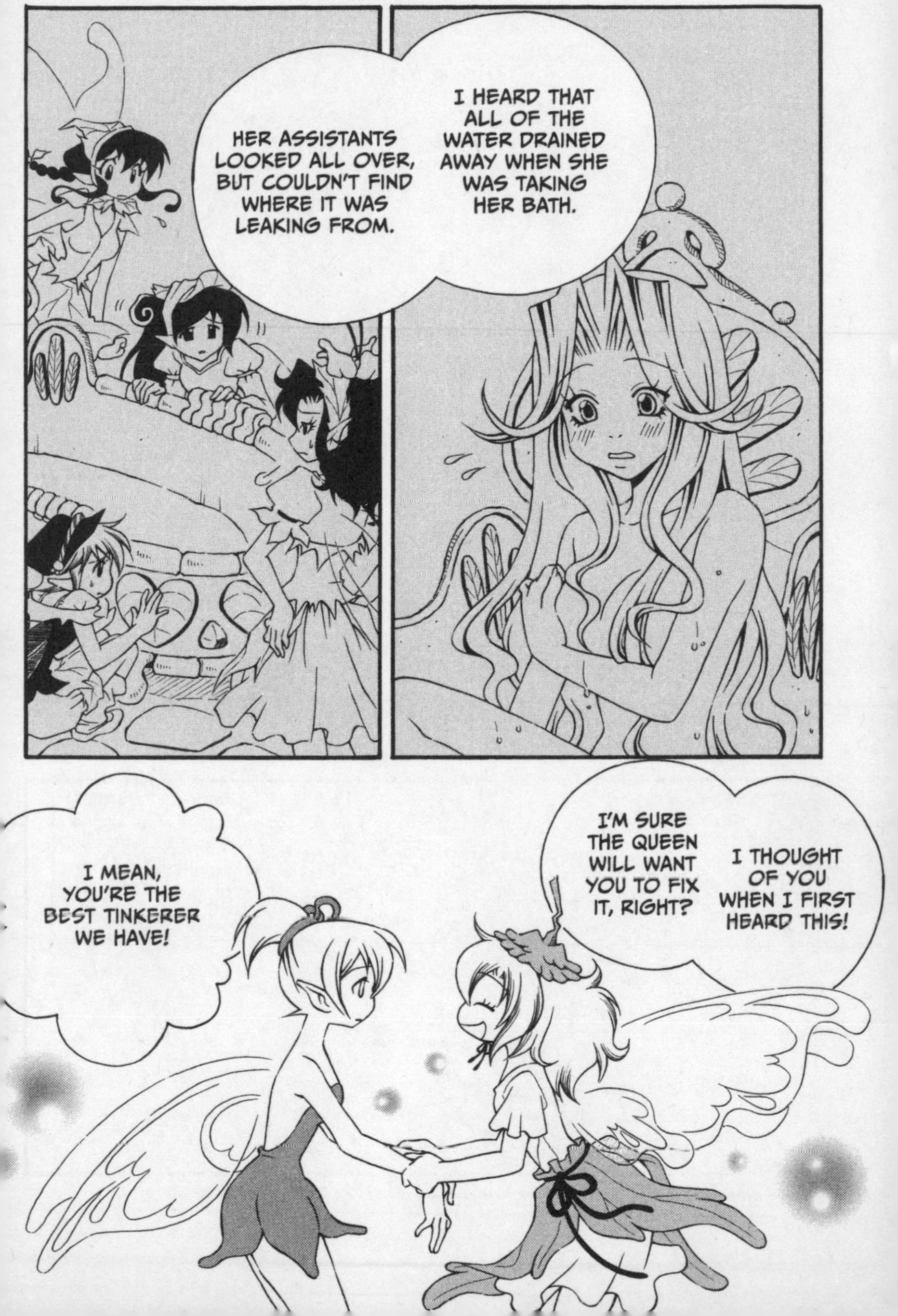
I HEARD THAT ALL OF THE WATER DRAINED AWAY WHEN SHE WAS TAKING HER BATH.
HER ASSISTANTS LOOKED ALL OVER, BUT COULDN'T FIND WHERE IT WAS LEAKING FROM.
I THOUGHT OF YOU WHEN I FIRST HEARD THIS!
I'M SURE THE QUEEN WILL WANT YOU TO FIX IT, RIGHT?
I MEAN, YOU'RE THE BEST TINKERER WE HAVE!

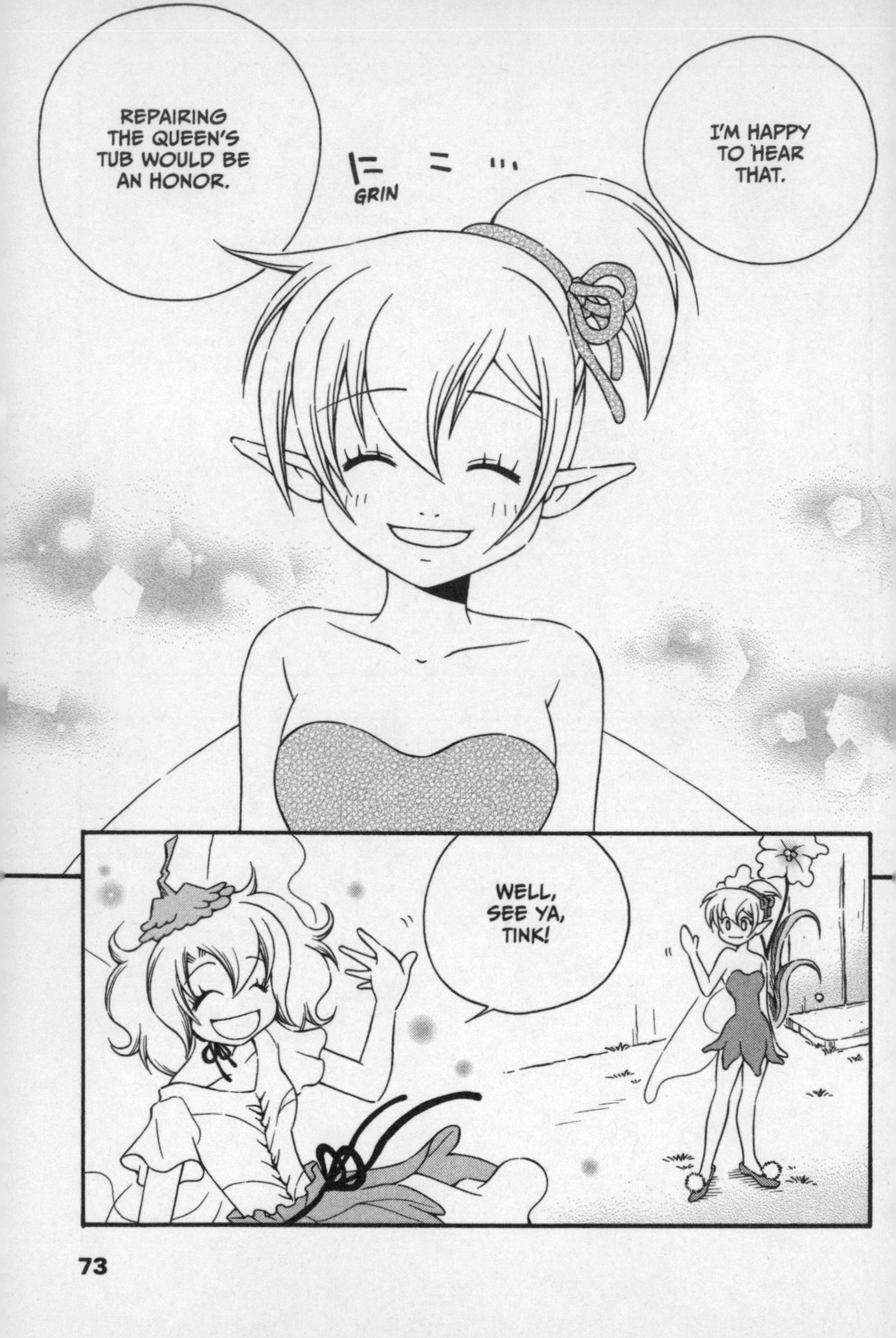
REPAIRING THE QUEEN'S TUB WOULD BE AN HONOR.
にこ…
GRIN
I'M HAPPY TO HEAR THAT.
WELL, SEE YA, TINK!

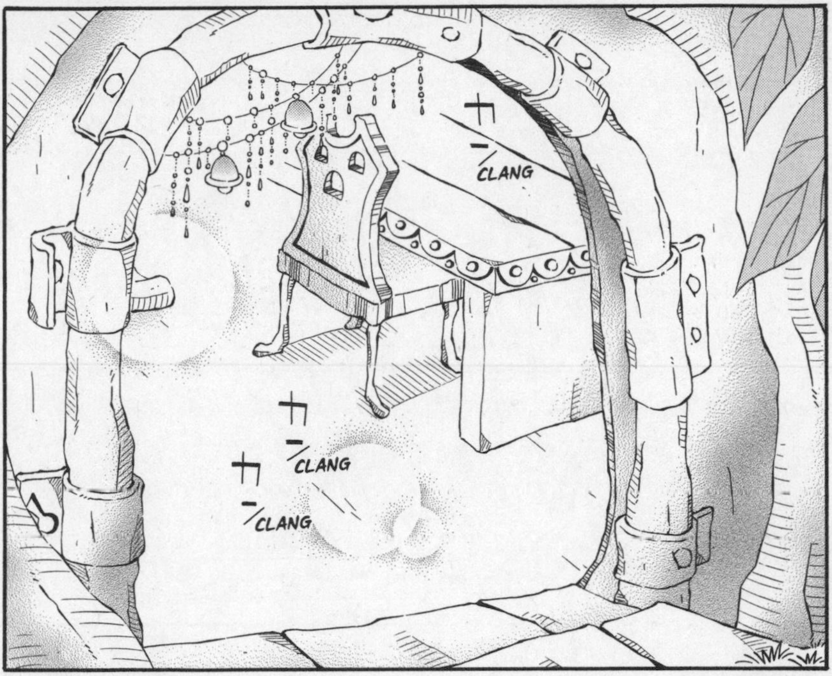
カー
CLANG
カー
CLANG
カー
CLANG

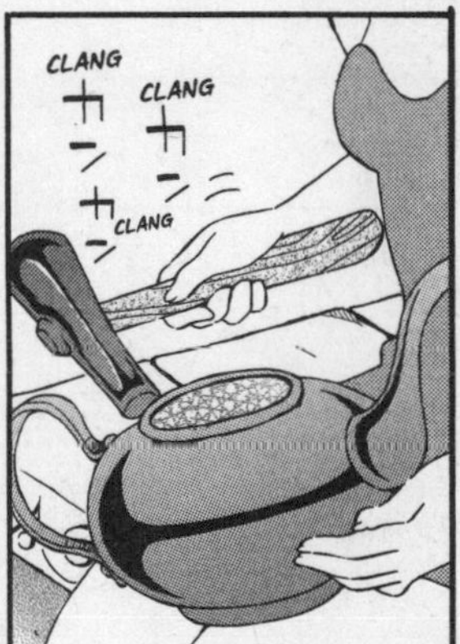
CLANG
カン
CLANG
カン
カン
CLANG

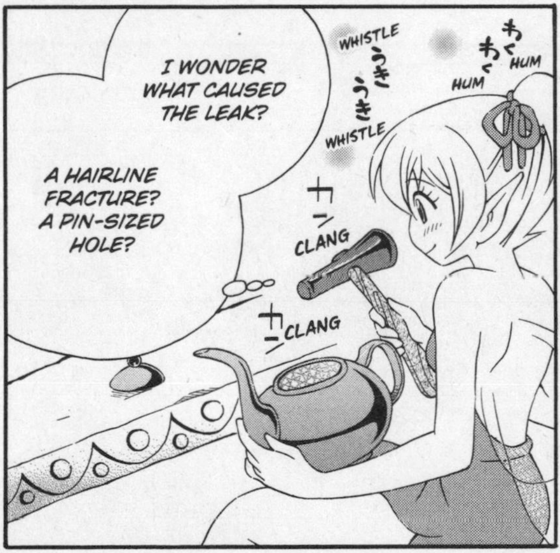
I WONDER WHAT CAUSED THE LEAK?
A HAIRLINE FRACTURE? A PIN-SIZED HOLE?
WHISTLE
うき
うき
WHISTLE
わく
HUM
わく
HUM
カー
CLANG
カー
CLANG

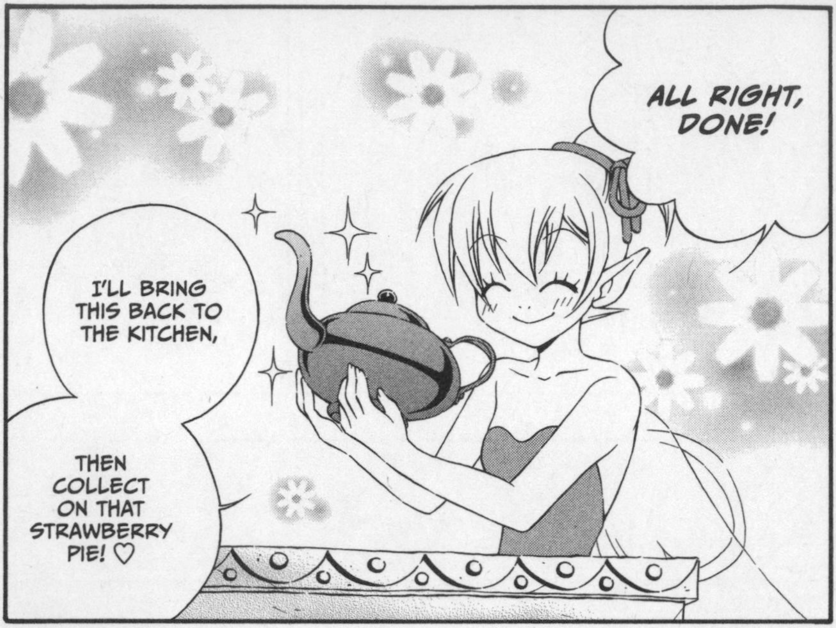
ALL RIGHT, DONE!
I'LL BRING THIS BACK TO THE KITCHEN,
THEN COLLECT ON THAT STRAWBERRY PIE! ♡

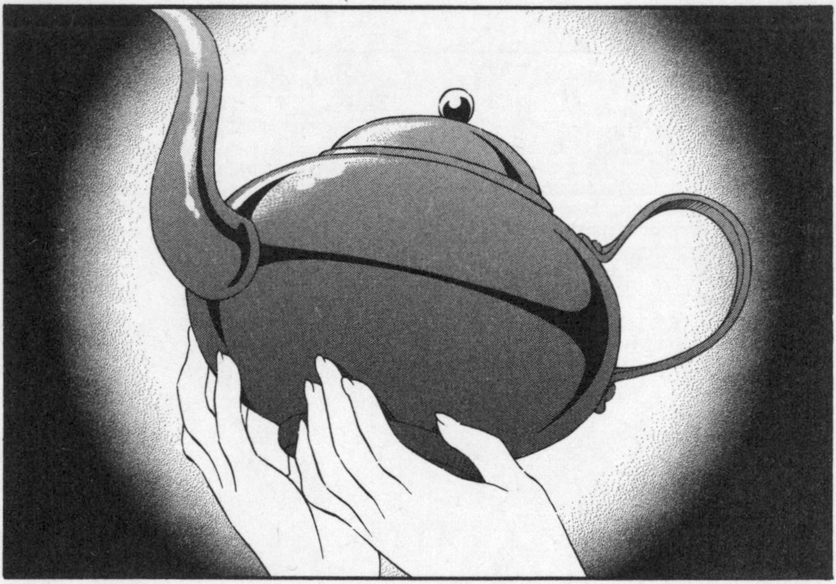

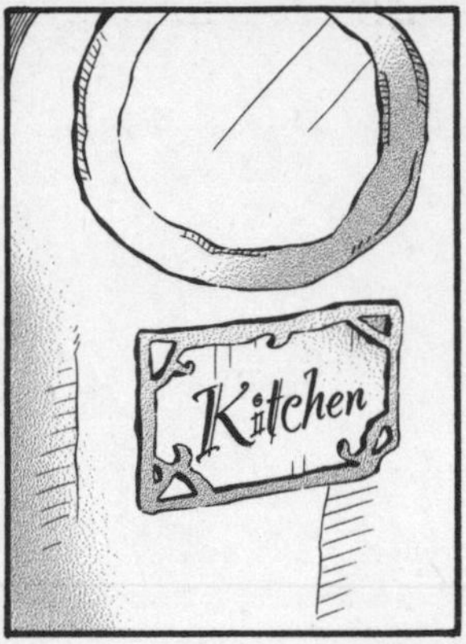
Kitchen

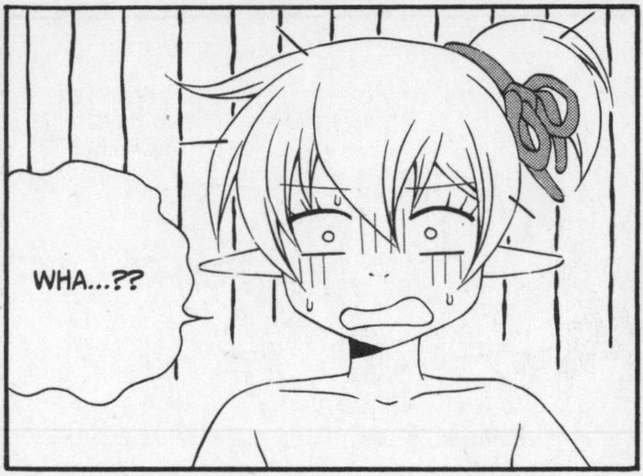
WHA...??

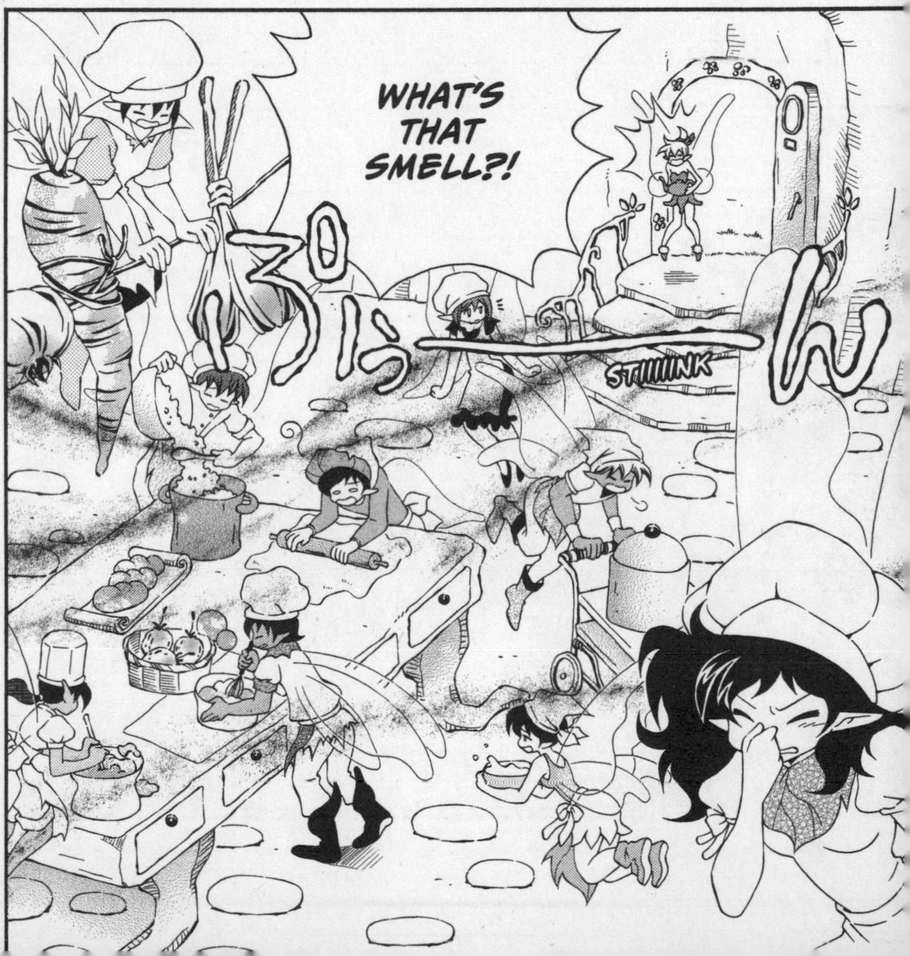
WHAT'S THAT SMELL?!
STIIIIIINK

READ THIS WAY

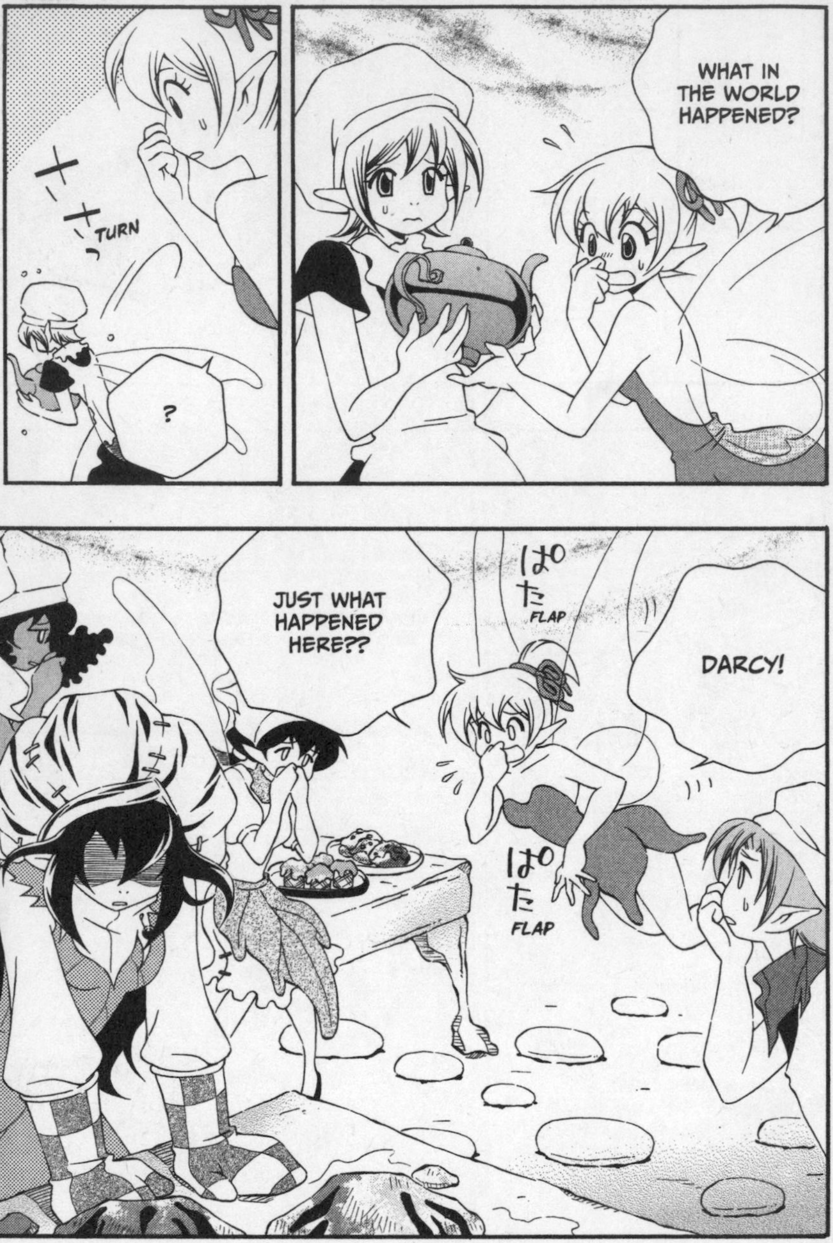
WHAT IN THE WORLD HAPPENED?
TURN
?
DARCY!
ぱた FLAP
ぱた FLAP
JUST WHAT HAPPENED HERE??

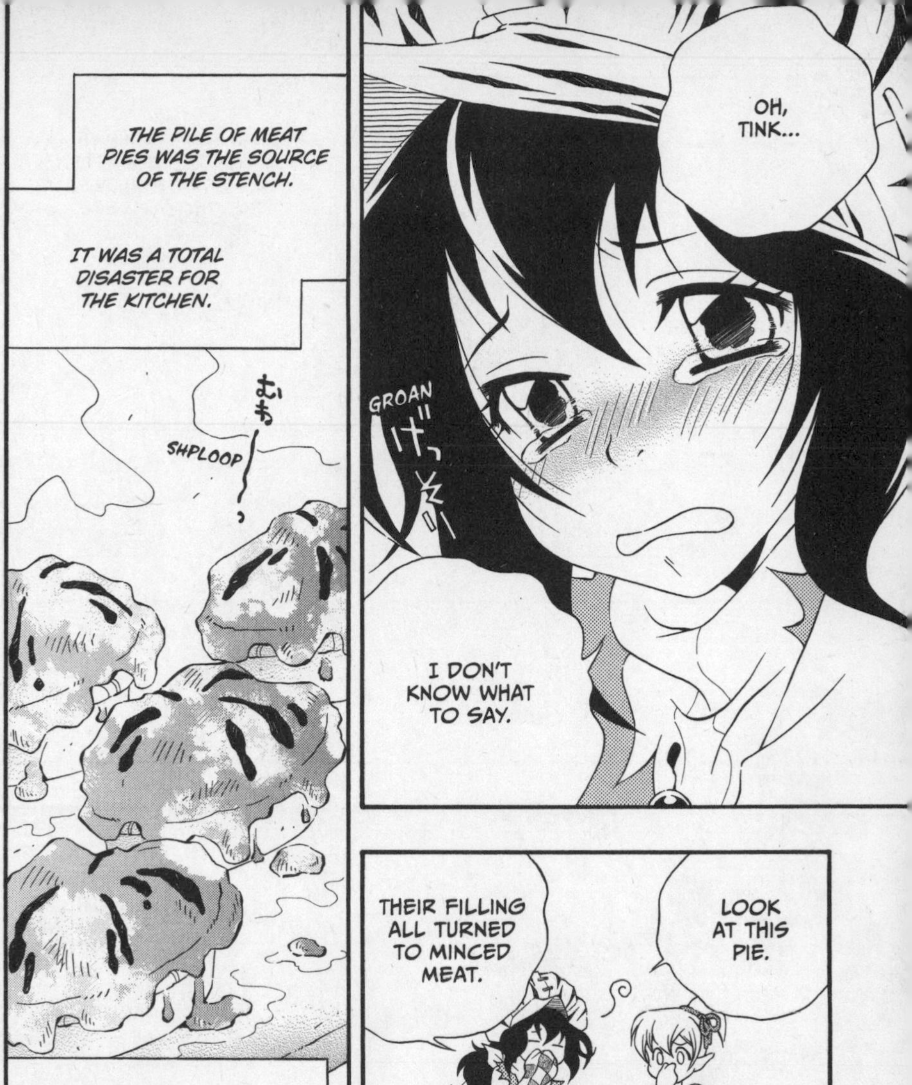
OH, TINK...
GROAN
I DON'T KNOW WHAT TO SAY.
LOOK AT THIS PIE.
THEIR FILLING ALL TURNED TO MINCED MEAT.
MUSH
MUSH
THE PILE OF MEAT PIES WAS THE SOURCE OF THE STENCH.
IT WAS A TOTAL DISASTER FOR THE KITCHEN.
SHPLOOP
TO FAIRIES, THE SMELL OF MINCED MEAT IS A HORRIBLE STENCH AKIN TO BURNT BROCCOLI MIXED WITH UNWASHED SOCKS.

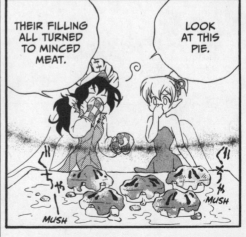

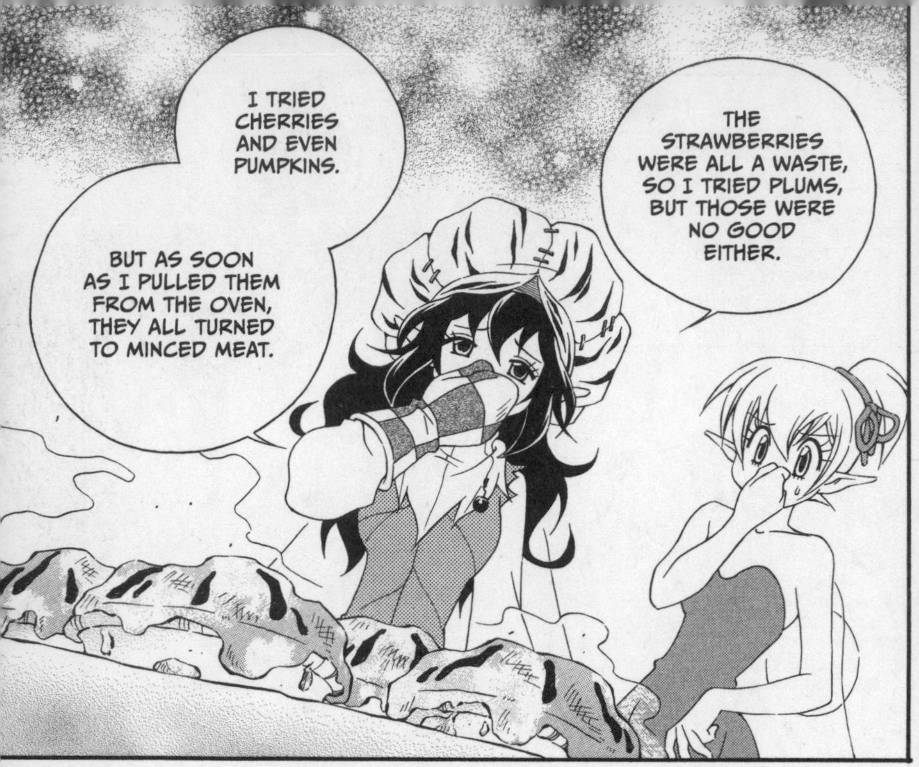
THE STRAWBERRIES WERE ALL A WASTE, SO I TRIED PLUMS, BUT THOSE WERE NO GOOD EITHER.
I TRIED CHERRIES AND EVEN PUMPKINS.
BUT AS SOON AS I PULLED THEM FROM THE OVEN, THEY ALL TURNED TO MINCED MEAT.
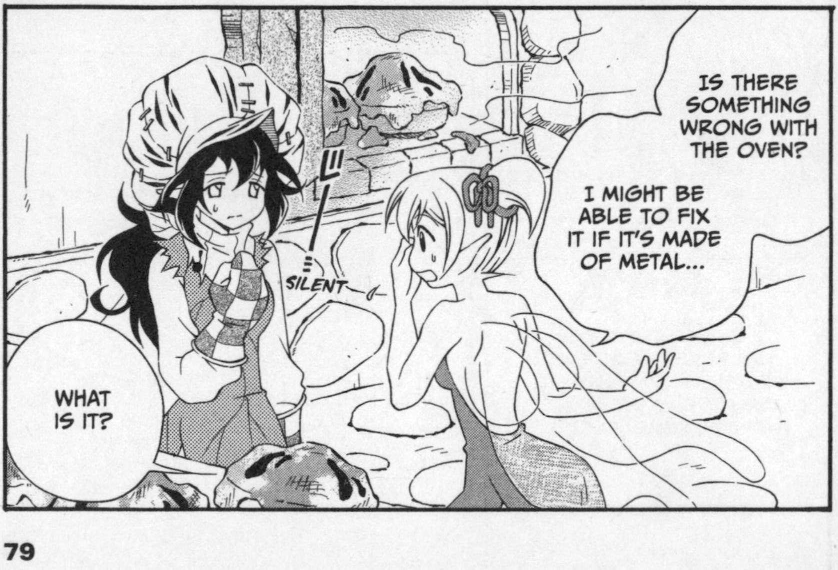
IS THERE SOMETHING WRONG WITH THE OVEN?
I MIGHT BE ABLE TO FIX IT IF IT'S MADE OF METAL...
SILENT
WHAT IS IT?

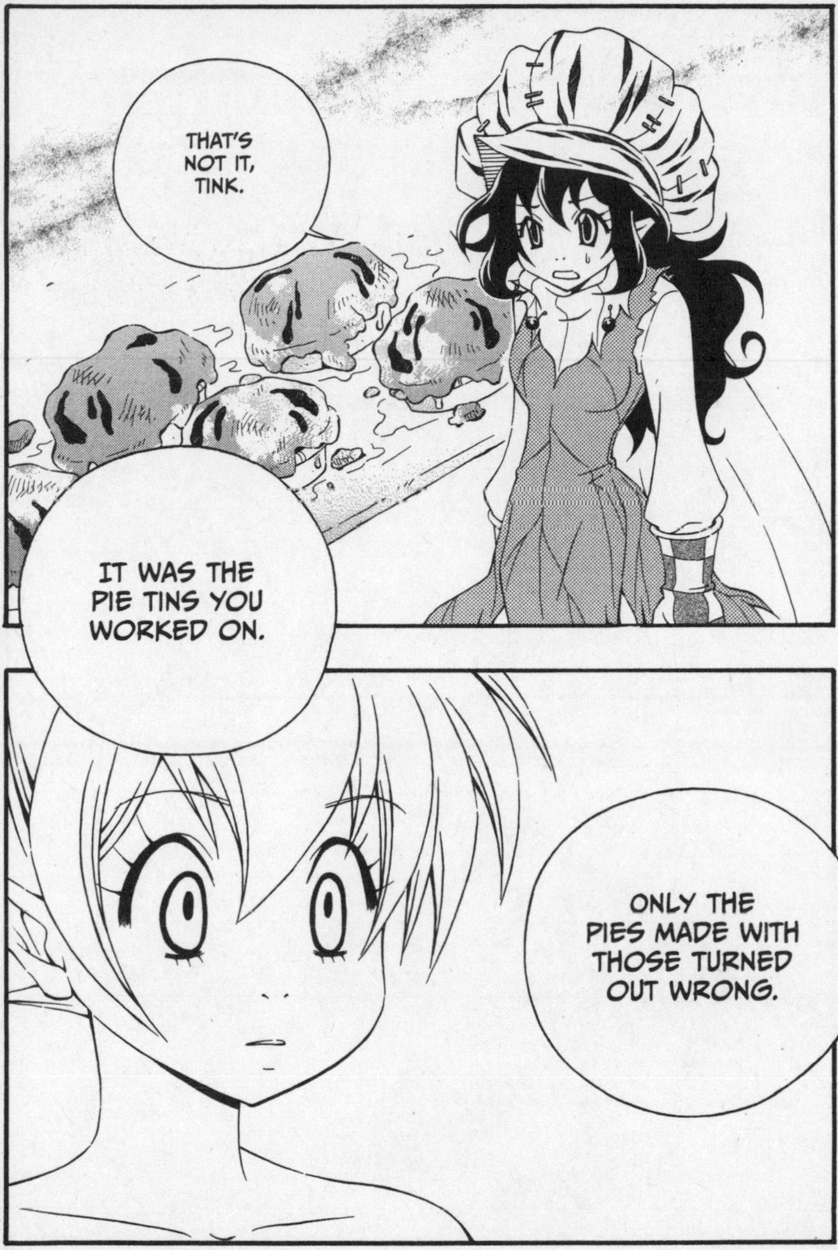
THAT'S NOT IT, TINK.
IT WAS THE PIE TINS YOU WORKED ON.
ONLY THE PIES MADE WITH THOSE TURNED OUT WRONG.

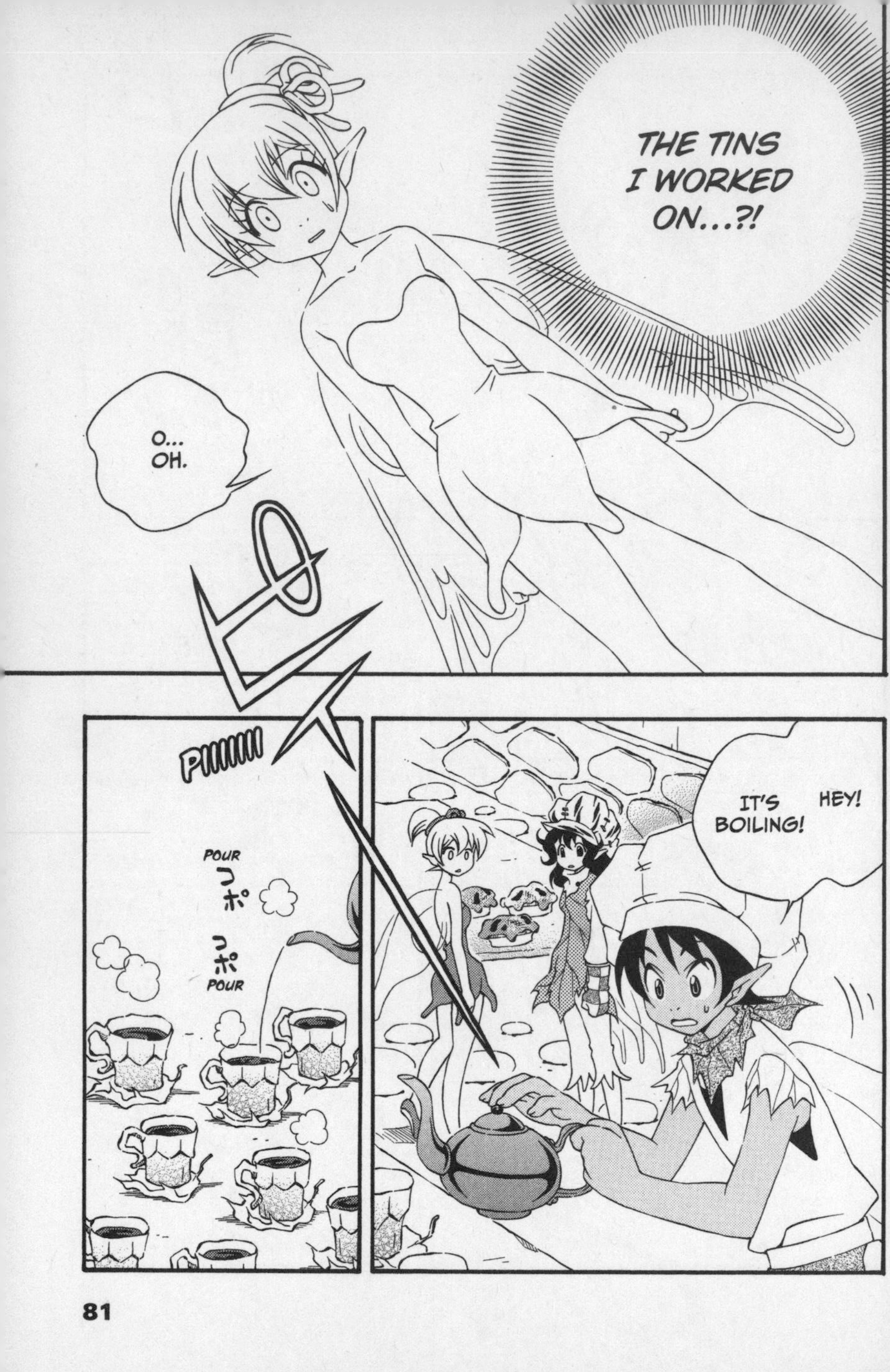
THE TINS I WORKED ON...?!
O... OH.
HEY!
IT'S BOILING!
PIIIIIII
POUR
コポ
コポ
POUR

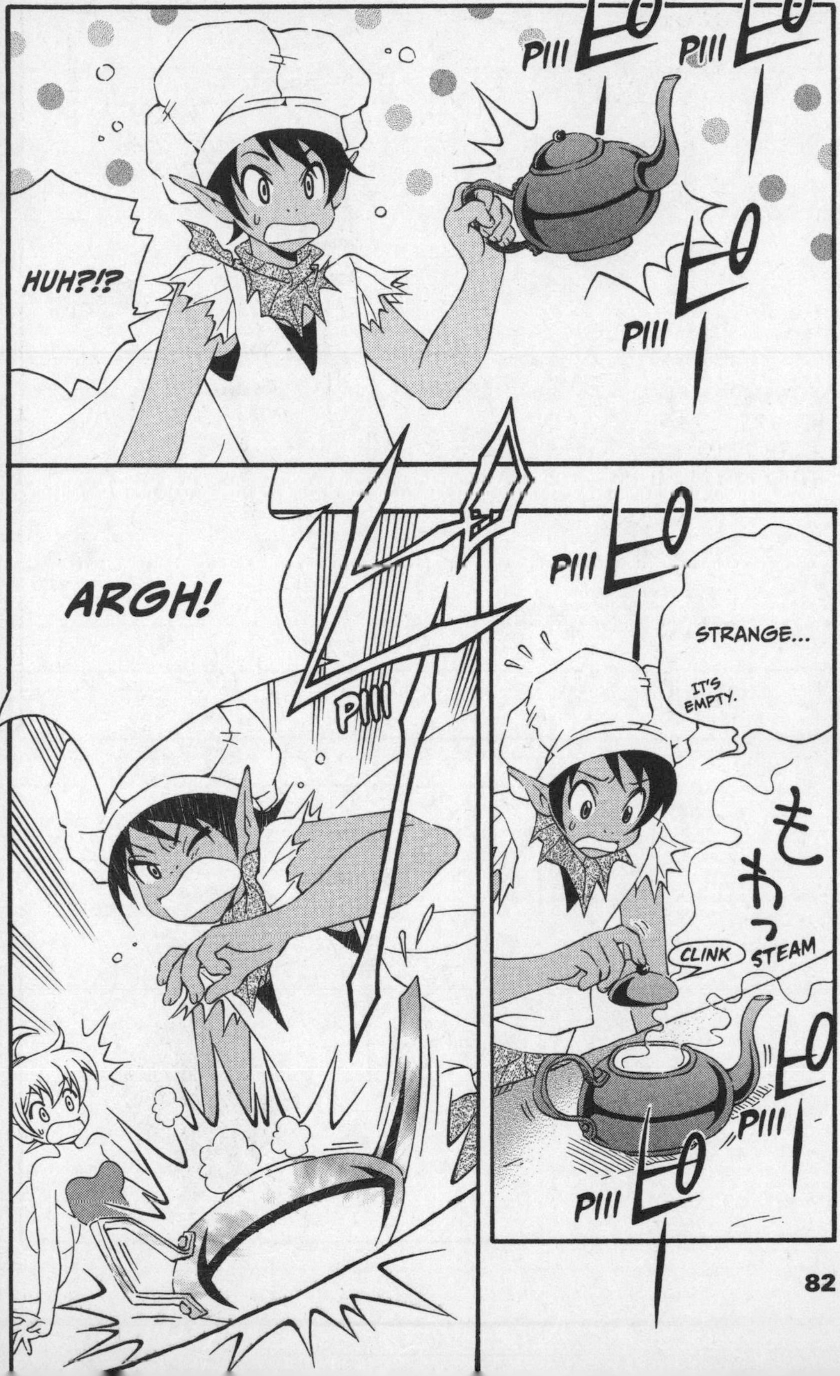
PIII
PIII
PIII
HUH?!?
PIII
STRANGE...
IT'S EMPTY.
CLINK
もわっ
STEAM
PIII
PIII
ARGH!
PIII

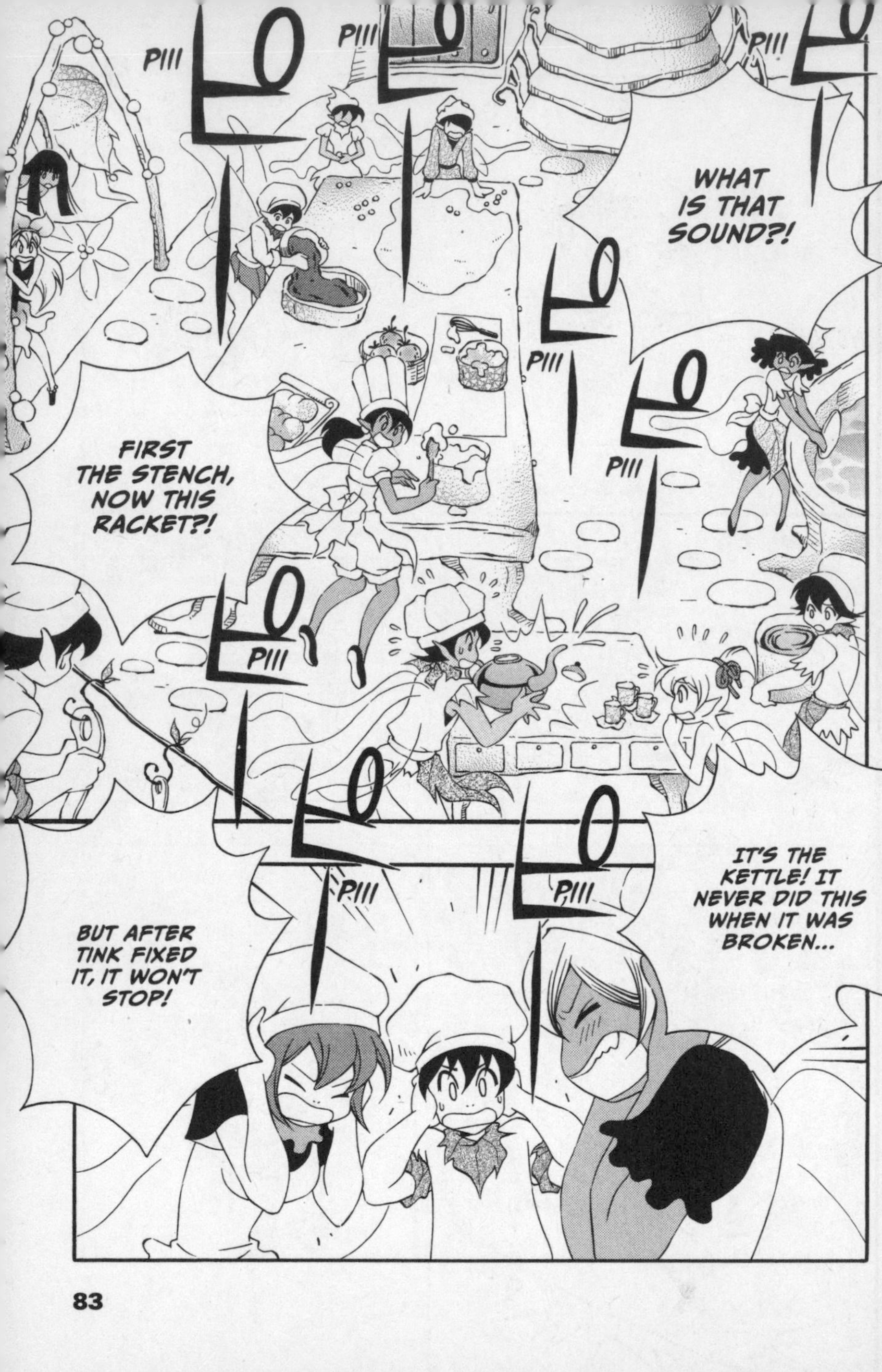
PIII
PIII
PIII
WHAT IS THAT SOUND?!
PIII
PIII
FIRST THE STENCH, NOW THIS RACKET?!
PIII
PIII
PIII
IT'S THE KETTLE! IT NEVER DID THIS WHEN IT WAS BROKEN...
BUT AFTER TINK FIXED IT, IT WON'T STOP!

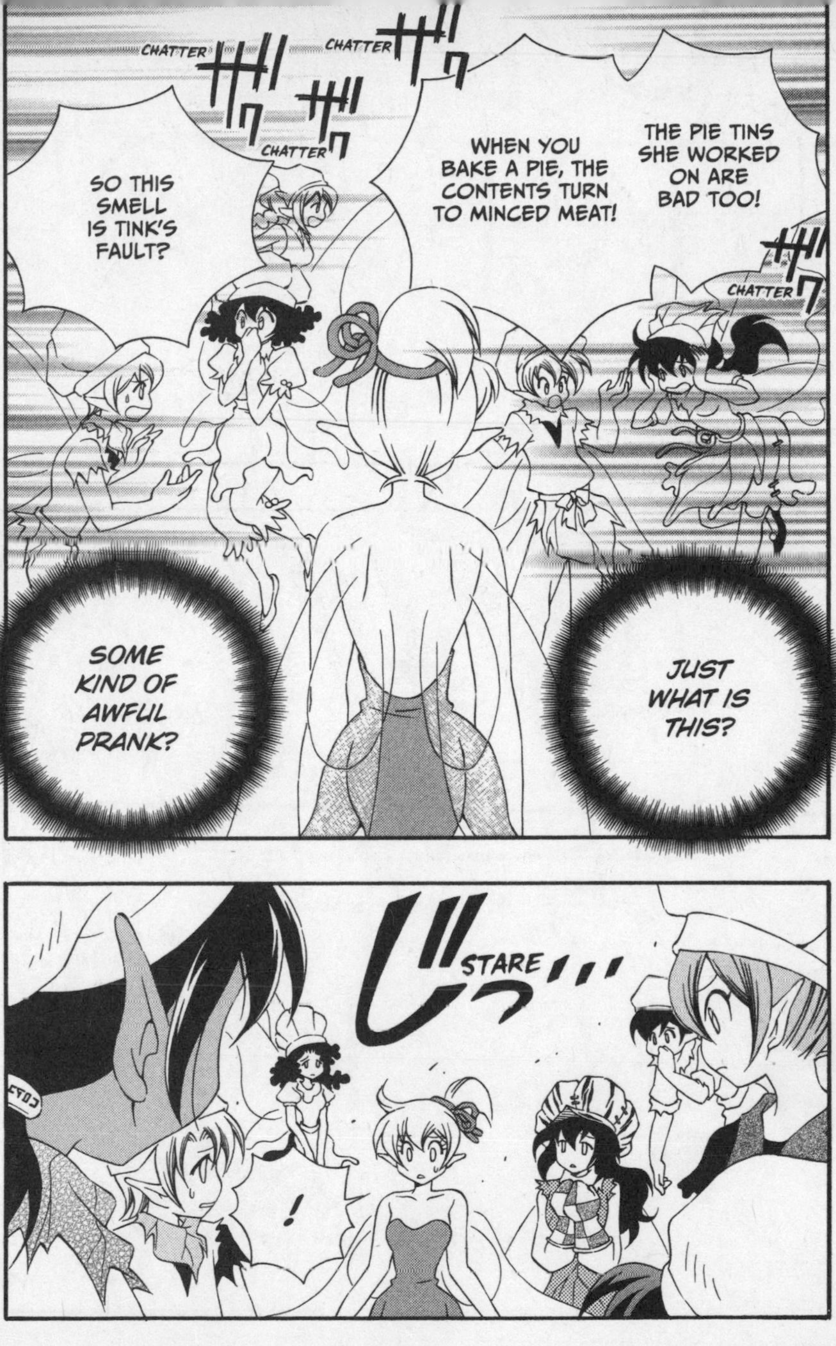
CHATTER
CHATTER
THE PIE TINS SHE WORKED ON ARE BAD TOO!
WHEN YOU BAKE A PIE, THE CONTENTS TURN TO MINCED MEAT!
CHATTER
CHATTER
SO THIS SMELL IS TINK'S FAULT?
JUST WHAT IS THIS?
SOME KIND OF AWFUL PRANK?
STARE
!

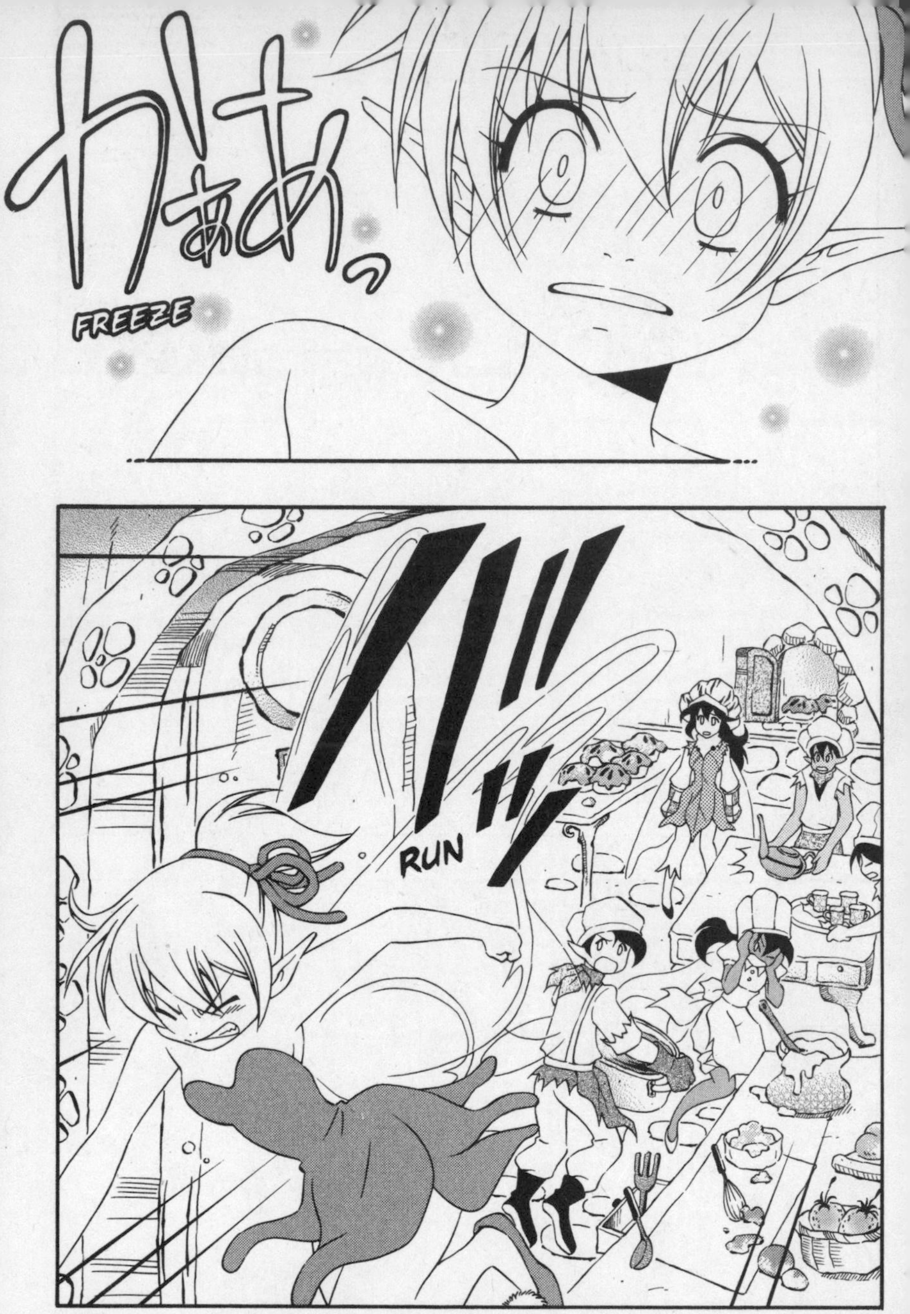
わ゛ぁあっ
FREEZE
バッ
RUN

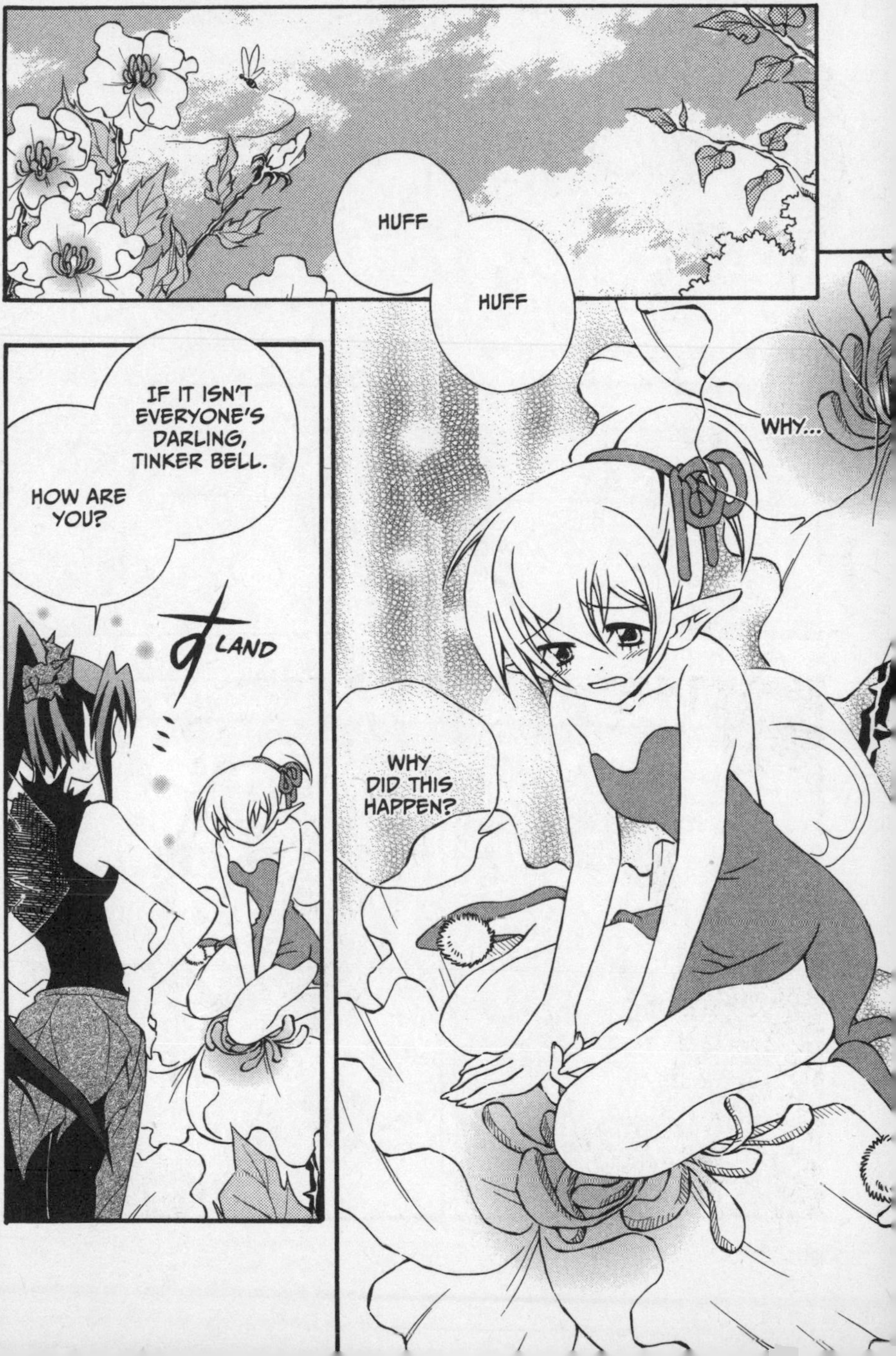
HUFF
HUFF
WHY...
WHY DID THIS HAPPEN?
IF IT ISN'T EVERYONE'S DARLING, TINKER BELL.
HOW ARE YOU?
LAND

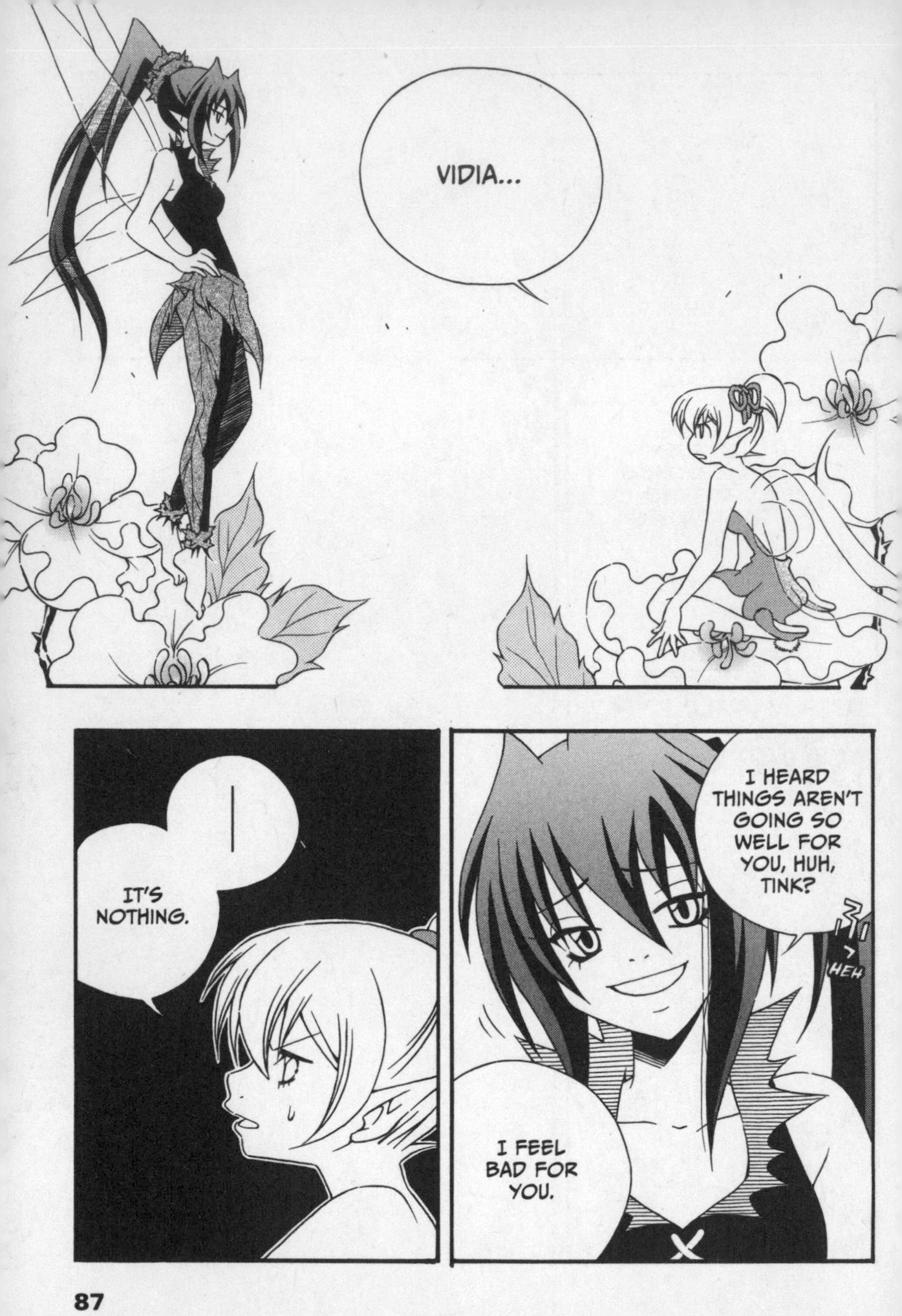
VIDIA...
I HEARD THINGS AREN'T GOING SO WELL FOR YOU, HUH, TINK?
HEH
I FEEL BAD FOR YOU.
IT'S NOTHING.

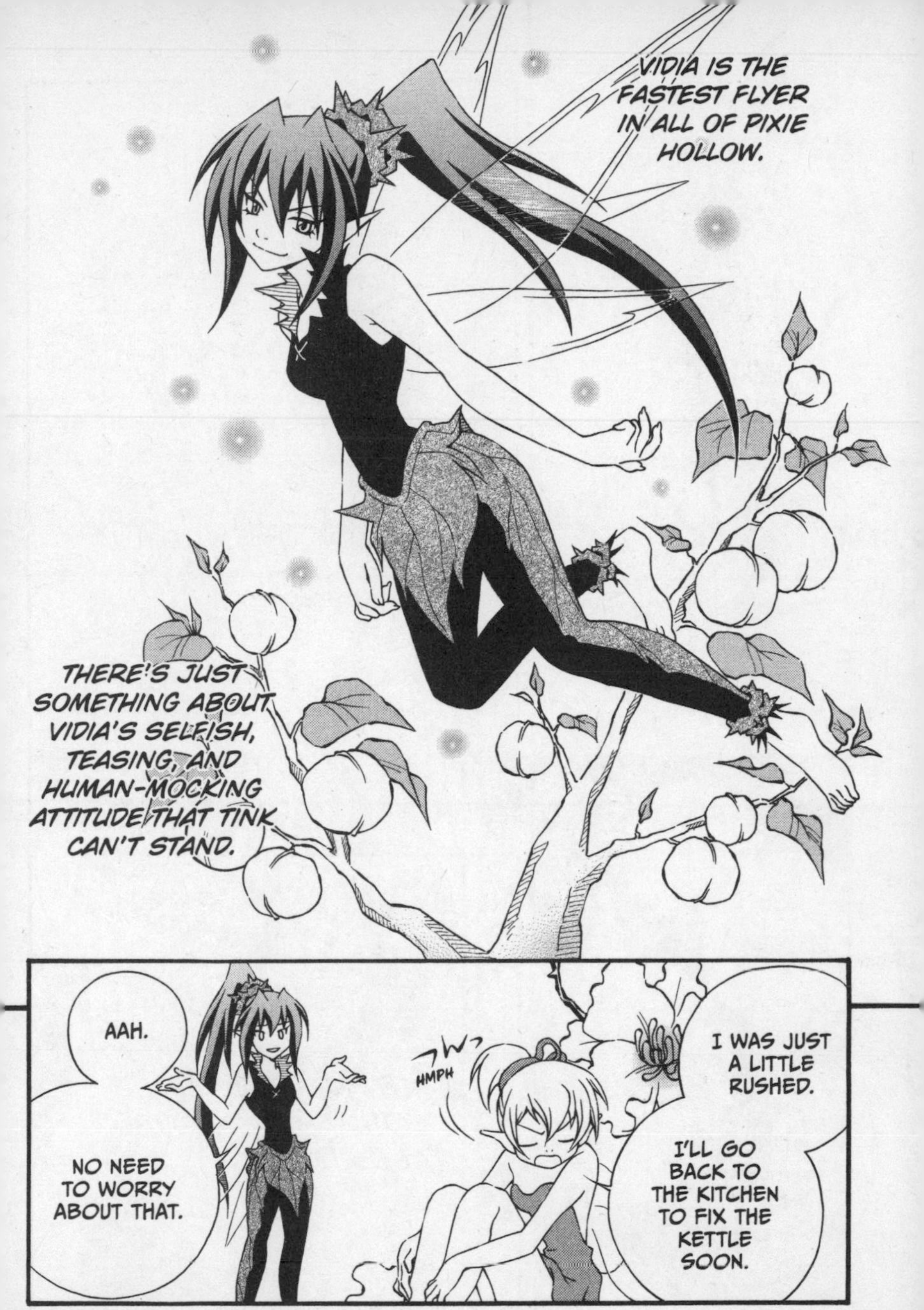
VIDIA IS THE FASTEST FLYER IN ALL OF PIXIE HOLLOW.
THERE'S JUST SOMETHING ABOUT VIDIA'S SELFISH, TEASING, AND HUMAN-MOCKING ATTITUDE THAT TINK CAN'T STAND.
I WAS JUST A LITTLE RUSHED.
I'LL GO BACK TO THE KITCHEN TO FIX THE KETTLE SOON.
HMPH
AAH.
NO NEED TO WORRY ABOUT THAT.

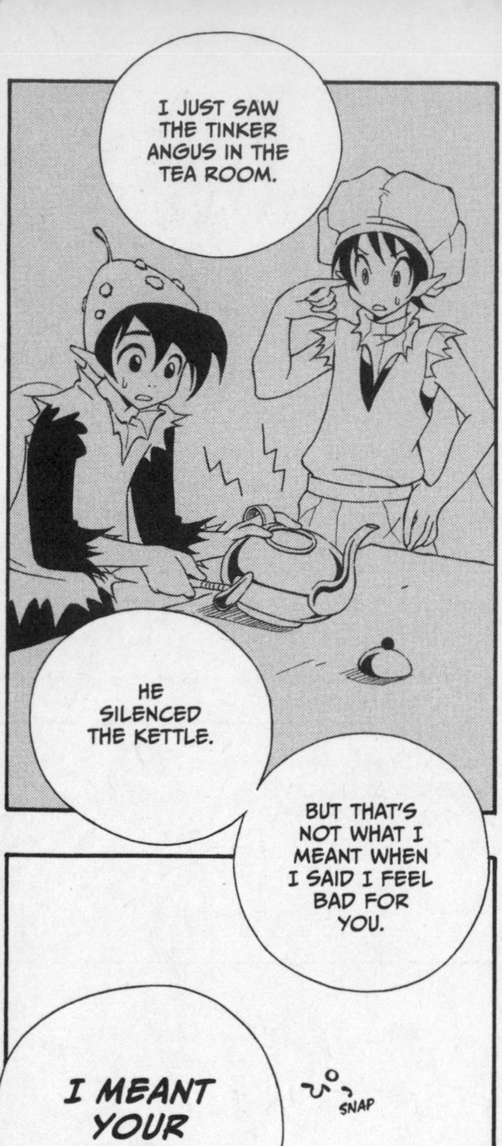
I JUST SAW THE TINKER ANGUS IN THE TEA ROOM.
HE SILENCED THE KETTLE.
BUT THAT'S NOT WHAT I MEANT WHEN I SAID I FEEL BAD FOR YOU.
SNAP
I MEANT YOUR TALENT.
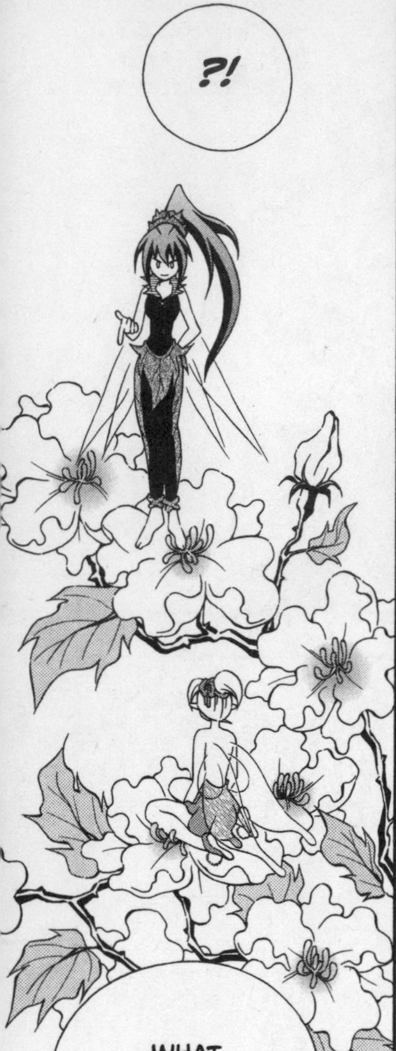
?!
WHAT DO YOU MEAN?

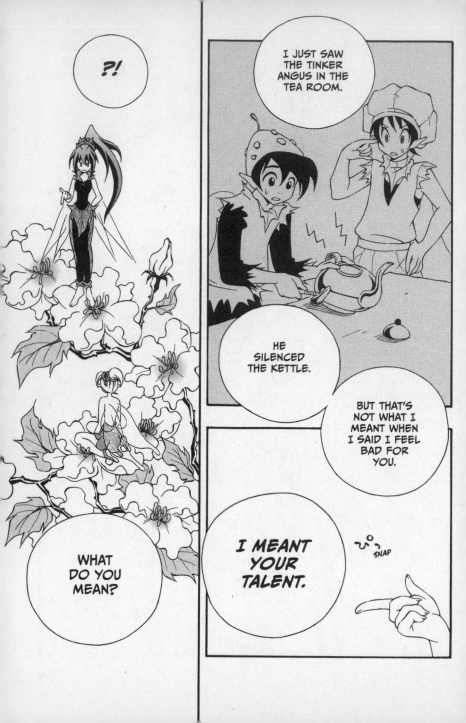

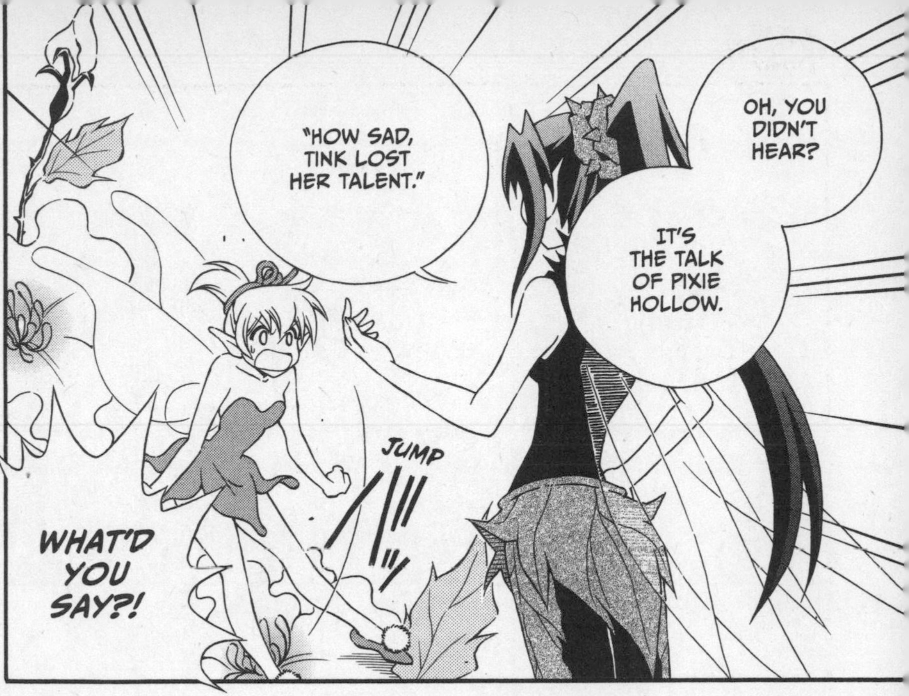
OH, YOU DIDN'T HEAR?
IT'S THE TALK OF PIXIE HOLLOW.
"HOW SAD, TINK LOST HER TALENT."
JUMP
WHAT'D YOU SAY?!

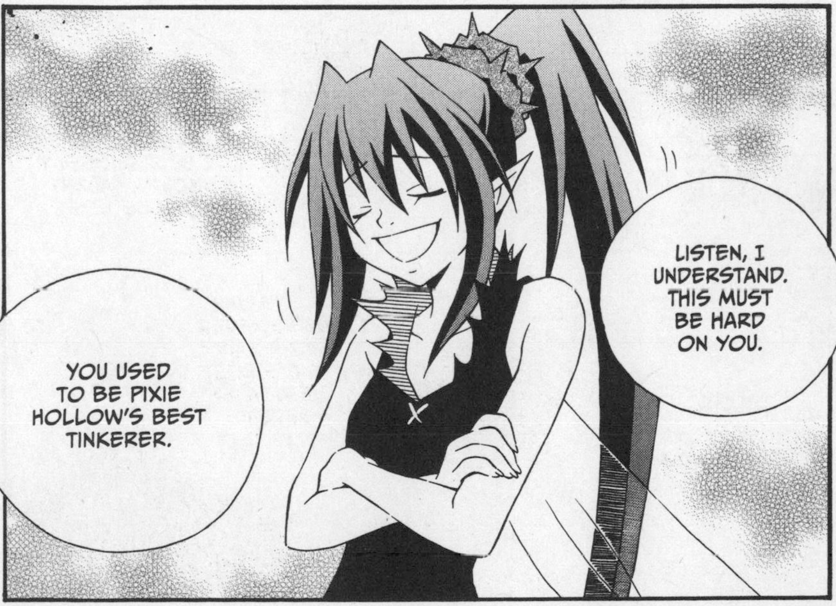
LISTEN, I UNDERSTAND. THIS MUST BE HARD ON YOU.
YOU USED TO BE PIXIE HOLLOW'S BEST TINKERER.

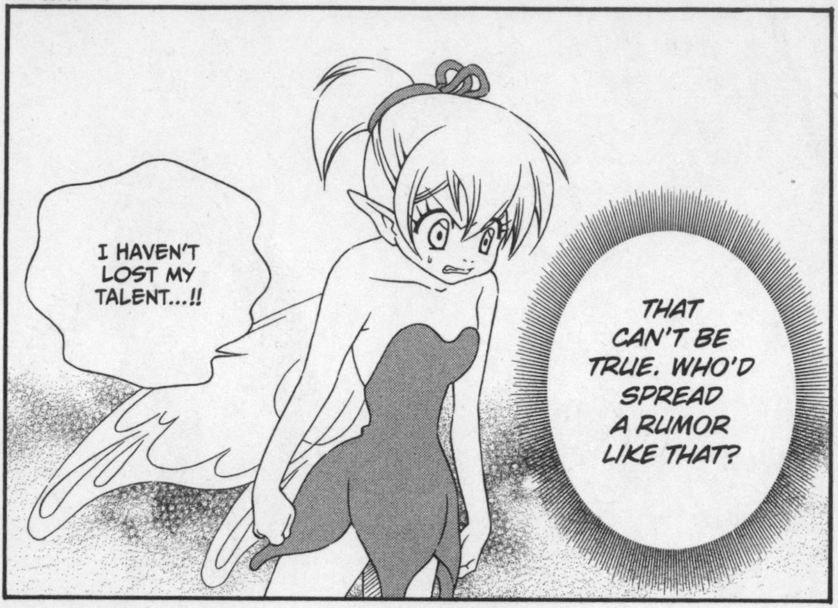
THAT CAN'T BE TRUE. WHO'D SPREAD A RUMOR LIKE THAT?
I HAVEN'T LOST MY TALENT...!!

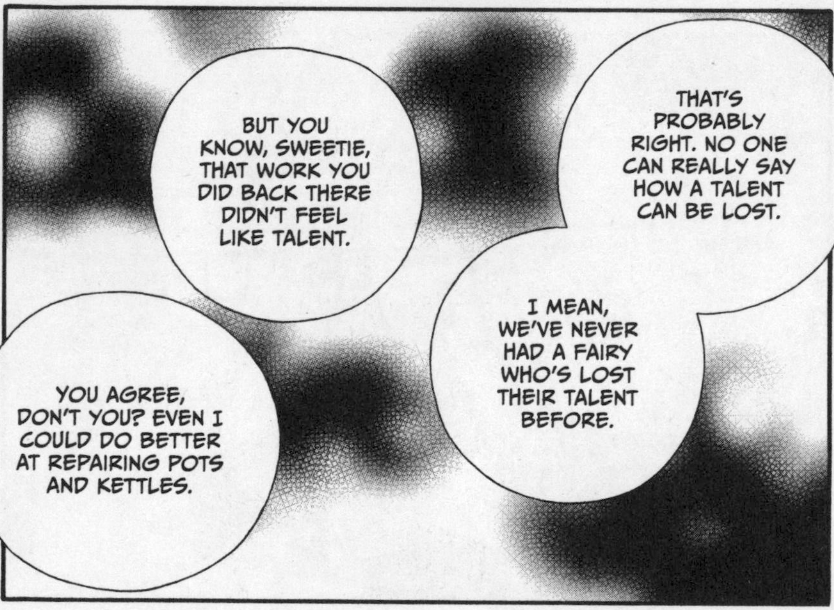
THAT'S PROBABLY RIGHT. NO ONE CAN REALLY SAY HOW A TALENT CAN BE LOST.
I MEAN, WE'VE NEVER HAD A FAIRY WHO'S LOST THEIR TALENT BEFORE.
BUT YOU KNOW, SWEETIE, THAT WORK YOU DID BACK THERE DIDN'T FEEL LIKE TALENT.
YOU AGREE, DON'T YOU? EVEN I COULD DO BETTER AT REPAIRING POTS AND KETTLES.

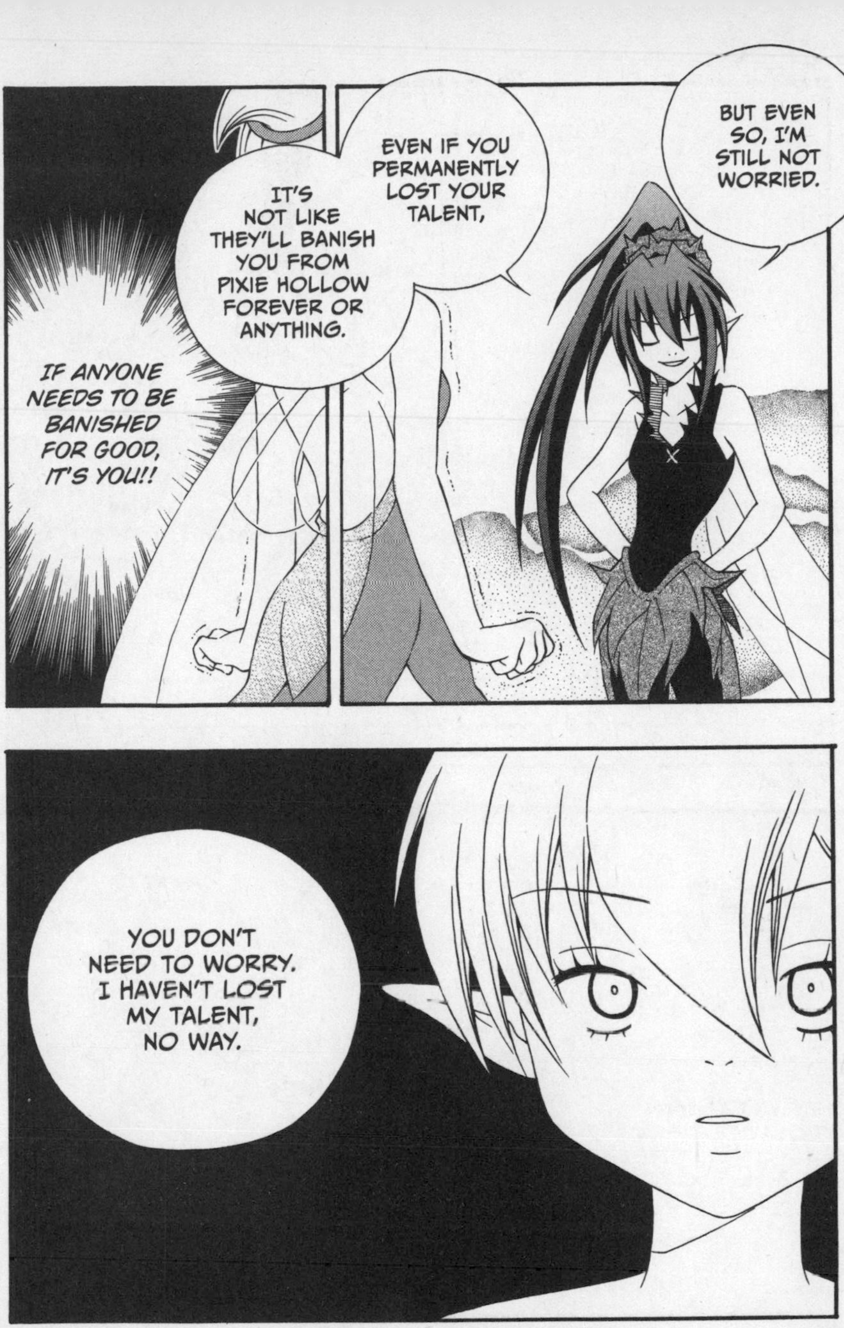
BUT EVEN SO, I'M STILL NOT WORRIED.
EVEN IF YOU PERMANENTLY LOST YOUR TALENT,
IT'S NOT LIKE THEY'LL BANISH YOU FROM PIXIE HOLLOW FOREVER OR ANYTHING.
IF ANYONE NEEDS TO BE BANISHED FOR GOOD, IT'S YOU!!
YOU DON'T NEED TO WORRY. I HAVEN'T LOST MY TALENT, NO WAY.

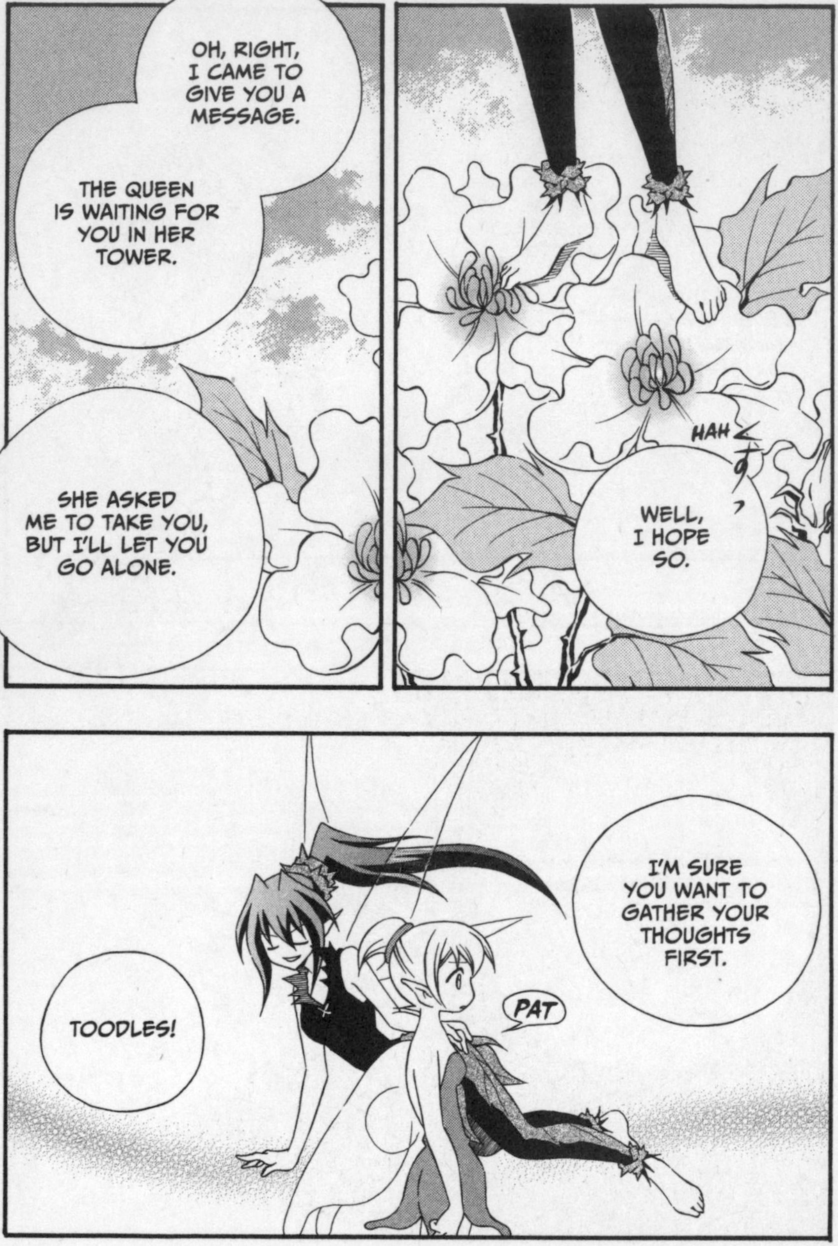
HAH
WELL, I HOPE SO.
OH, RIGHT, I CAME TO GIVE YOU A MESSAGE.
THE QUEEN IS WAITING FOR YOU IN HER TOWER.
SHE ASKED ME TO TAKE YOU, BUT I'LL LET YOU GO ALONE.
I'M SURE YOU WANT TO GATHER YOUR THOUGHTS FIRST.
PAT
TOODLES!

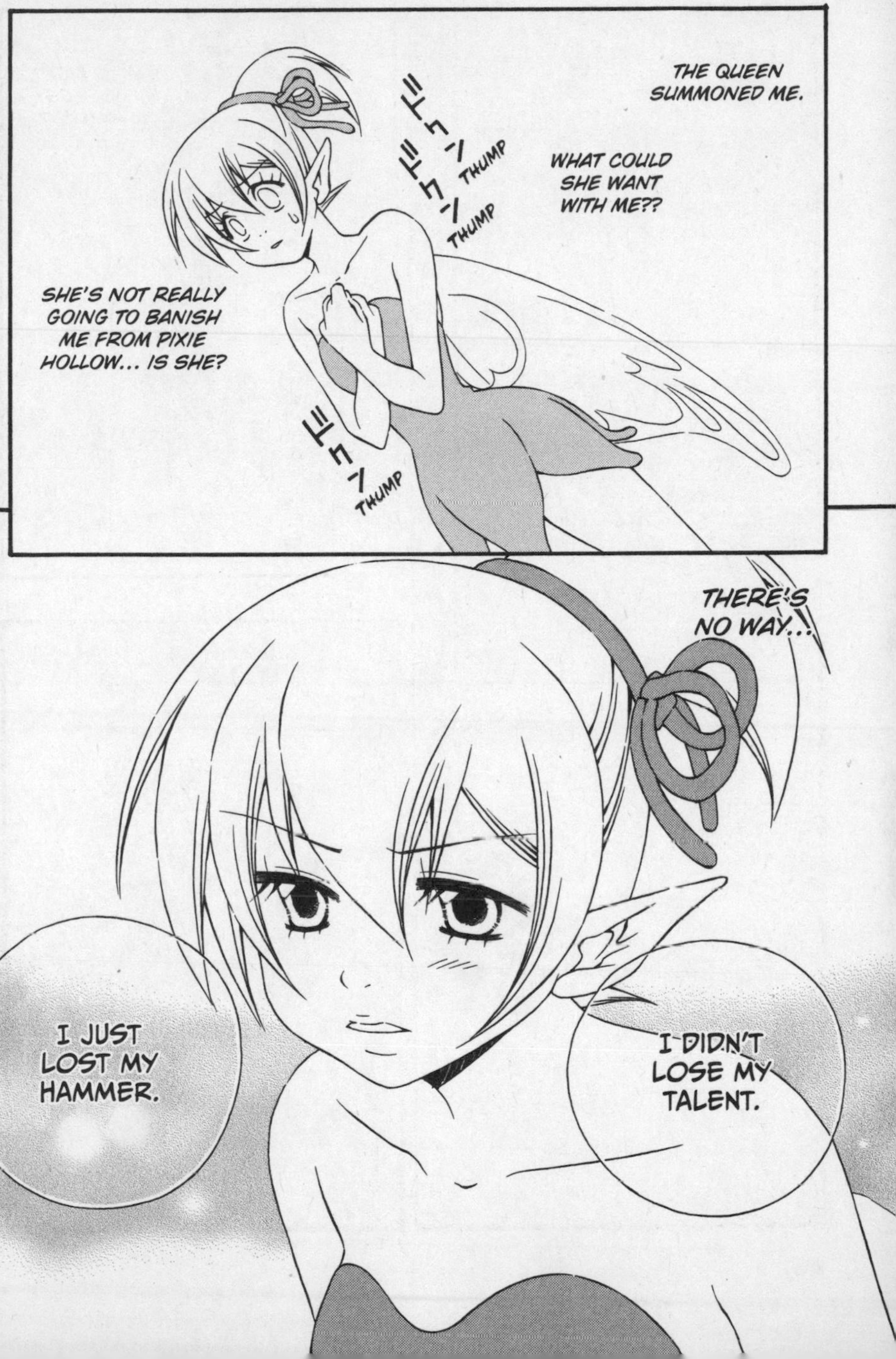
THE QUEEN SUMMONED ME.
WHAT COULD SHE WANT WITH ME??
ドキン THUMP
ドキン THUMP
SHE'S NOT REALLY GOING TO BANISH ME FROM PIXIE HOLLOW... IS SHE?
ドキン THUMP
THERE'S NO WAY...
I DIDN'T LOSE MY TALENT.
I JUST LOST MY HAMMER.

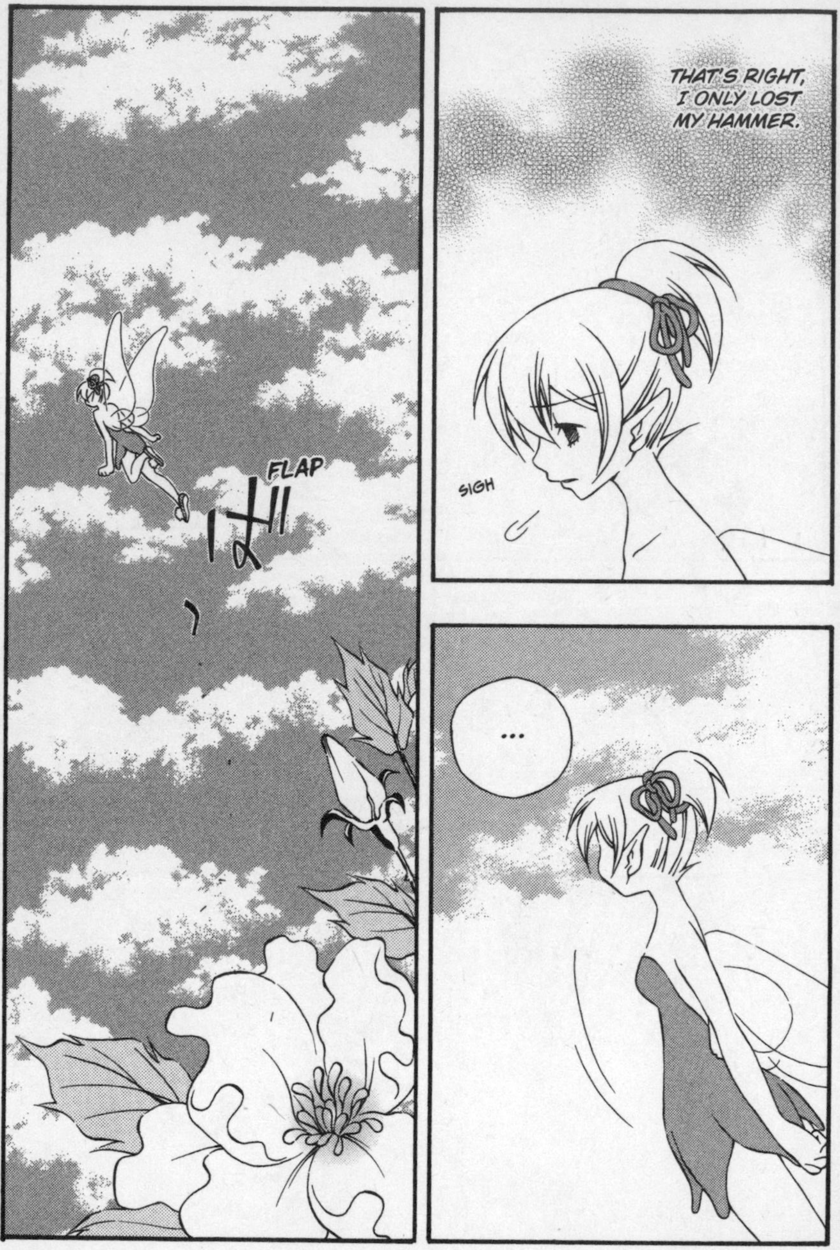
THAT'S RIGHT, I ONLY LOST MY HAMMER.
SIGH
...
FLAP

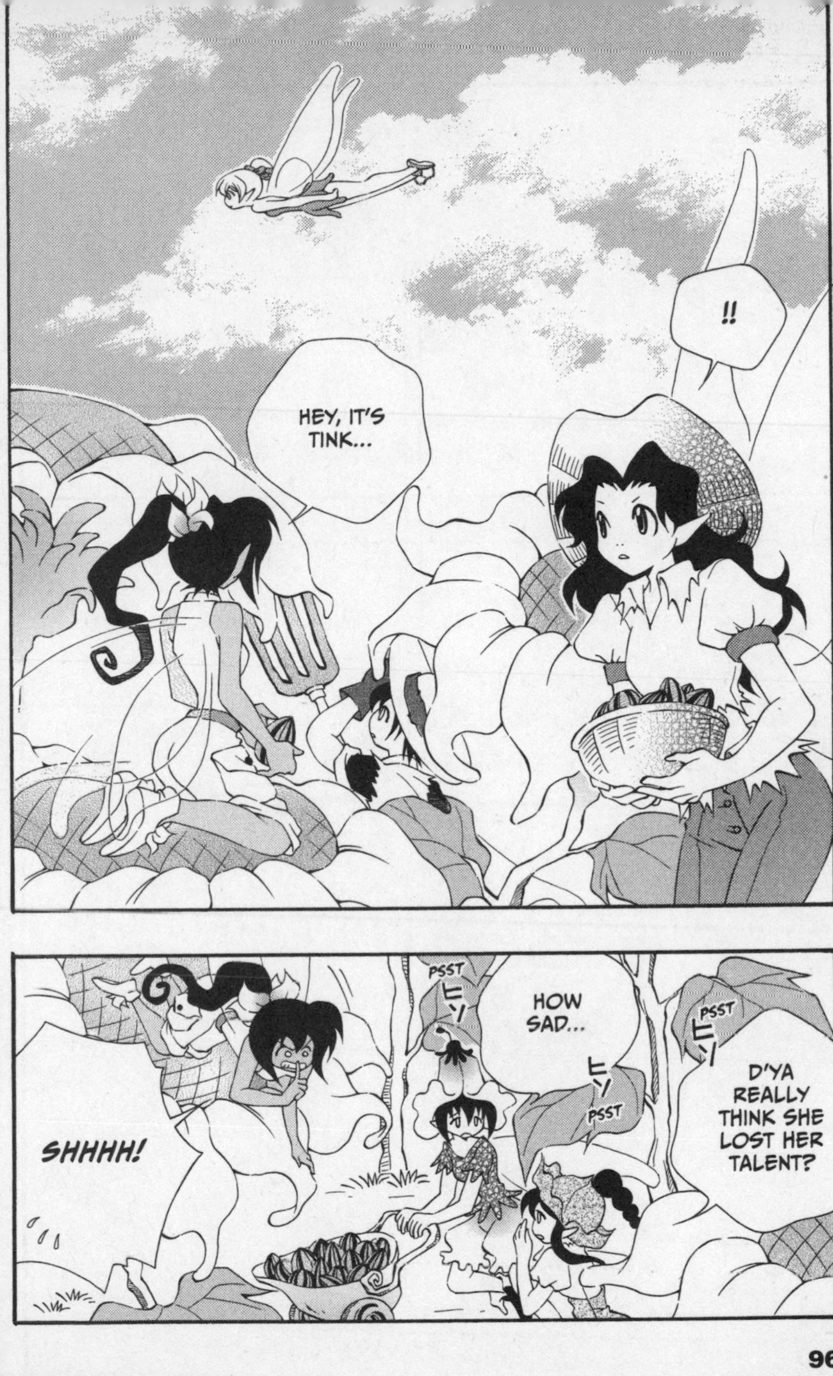
!!
HEY, IT'S TINK...
PSST
ヒソ
D'YA REALLY THINK SHE LOST HER TALENT?
PSST
ヒソ
HOW SAD...
ヒソ
PSST
SHHHH!

READ THIS WAY

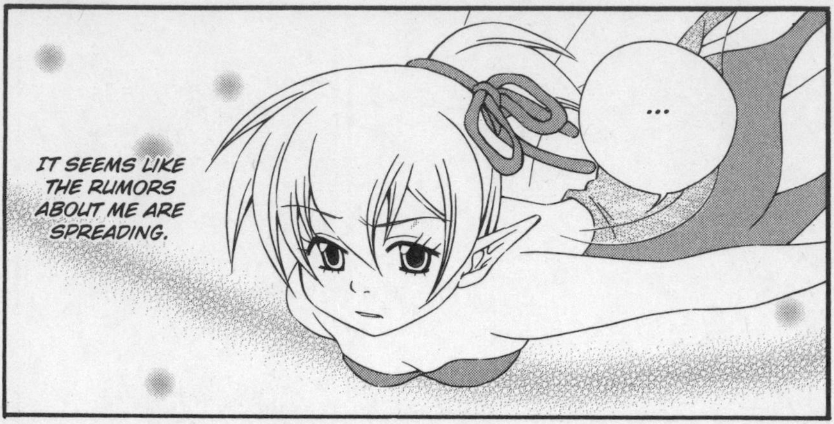
...
IT SEEMS LIKE THE RUMORS ABOUT ME ARE SPREADING.

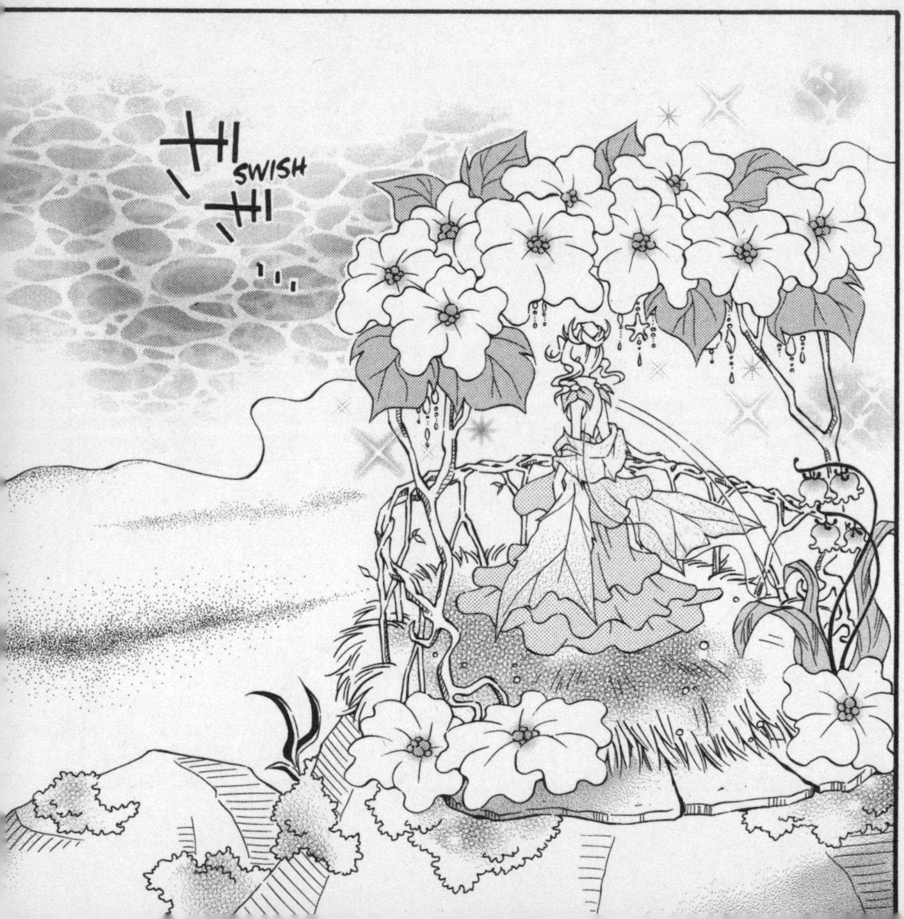
SWISH

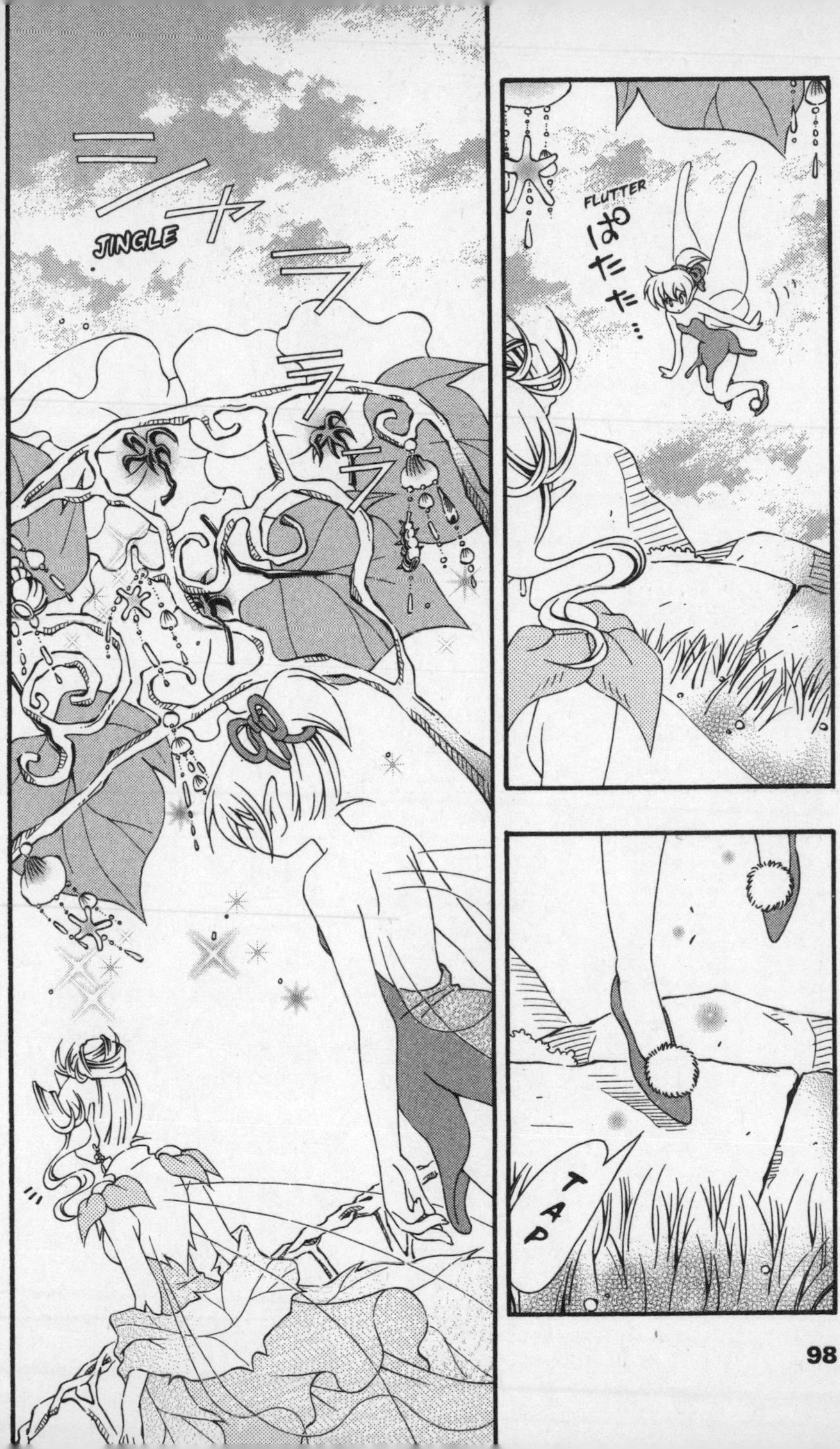
FLUTTER
ぱたた…
TAP
JINGLE
シャラララ

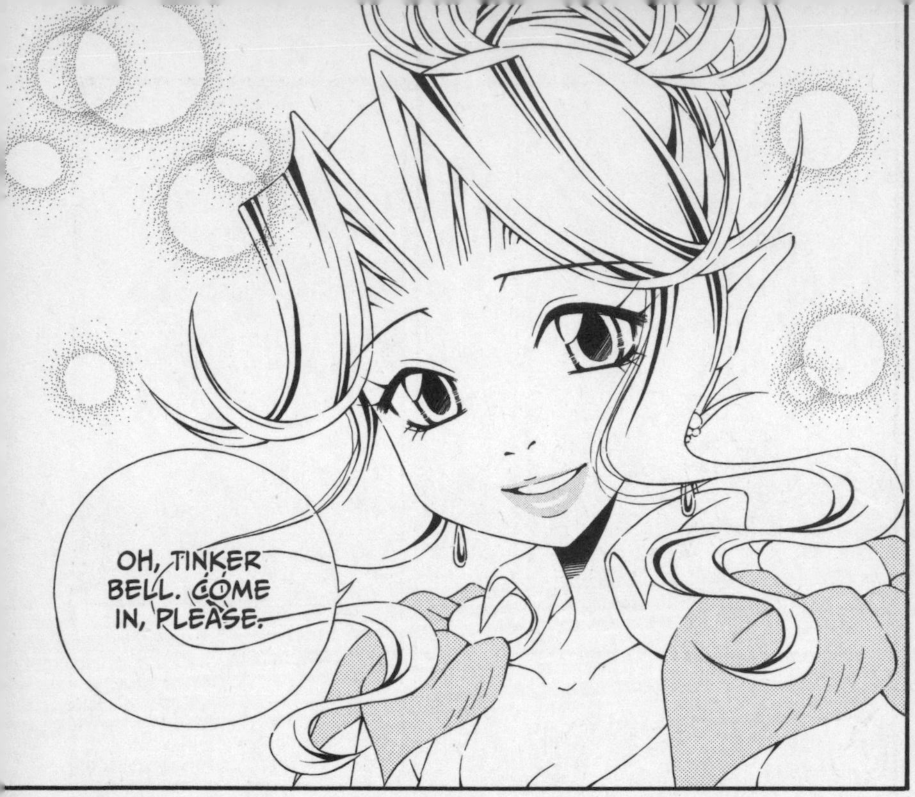
OH, TINKER BELL. COME IN, PLEASE.

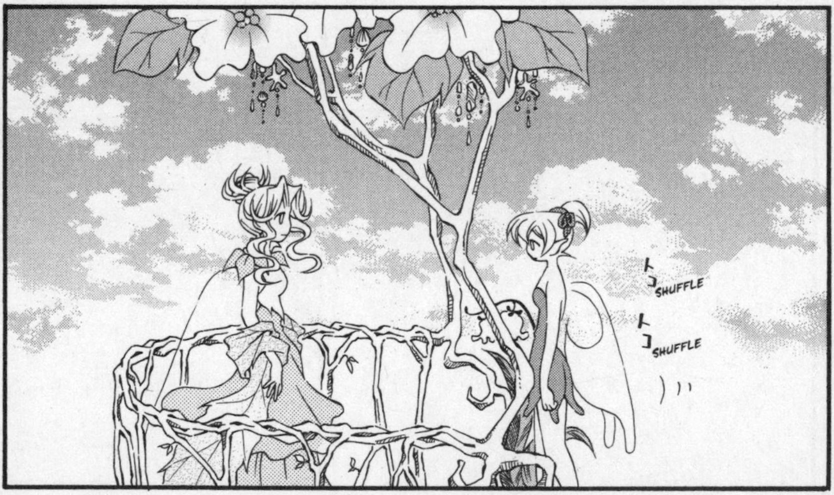
トコ SHUFFLE
トコ SHUFFLE

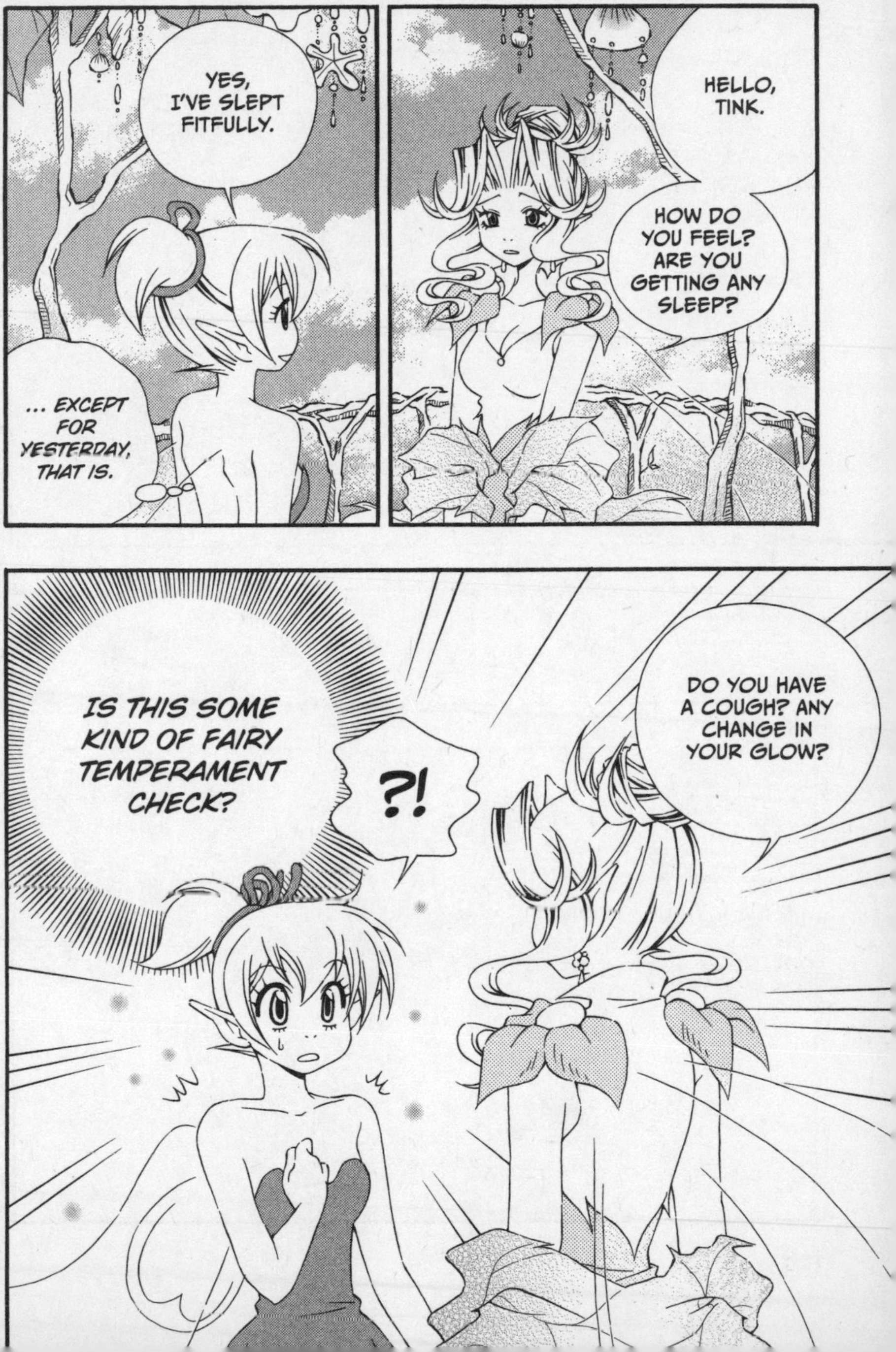
HELLO, TINK.
HOW DO YOU FEEL? ARE YOU GETTING ANY SLEEP?
YES, I'VE SLEPT FITFULLY.
... EXCEPT FOR YESTERDAY, THAT IS.
DO YOU HAVE A COUGH? ANY CHANGE IN YOUR GLOW?
?!
IS THIS SOME KIND OF FAIRY TEMPERAMENT CHECK?

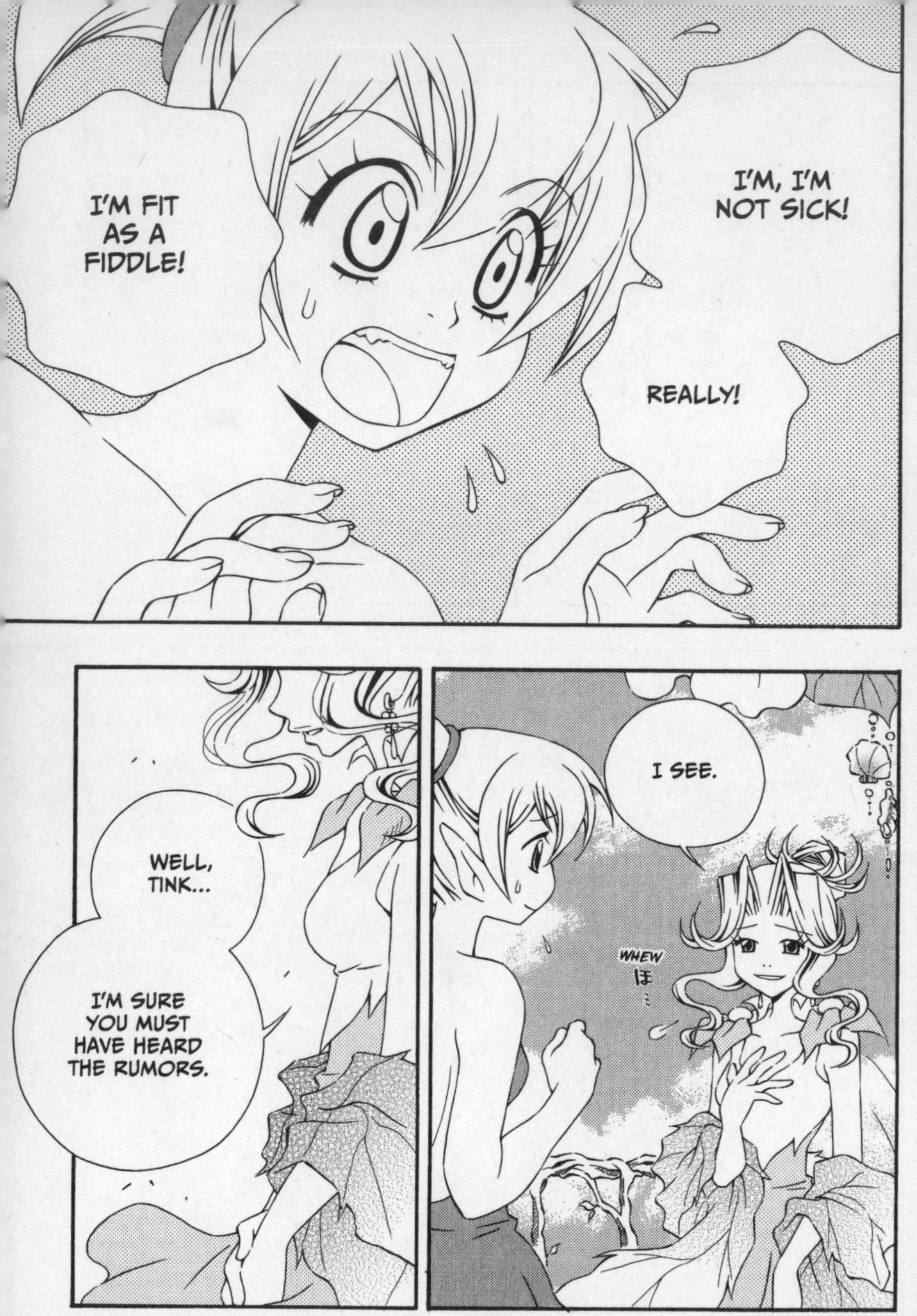
I'M, I'M NOT SICK!
REALLY!
I'M FIT AS A FIDDLE!
I SEE.
WHEW
ほ
WELL, TINK...
I'M SURE YOU MUST HAVE HEARD THE RUMORS.

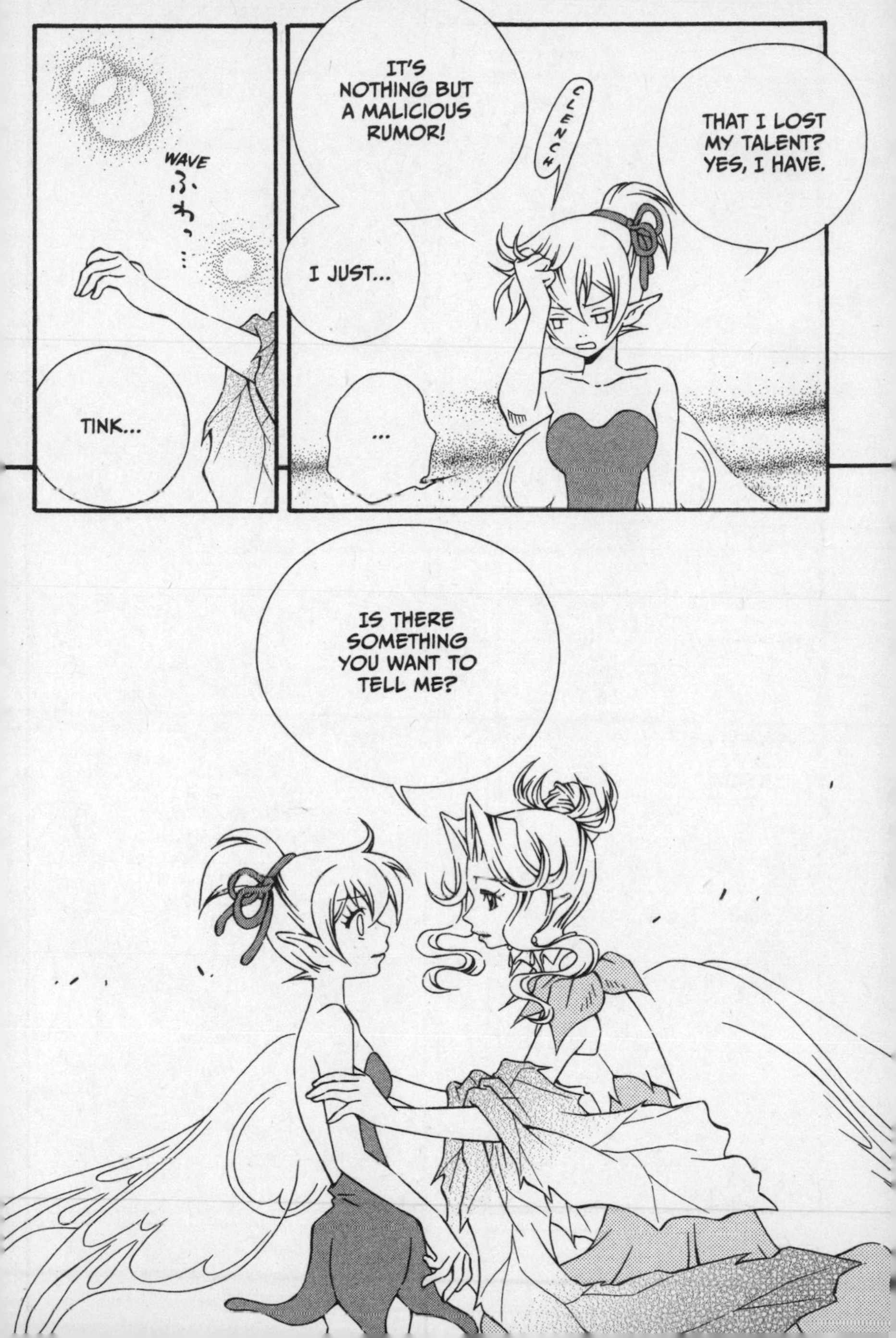
THAT I LOST MY TALENT? YES, I HAVE.
CLENCH
IT'S NOTHING BUT A MALICIOUS RUMOR!
I JUST...
...
WAVE
ふわっ…
TINK...
IS THERE SOMETHING YOU WANT TO TELL ME?

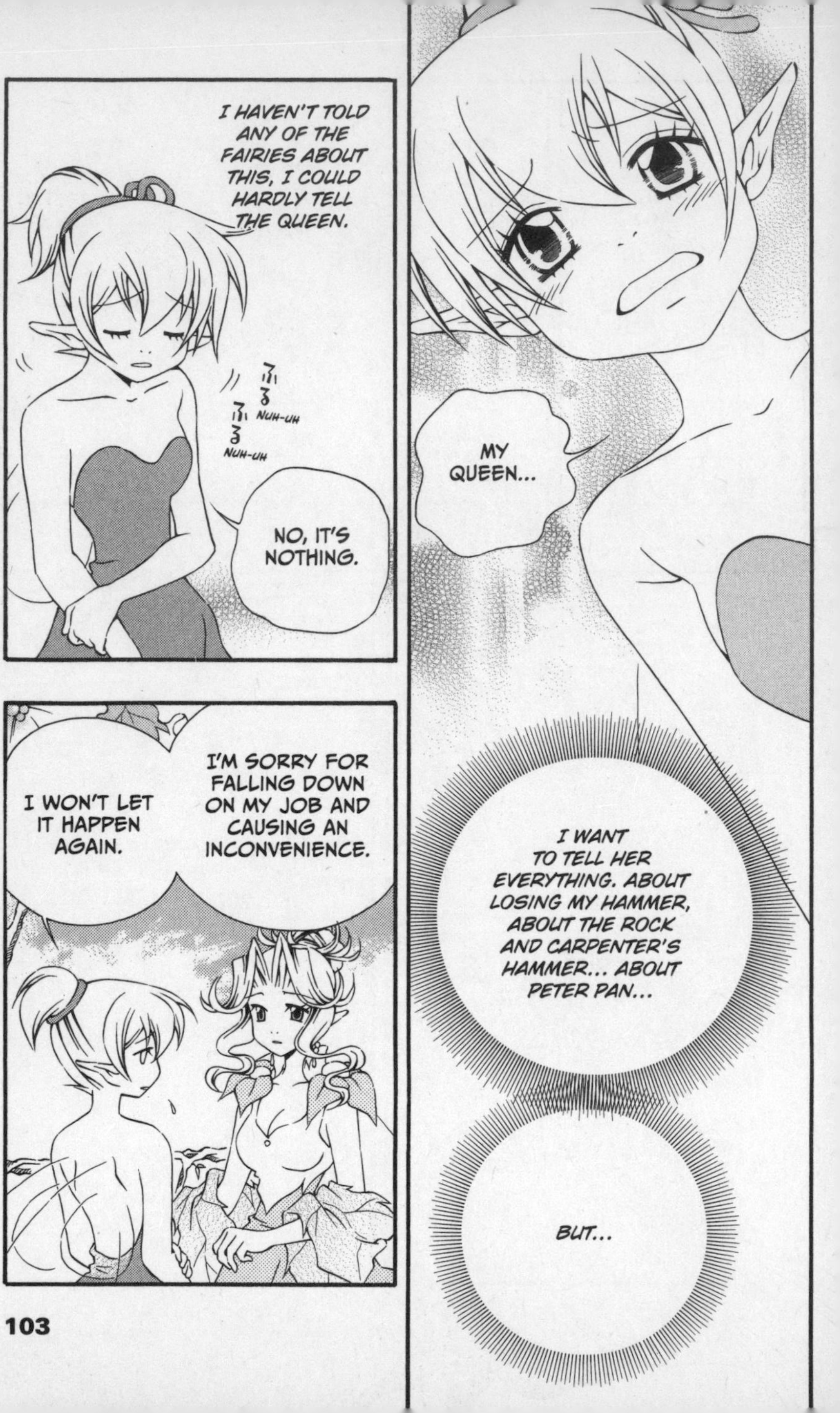
MY QUEEN...
I WANT TO TELL HER EVERYTHING. ABOUT LOSING MY HAMMER, ABOUT THE ROCK AND CARPENTER'S HAMMER... ABOUT PETER PAN...
BUT...
I HAVEN'T TOLD ANY OF THE FAIRIES ABOUT THIS, I COULD HARDLY TELL THE QUEEN.
ふるふる NUH-UH NUH-UH
NO, IT'S NOTHING.
I'M SORRY FOR FALLING DOWN ON MY JOB AND CAUSING AN INCONVENIENCE.
I WON'T LET IT HAPPEN AGAIN.

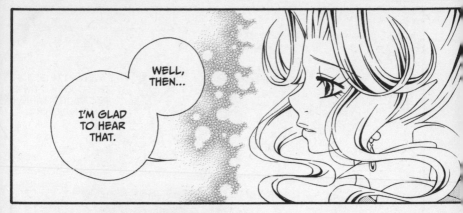

WELL, THEN...

I'M GLAD TO HEAR THAT.

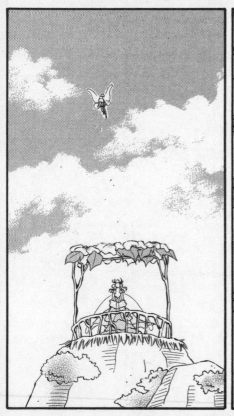

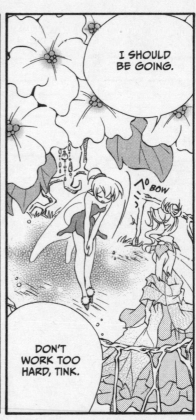

I SHOULD BE GOING.

BOW

DON'T WORK TOO HARD, TINK.

READ THIS WAY

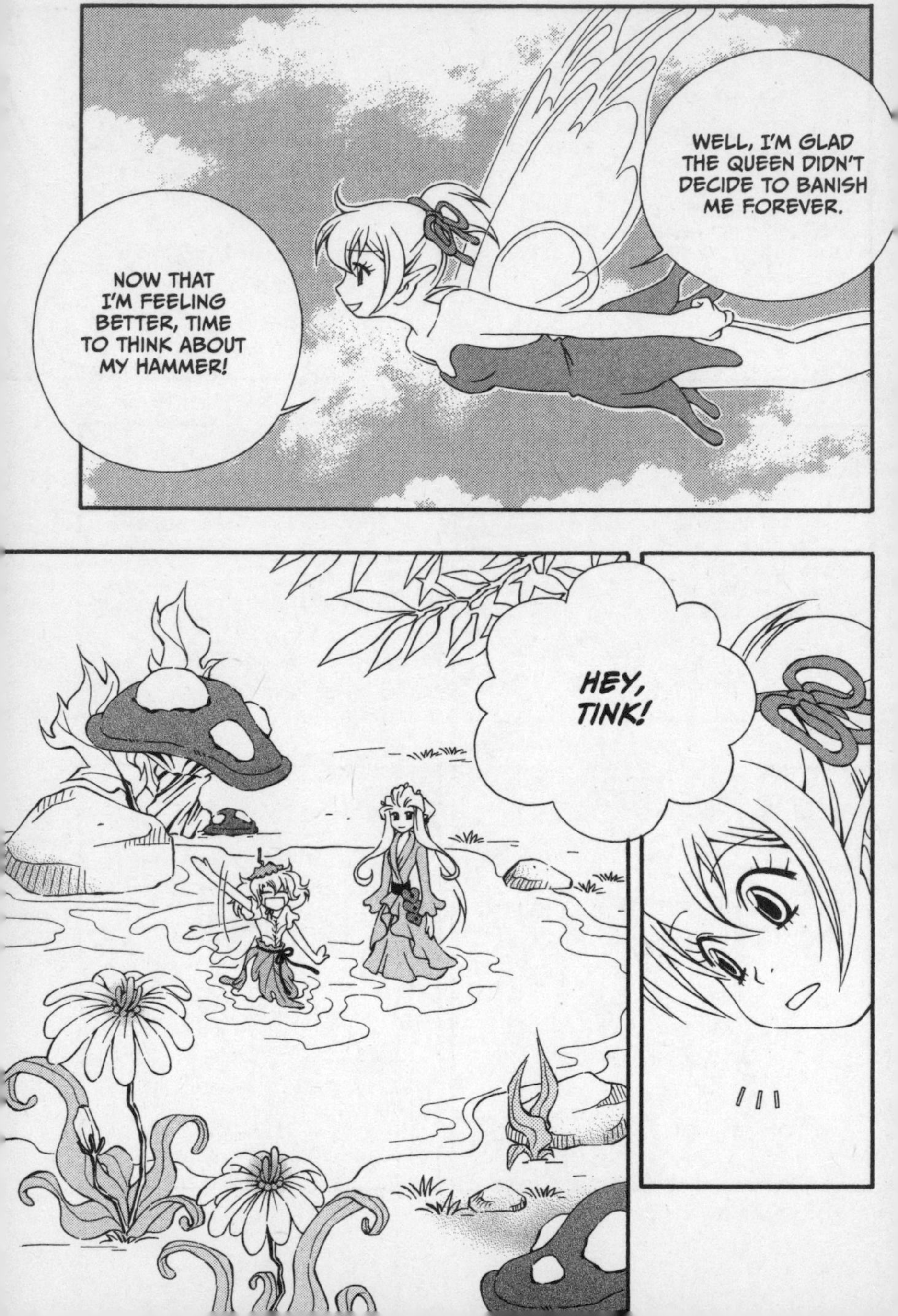

WELL, I'M GLAD THE QUEEN DIDN'T DECIDE TO BANISH ME FOREVER.
NOW THAT I'M FEELING BETTER, TIME TO THINK ABOUT MY HAMMER!
HEY, TINK!

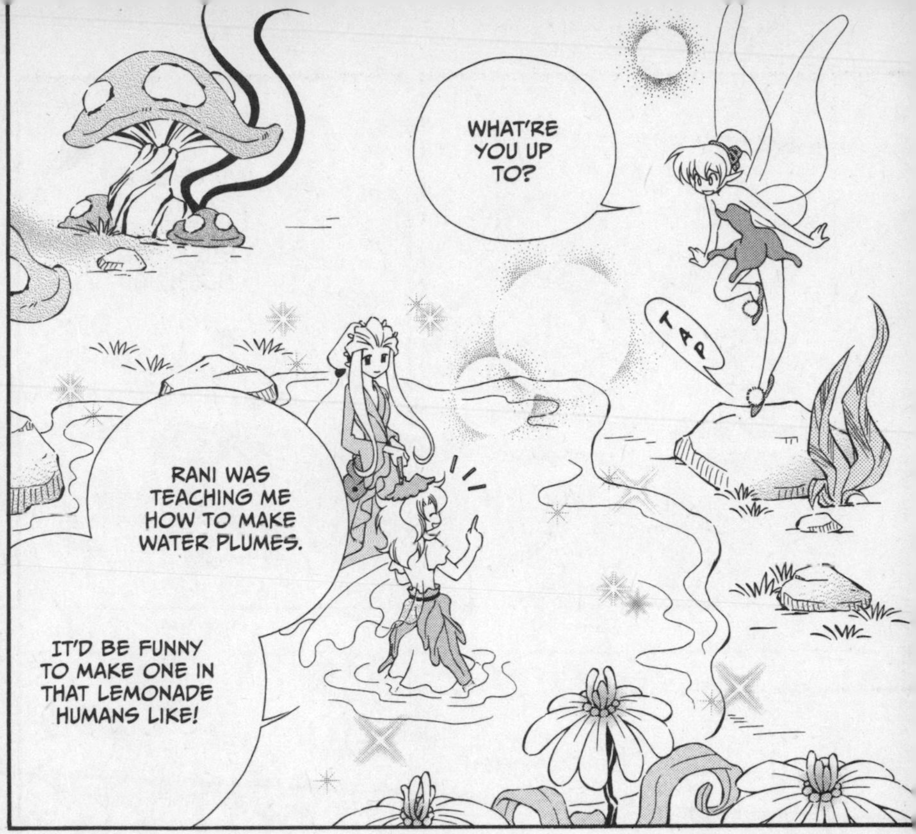
WHAT'RE YOU UP TO?
TAP
RANI WAS TEACHING ME HOW TO MAKE WATER PLUMES.
IT'D BE FUNNY TO MAKE ONE IN THAT LEMONADE HUMANS LIKE!
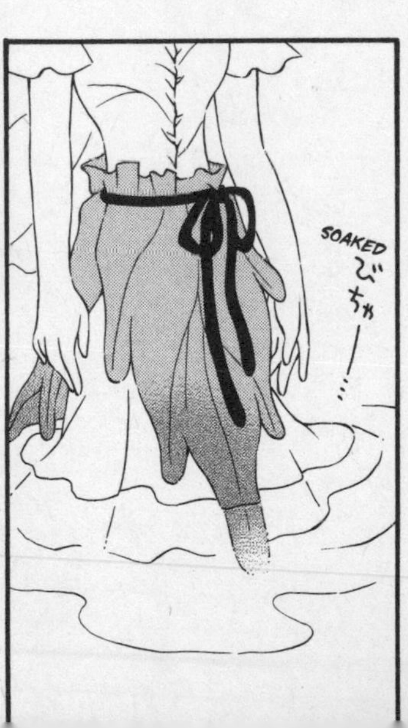
SOAKED
びちゃ
......
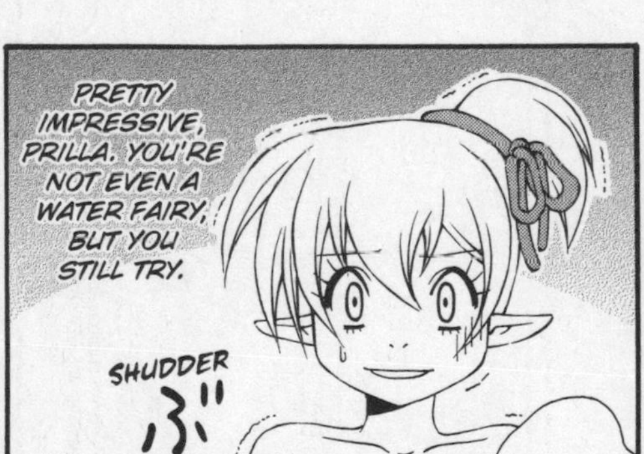
PRETTY IMPRESSIVE, PRILLA. YOU'RE NOT EVEN A WATER FAIRY, BUT YOU STILL TRY.
SHUDDER
ぶるっ
...

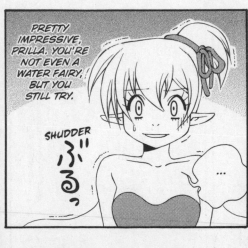

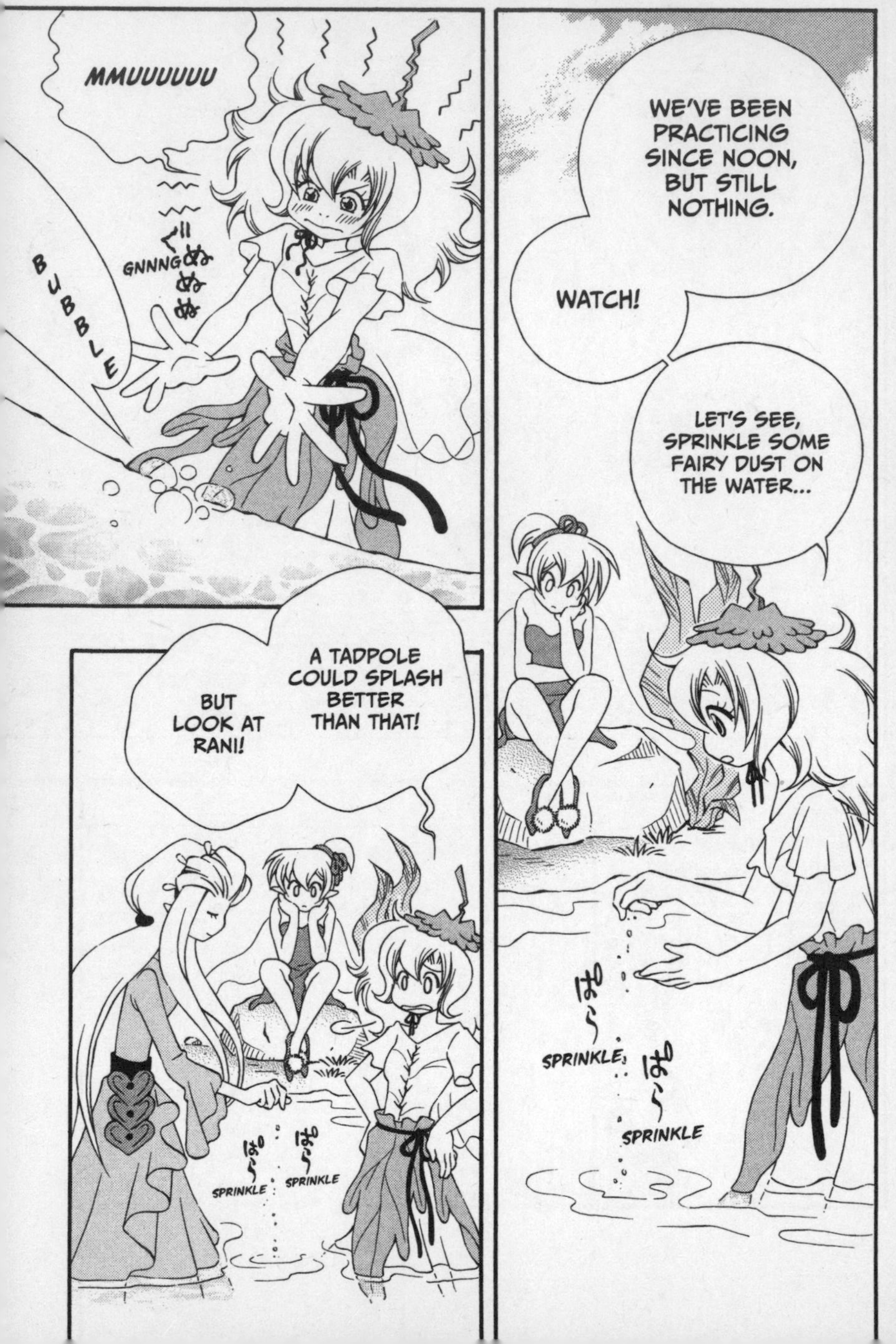
WE'VE BEEN PRACTICING SINCE NOON, BUT STILL NOTHING.
WATCH!
LET'S SEE, SPRINKLE SOME FAIRY DUST ON THE WATER...
ぱら
SPRINKLE
ぱら
SPRINKLE
MMUUUUUU
ぐぬぬぬ
GNNNG
BUBBLE
A TADPOLE COULD SPLASH BETTER THAN THAT!
BUT LOOK AT RANI!
ぱら
SPRINKLE
ぱら
SPRINKLE

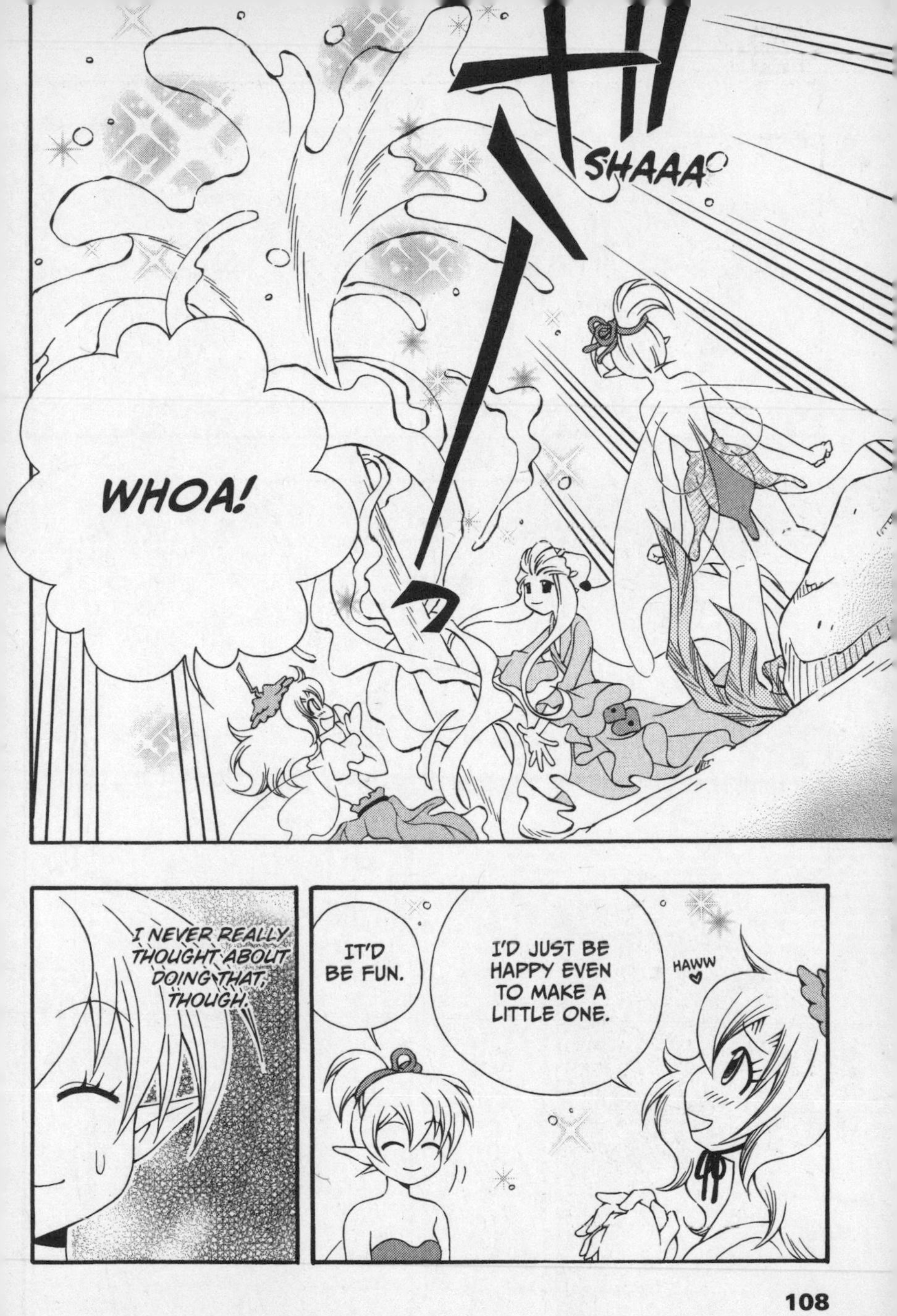
SHAAA
WHOA!
HAWW
I'D JUST BE HAPPY EVEN TO MAKE A LITTLE ONE.
IT'D BE FUN.
I NEVER REALLY THOUGHT ABOUT DOING THAT, THOUGH.

READ THIS WAY

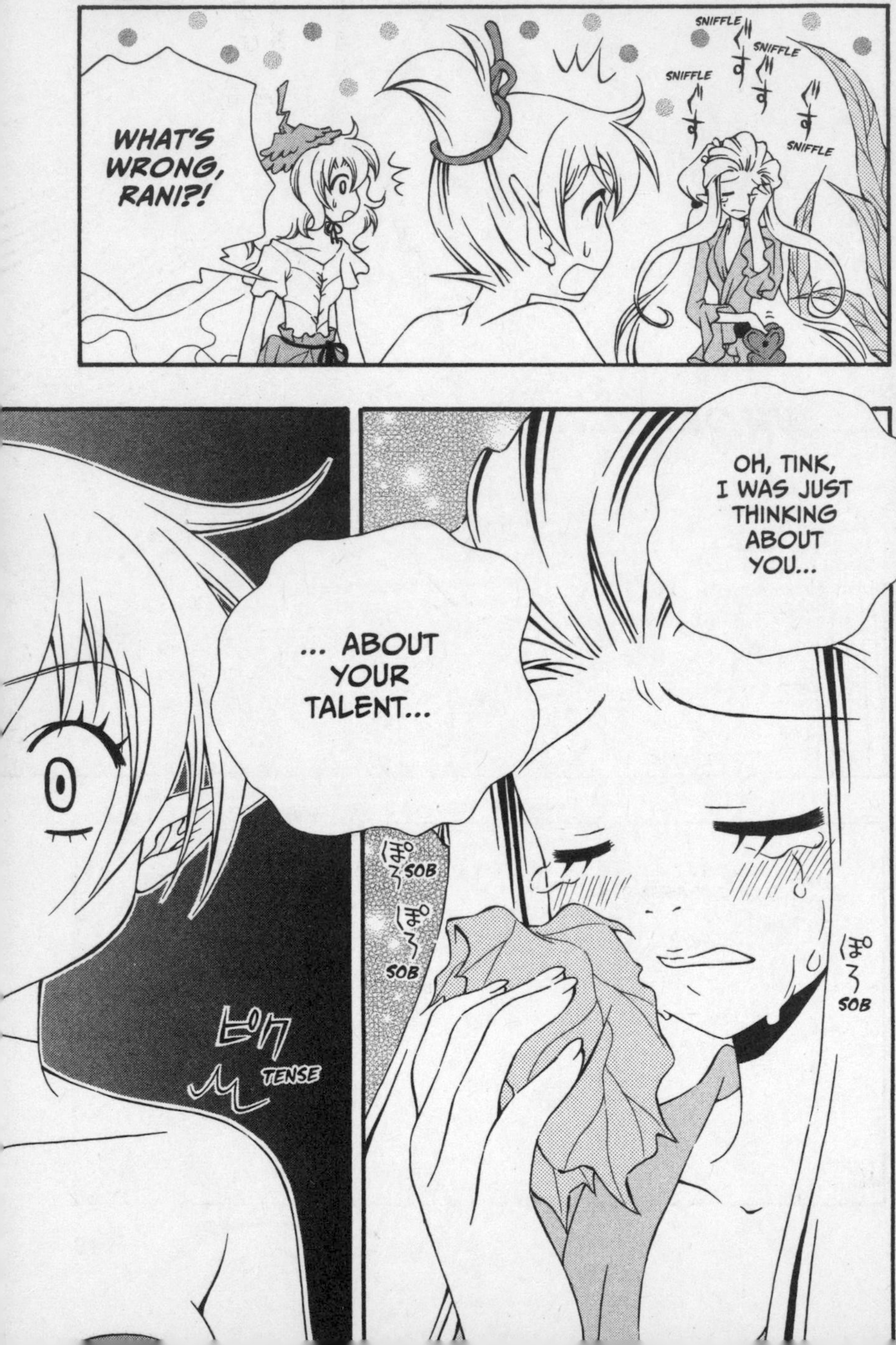

ぐす SNIFFLE
ぐす SNIFFLE
ぐす SNIFFLE
ぐす SNIFFLE
WHAT'S WRONG, RANI?!
OH, TINK, I WAS JUST THINKING ABOUT YOU...
... ABOUT YOUR TALENT...
ぽろ SOB
ぽろ SOB
ぽろ SOB
ピク TENSE

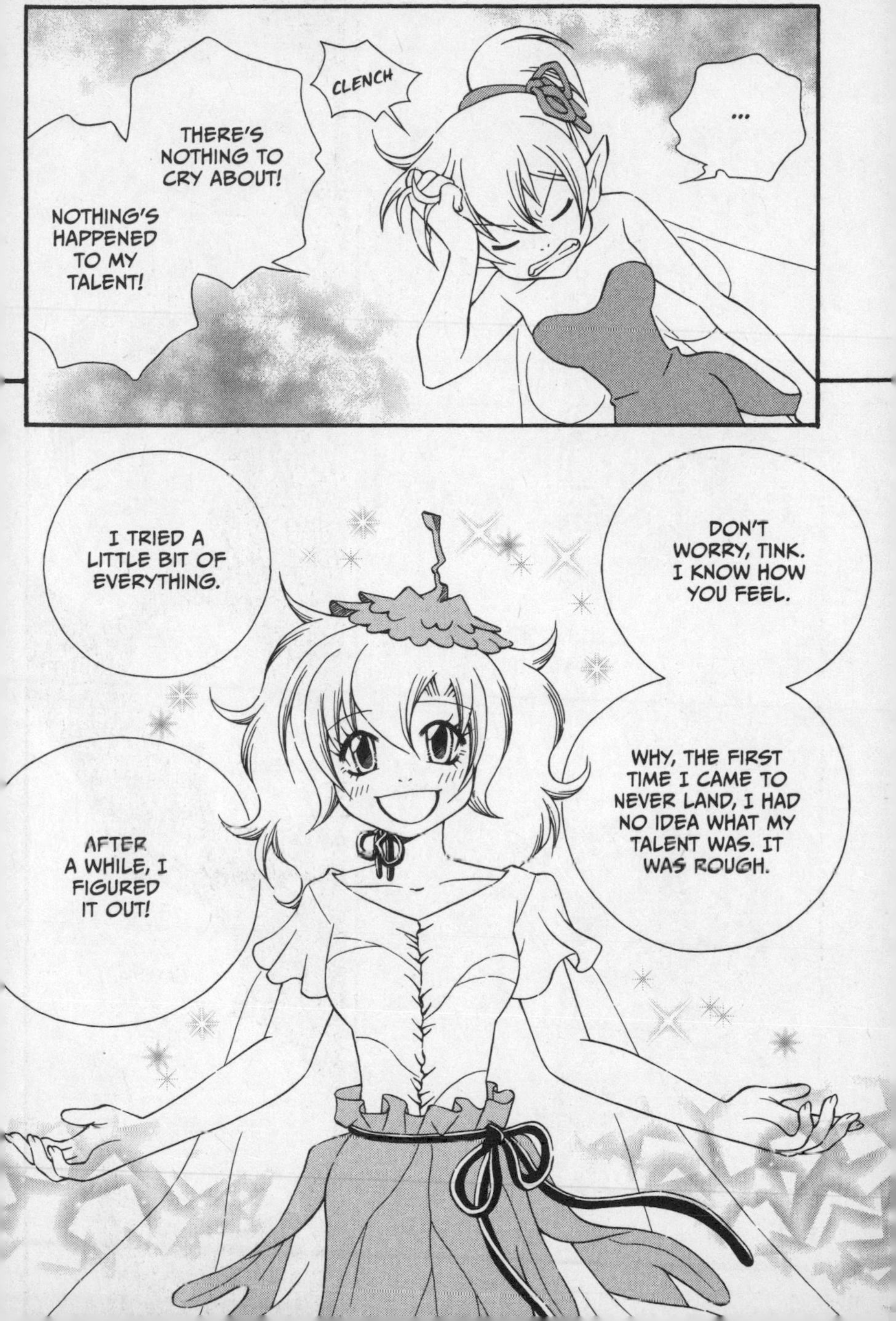
...
CLENCH
THERE'S NOTHING TO CRY ABOUT!
NOTHING'S HAPPENED TO MY TALENT!
DON'T WORRY, TINK. I KNOW HOW YOU FEEL.
WHY, THE FIRST TIME I CAME TO NEVER LAND, I HAD NO IDEA WHAT MY TALENT WAS. IT WAS ROUGH.
I TRIED A LITTLE BIT OF EVERYTHING.
AFTER A WHILE, I FIGURED IT OUT!

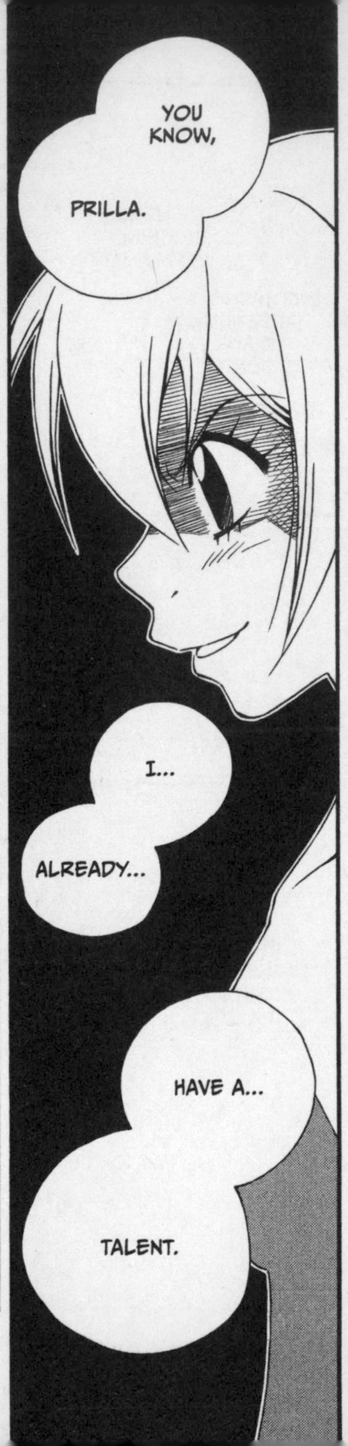
YOU KNOW,
PRILLA.
I...
ALREADY...
HAVE A...
TALENT.

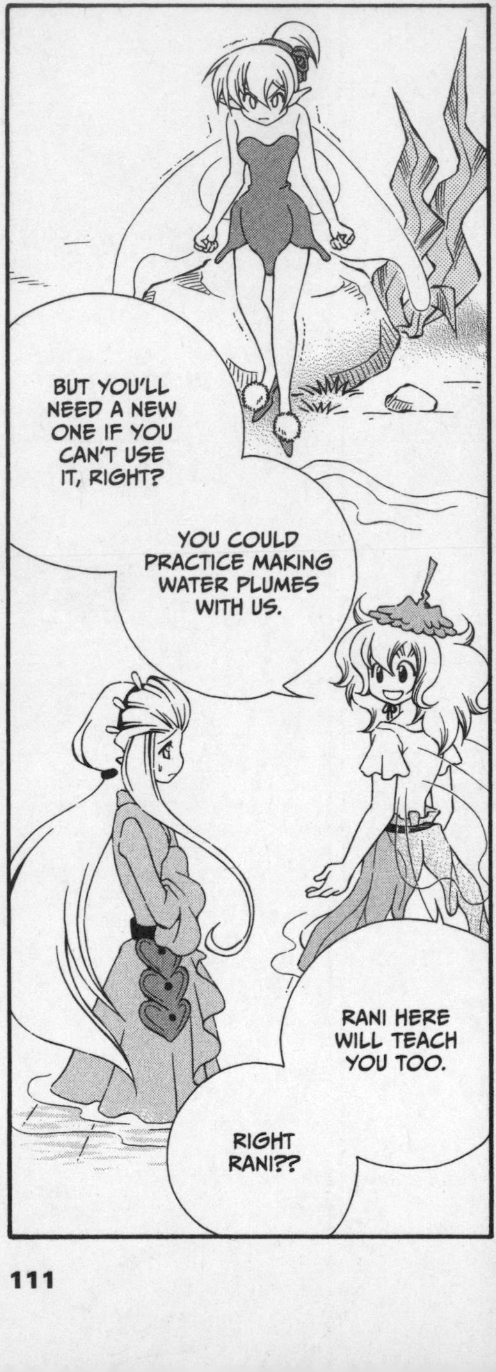
BUT YOU'LL NEED A NEW ONE IF YOU CAN'T USE IT, RIGHT?
YOU COULD PRACTICE MAKING WATER PLUMES WITH US.
RANI HERE WILL TEACH YOU TOO.
RIGHT RANI??

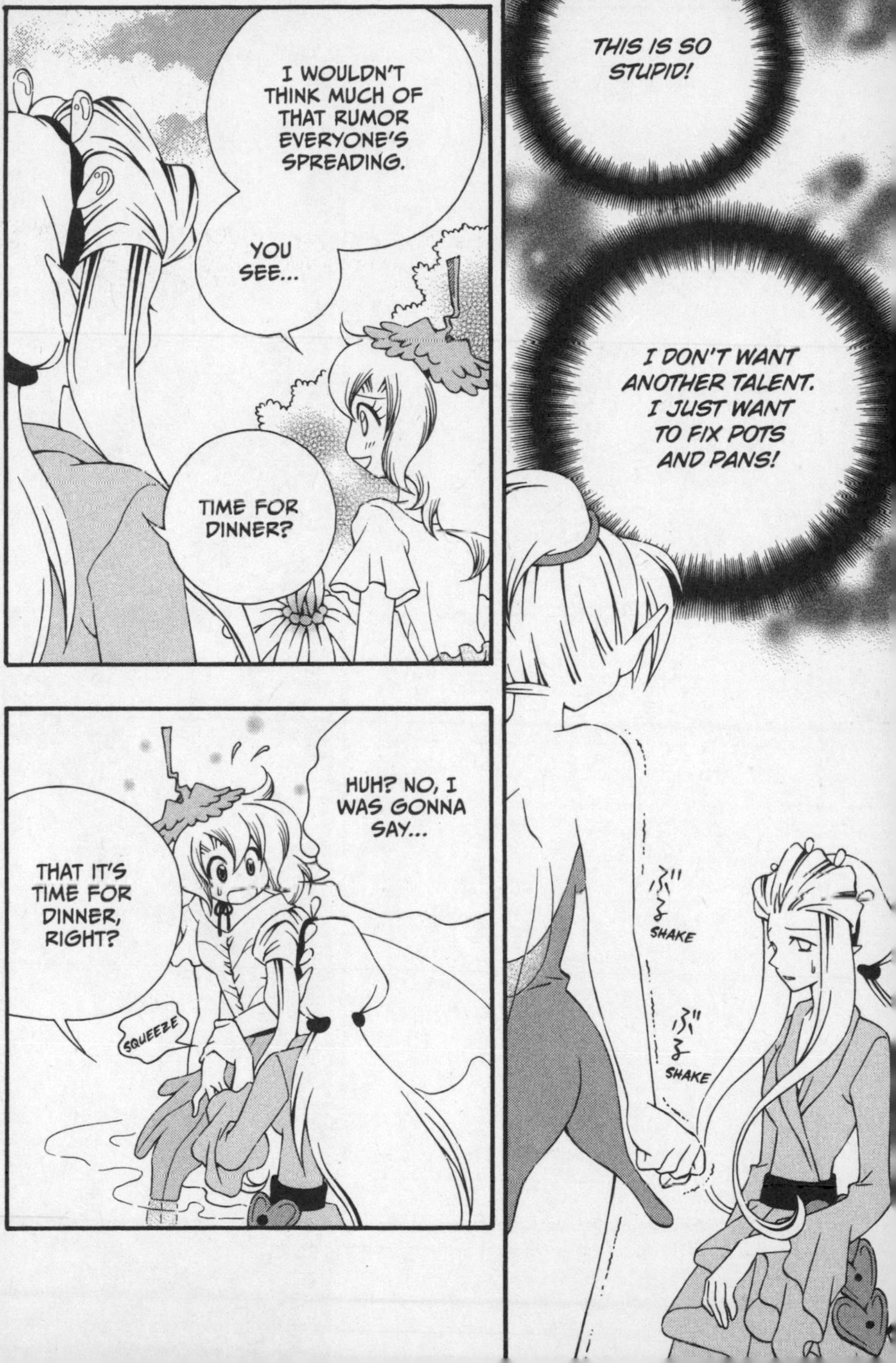
THIS IS SO STUPID!
I DON'T WANT ANOTHER TALENT. I JUST WANT TO FIX POTS AND PANS!
ぶる
SHAKE
ぶる
SHAKE
I WOULDN'T THINK MUCH OF THAT RUMOR EVERYONE'S SPREADING.
YOU SEE...
TIME FOR DINNER?
HUH? NO, I WAS GONNA SAY...
THAT IT'S TIME FOR DINNER, RIGHT?
SQUEEZE

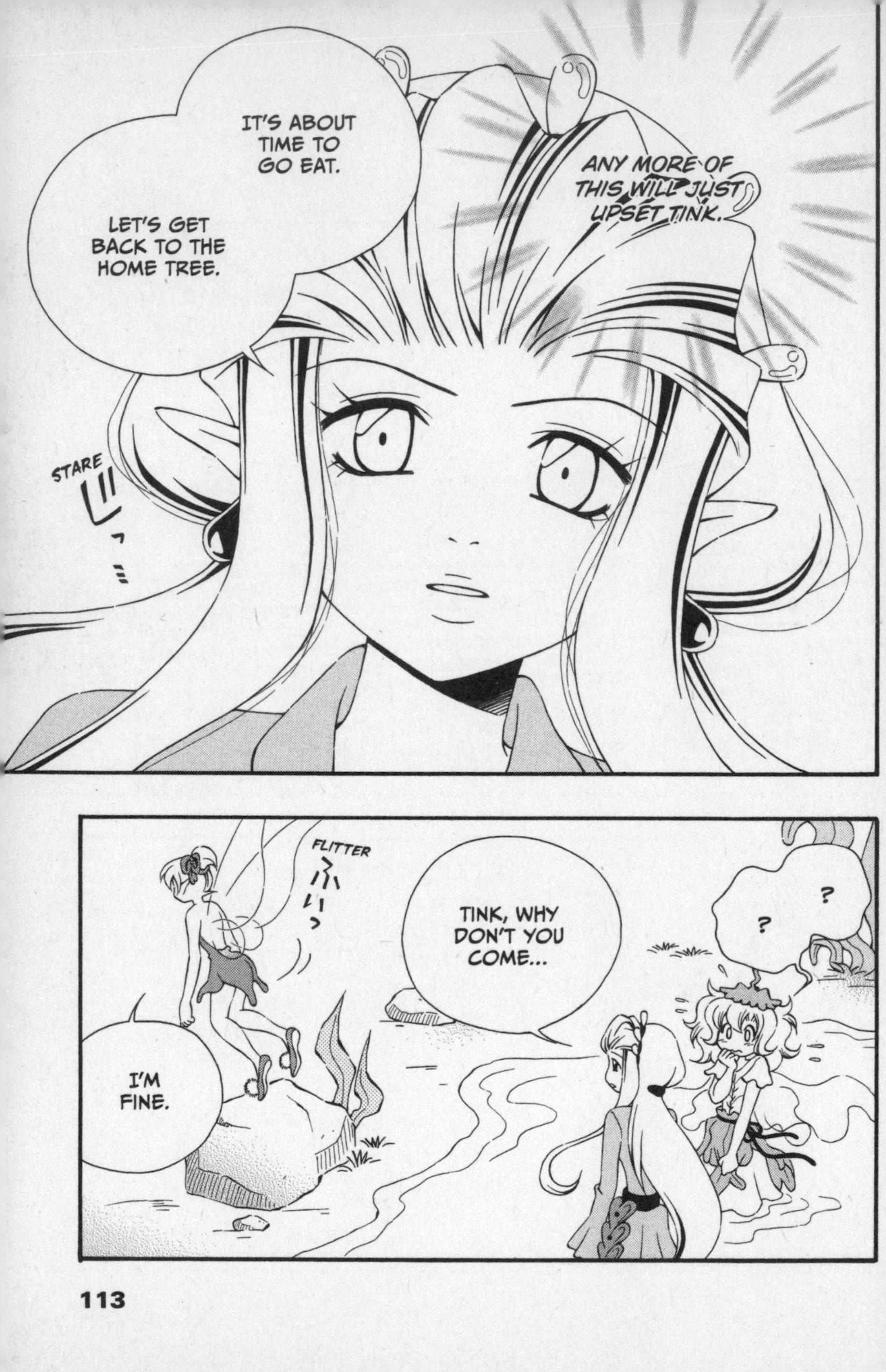
ANY MORE OF THIS WILL JUST UPSET TINK.
IT'S ABOUT TIME TO GO EAT.
LET'S GET BACK TO THE HOME TREE.
STARE
じーっ
? ?
TINK, WHY DON'T YOU COME...
FLITTER
ふいっ
I'M FINE.

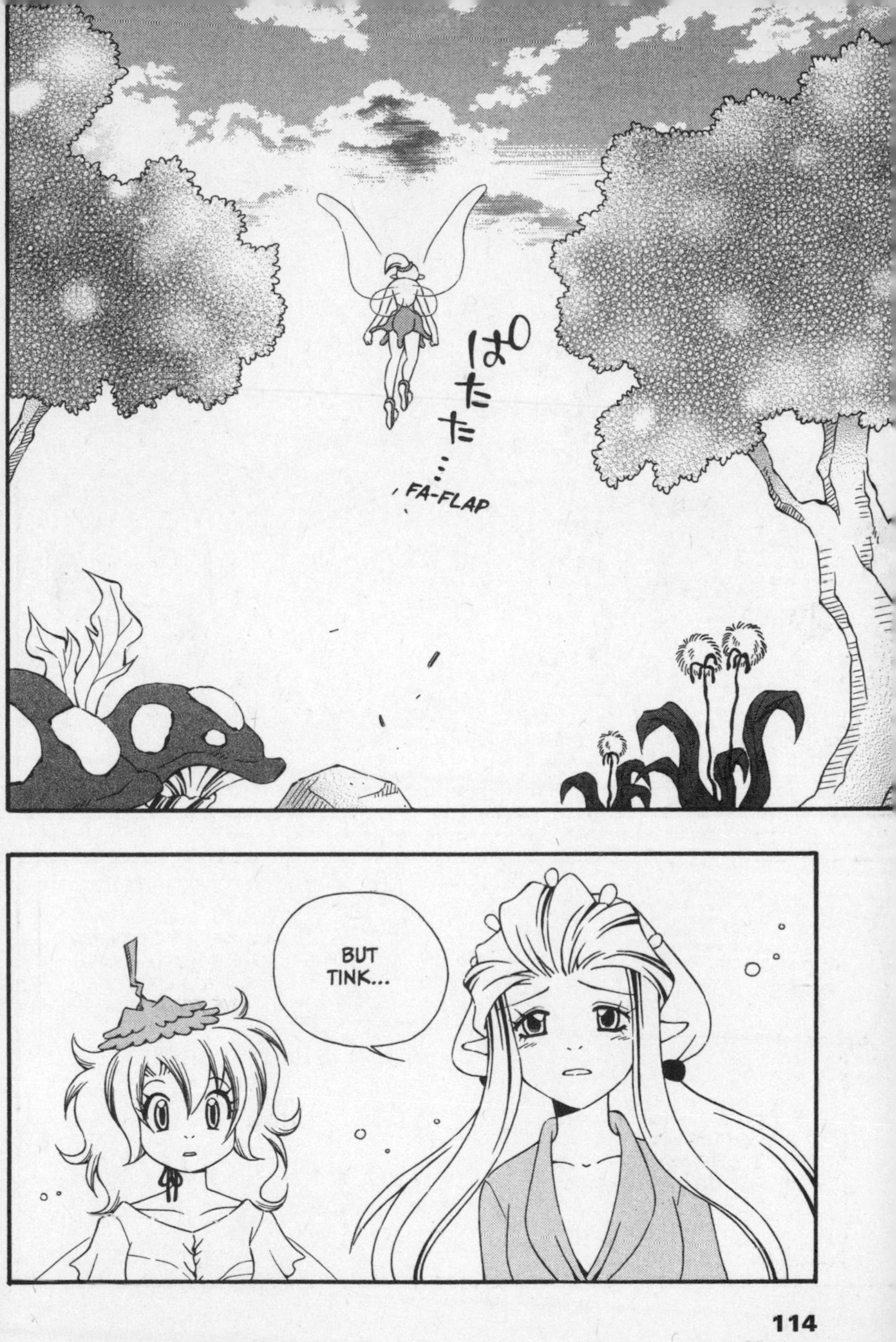
ぱたた…
FA-FLAP
BUT TINK...

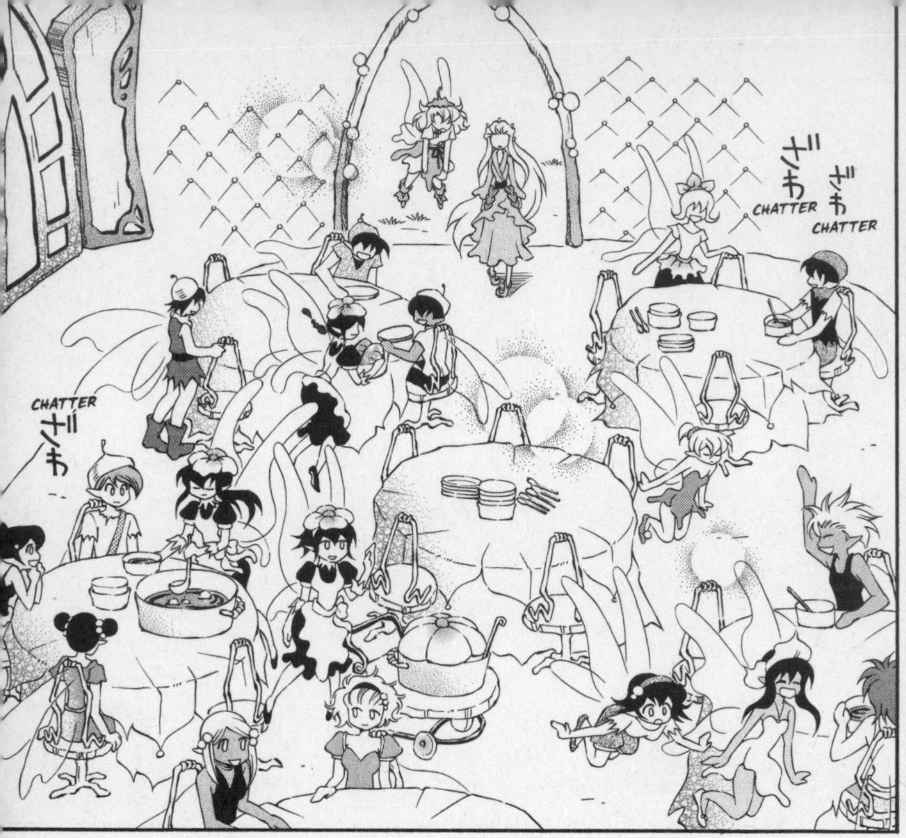
ざわ ざわ
CHATTER
CHATTER
ざわ
CHATTER

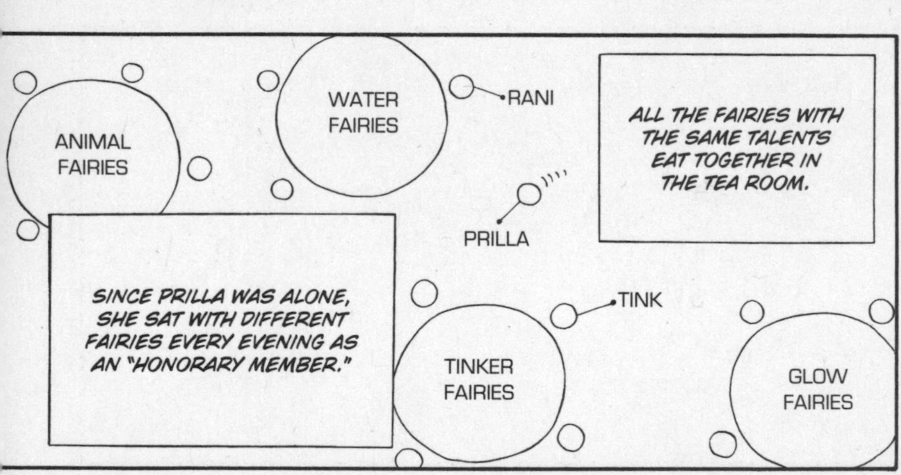
ALL THE FAIRIES WITH THE SAME TALENTS EAT TOGETHER IN THE TEA ROOM.
RANI
WATER FAIRIES
ANIMAL FAIRIES
PRILLA
TINK
GLOW FAIRIES
TINKER FAIRIES
SINCE PRILLA WAS ALONE, SHE SAT WITH DIFFERENT FAIRIES EVERY EVENING AS AN "HONORARY MEMBER."

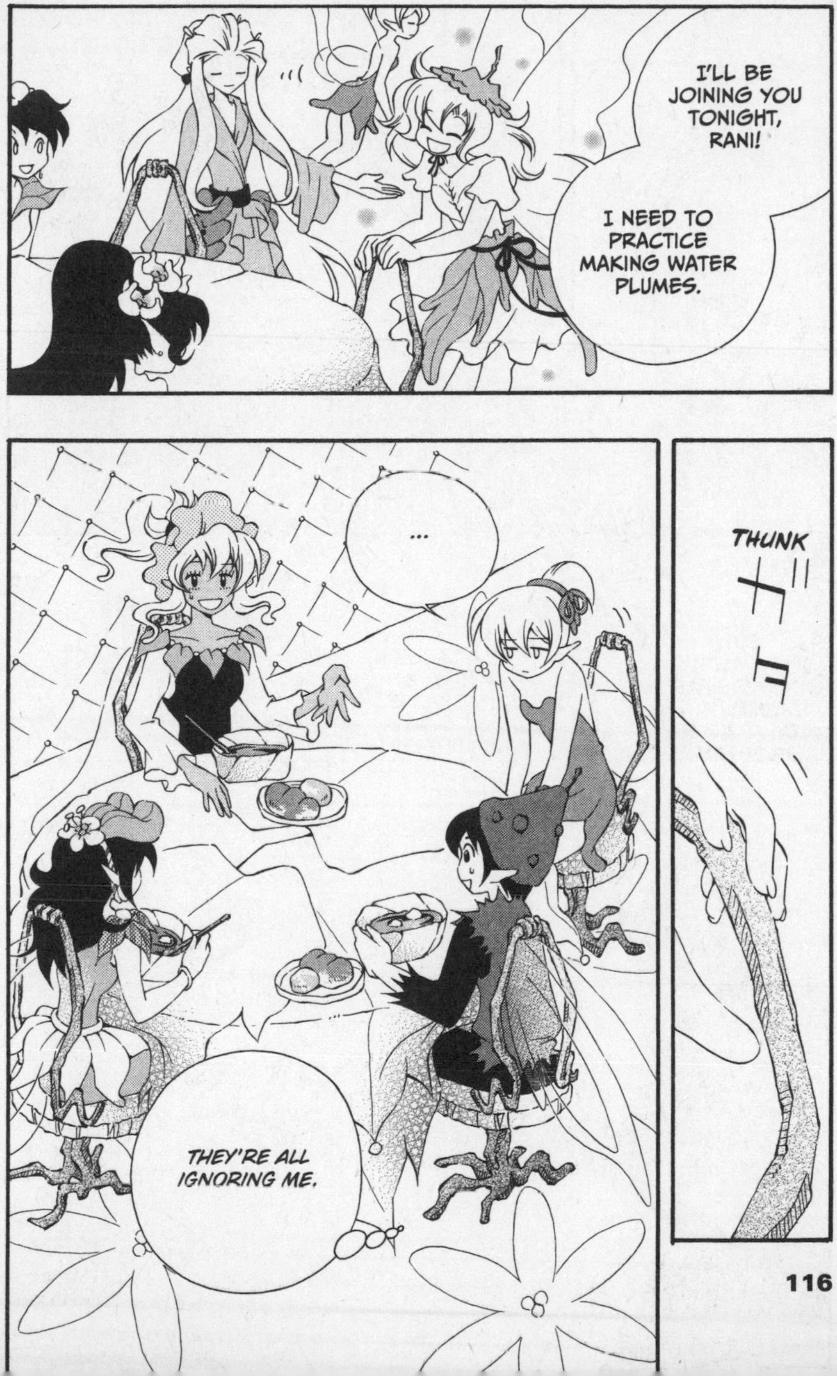
I'LL BE JOINING YOU TONIGHT, RANI!
I NEED TO PRACTICE MAKING WATER PLUMES.
THUNK
...
THEY'RE ALL IGNORING ME.

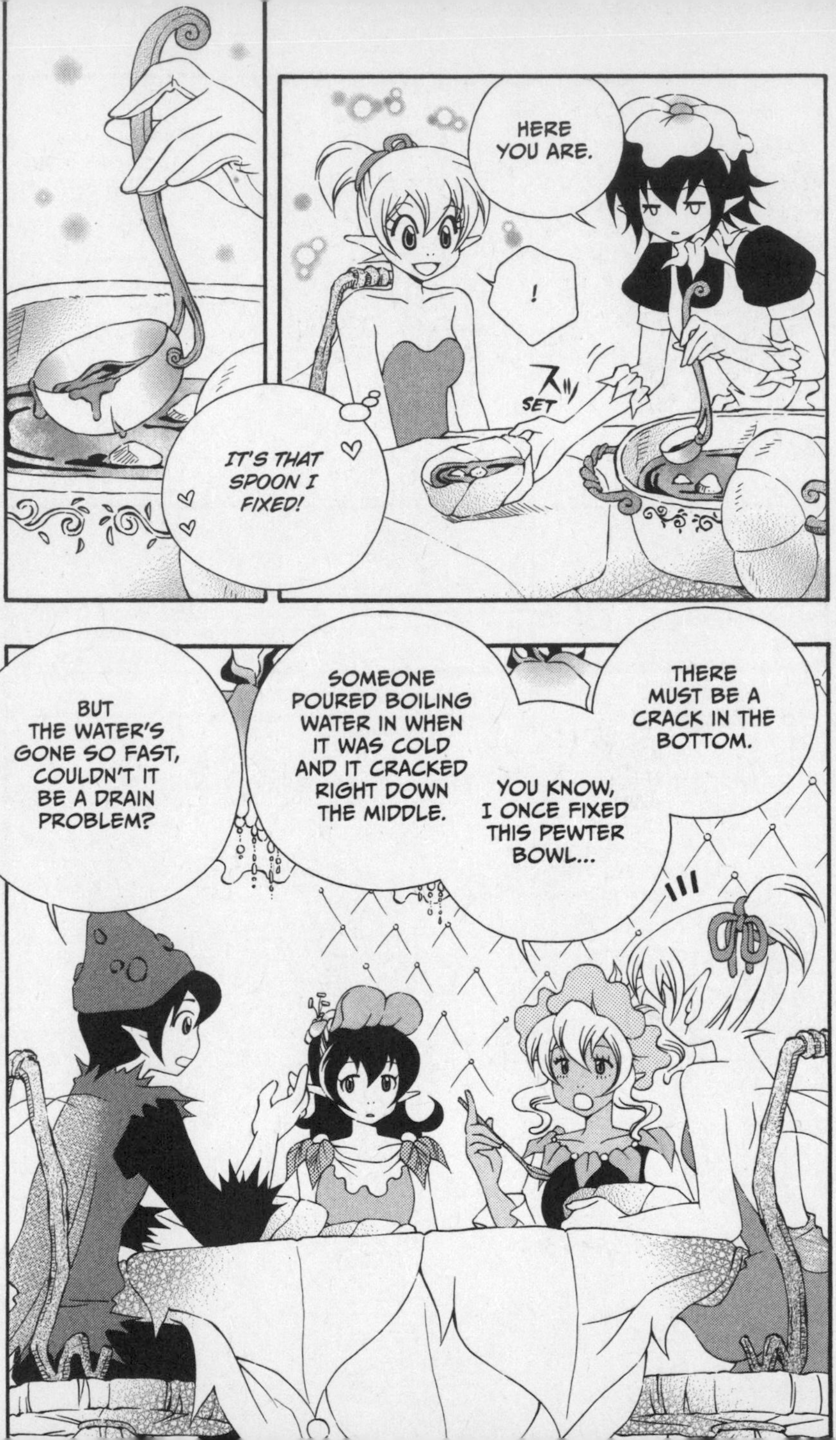
HERE YOU ARE.
!
スッ SET
IT'S THAT SPOON I FIXED!
THERE MUST BE A CRACK IN THE BOTTOM.
YOU KNOW, I ONCE FIXED THIS PEWTER BOWL...
SOMEONE POURED BOILING WATER IN WHEN IT WAS COLD AND IT CRACKED RIGHT DOWN THE MIDDLE.
BUT THE WATER'S GONE SO FAST, COULDN'T IT BE A DRAIN PROBLEM?

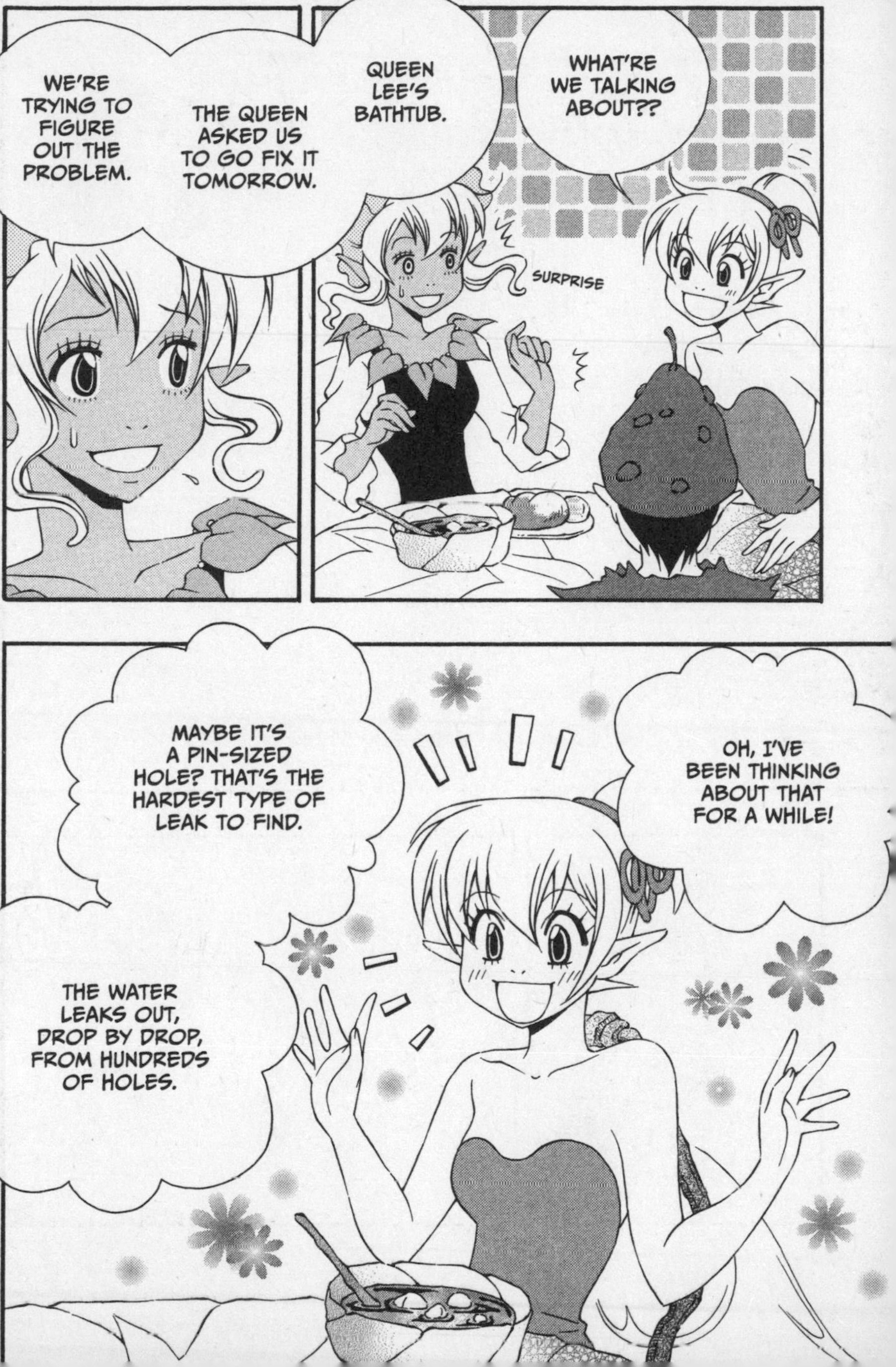
WHAT'RE WE TALKING ABOUT??
QUEEN LEE'S BATHTUB.
SURPRISE
THE QUEEN ASKED US TO GO FIX IT TOMORROW.
WE'RE TRYING TO FIGURE OUT THE PROBLEM.
OH, I'VE BEEN THINKING ABOUT THAT FOR A WHILE!
MAYBE IT'S A PIN-SIZED HOLE? THAT'S THE HARDEST TYPE OF LEAK TO FIND.
THE WATER LEAKS OUT, DROP BY DROP, FROM HUNDREDS OF HOLES.

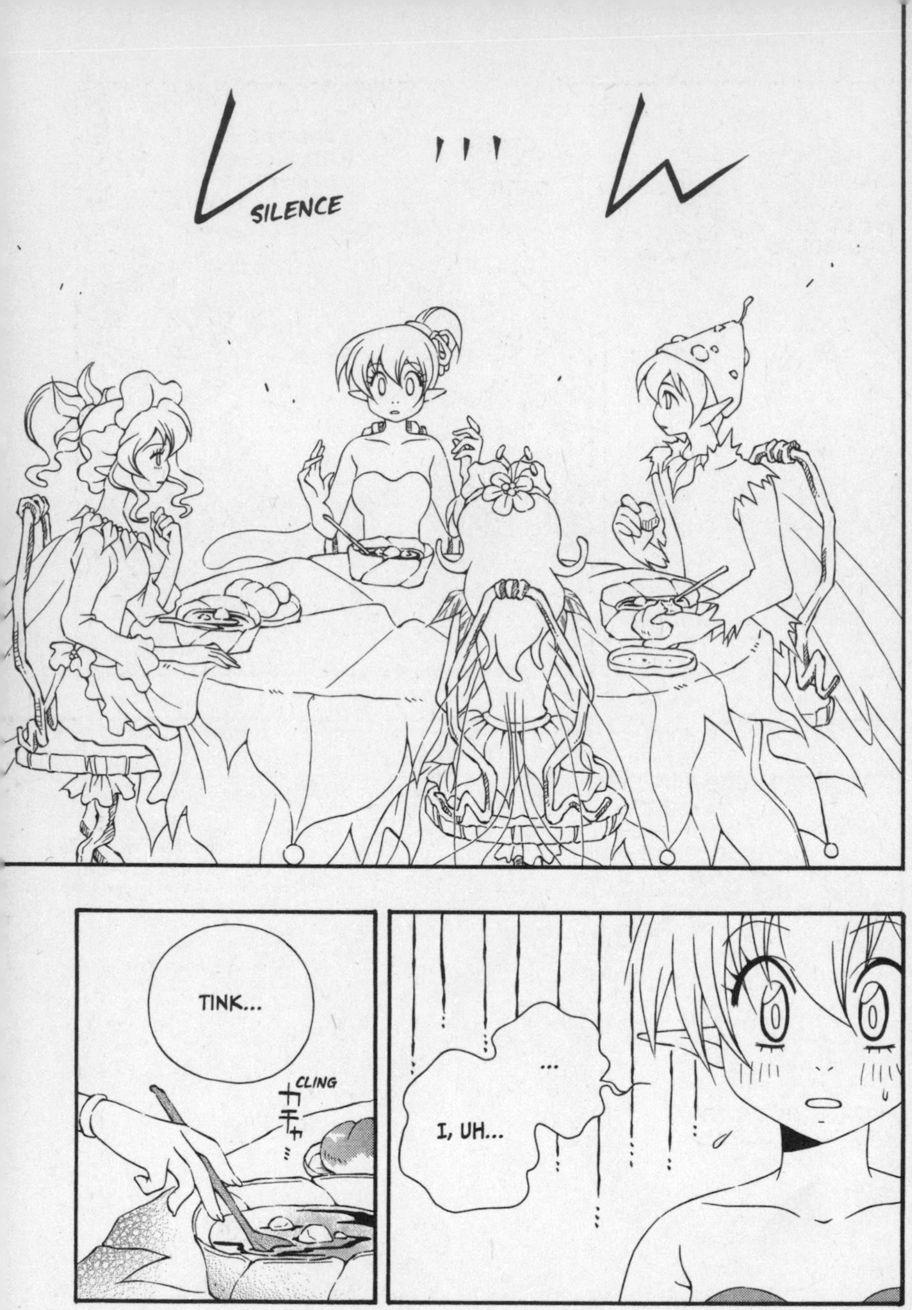
SILENCE
...
I, UH...
TINK...
CLING
カチャ

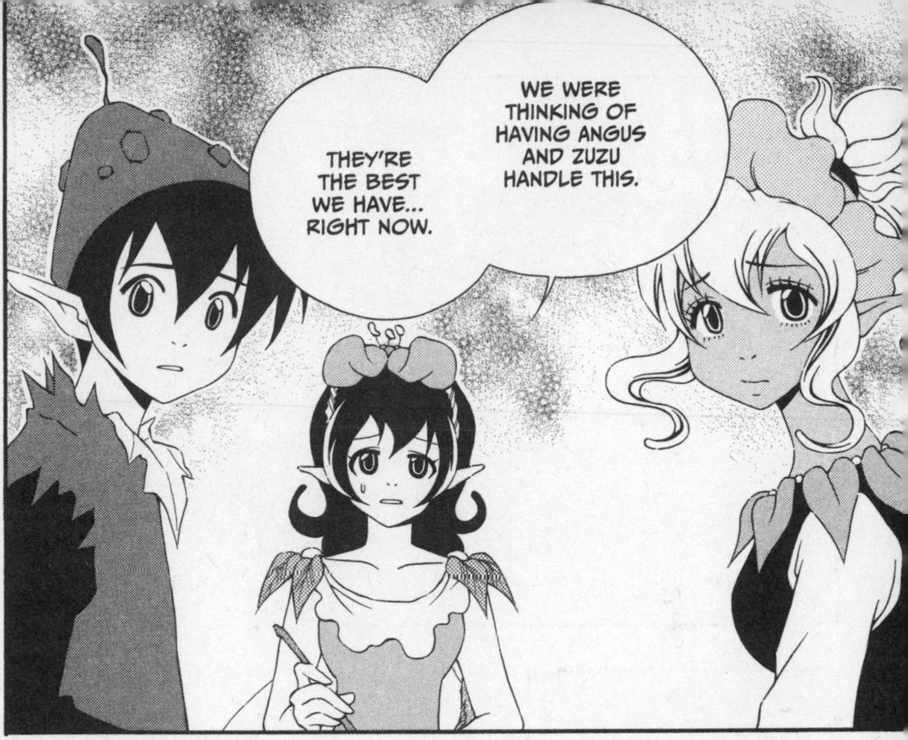
WE WERE THINKING OF HAVING ANGUS AND ZUZU HANDLE THIS.
THEY'RE THE BEST WE HAVE... RIGHT NOW.

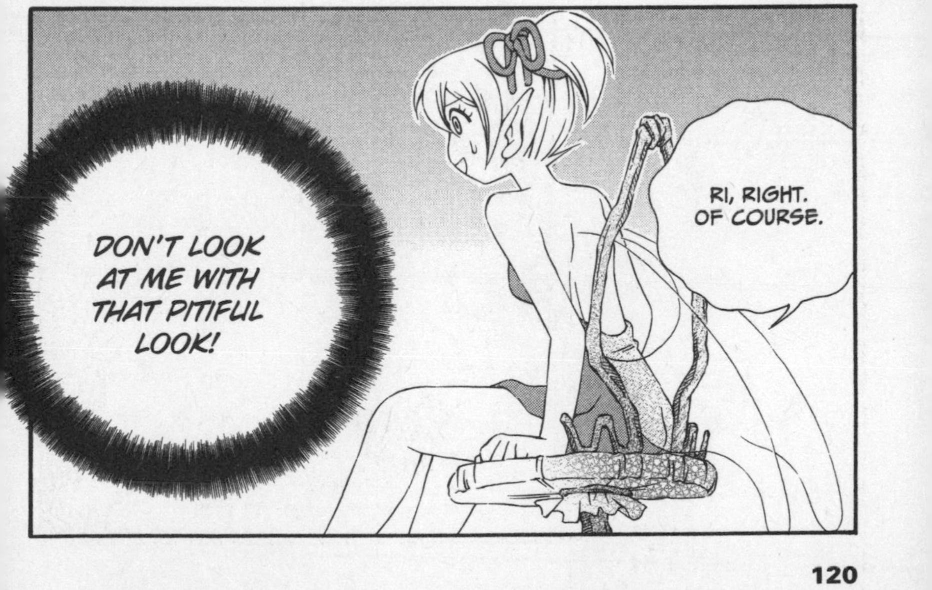
RI, RIGHT. OF COURSE.
DON'T LOOK AT ME WITH THAT PITIFUL LOOK!

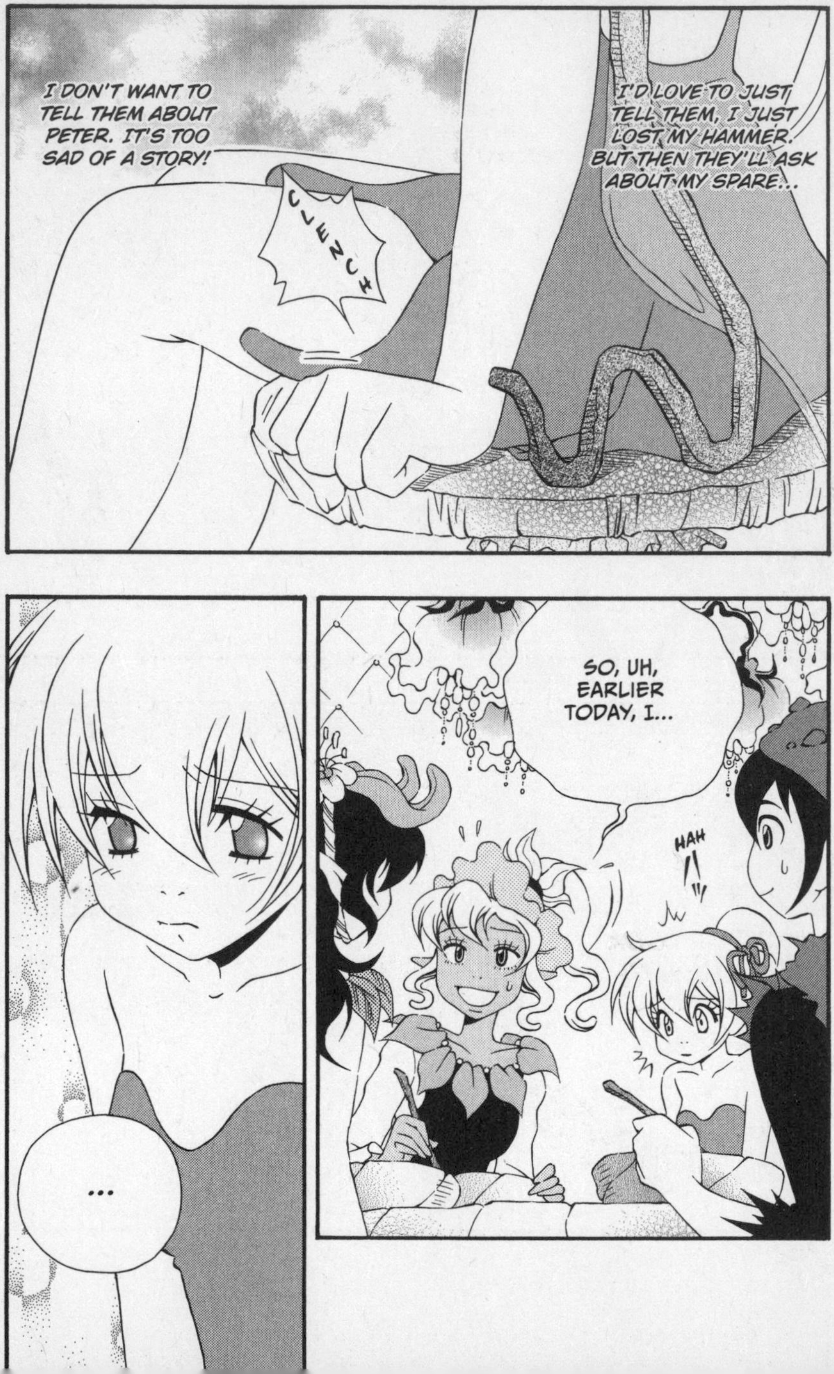
I'D LOVE TO JUST TELL THEM, I JUST LOST MY HAMMER. BUT THEN THEY'LL ASK ABOUT MY SPARE...
I DON'T WANT TO TELL THEM ABOUT PETER. IT'S TOO SAD OF A STORY!
CLENCH
SO, UH, EARLIER TODAY, I...
HAH
...

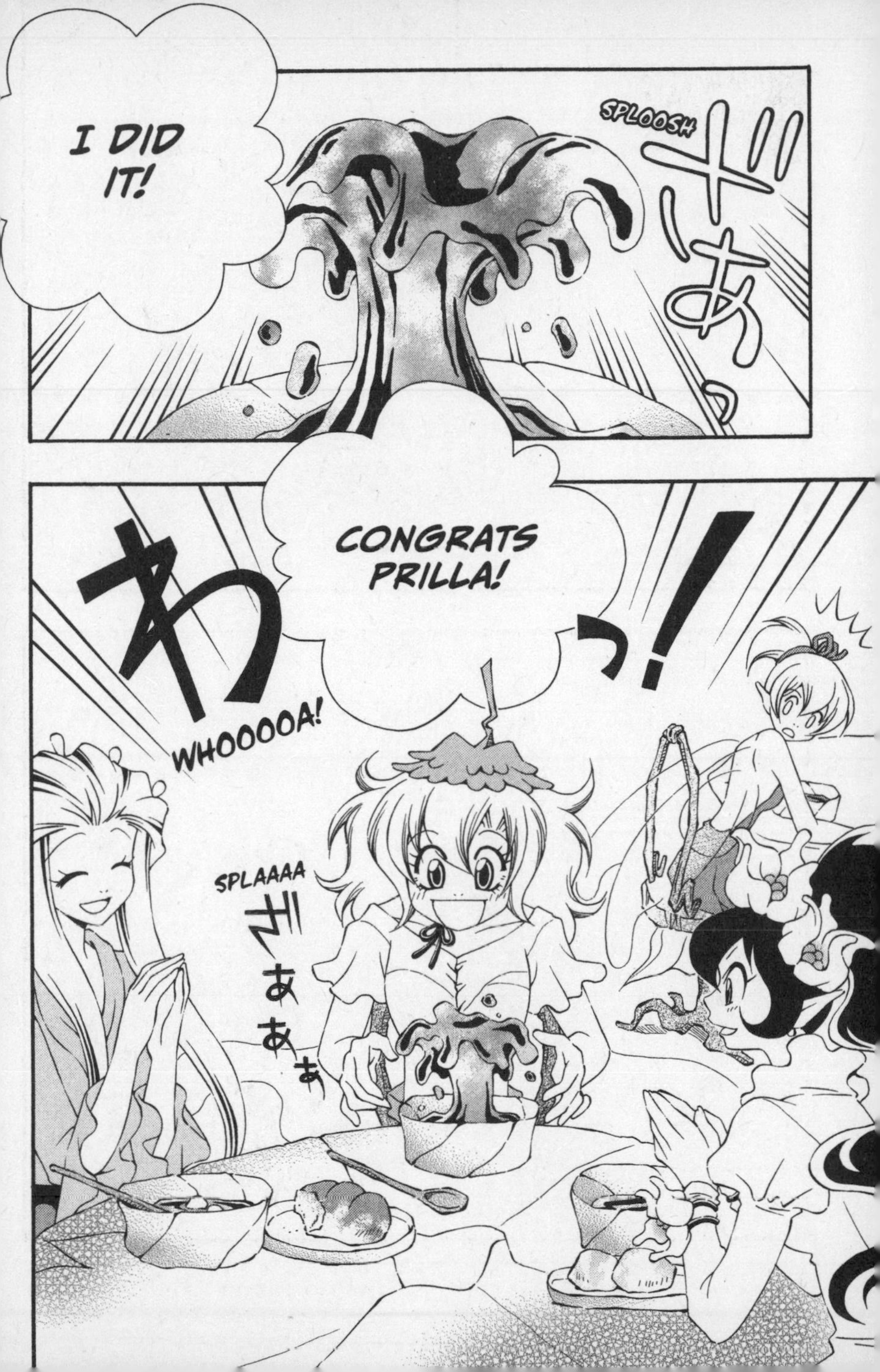
SPLOOSH
ざぁっ
I DID IT!
CONGRATS PRILLA!
やっ!
WHOOOOA!
SPLAAAA
ざあああ

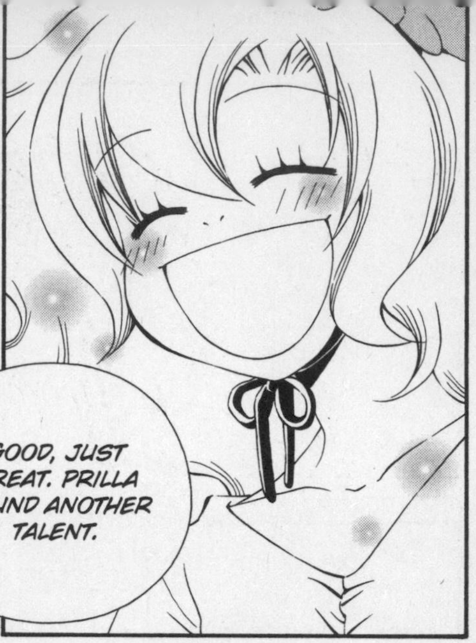
GOOD, JUST GREAT. PRILLA FOUND ANOTHER TALENT.

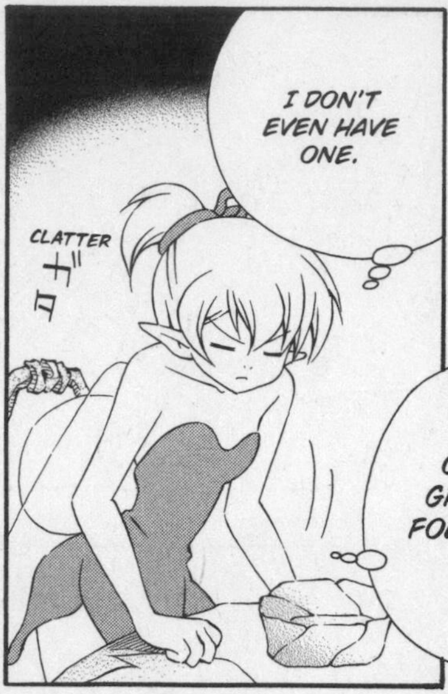
I DON'T EVEN HAVE ONE.
CLATTER
ガタ

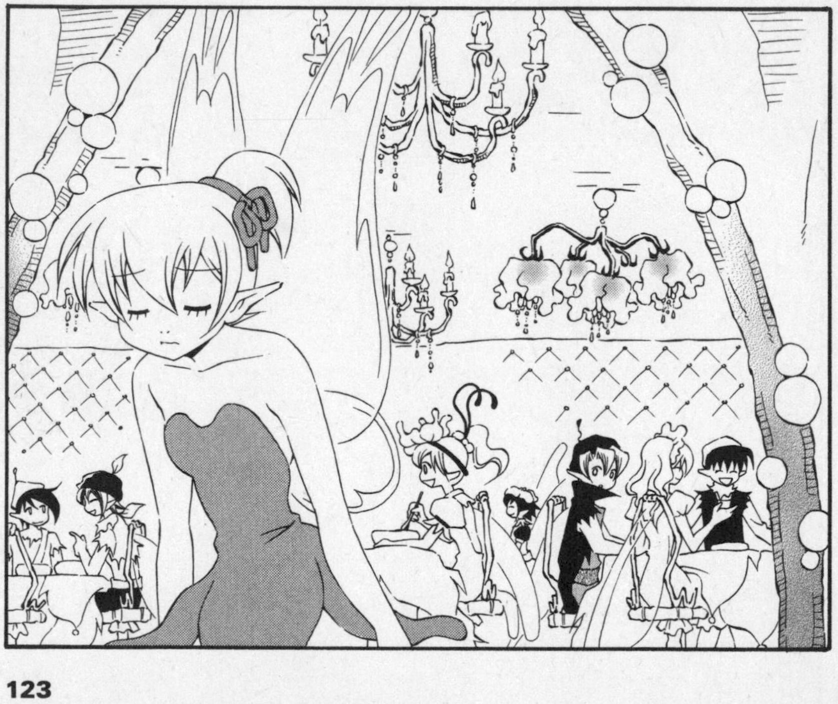

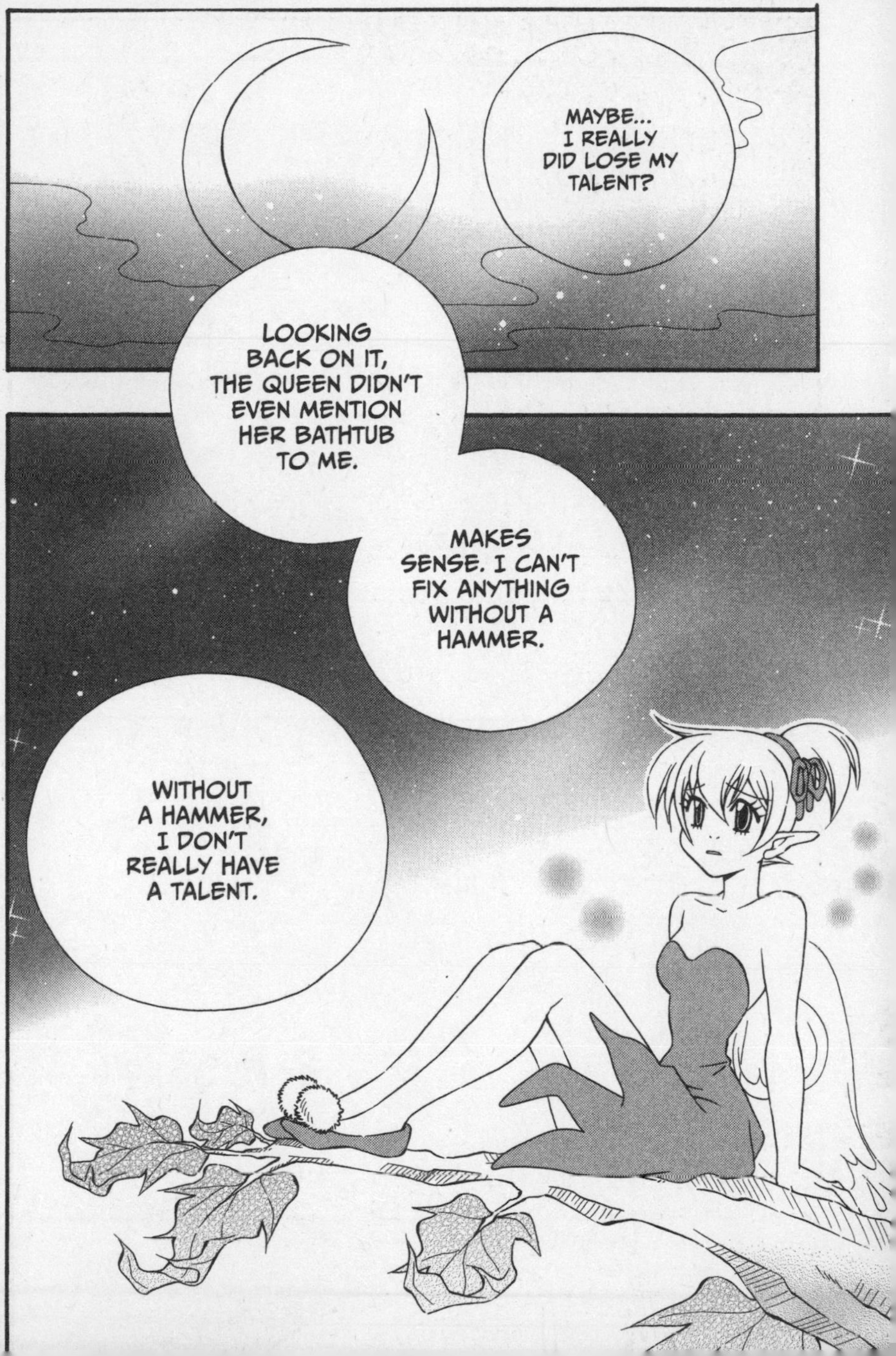
MAYBE... I REALLY DID LOSE MY TALENT?
LOOKING BACK ON IT, THE QUEEN DIDN'T EVEN MENTION HER BATHTUB TO ME.
MAKES SENSE. I CAN'T FIX ANYTHING WITHOUT A HAMMER.
WITHOUT A HAMMER, I DON'T REALLY HAVE A TALENT.

READ THIS WAY

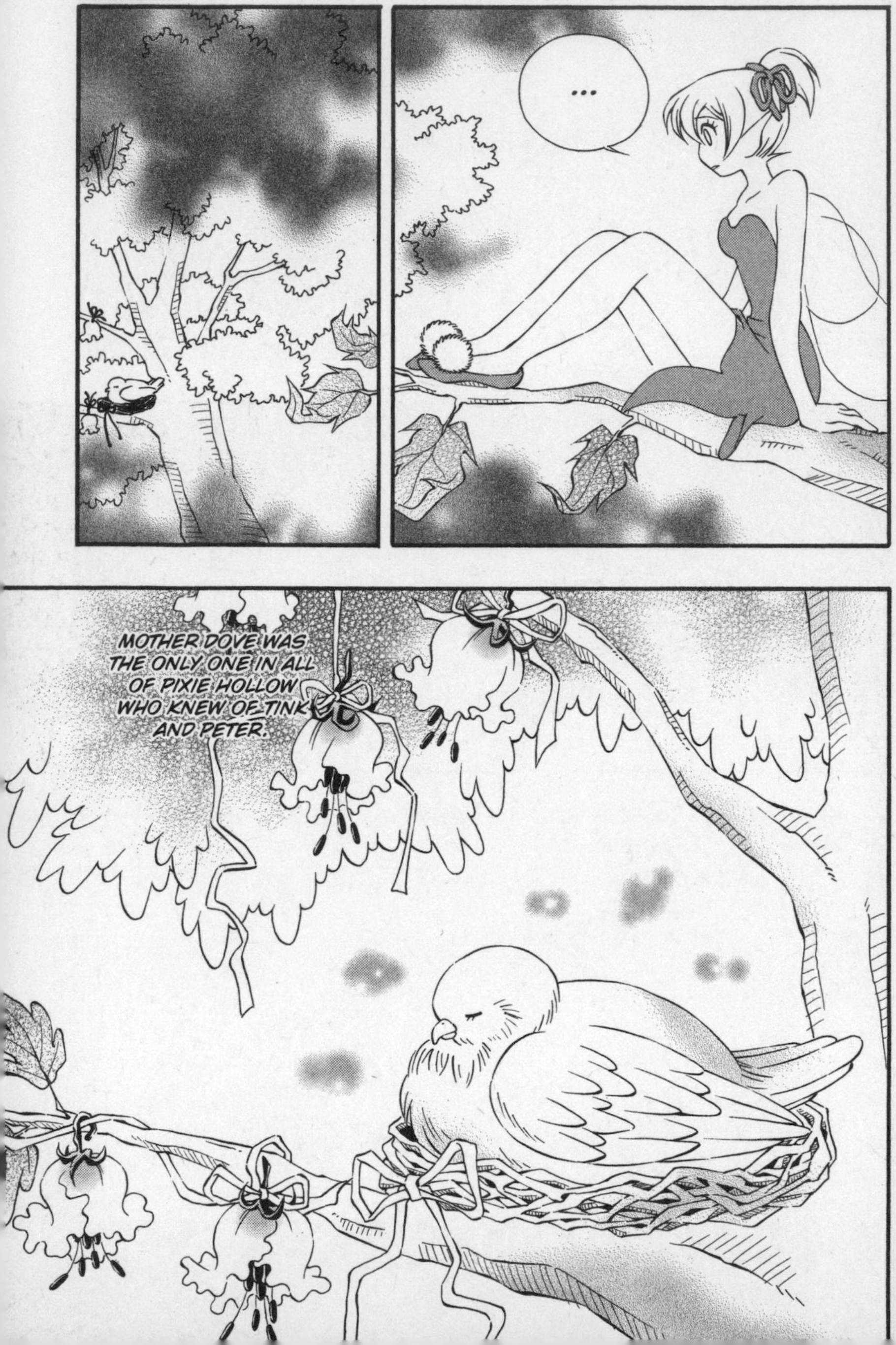
...
MOTHER DOVE WAS THE ONLY ONE IN ALL OF PIXIE HOLLOW WHO KNEW OF TINK AND PETER.

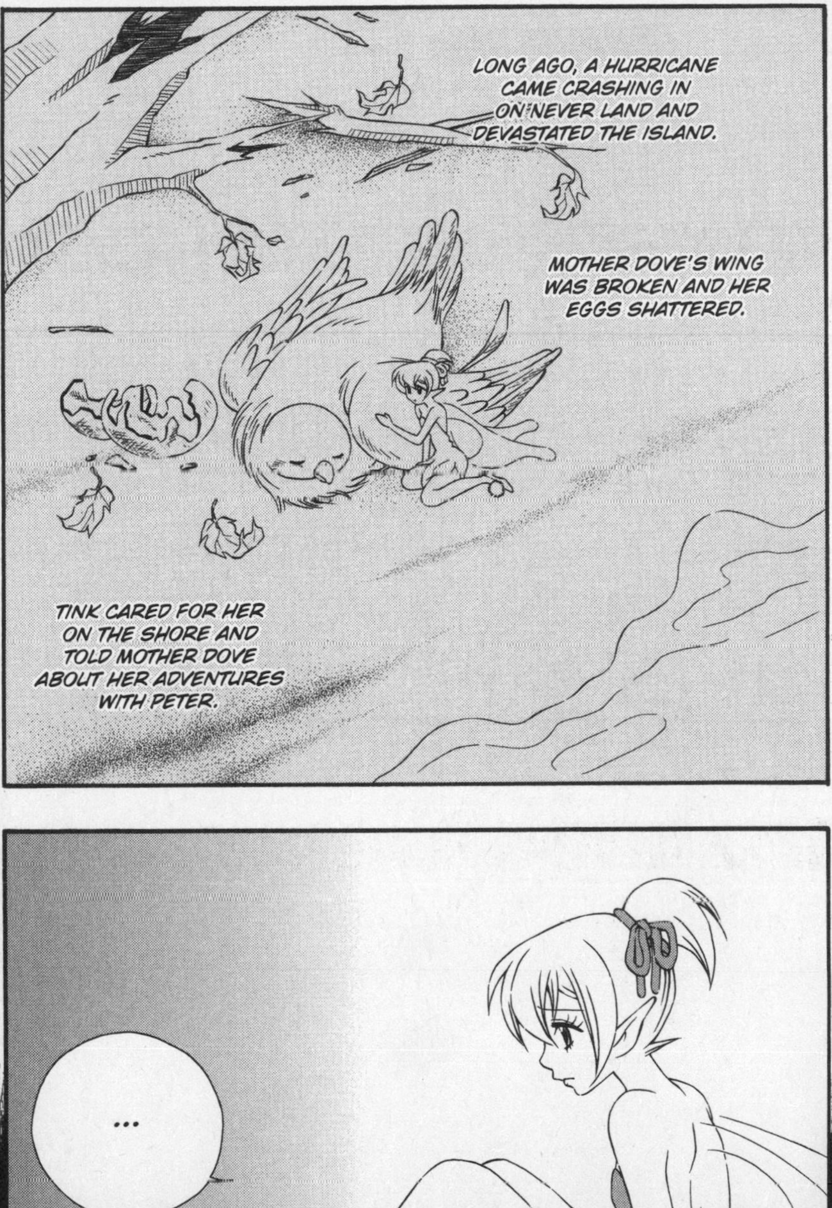
LONG AGO, A HURRICANE CAME CRASHING IN ON NEVER LAND AND DEVASTATED THE ISLAND.
MOTHER DOVE'S WING WAS BROKEN AND HER EGGS SHATTERED.
TINK CARED FOR HER ON THE SHORE AND TOLD MOTHER DOVE ABOUT HER ADVENTURES WITH PETER.
...

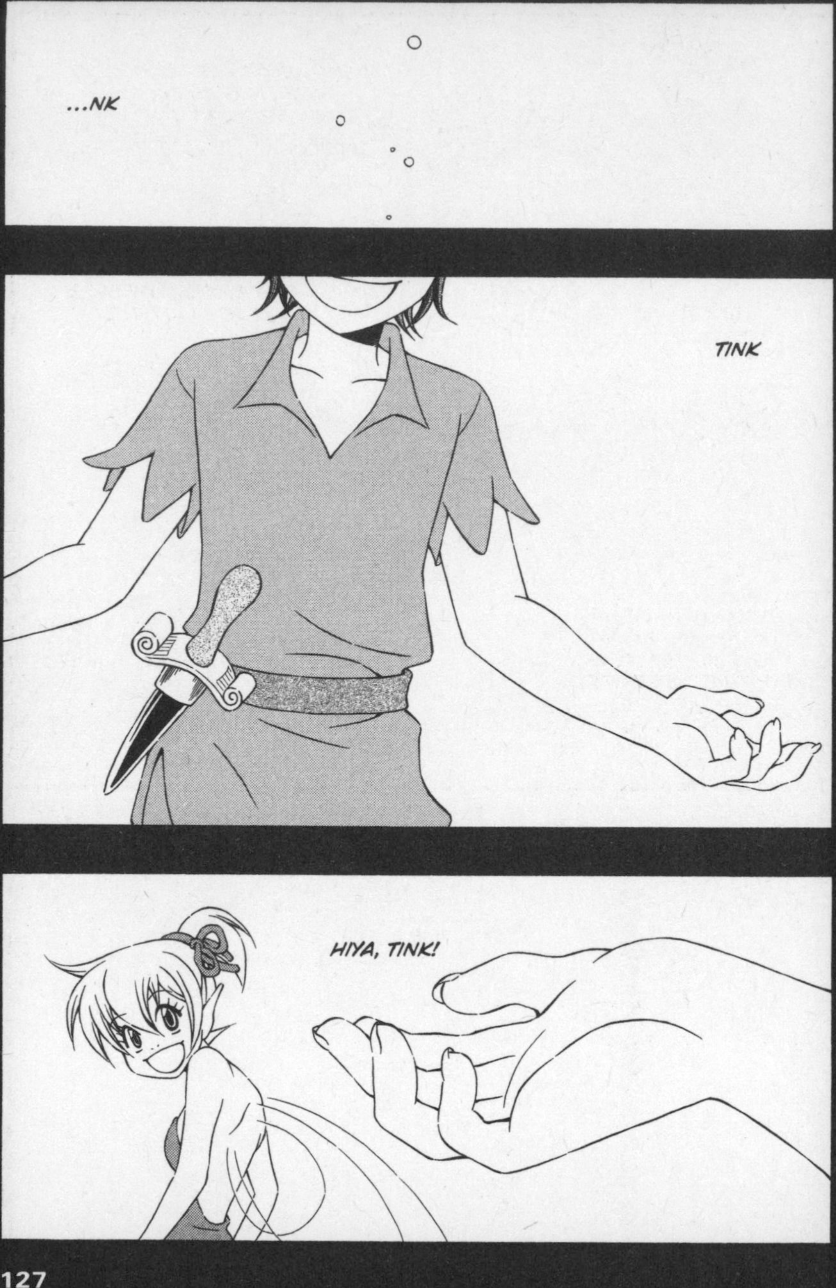
...NK
TINK
HIYA, TINK!

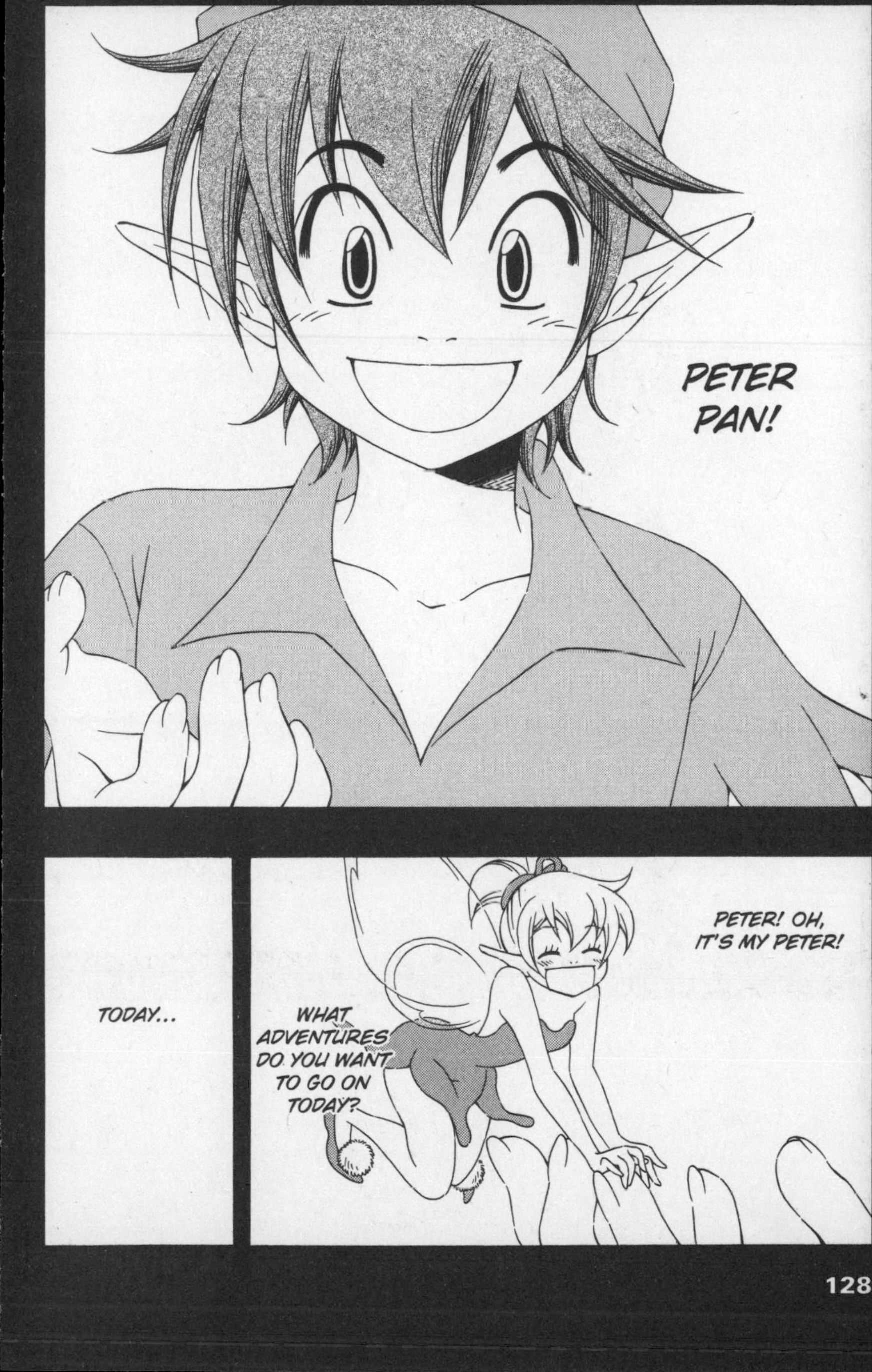
PETER PAN!
PETER! OH, IT'S MY PETER!
WHAT ADVENTURES DO YOU WANT TO GO ON TODAY?
TODAY...

READ THIS WAY

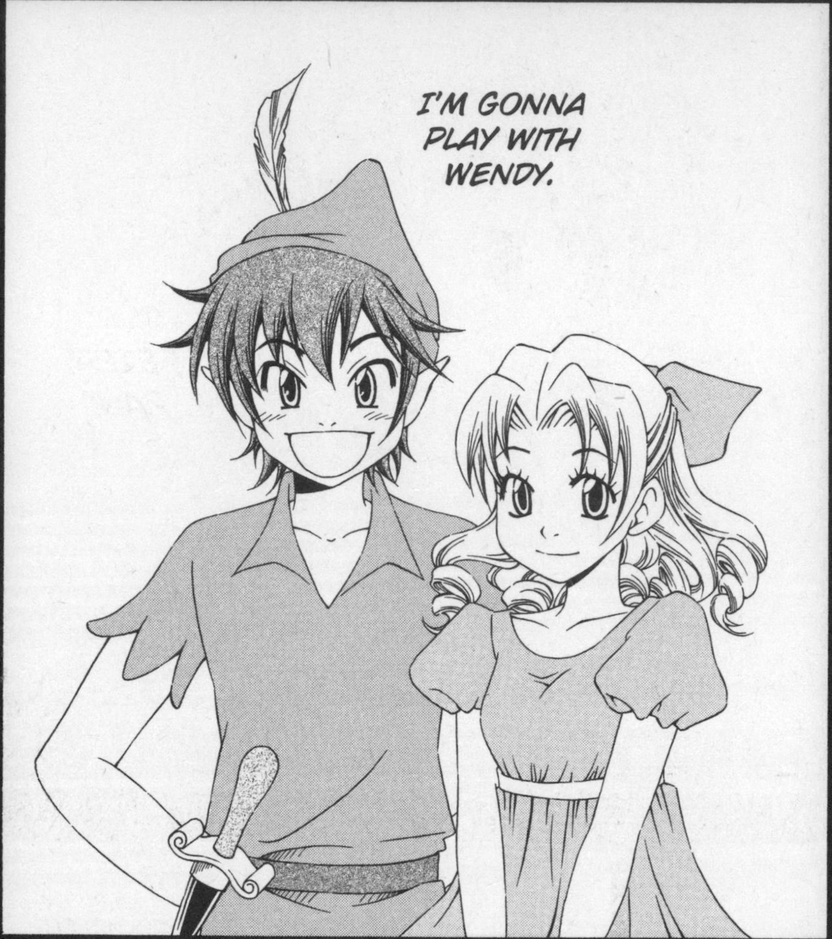
I'M GONNA PLAY WITH WENDY.

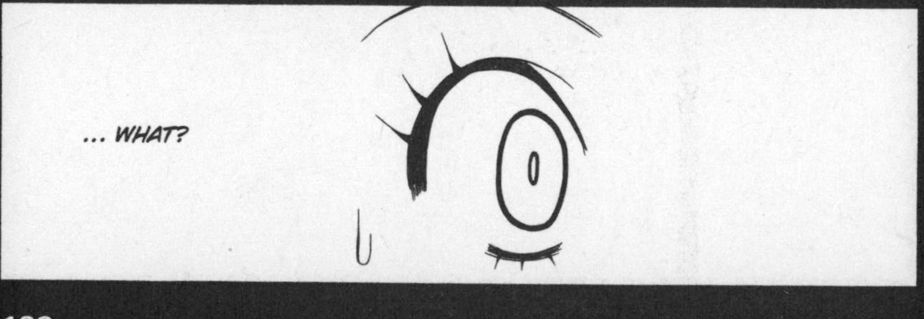
... WHAT?

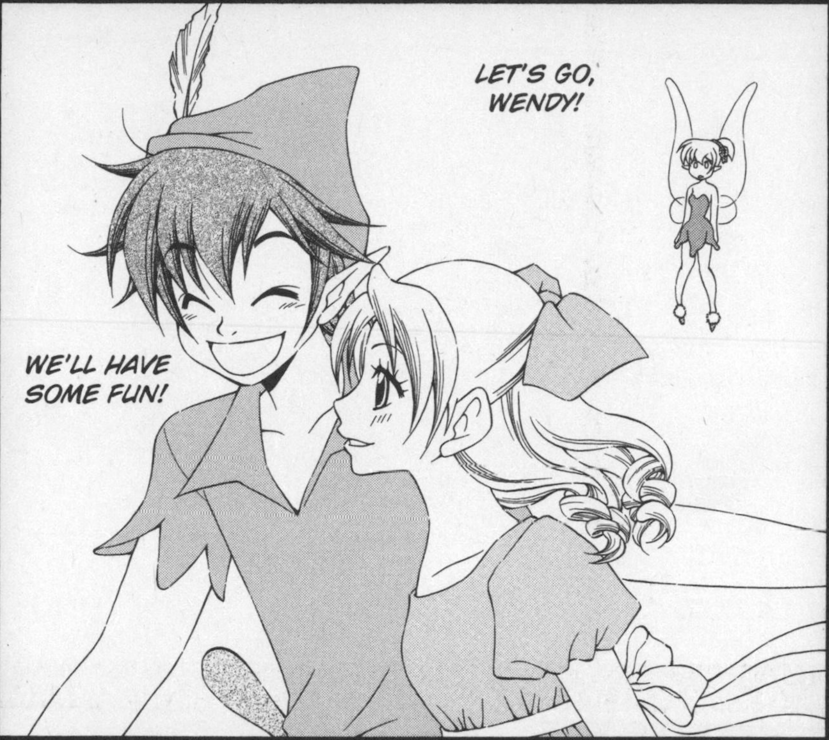
LET'S GO, WENDY!
WE'LL HAVE SOME FUN!
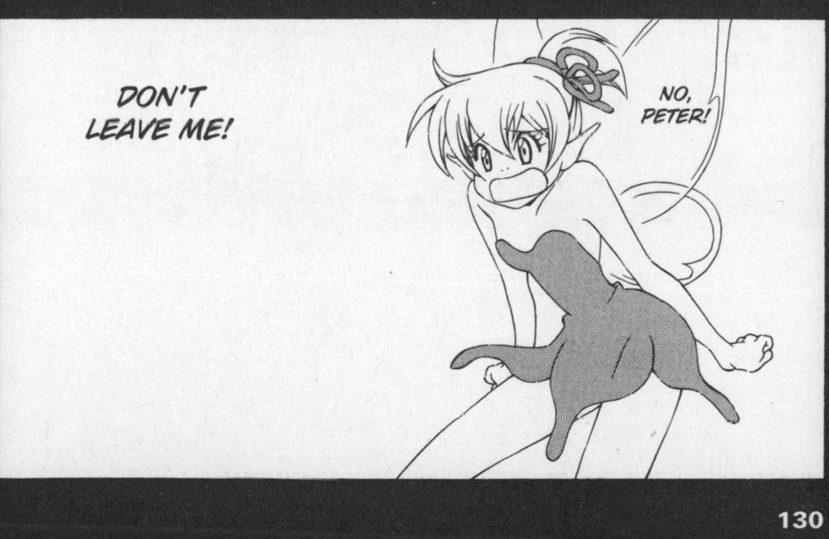
NO, PETER!
DON'T LEAVE ME!

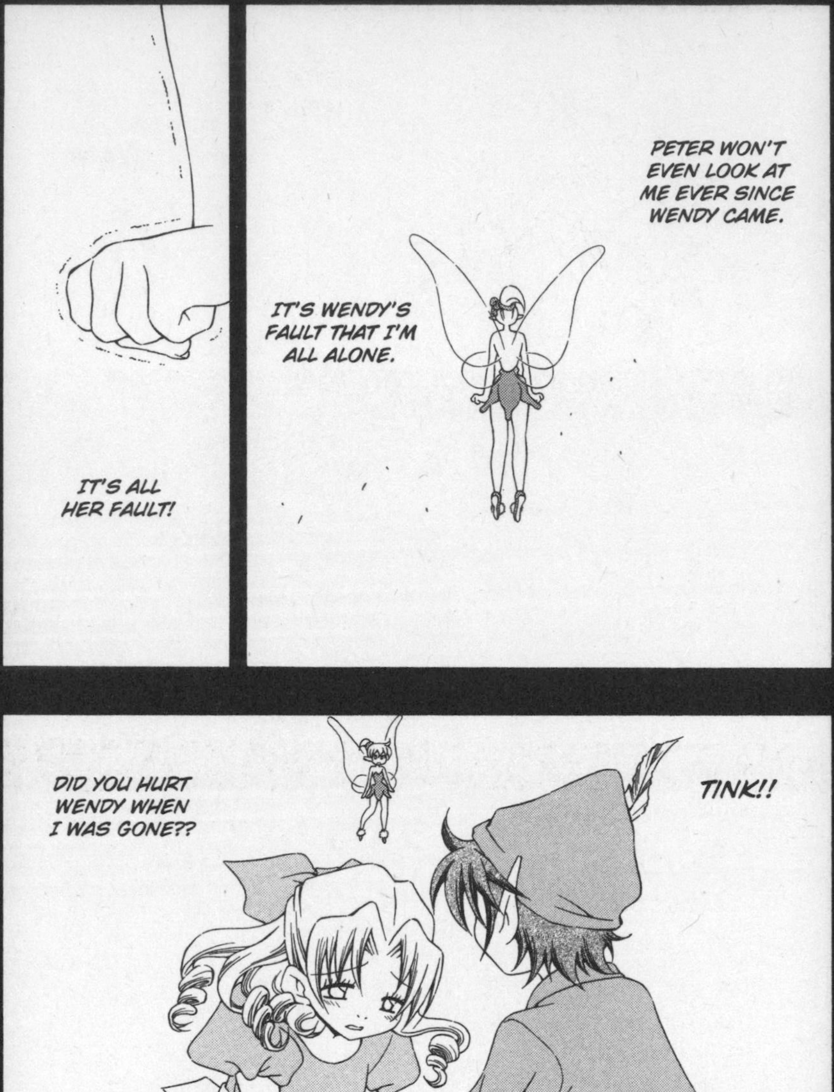
PETER WON'T EVEN LOOK AT ME EVER SINCE WENDY CAME.
IT'S WENDY'S FAULT THAT I'M ALL ALONE.
IT'S ALL HER FAULT!
TINK!!
DID YOU HURT WENDY WHEN I WAS GONE??

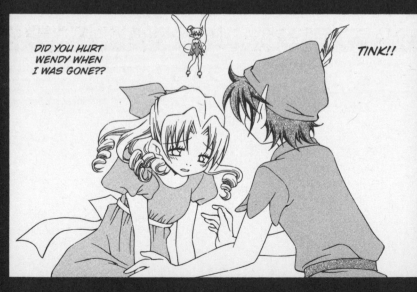

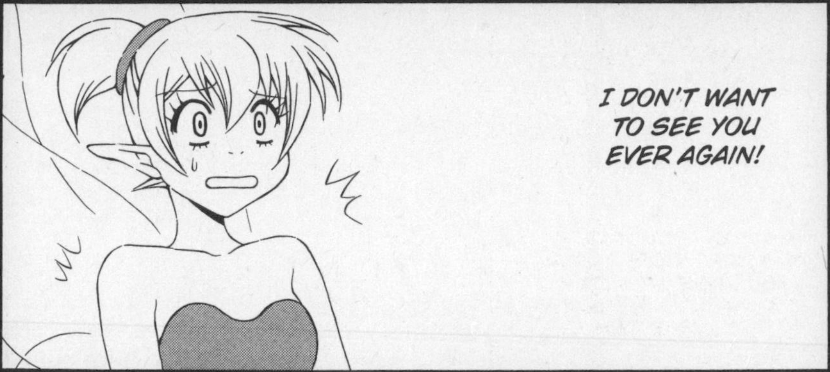
I DON'T WANT TO SEE YOU EVER AGAIN!

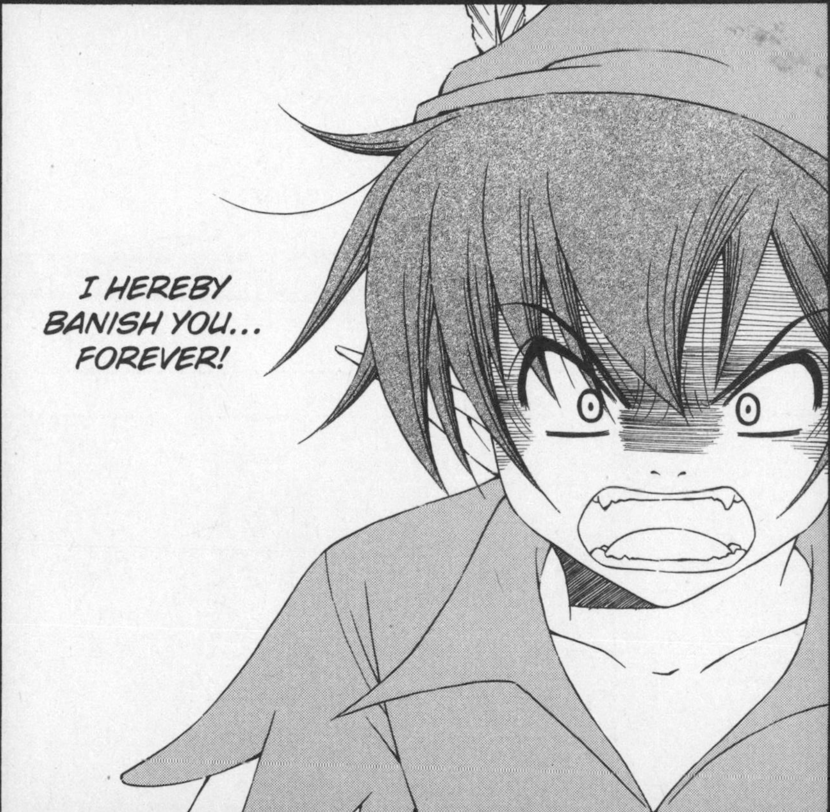
I HEREBY BANISH YOU... FOREVER!

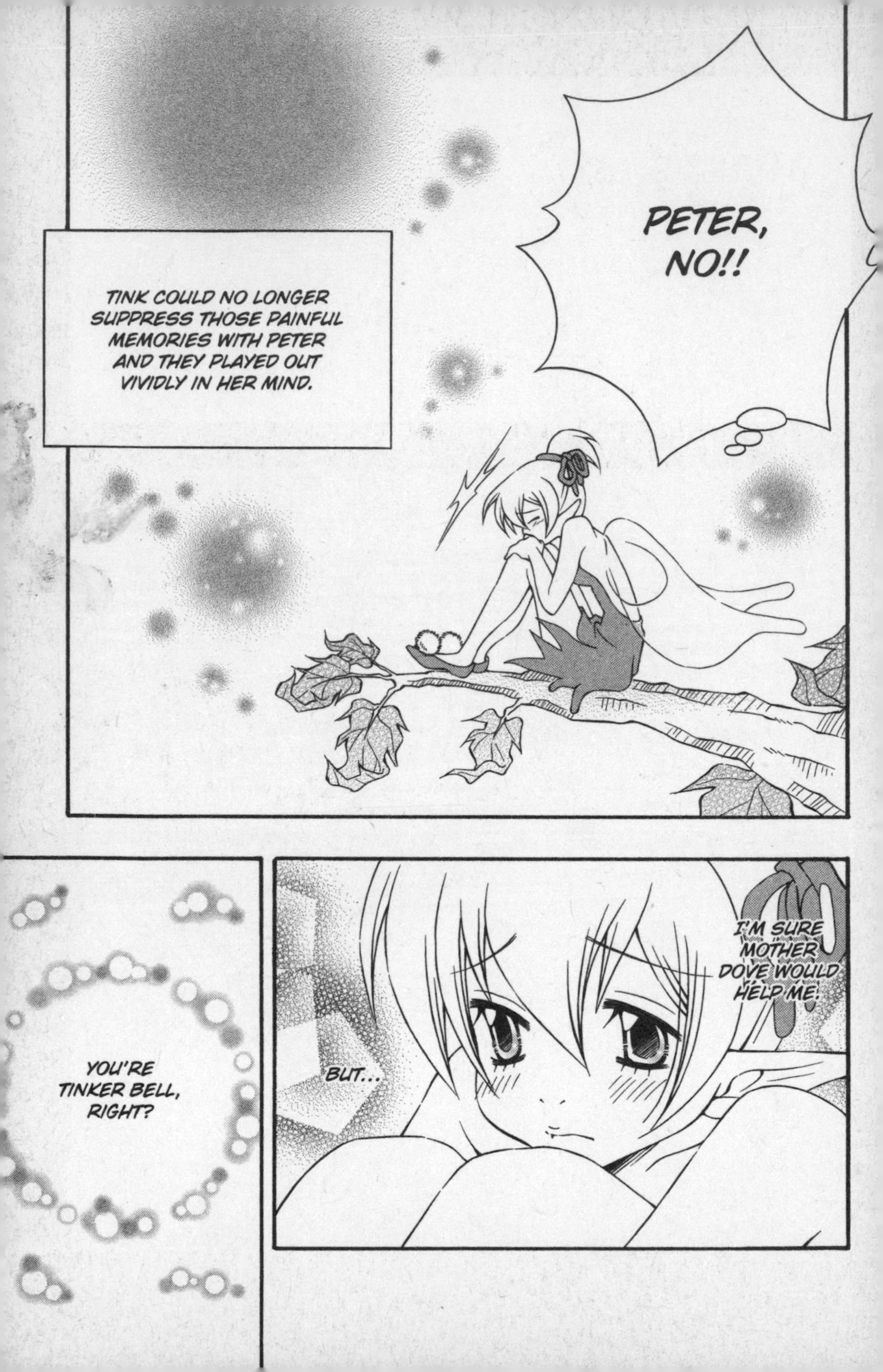
PETER, NO!!
TINK COULD NO LONGER SUPPRESS THOSE PAINFUL MEMORIES WITH PETER AND THEY PLAYED OUT VIVIDLY IN HER MIND.
I'M SURE MOTHER DOVE WOULD HELP ME.
BUT...
YOU'RE TINKER BELL, RIGHT?

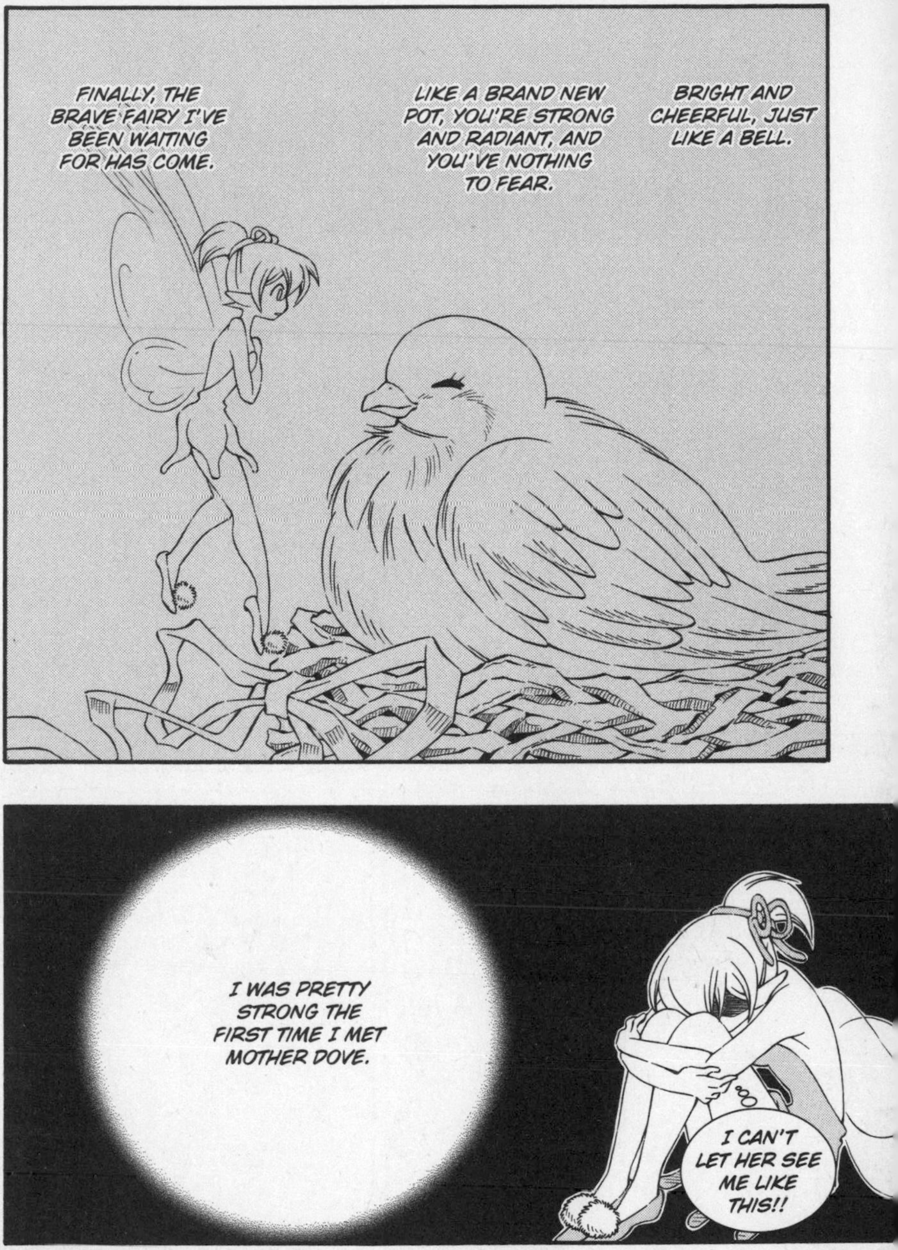
BRIGHT AND CHEERFUL, JUST LIKE A BELL.
LIKE A BRAND NEW POT, YOU'RE STRONG AND RADIANT, AND YOU'VE NOTHING TO FEAR.
FINALLY, THE BRAVE FAIRY I'VE BEEN WAITING FOR HAS COME.
I WAS PRETTY STRONG THE FIRST TIME I MET MOTHER DOVE.
I CAN'T LET HER SEE ME LIKE THIS!!

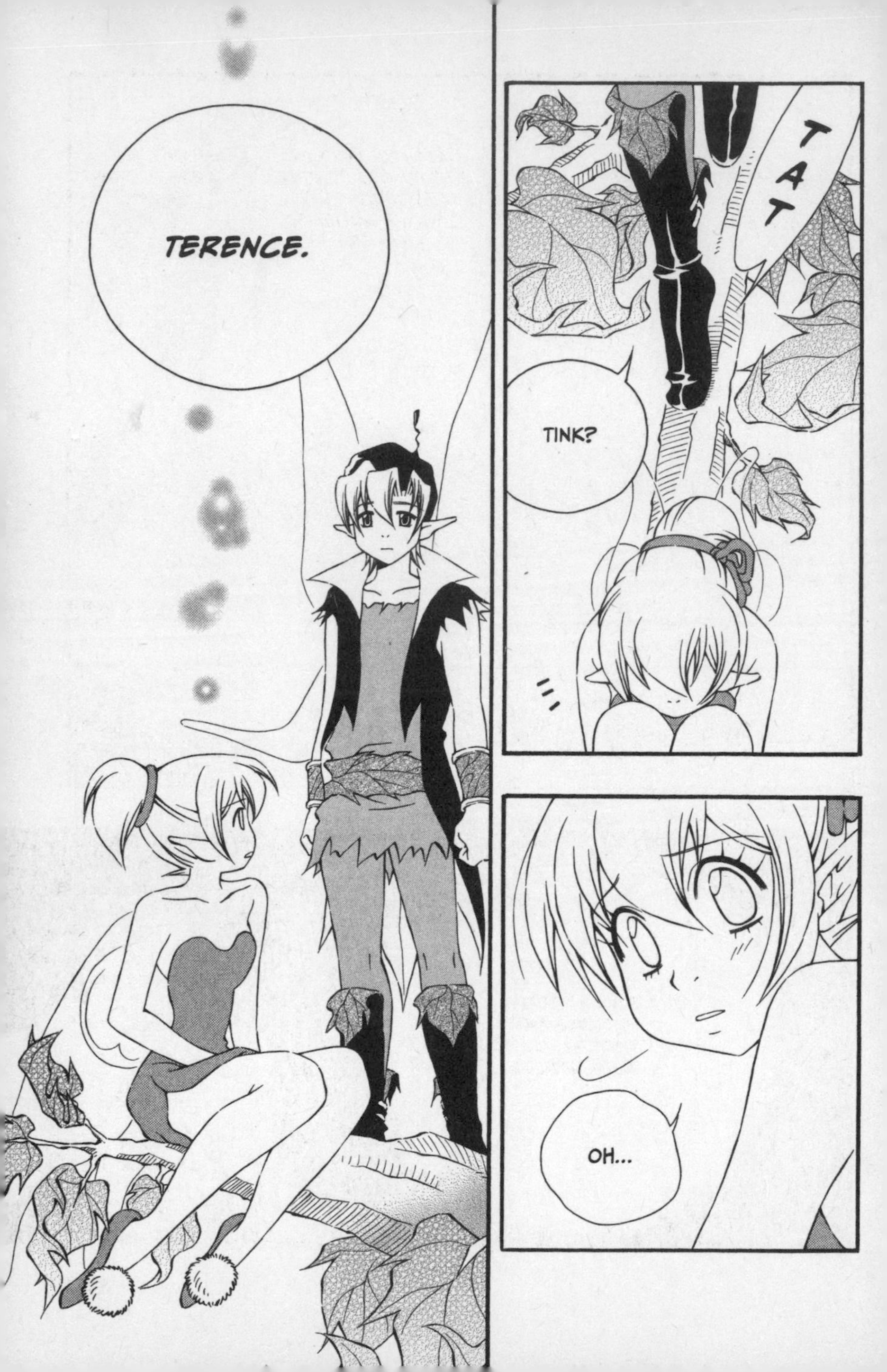
TAT
TINK?
OH...
TERENCE.

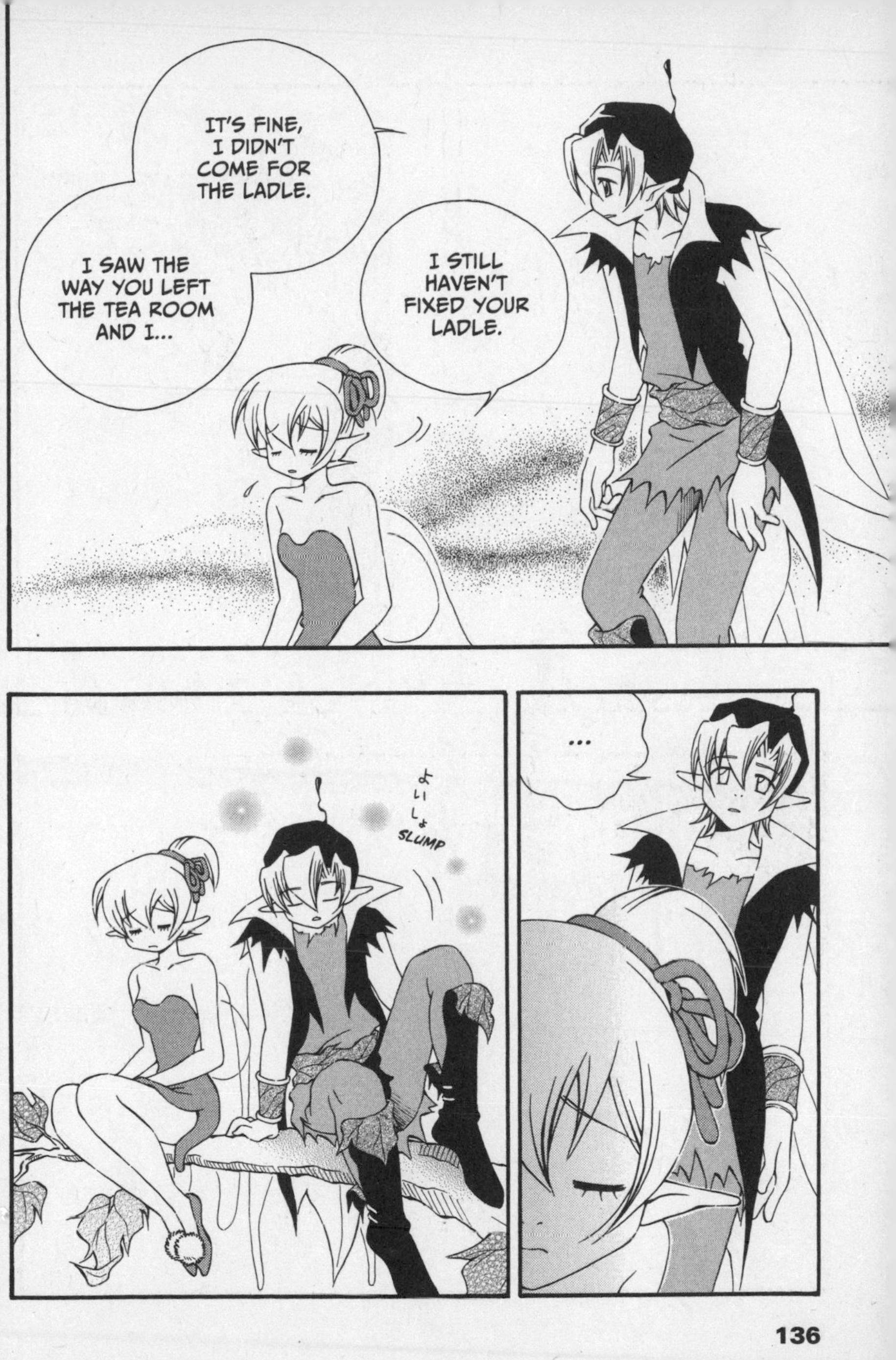
I STILL HAVEN'T FIXED YOUR LADLE.
IT'S FINE, I DIDN'T COME FOR THE LADLE.
I SAW THE WAY YOU LEFT THE TEA ROOM AND I...
...
よいしょ
SLUMP

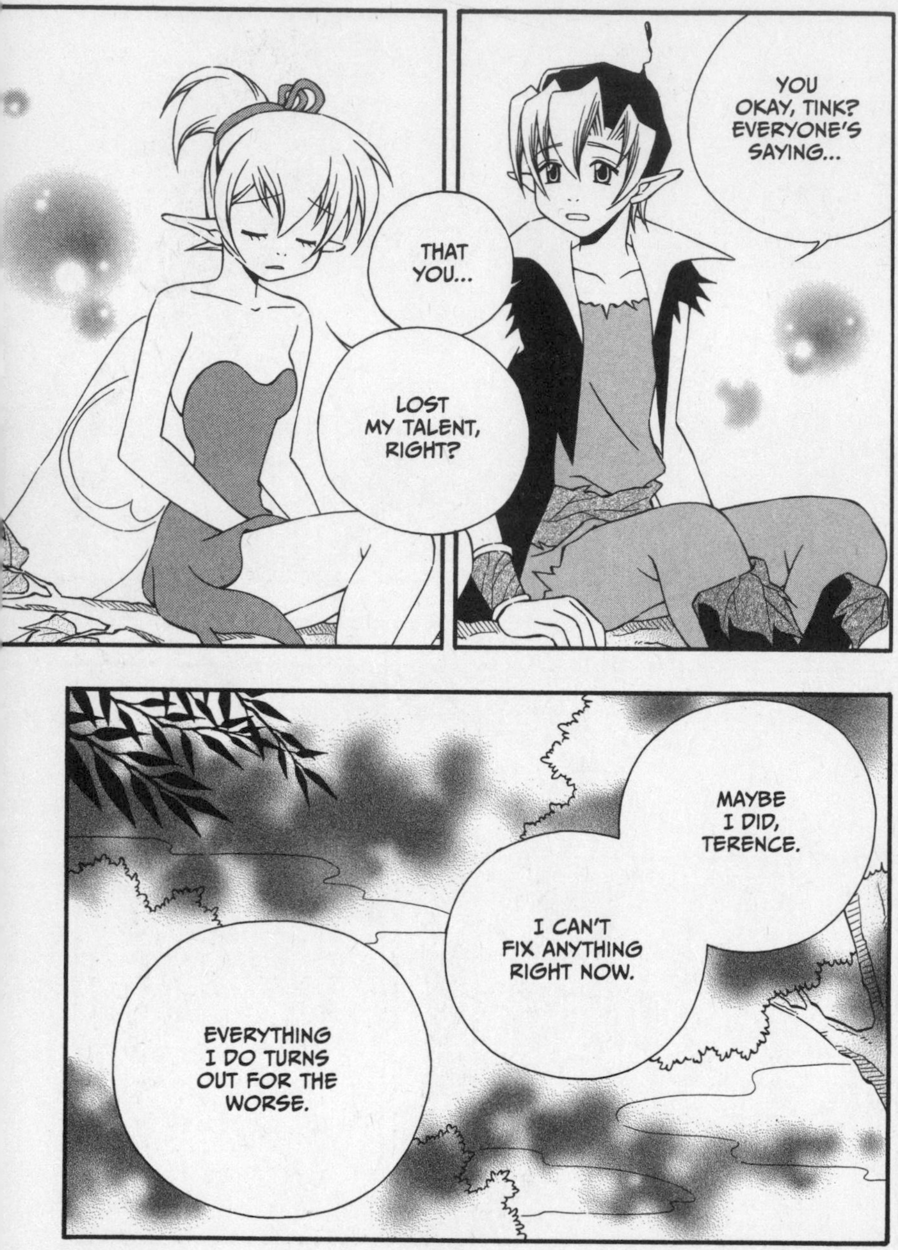
YOU OKAY, TINK? EVERYONE'S SAYING...
THAT YOU...
LOST MY TALENT, RIGHT?
MAYBE I DID, TERENCE.
I CAN'T FIX ANYTHING RIGHT NOW.
EVERYTHING I DO TURNS OUT FOR THE WORSE.

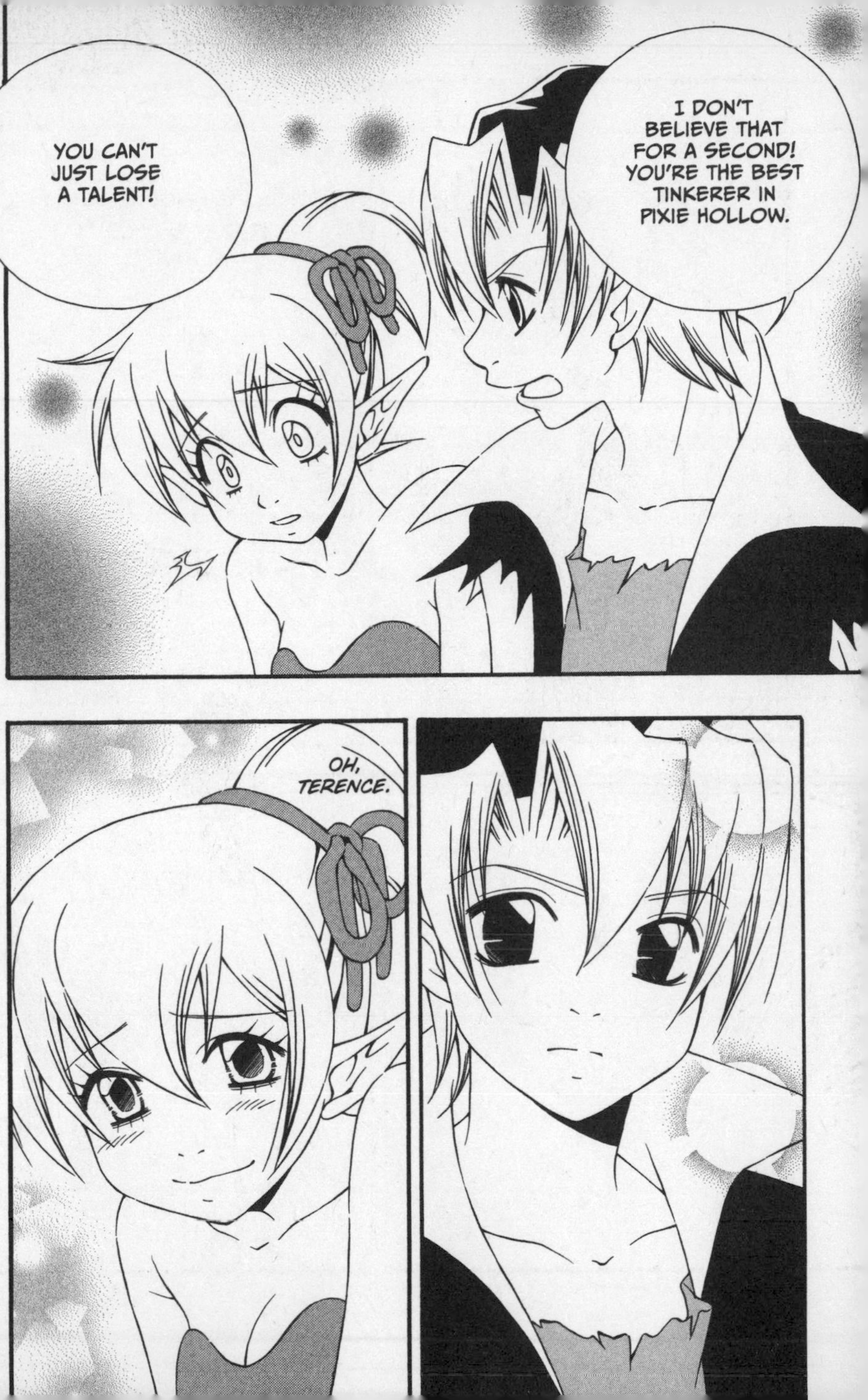
I DON'T BELIEVE THAT FOR A SECOND! YOU'RE THE BEST TINKERER IN PIXIE HOLLOW.
YOU CAN'T JUST LOSE A TALENT!
OH, TERENCE.

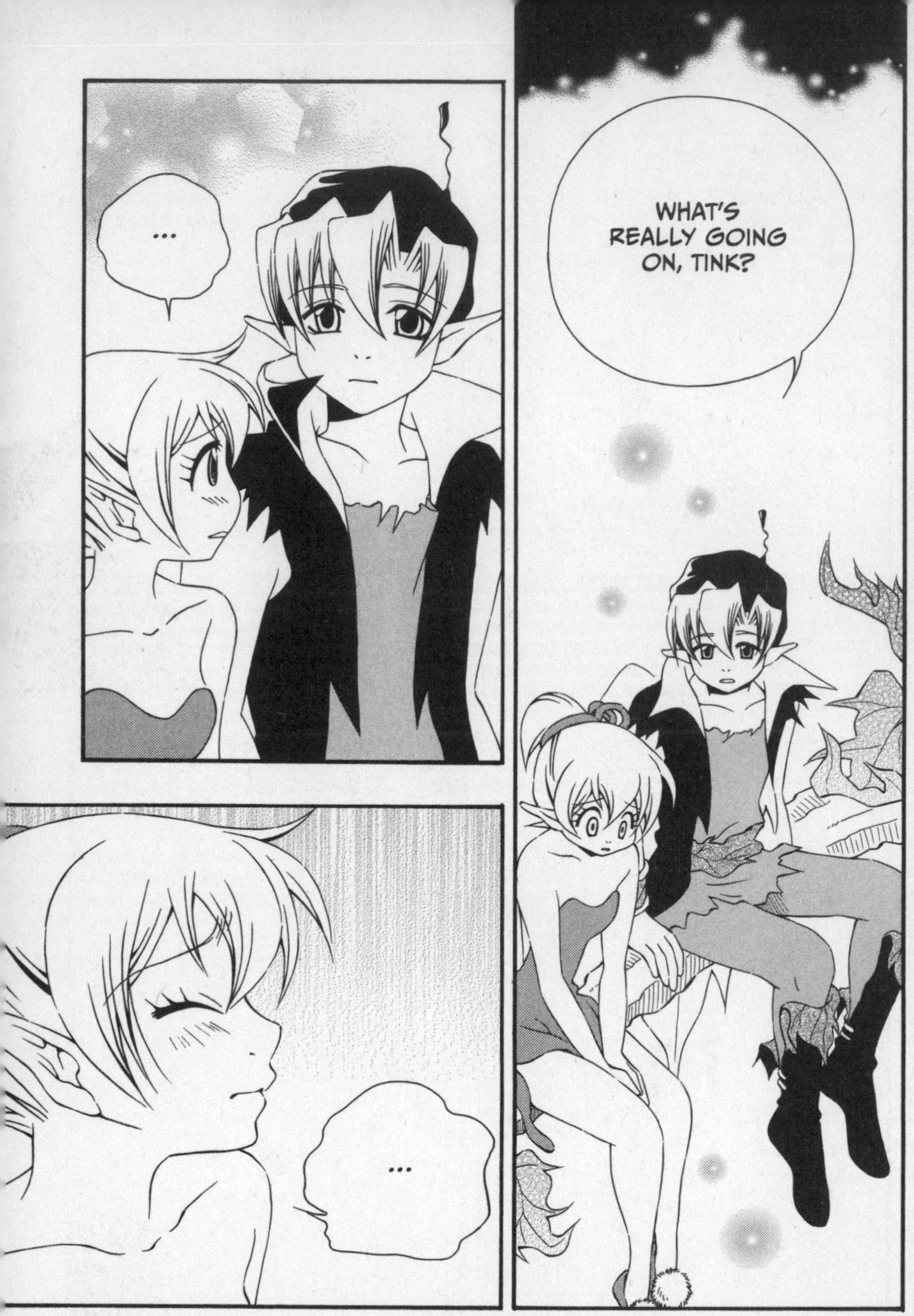
WHAT'S REALLY GOING ON, TINK?
...
...

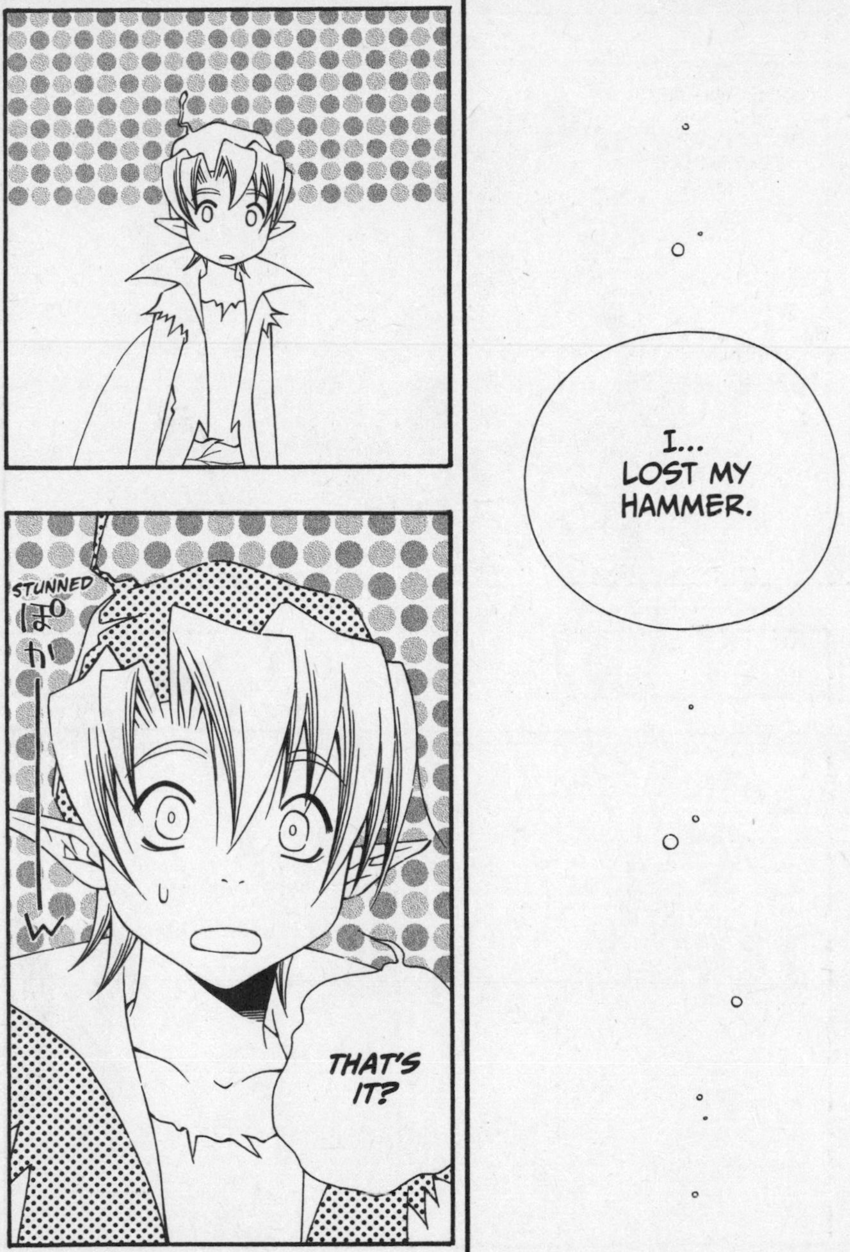
I... LOST MY HAMMER.
STUNNED
ぽかーん
THAT'S IT?

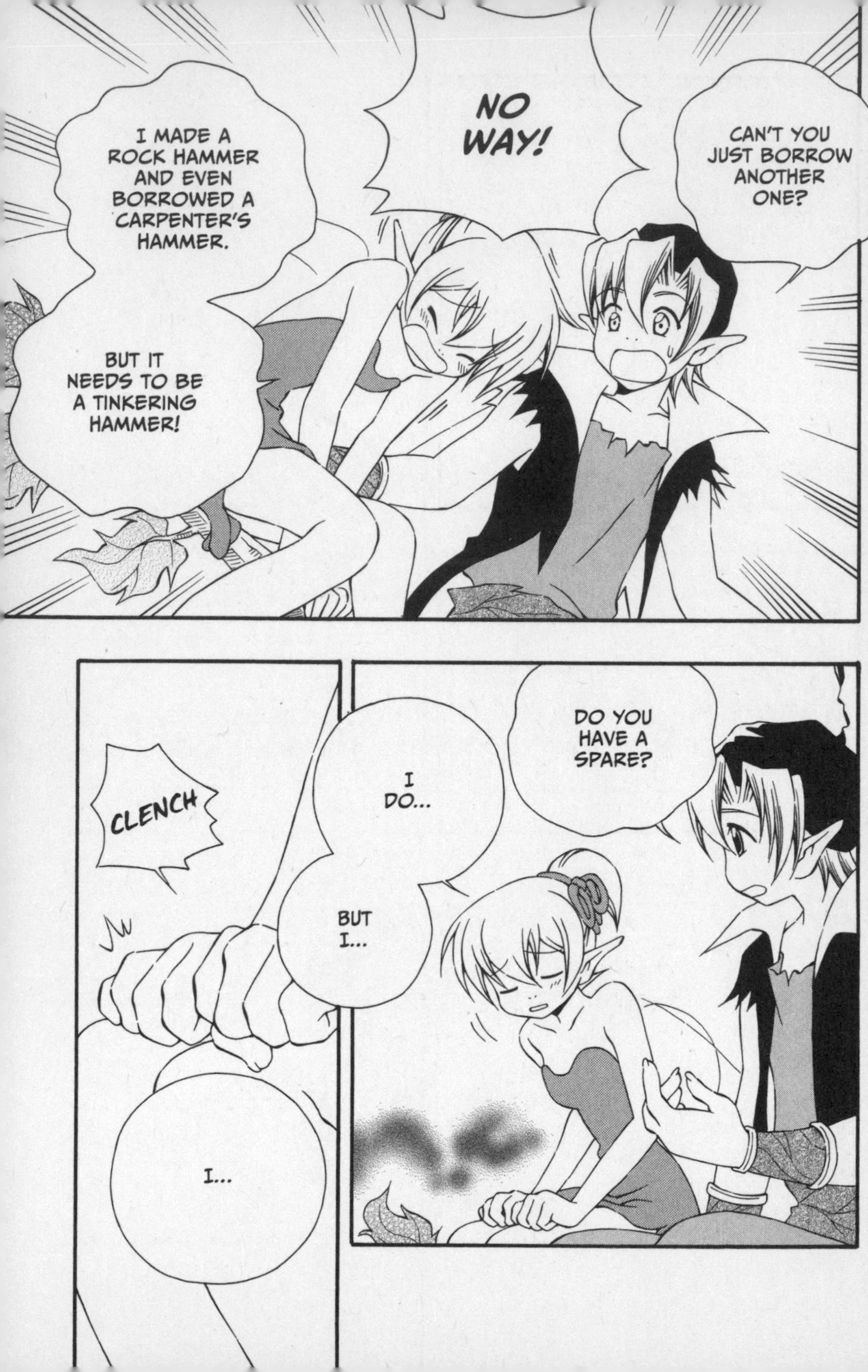
CAN'T YOU JUST BORROW ANOTHER ONE?
NO WAY!
I MADE A ROCK HAMMER AND EVEN BORROWED A CARPENTER'S HAMMER.
BUT IT NEEDS TO BE A TINKERING HAMMER!
DO YOU HAVE A SPARE?
I DO...
BUT I...
CLENCH
I...

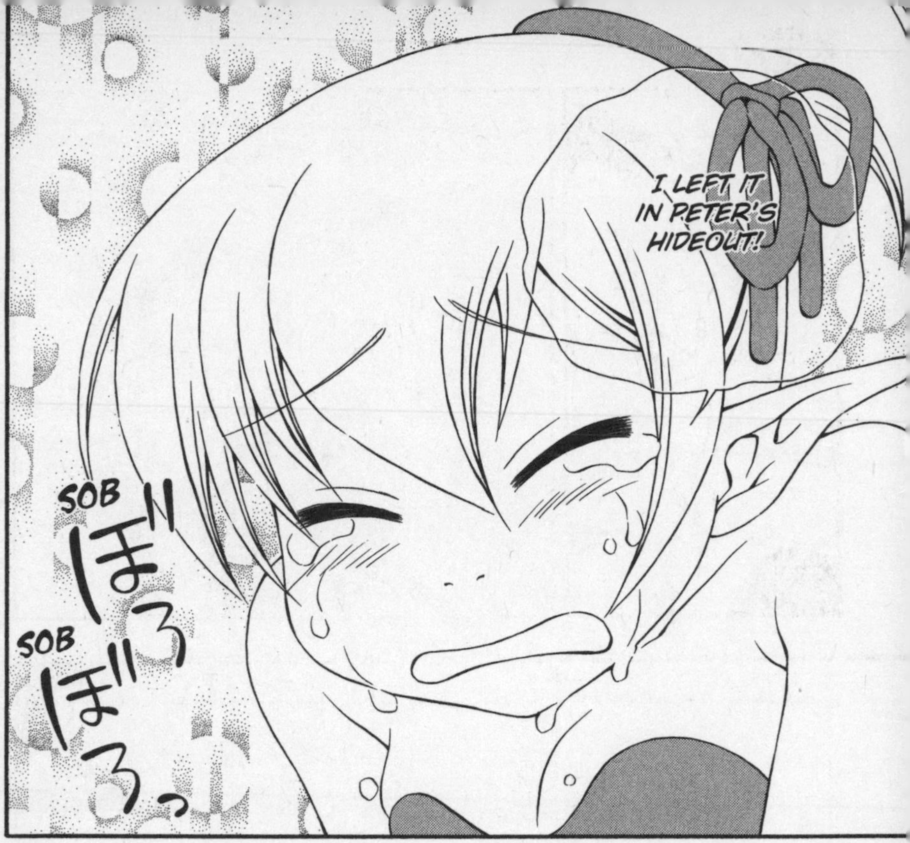
I LEFT IT IN PETER'S HIDEOUT!
SOB ぼろ
SOB ぼろっ

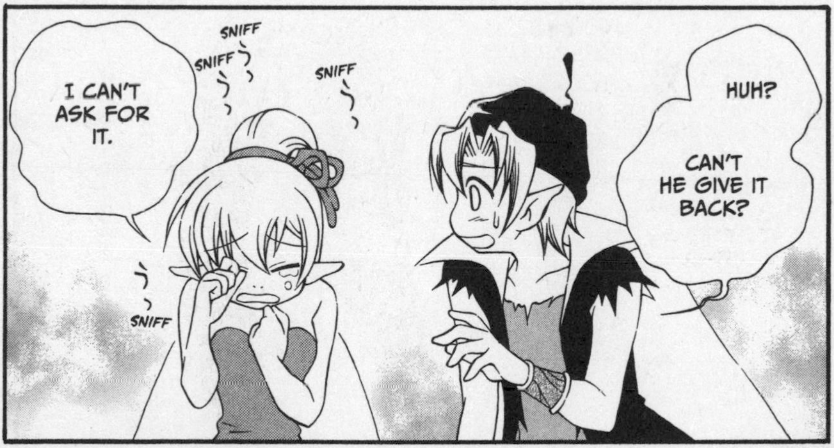
HUH?
CAN'T HE GIVE IT BACK?
SNIFF うっ
SNIFF うっ
SNIFF うっ
I CAN'T ASK FOR IT.
うっ SNIFF

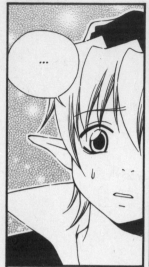

...

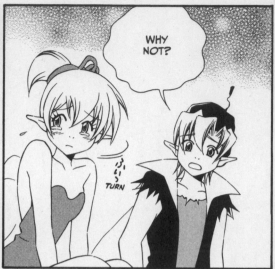

WHY NOT?

ふらふら
TURN

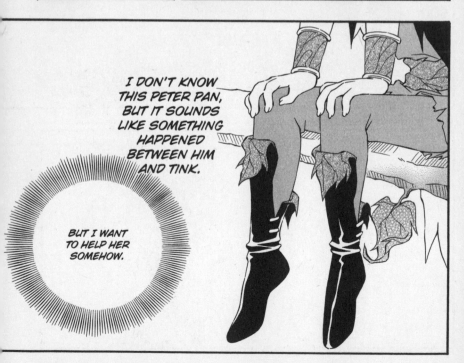

I DON'T KNOW THIS PETER PAN, BUT IT SOUNDS LIKE SOMETHING HAPPENED BETWEEN HIM AND TINK.

BUT I WANT TO HELP HER SOMEHOW.

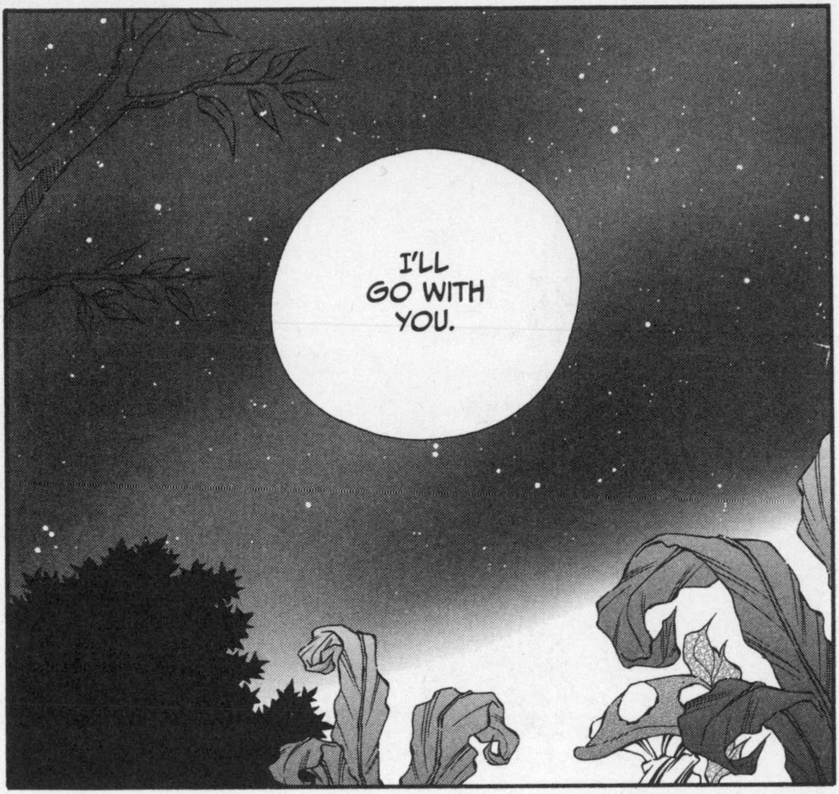
I'LL
GO WITH
YOU.

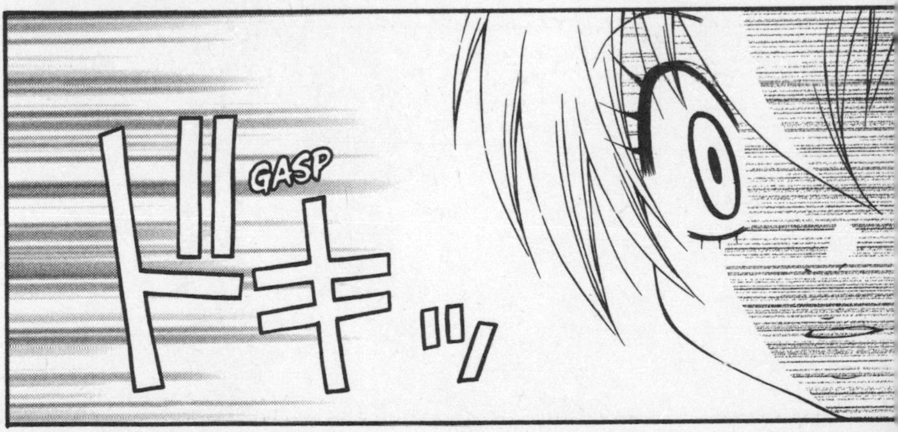
ドキッ
GASP

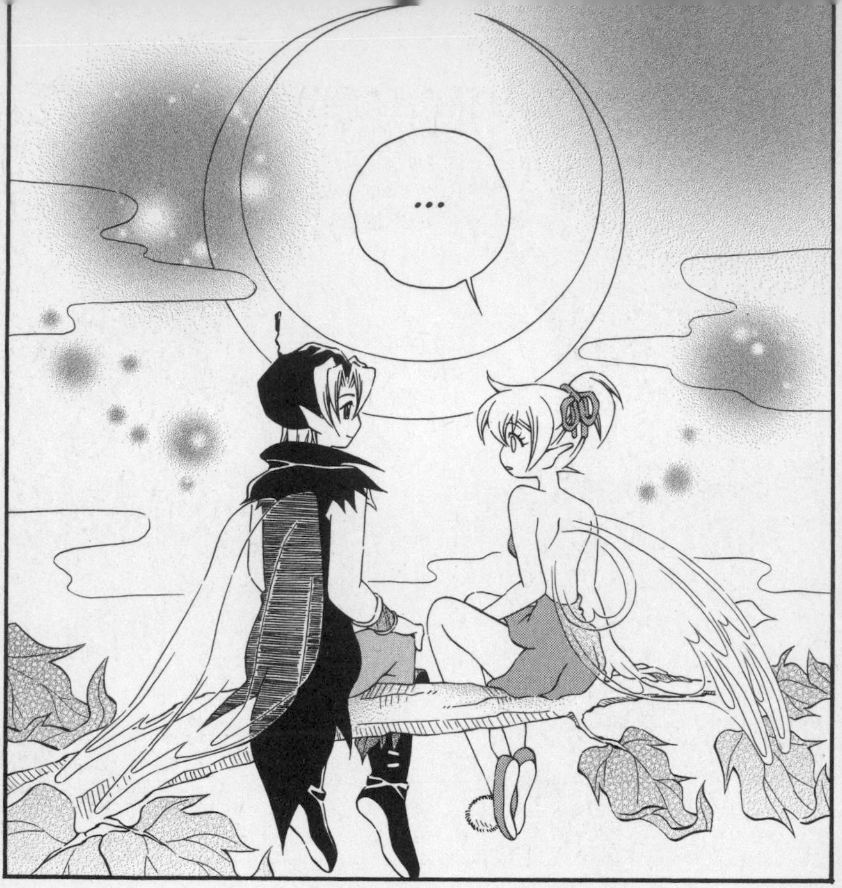
...

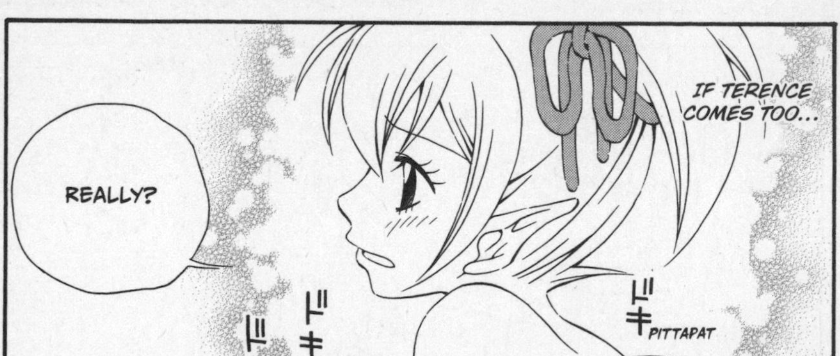
IF TERENCE COMES TOO...
ドキ PITTAPAT
REALLY?
ドキ PITTAPAT
ドキ PITTAPAT

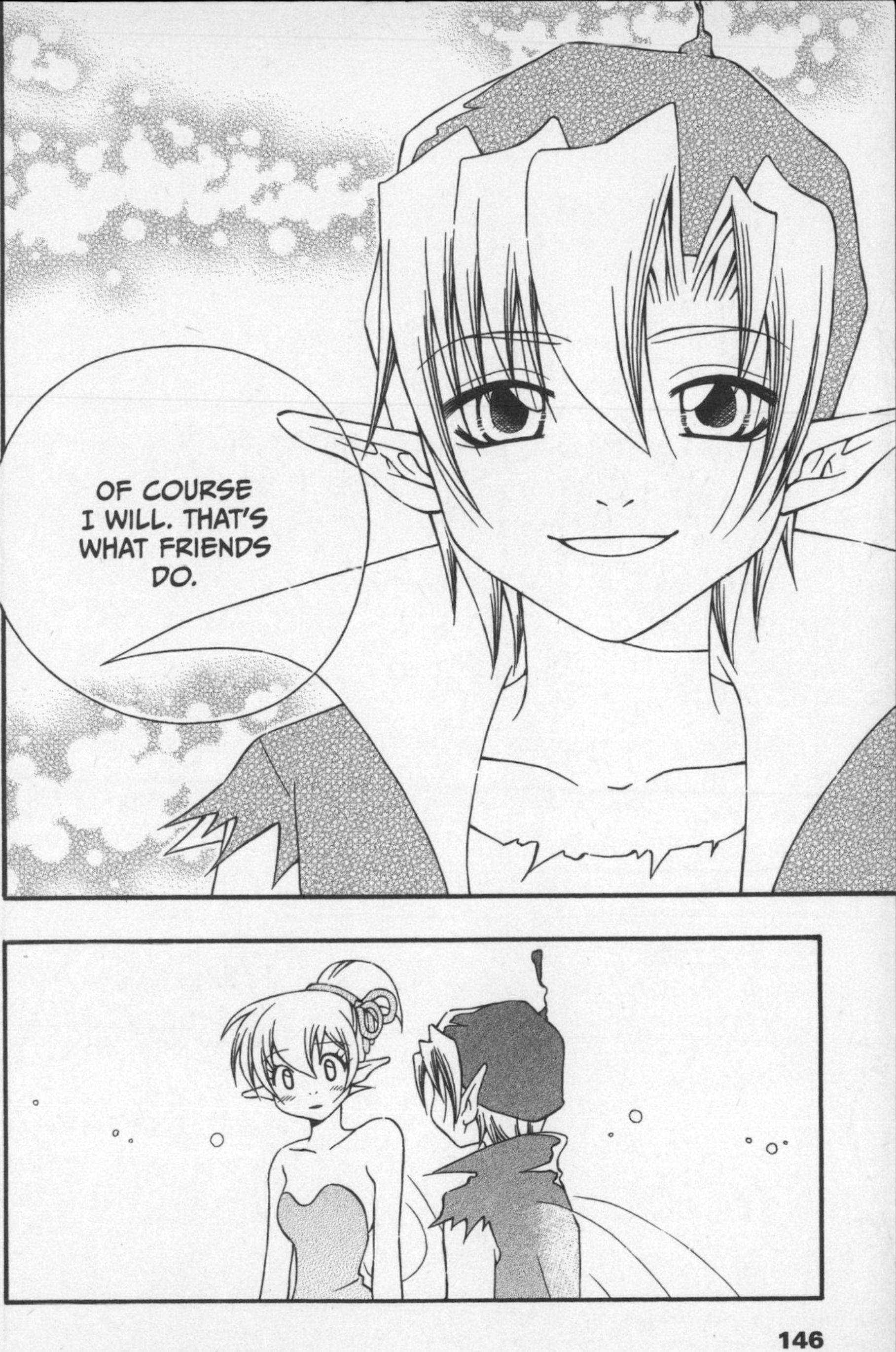
OF COURSE I WILL. THAT'S WHAT FRIENDS DO.

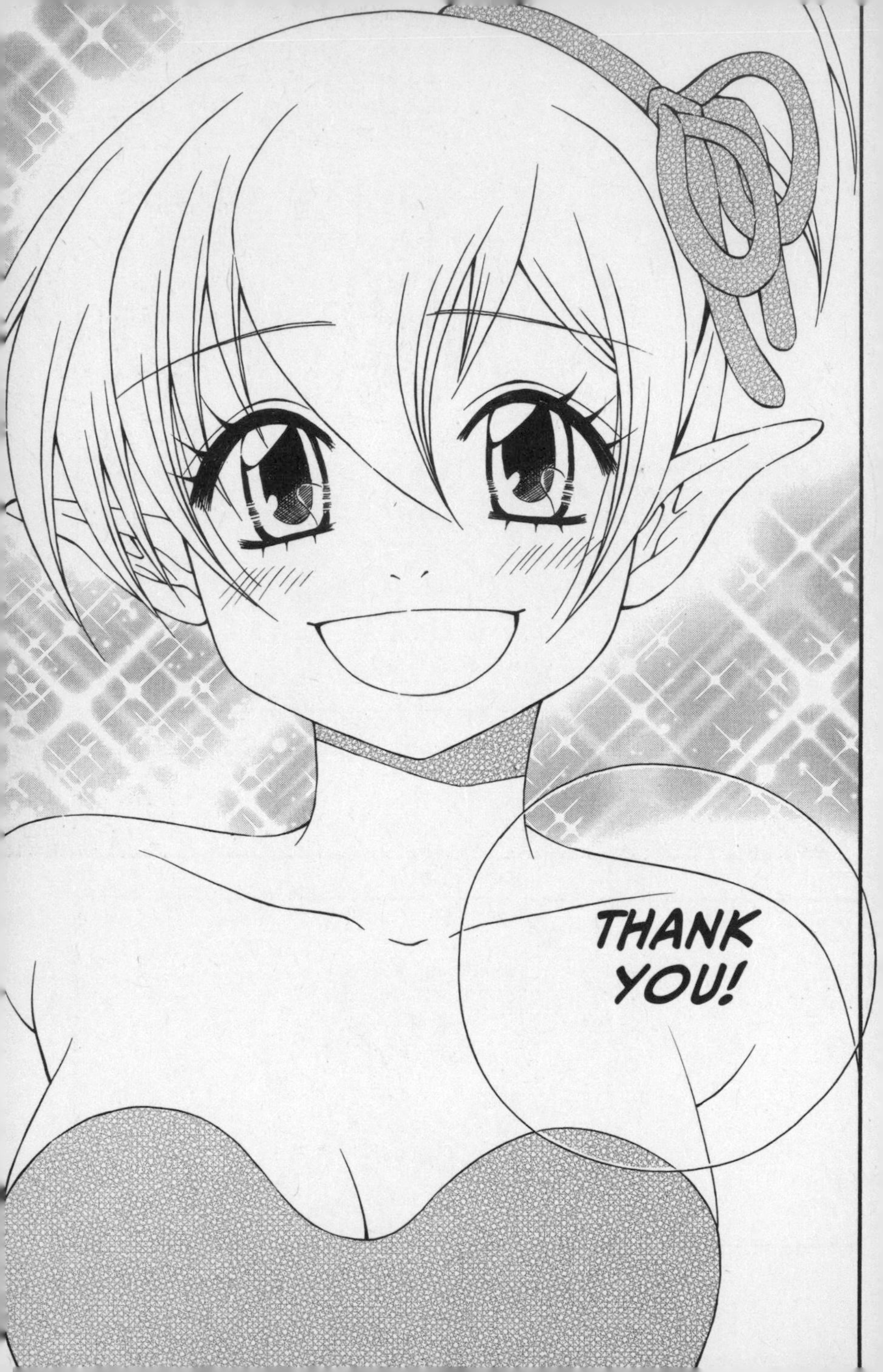
THANK YOU!

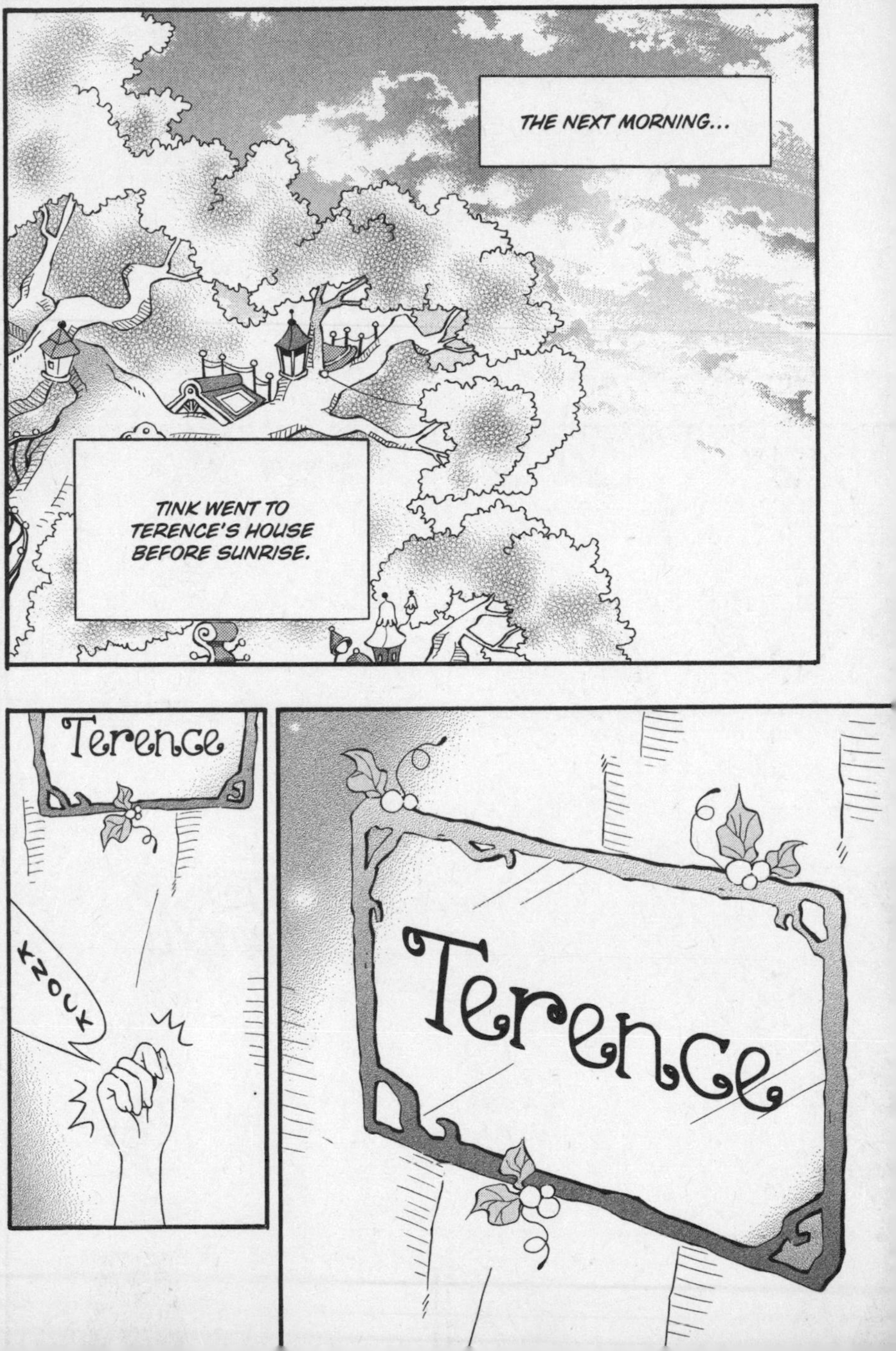
THE NEXT MORNING...
TINK WENT TO TERENCE'S HOUSE BEFORE SUNRISE.
Terence
Terence
KNOCK

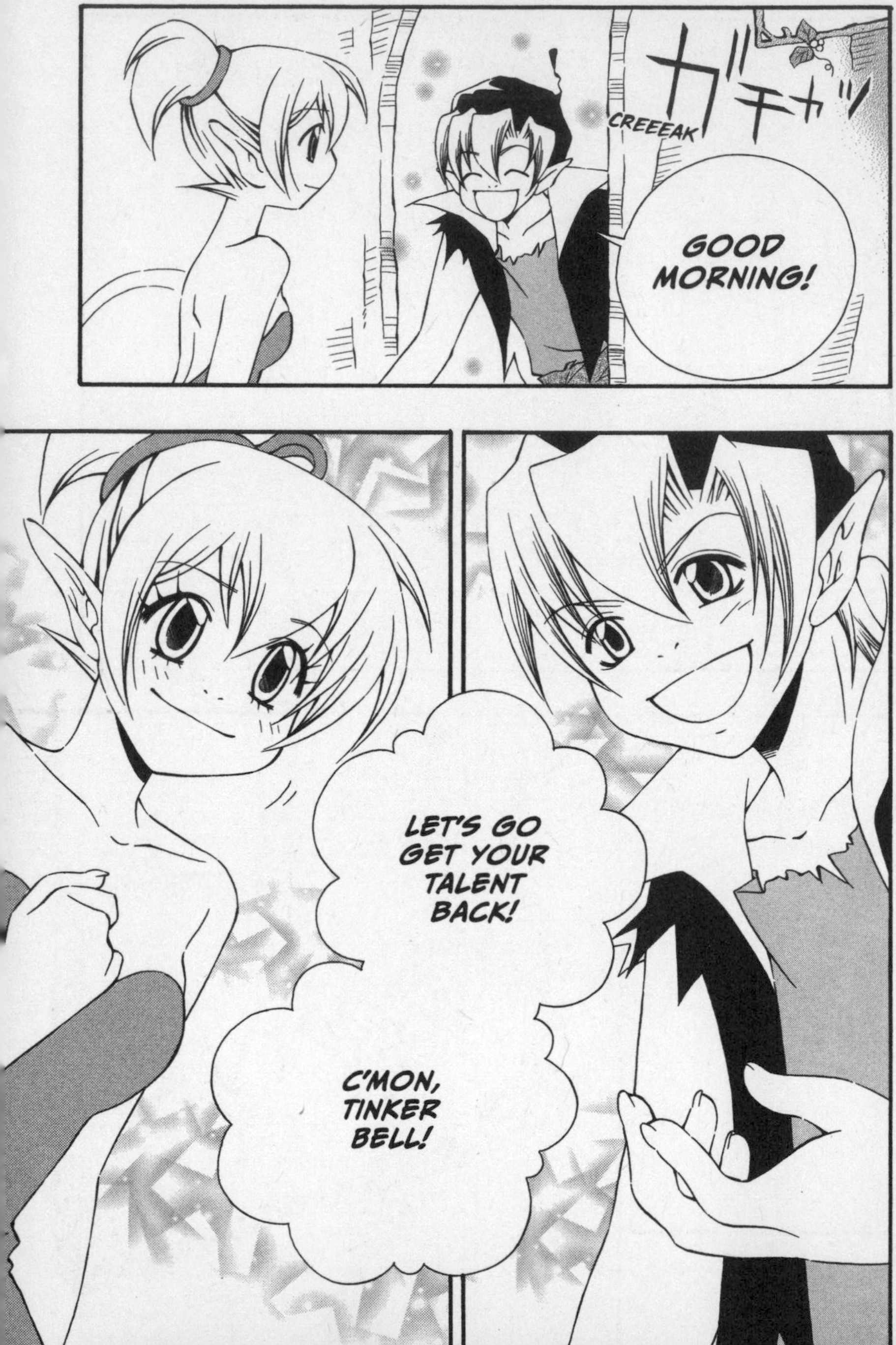
ガチャッ
CREEEAK
GOOD MORNING!
LET'S GO GET YOUR TALENT BACK!
C'MON, TINKER BELL!

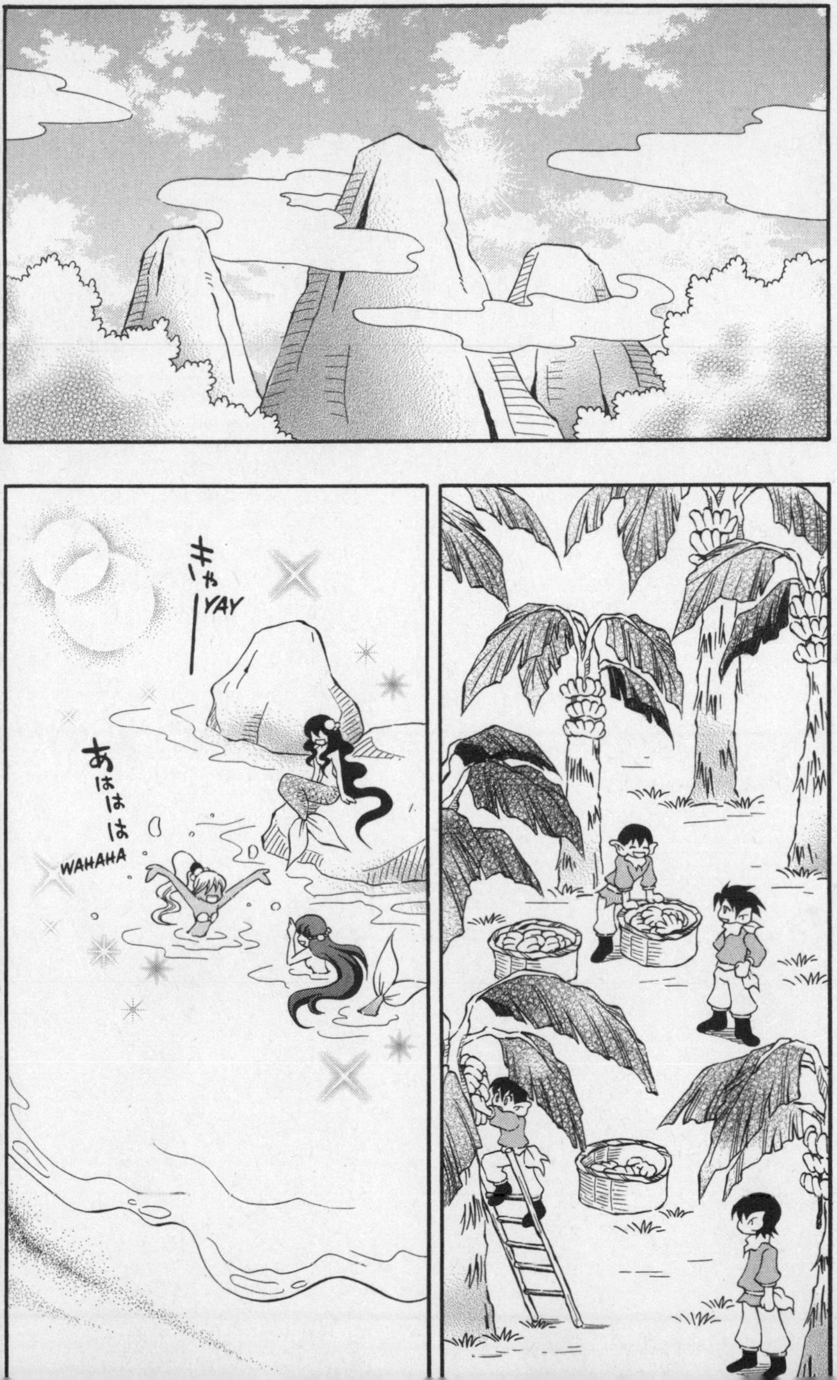
きゃー
YAY
あははは
WAHAHA

READ THIS WAY

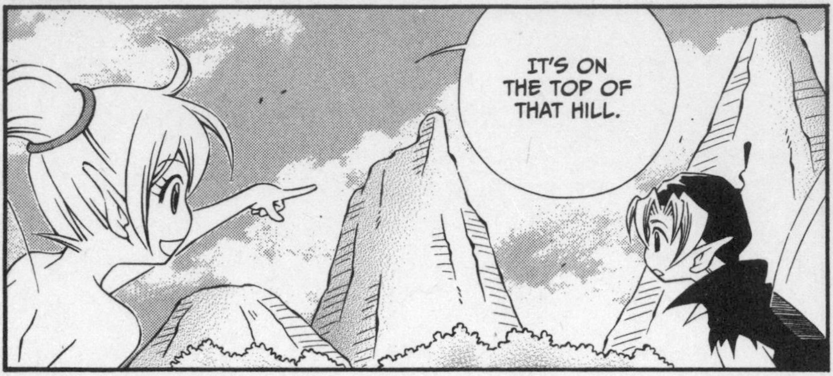
IT'S ON THE TOP OF THAT HILL.

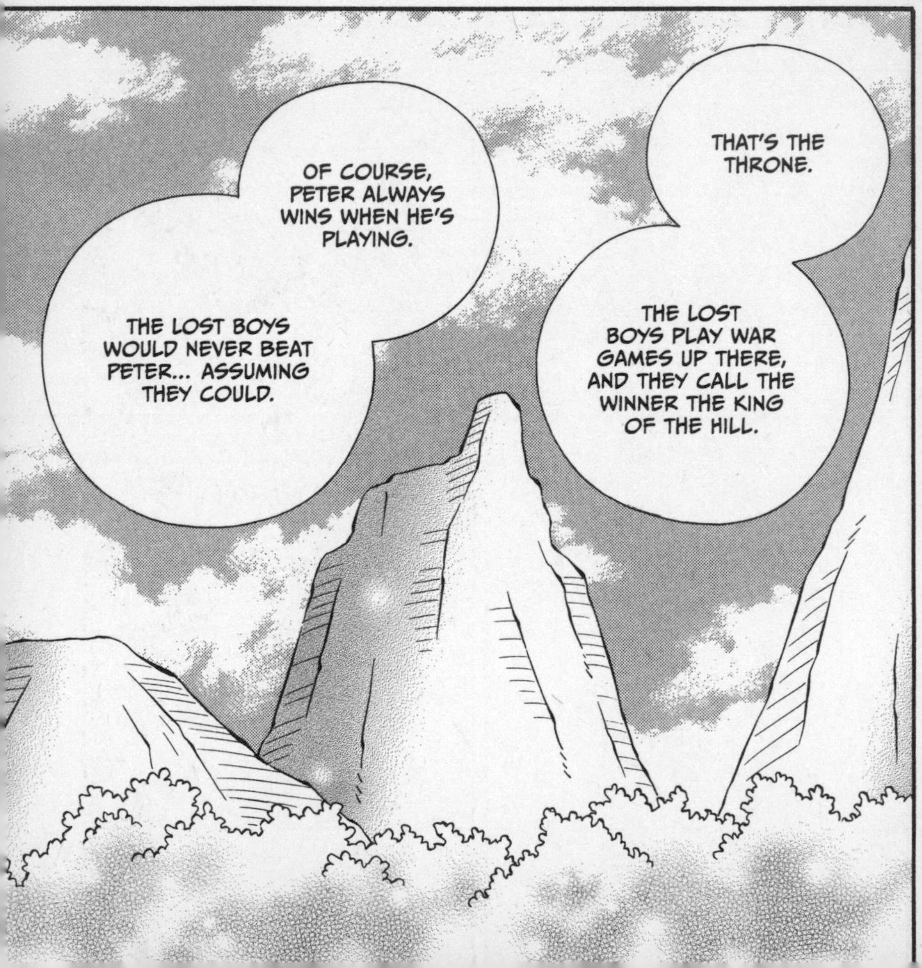
THAT'S THE THRONE.
THE LOST BOYS PLAY WAR GAMES UP THERE, AND THEY CALL THE WINNER THE KING OF THE HILL.
OF COURSE, PETER ALWAYS WINS WHEN HE'S PLAYING.
THE LOST BOYS WOULD NEVER BEAT PETER... ASSUMING THEY COULD.

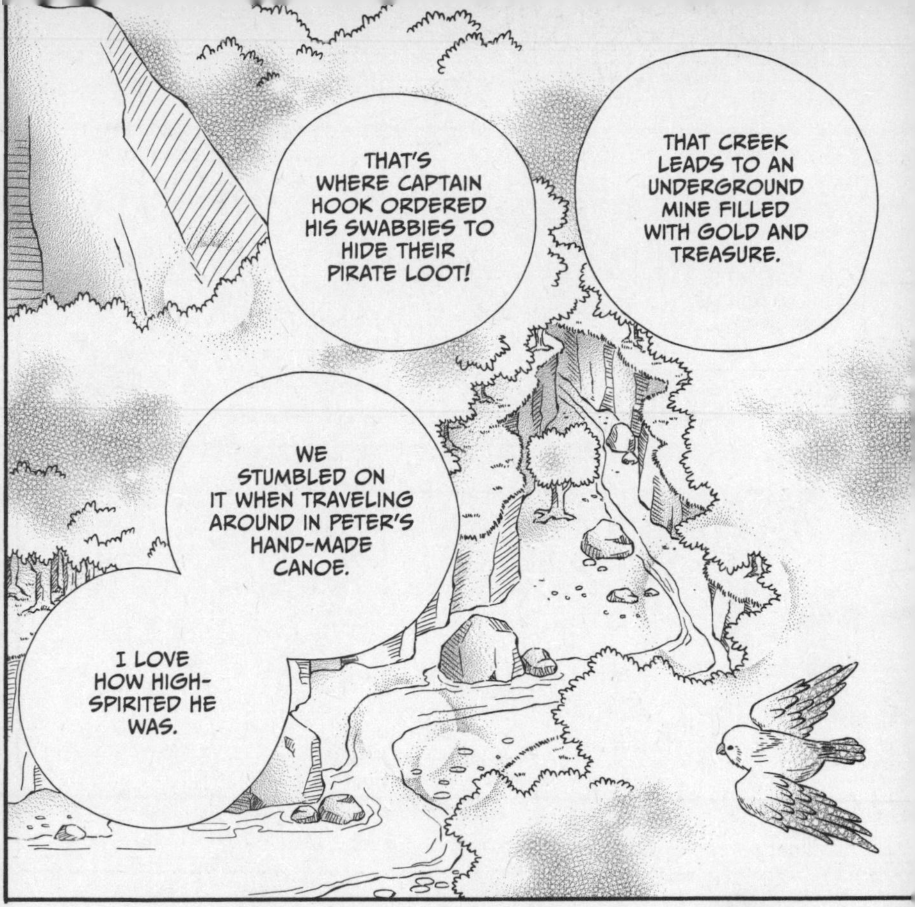
THAT CREEK LEADS TO AN UNDERGROUND MINE FILLED WITH GOLD AND TREASURE.
THAT'S WHERE CAPTAIN HOOK ORDERED HIS SWABBIES TO HIDE THEIR PIRATE LOOT!
WE STUMBLED ON IT WHEN TRAVELING AROUND IN PETER'S HAND-MADE CANOE.
I LOVE HOW HIGH-SPIRITED HE WAS.

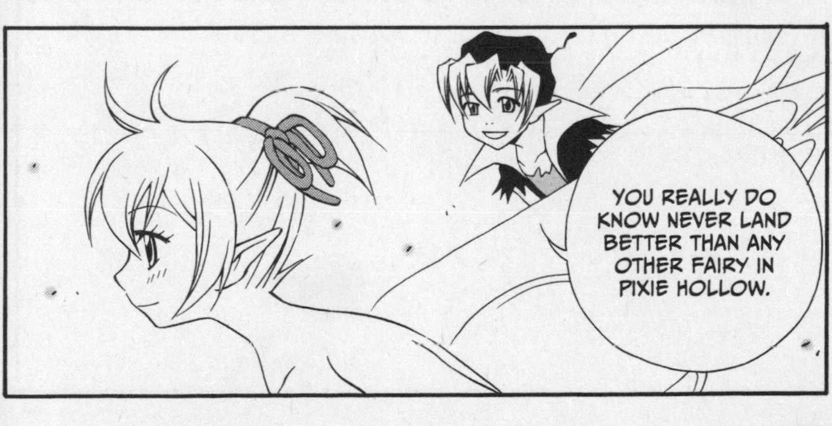
YOU REALLY DO KNOW NEVER LAND BETTER THAN ANY OTHER FAIRY IN PIXIE HOLLOW.

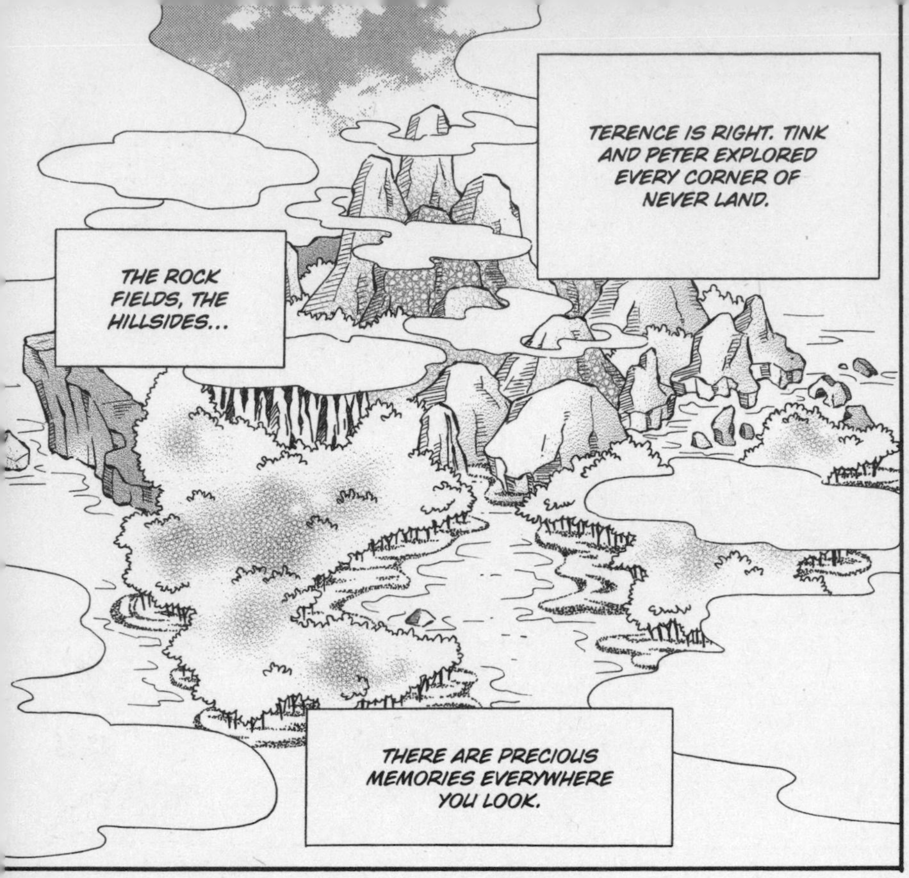
TERENCE IS RIGHT. TINK AND PETER EXPLORED EVERY CORNER OF NEVER LAND.
THE ROCK FIELDS, THE HILLSIDES...
THERE ARE PRECIOUS MEMORIES EVERYWHERE YOU LOOK.

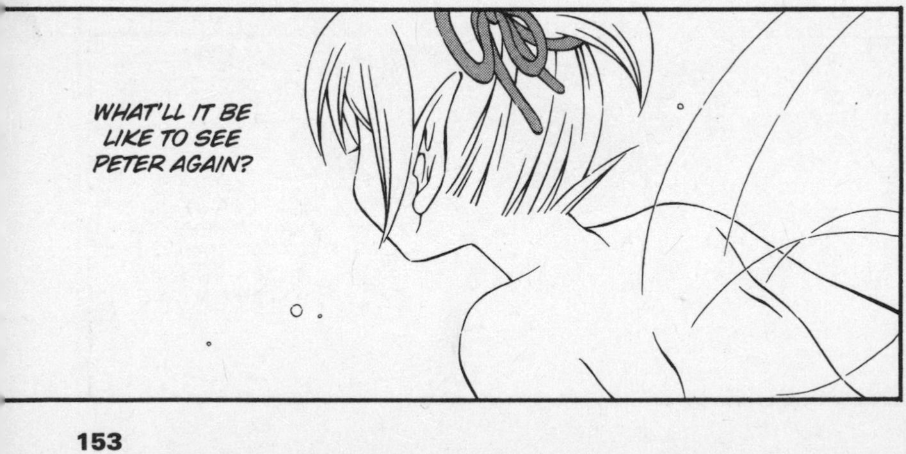
WHAT'LL IT BE LIKE TO SEE PETER AGAIN?

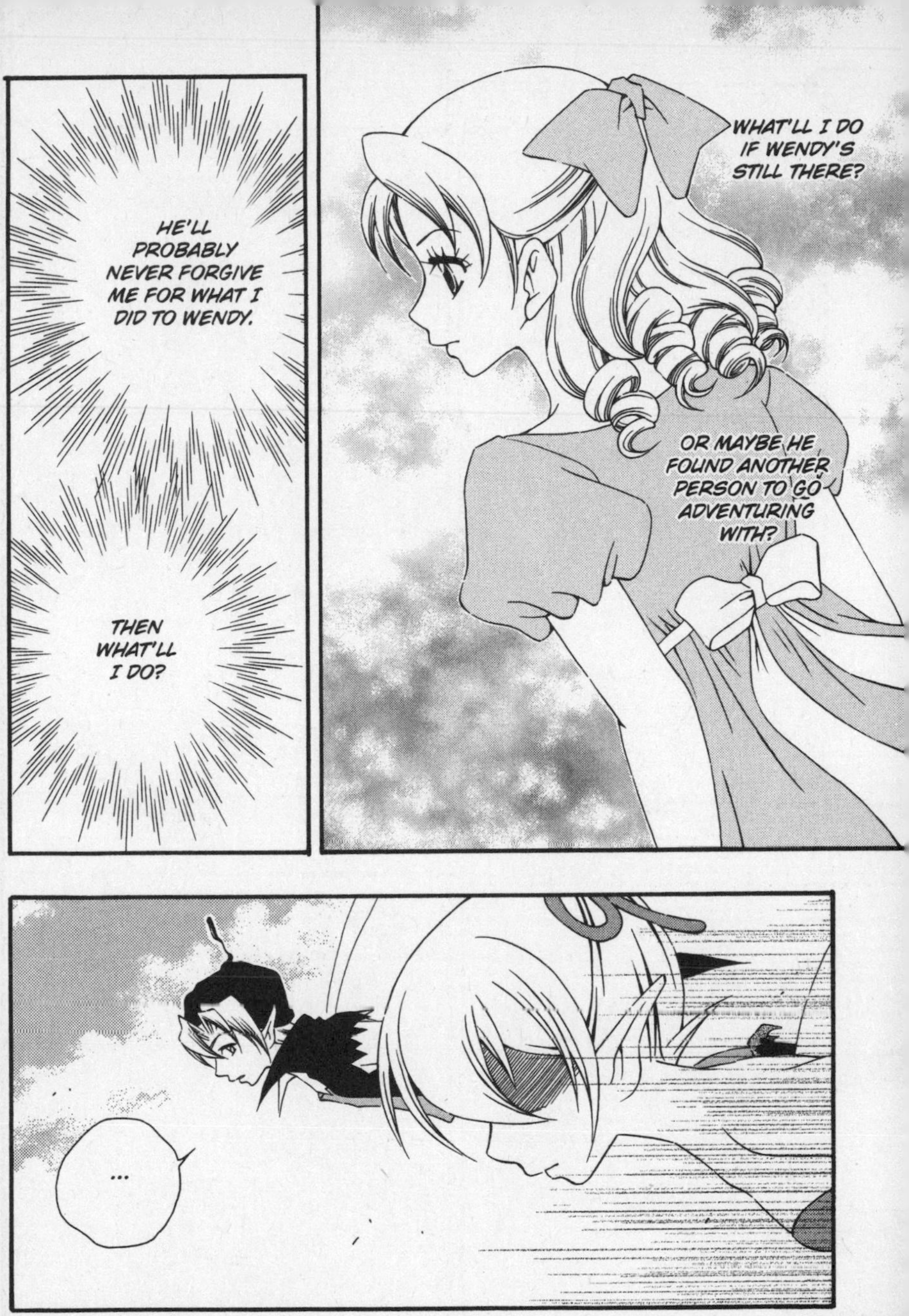
WHAT'LL I DO IF WENDY'S STILL THERE?
OR MAYBE HE FOUND ANOTHER PERSON TO GO ADVENTURING WITH?
HE'LL PROBABLY NEVER FORGIVE ME FOR WHAT I DID TO WENDY.
THEN WHAT'LL I DO?
...

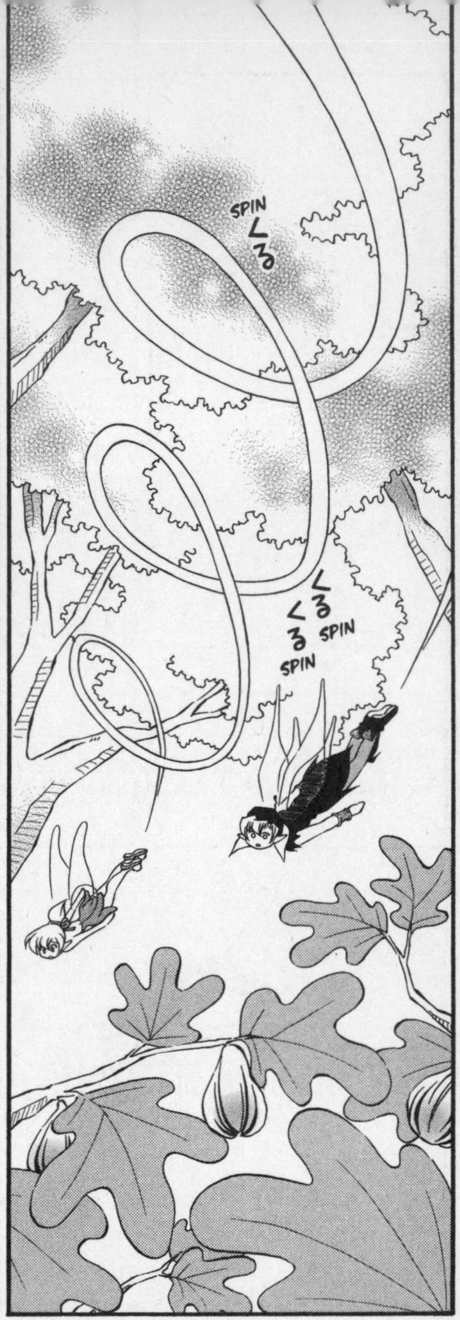
SPIN
くる
くる
くる
SPIN
SPIN
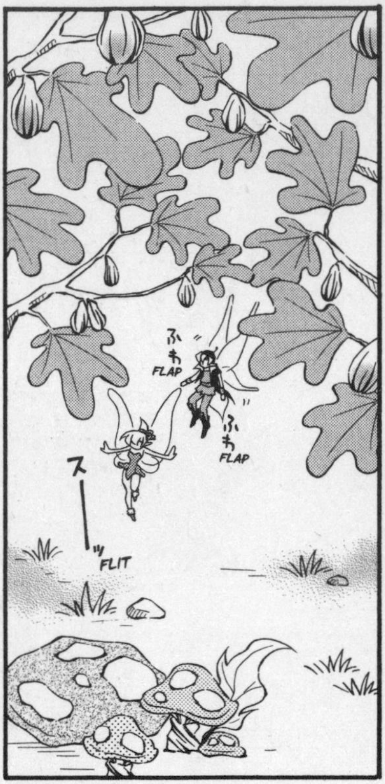
ふわ
FLAP
ふわ
FLAP
スーッ
FLIT
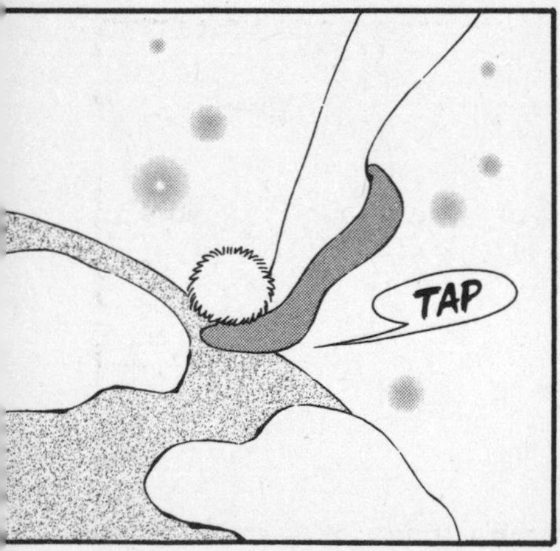
TAP

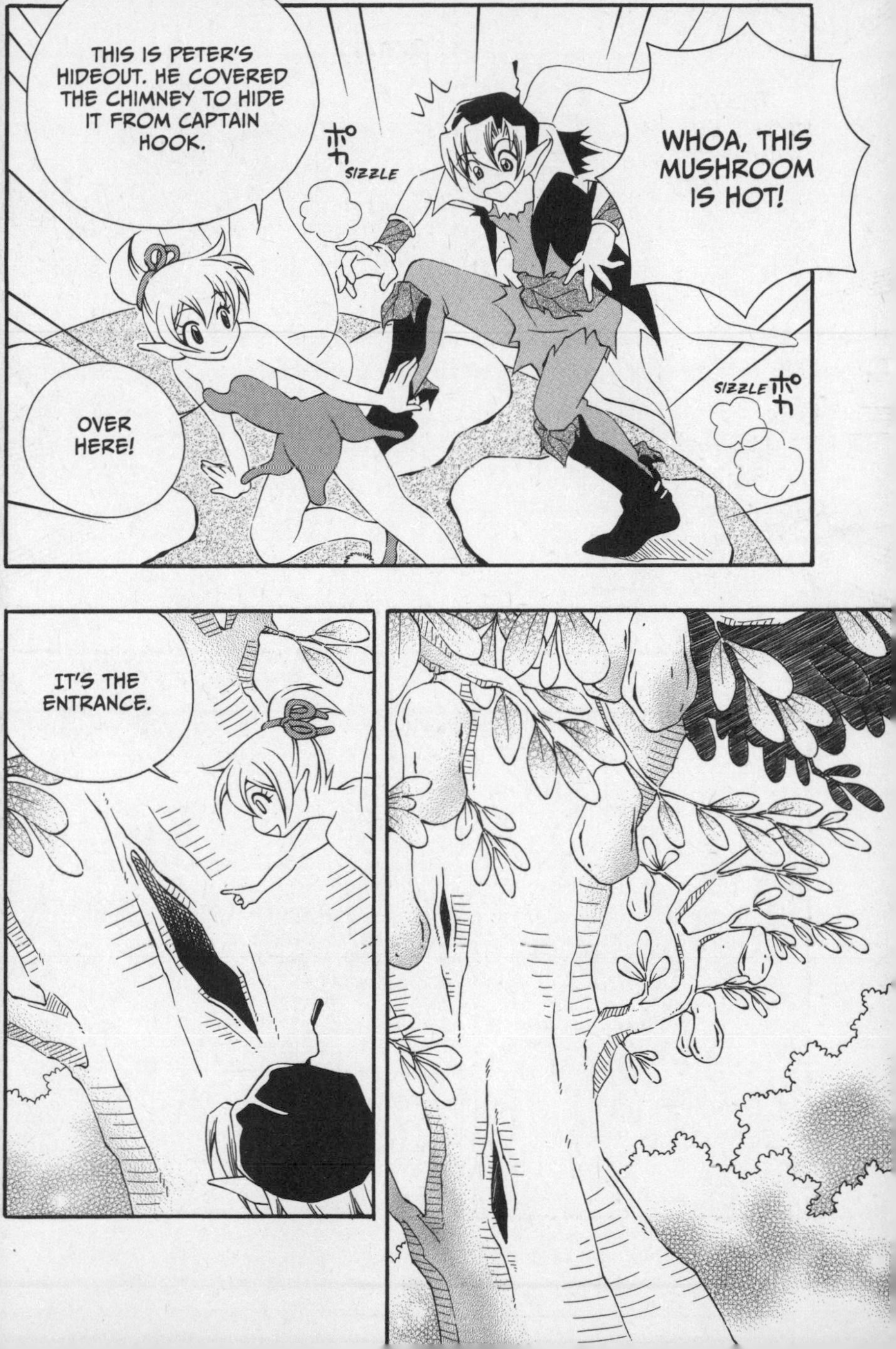
WHOA, THIS MUSHROOM IS HOT!
THIS IS PETER'S HIDEOUT. HE COVERED THE CHIMNEY TO HIDE IT FROM CAPTAIN HOOK.
ポカ SIZZLE
SIZZLE ポカ
OVER HERE!
IT'S THE ENTRANCE.

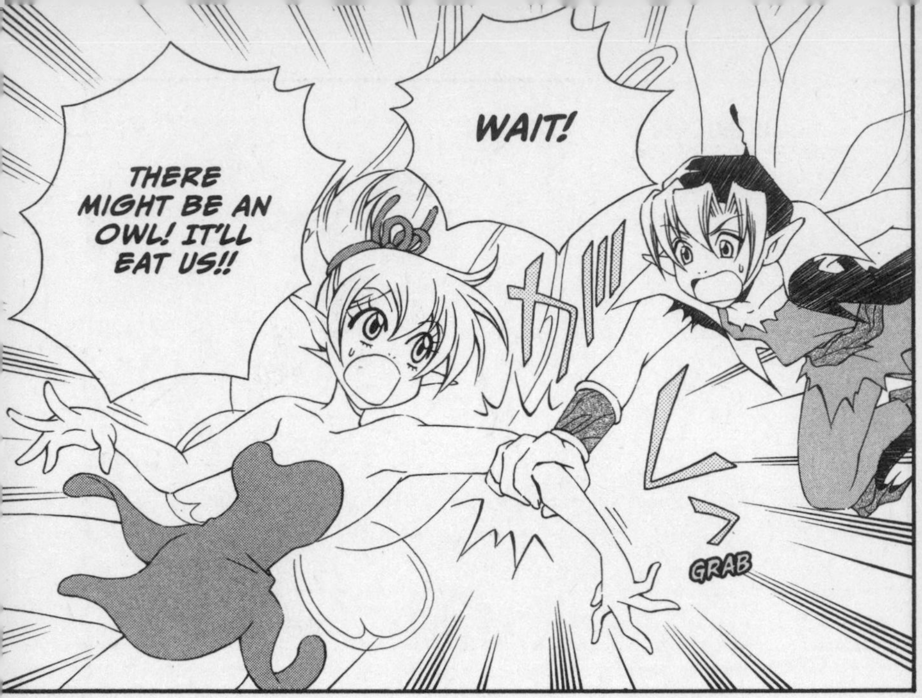
WAIT!
THERE MIGHT BE AN OWL! IT'LL EAT US!!
GRAB

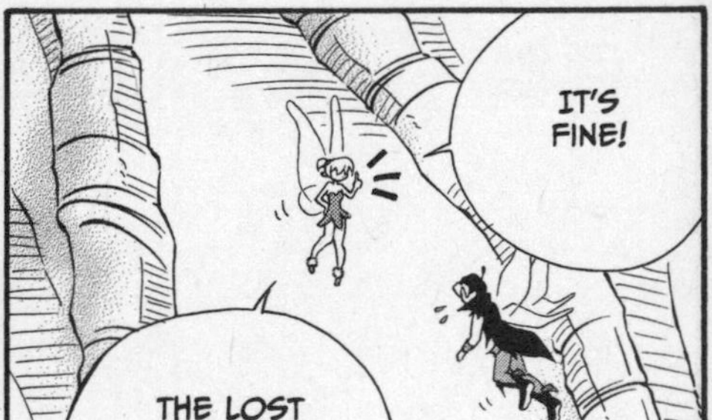
IT'S FINE!
THE LOST BOYS CHASE THE ANIMALS AWAY FROM HERE.
THIS IS THE ENTRANCE TO THE HIDEOUT.

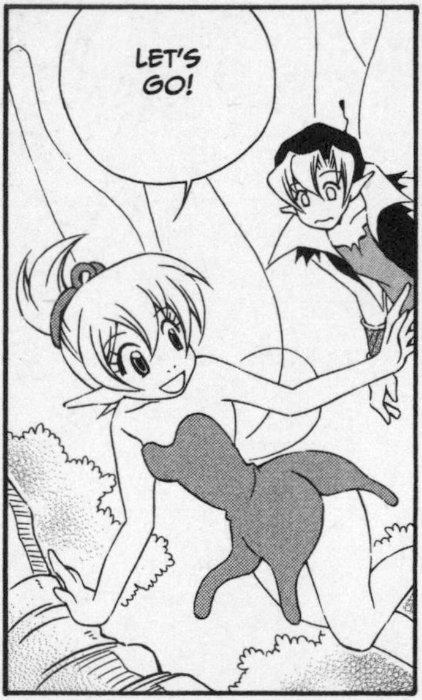
LET'S GO!

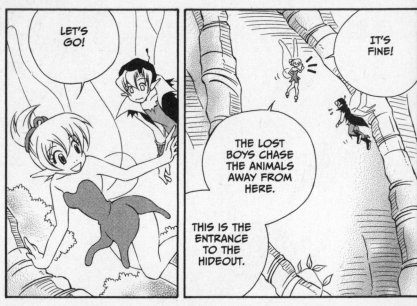

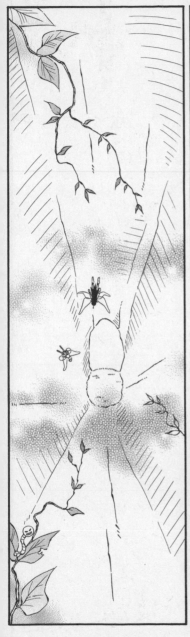

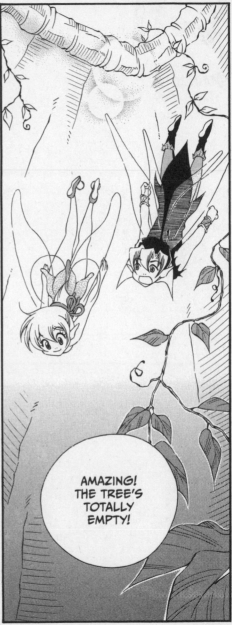

AMAZING!
THE TREE'S
TOTALLY
EMPTY!

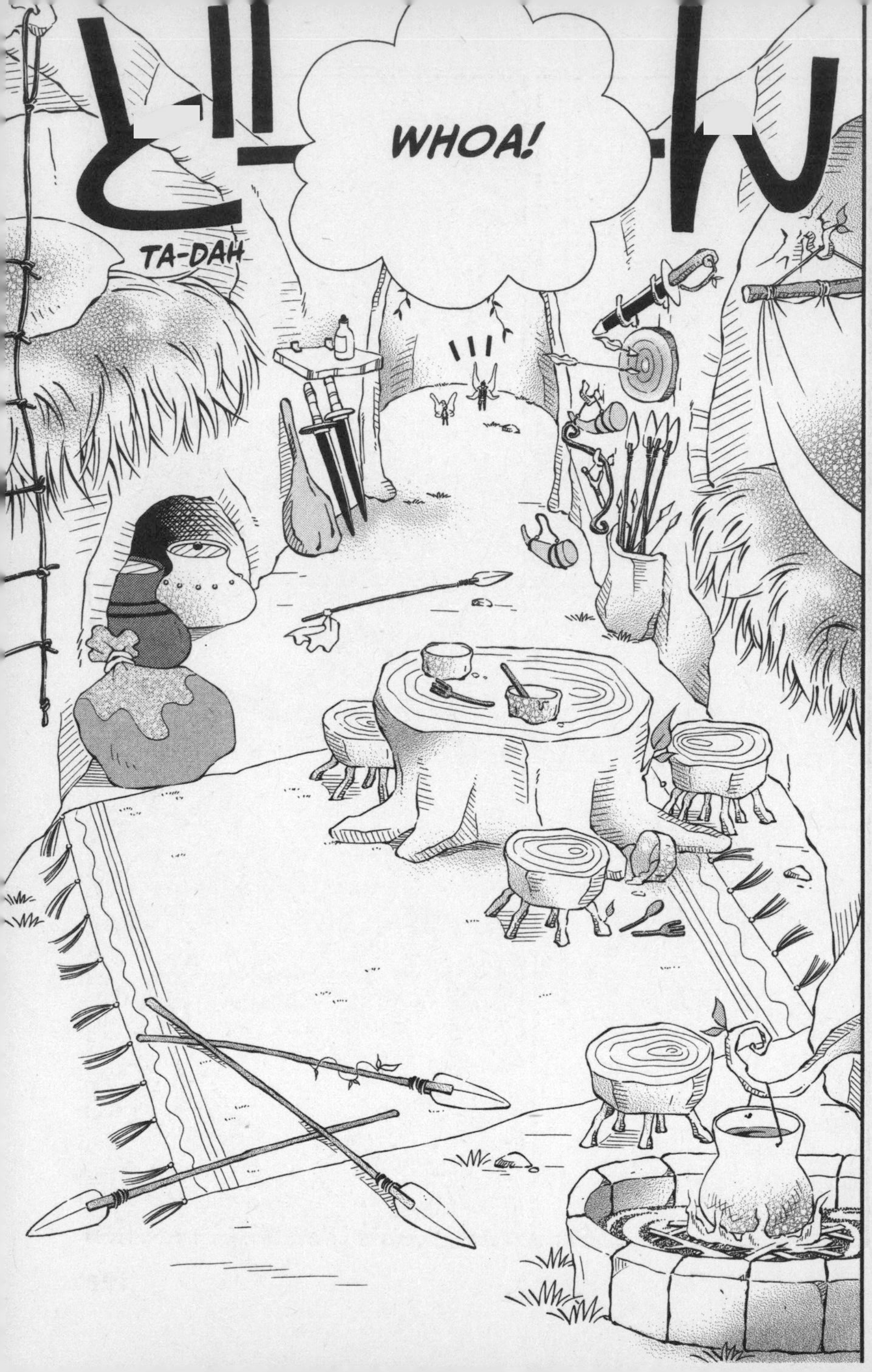
WHOA!
TA-DAH

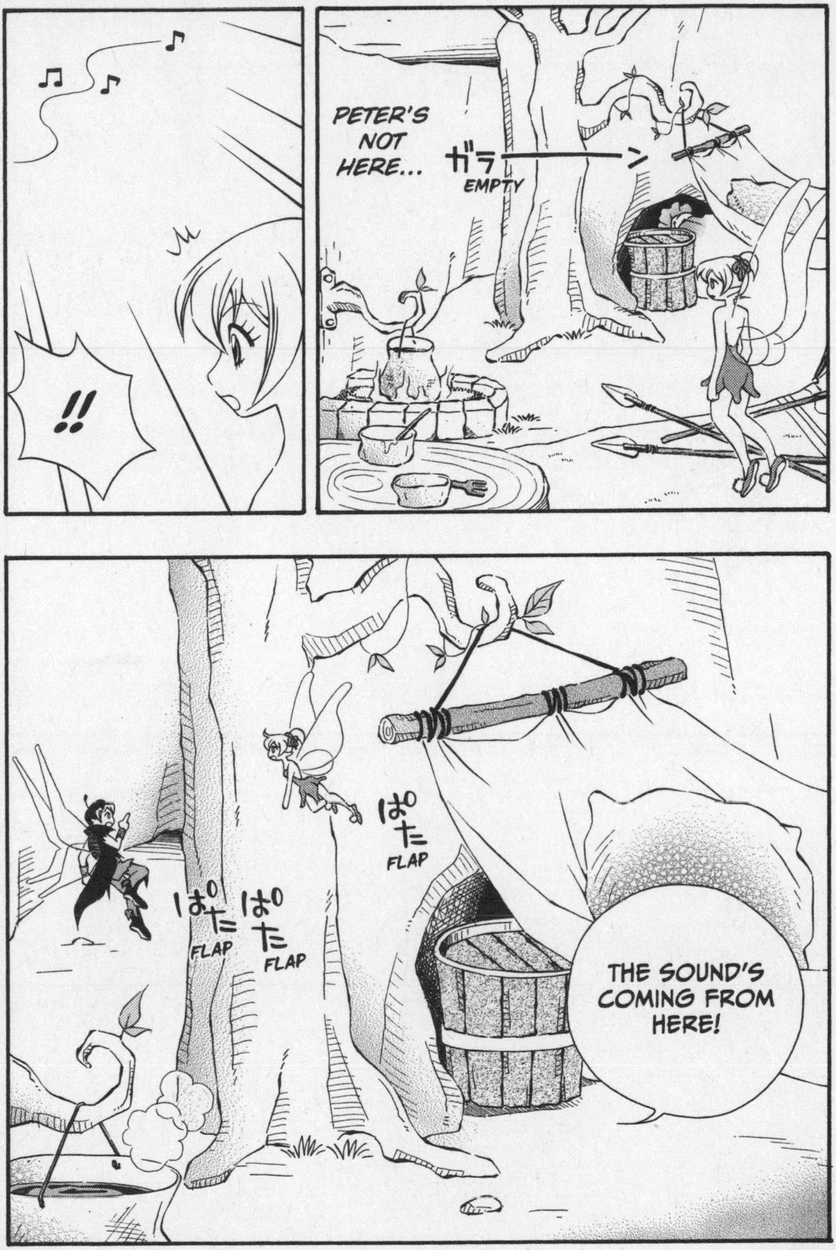
PETER'S NOT HERE...
ガラーン
EMPTY
!!
THE SOUND'S COMING FROM HERE!
ぱた
FLAP
ぱた ぱた
FLAP FLAP

READ THIS WAY

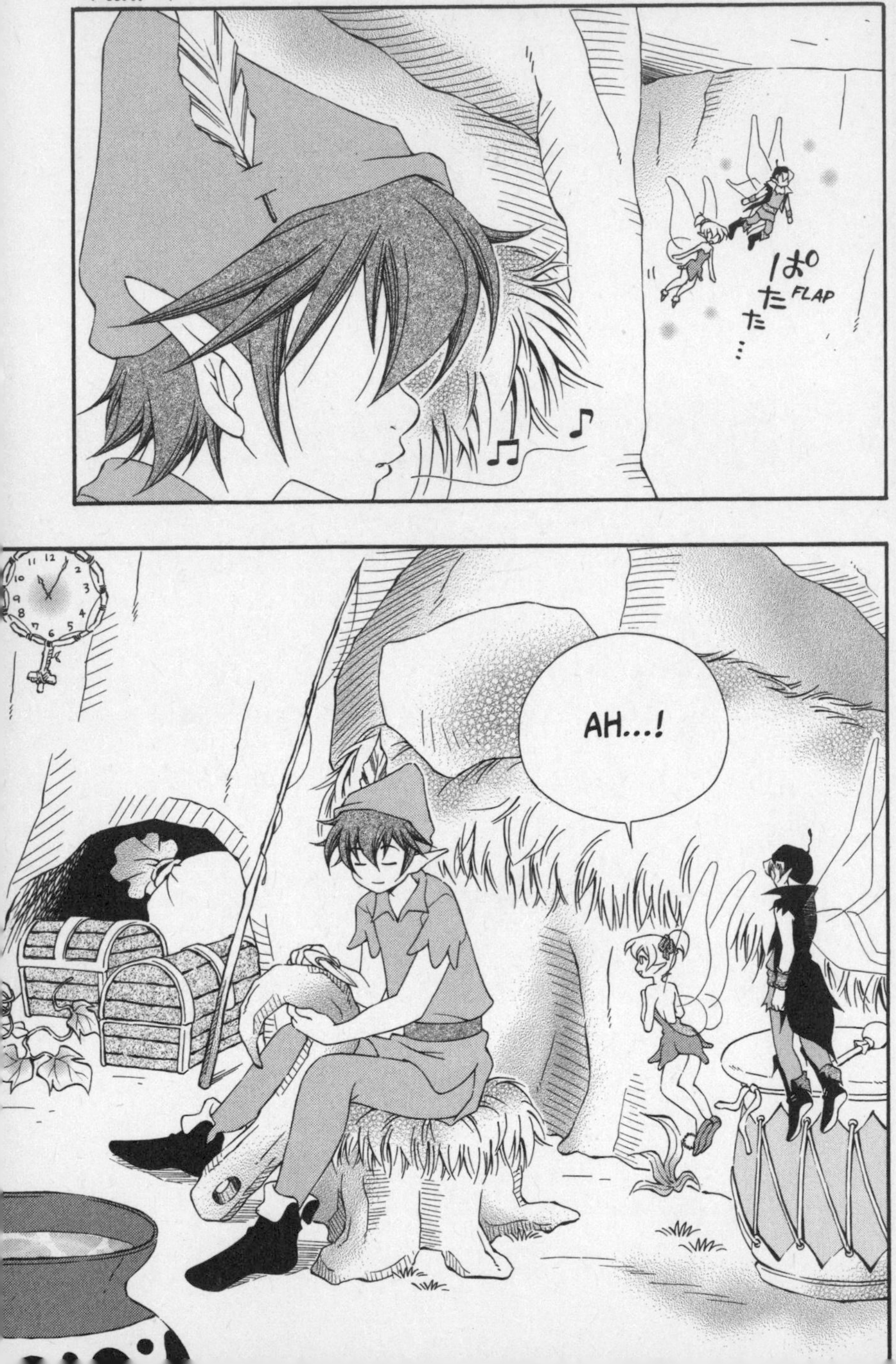
ぱたた…
FLAP
AH...!

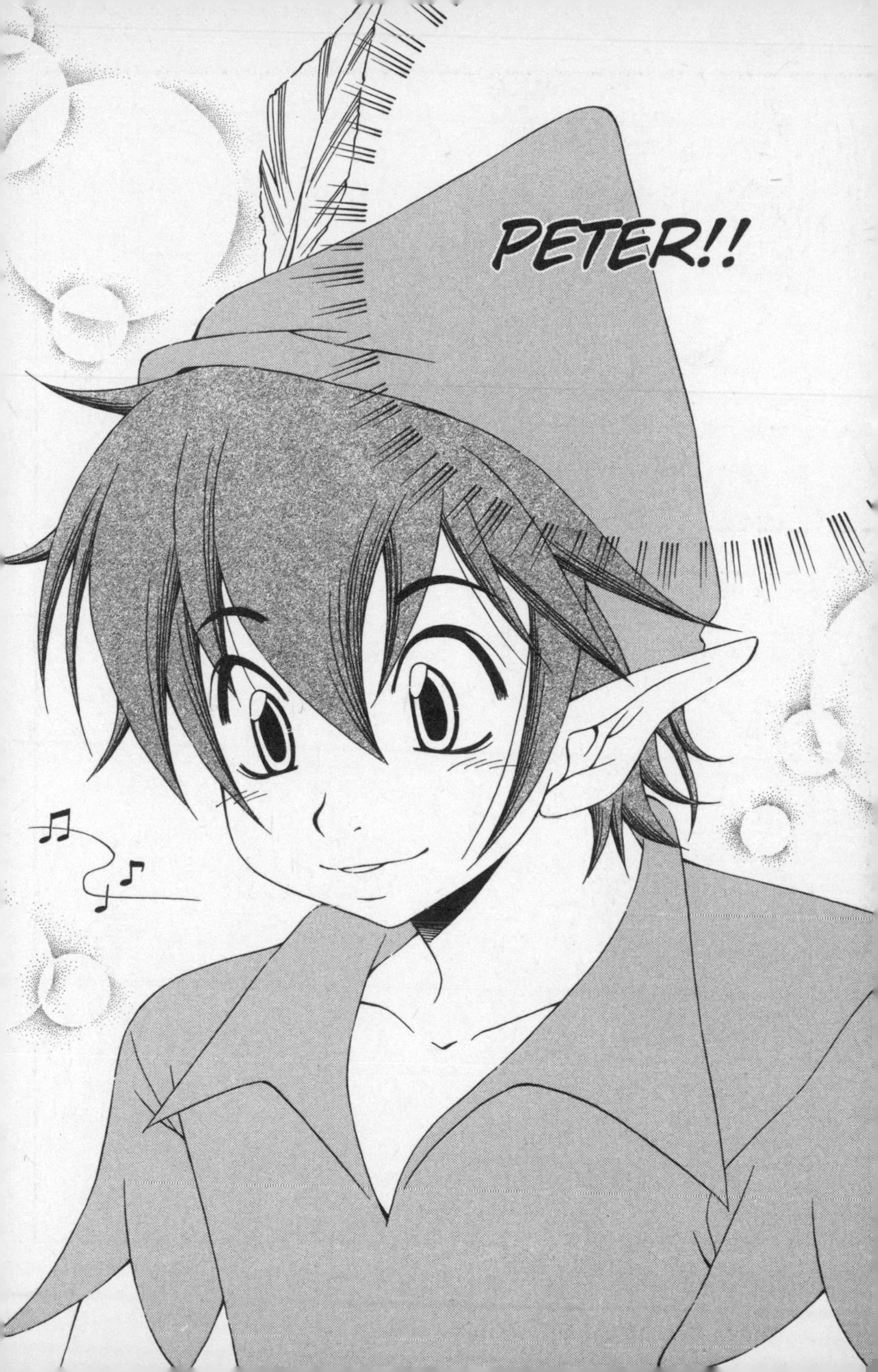
PETER!!

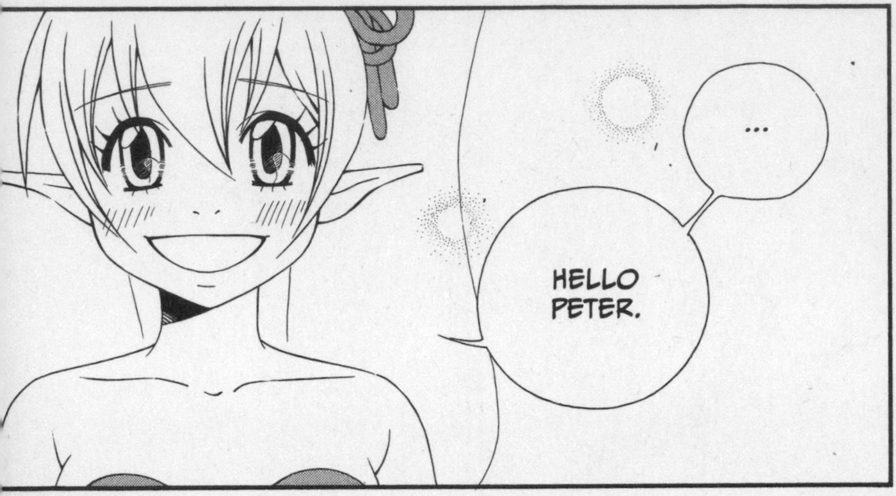
...
HELLO PETER.

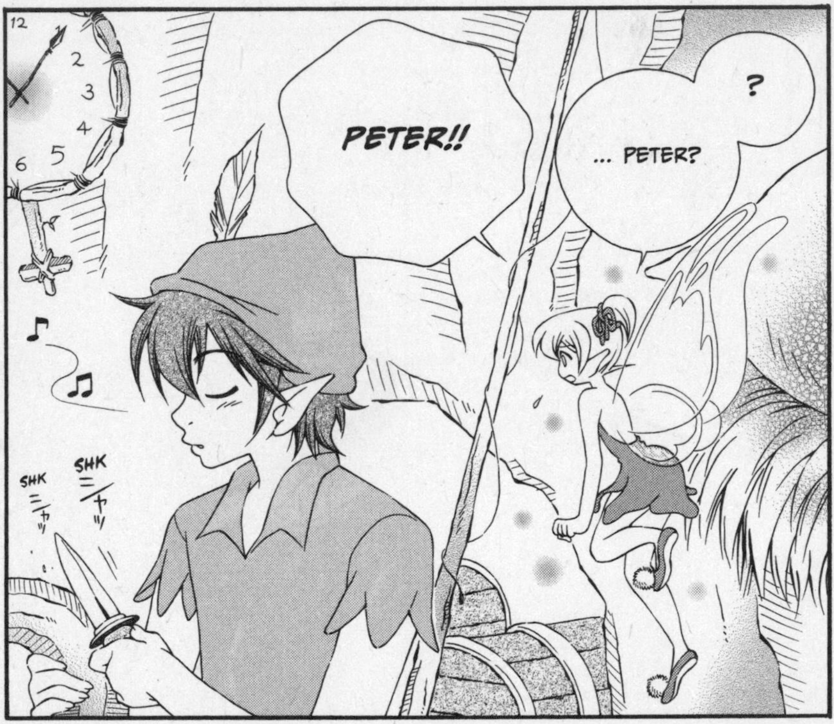
?
... PETER?
PETER!!
SHK
SHK

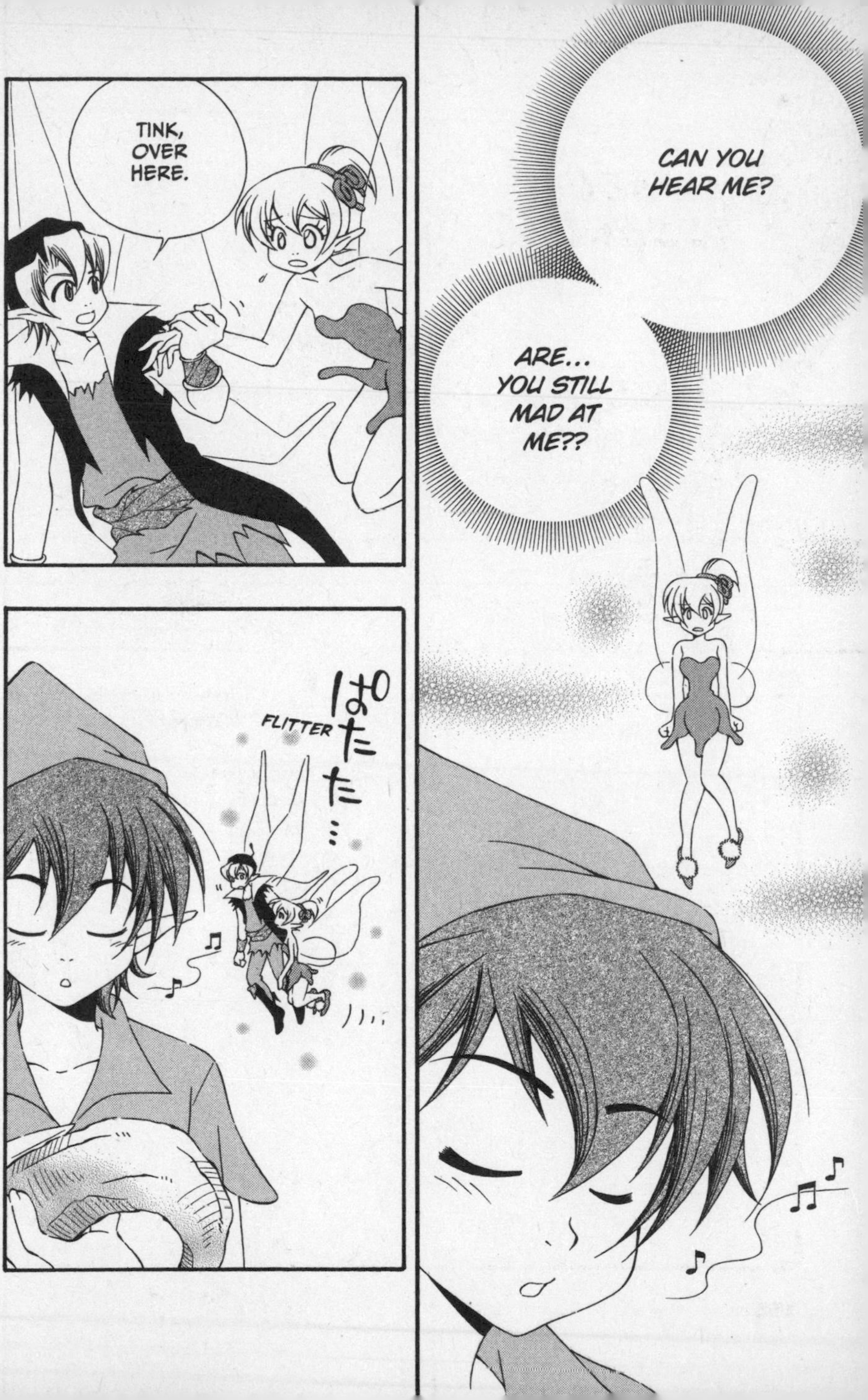
CAN YOU HEAR ME?
ARE... YOU STILL MAD AT ME??
TINK, OVER HERE.
ぱたた…
FLITTER

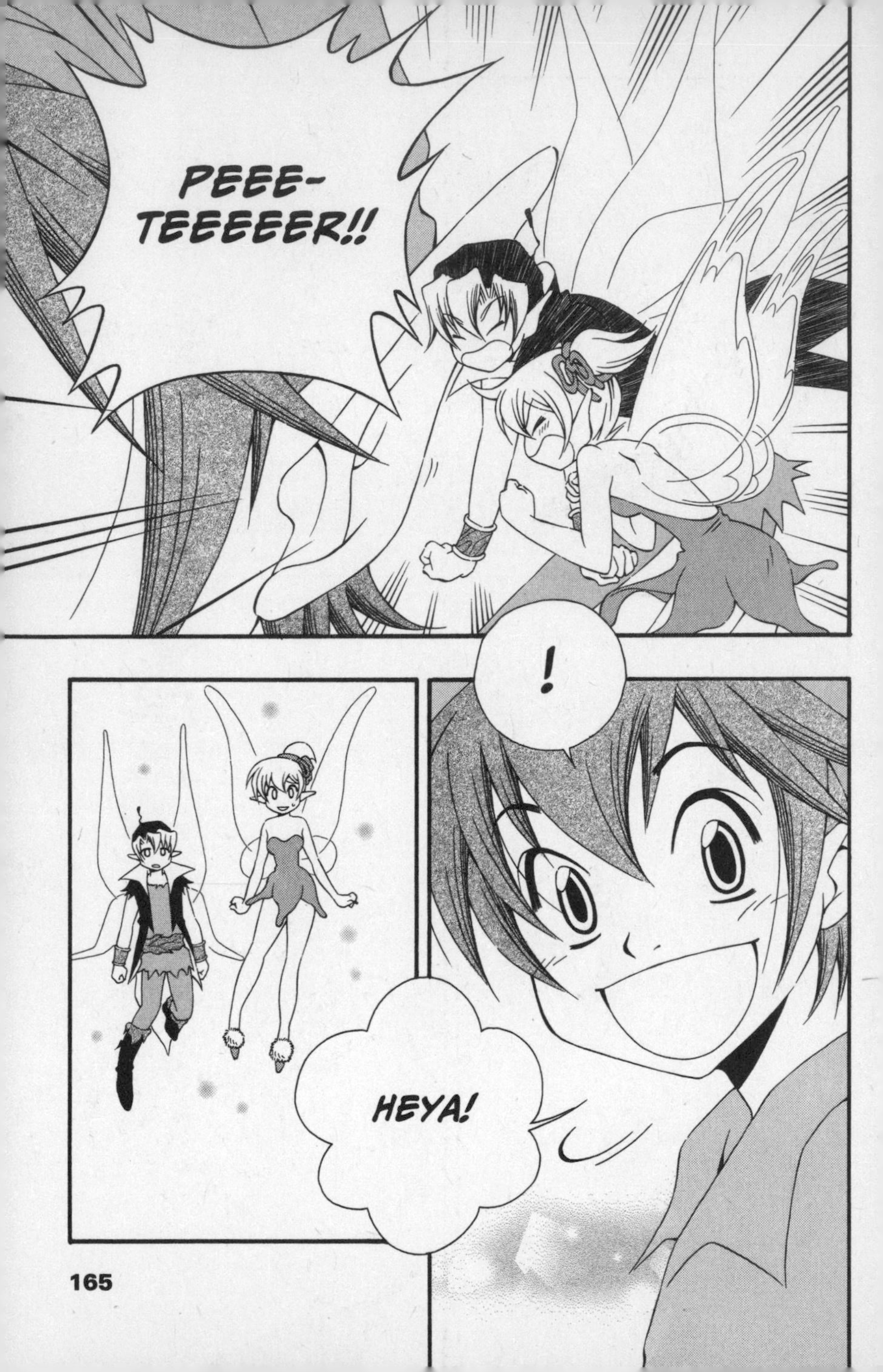
PEEEE-TEEEEEER!!
!
HEYA!

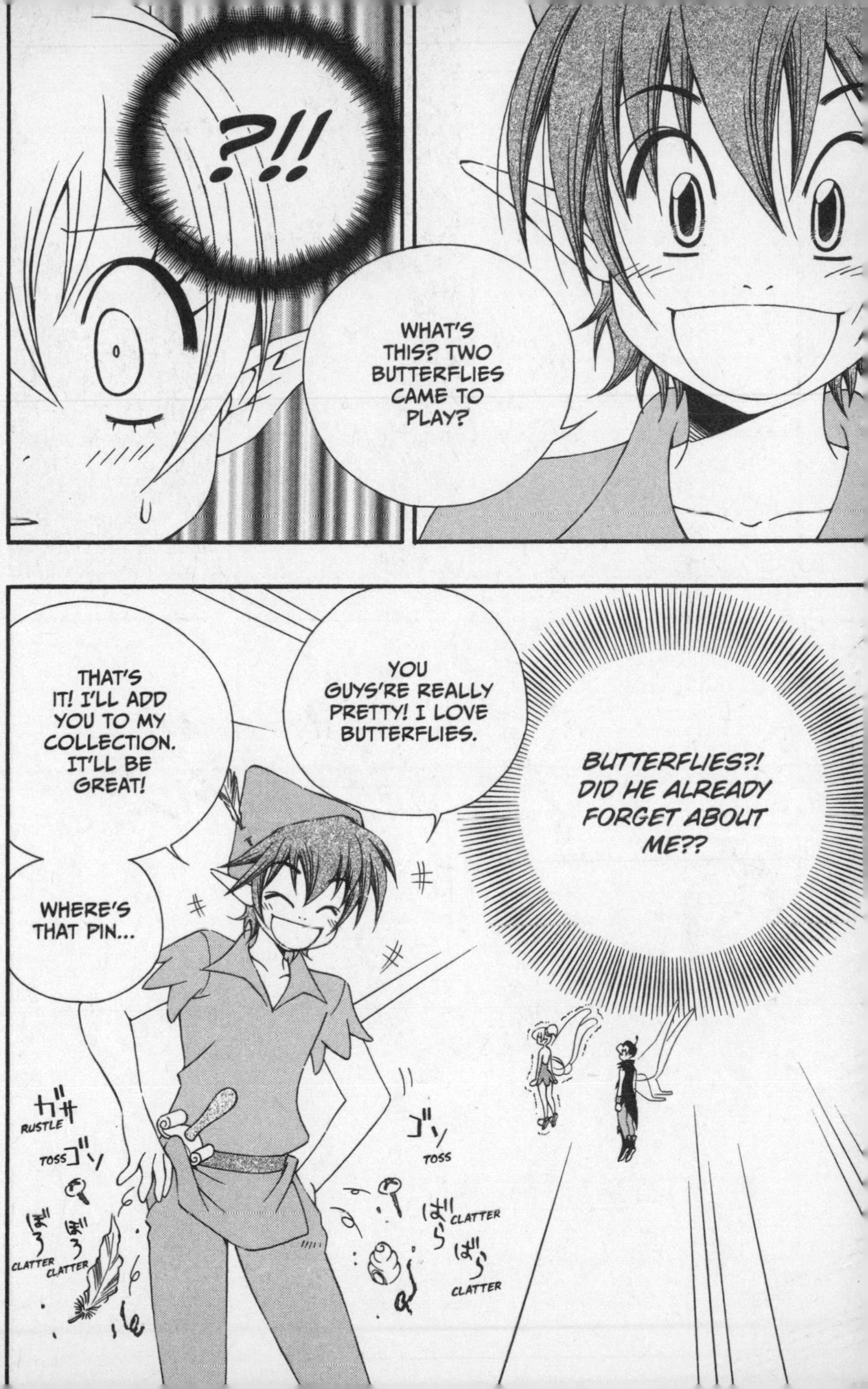
WHAT'S THIS? TWO BUTTERFLIES CAME TO PLAY?
?!!
BUTTERFLIES?! DID HE ALREADY FORGET ABOUT ME??
YOU GUYS'RE REALLY PRETTY! I LOVE BUTTERFLIES.
THAT'S IT! I'LL ADD YOU TO MY COLLECTION. IT'LL BE GREAT!
WHERE'S THAT PIN...
ゴッ TOSS
ばらばら CLATTER CLATTER
ガサ RUSTLE
ゴッ TOSS
ぼろぼろ CLATTER CLATTER

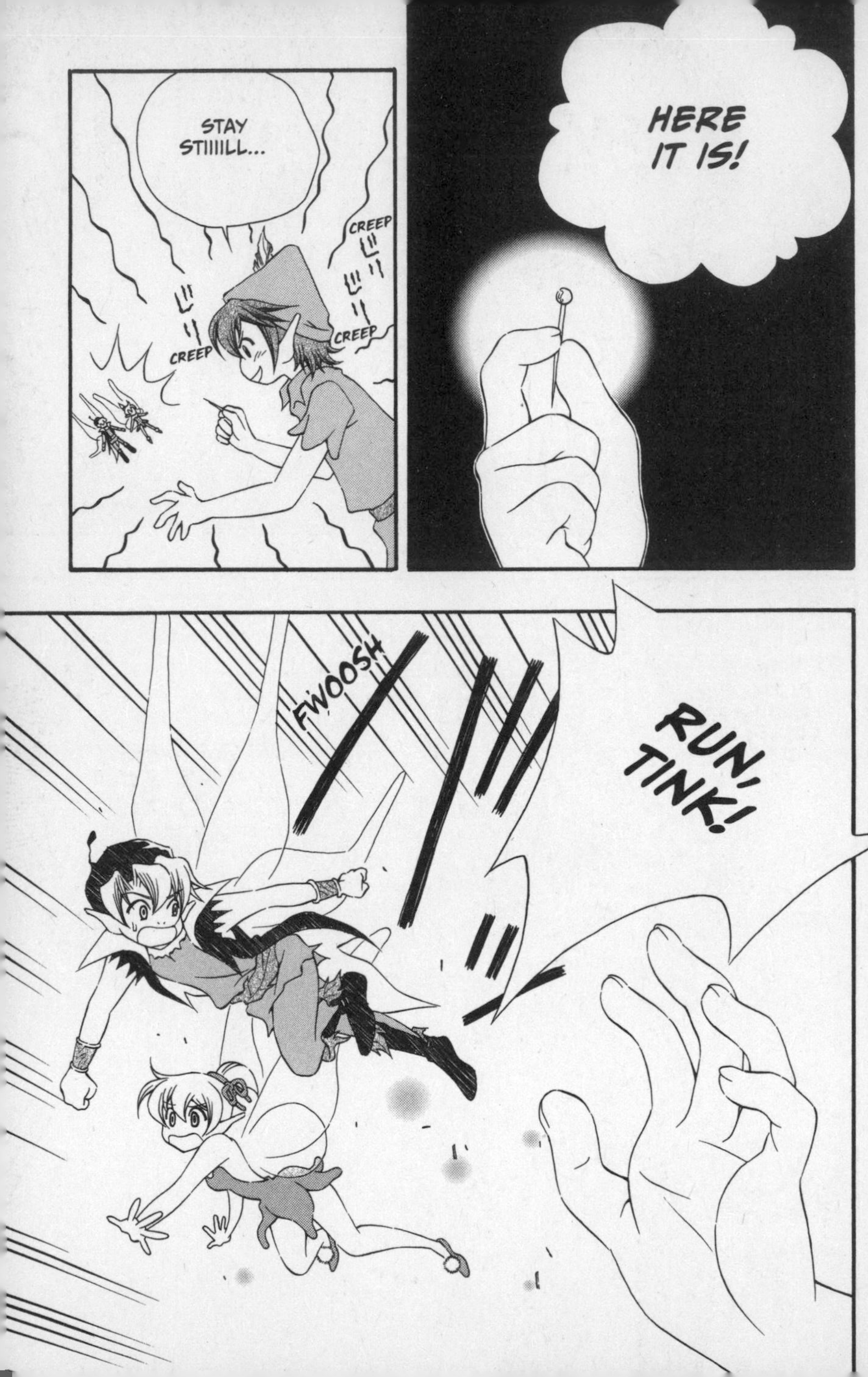
HERE IT IS!
STAY STIIIILL...
CREEP
CREEP
CREEP
RUN, TINK!
FWOOSH

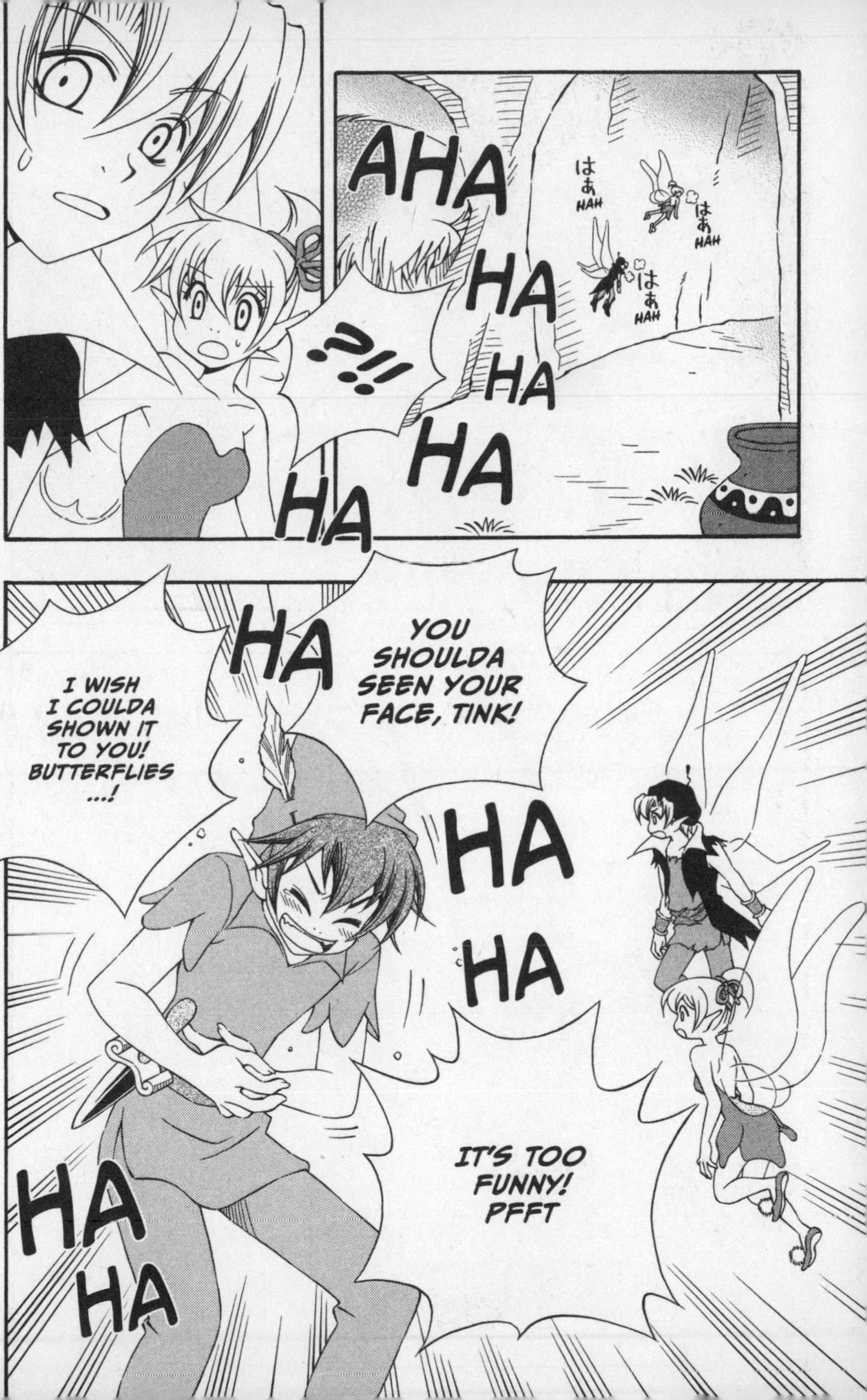
AHA
HA
HA
HA
HA
はあ
HAH
はあ
HAH
はあ
HAH
?!!
HA
YOU SHOULDA SEEN YOUR FACE, TINK!
I WISH I COULDA SHOWN IT TO YOU! BUTTERFLIES ...!
HA
HA
IT'S TOO FUNNY! PFFT
HA
HA

READ THIS WAY

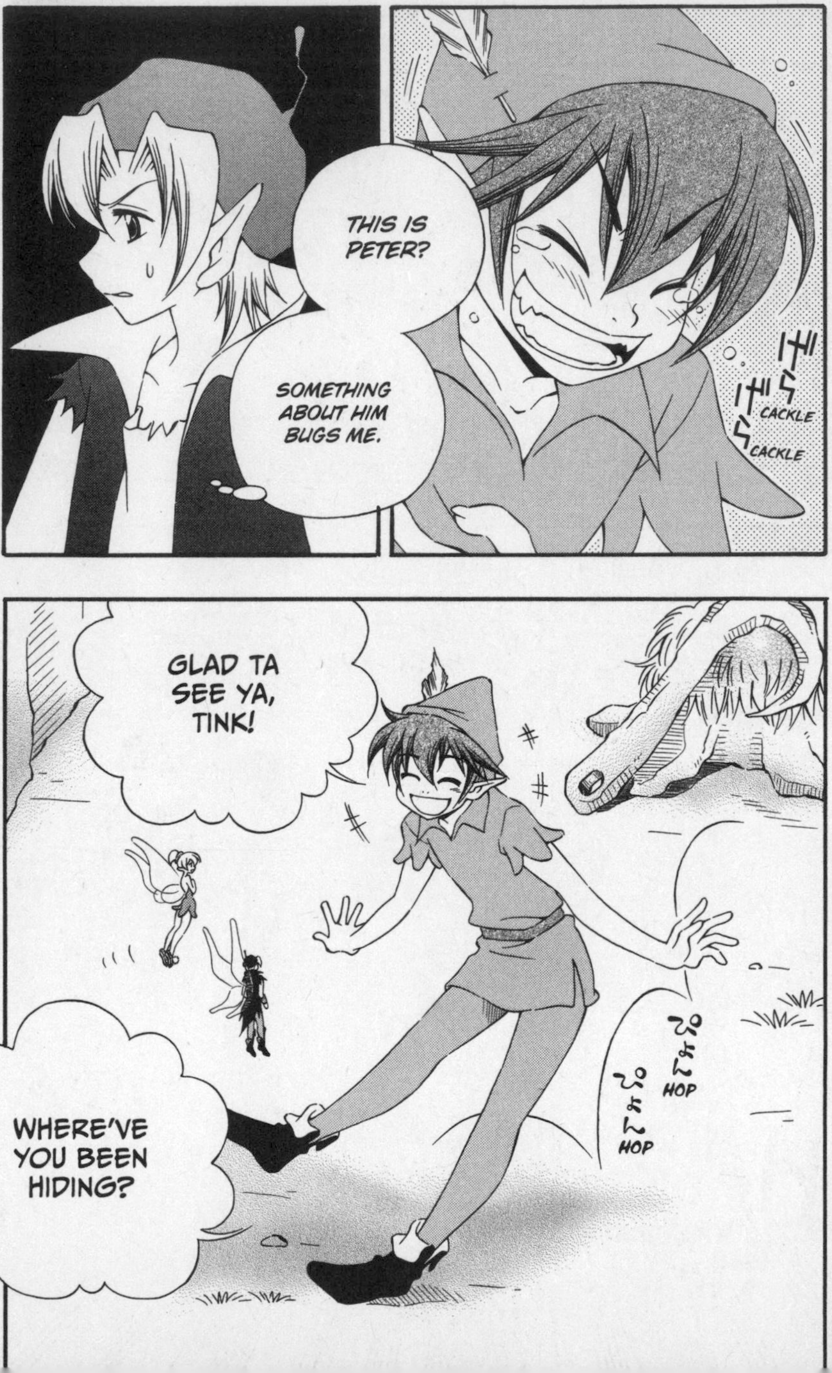
ゲラ CACKLE
ゲラ CACKLE
THIS IS PETER?
SOMETHING ABOUT HIM BUGS ME.
GLAD TA SEE YA, TINK!
ぴょん HOP
ぴょん HOP
WHERE'VE YOU BEEN HIDING?

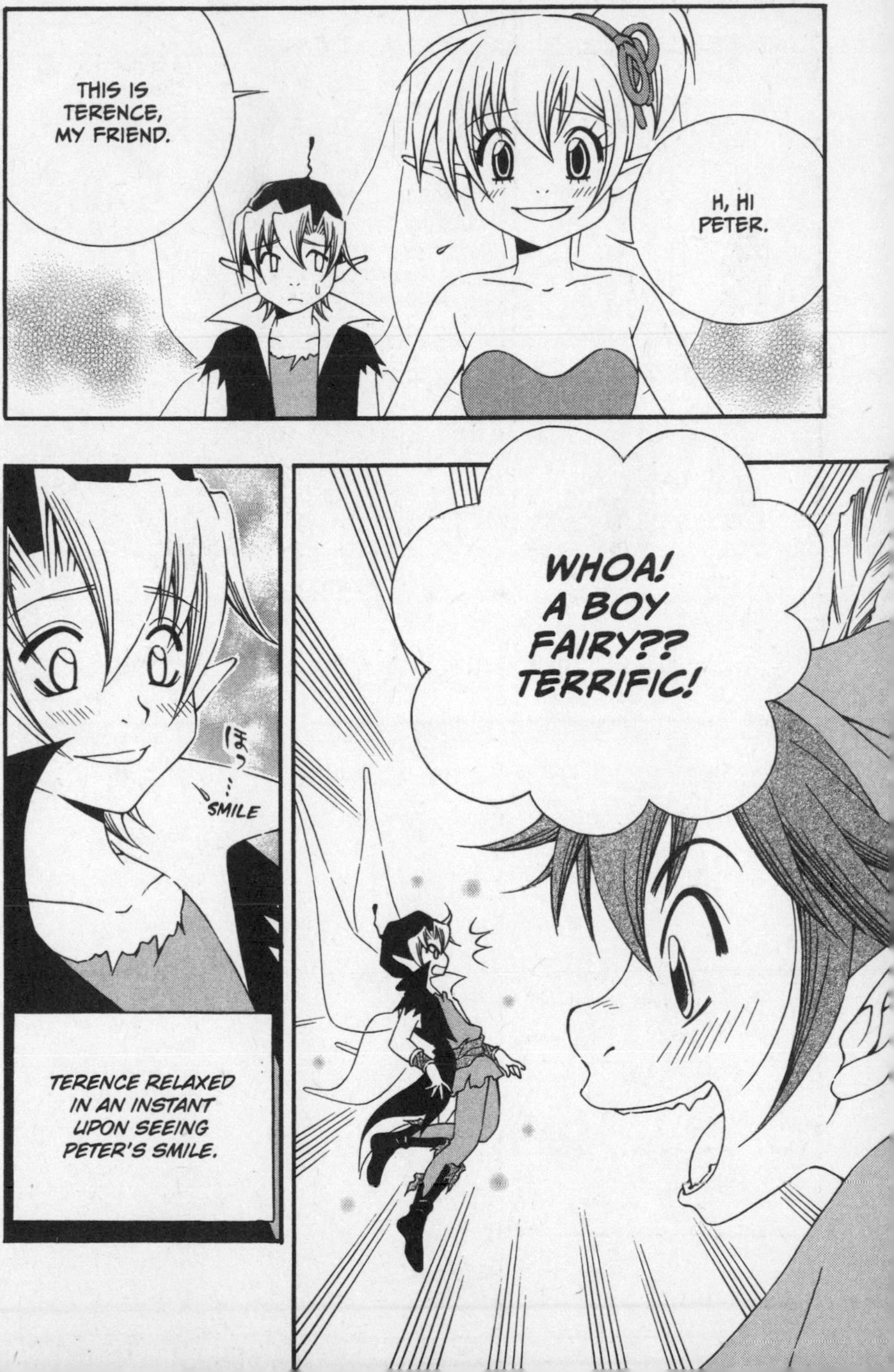
THIS IS TERENCE, MY FRIEND.
H, HI PETER.
WHOA! A BOY FAIRY?? TERRIFIC!
ほっ…
SMILE
TERENCE RELAXED IN AN INSTANT UPON SEEING PETER'S SMILE.

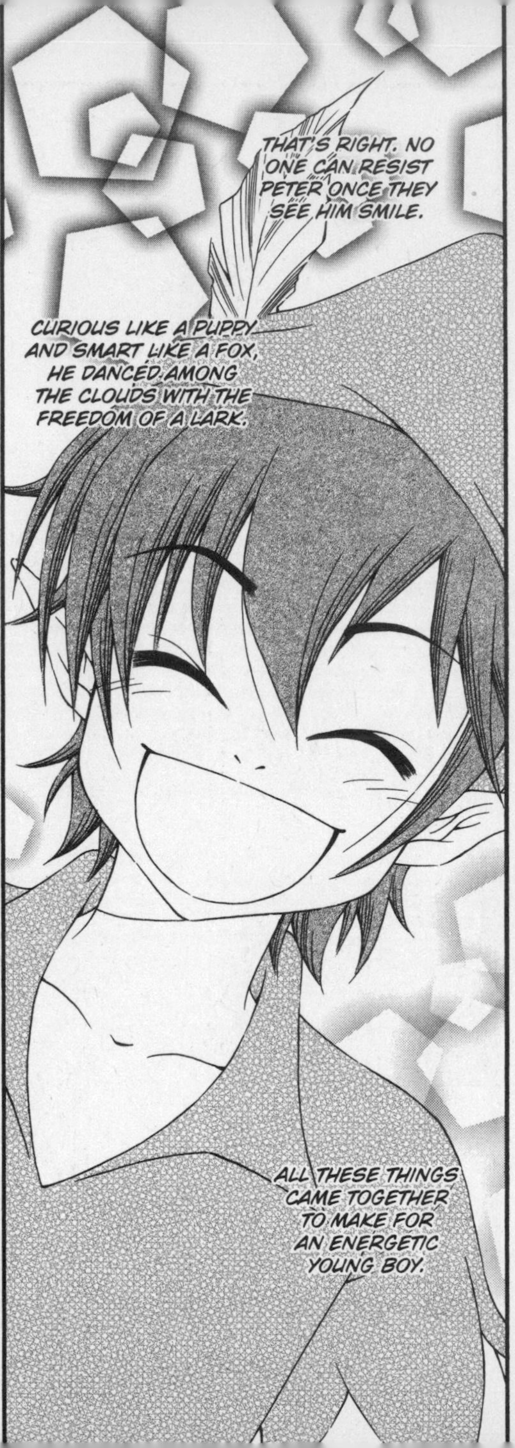
THAT'S RIGHT. NO ONE CAN RESIST PETER ONCE THEY SEE HIM SMILE.
CURIOUS LIKE A PUPPY AND SMART LIKE A FOX, HE DANCED AMONG THE CLOUDS WITH THE FREEDOM OF A LARK.
ALL THESE THINGS CAME TOGETHER TO MAKE FOR AN ENERGETIC YOUNG BOY.

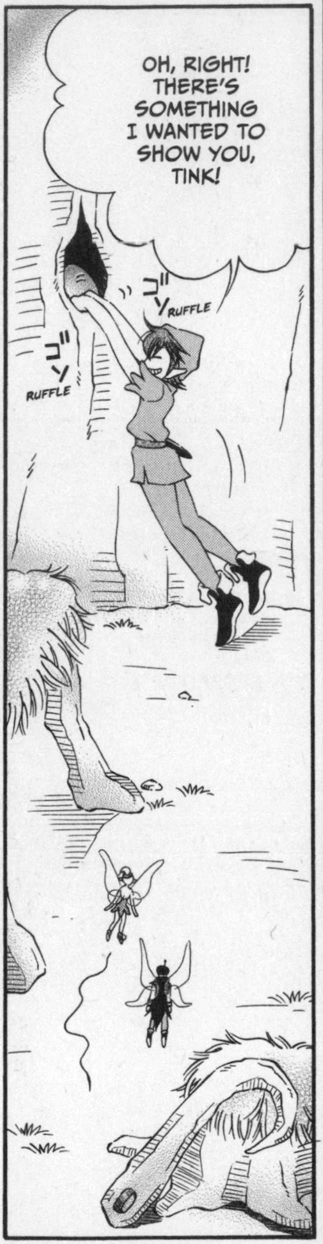
OH, RIGHT! THERE'S SOMETHING I WANTED TO SHOW YOU, TINK!
ゴソ RUFFLE
ゴソ RUFFLE

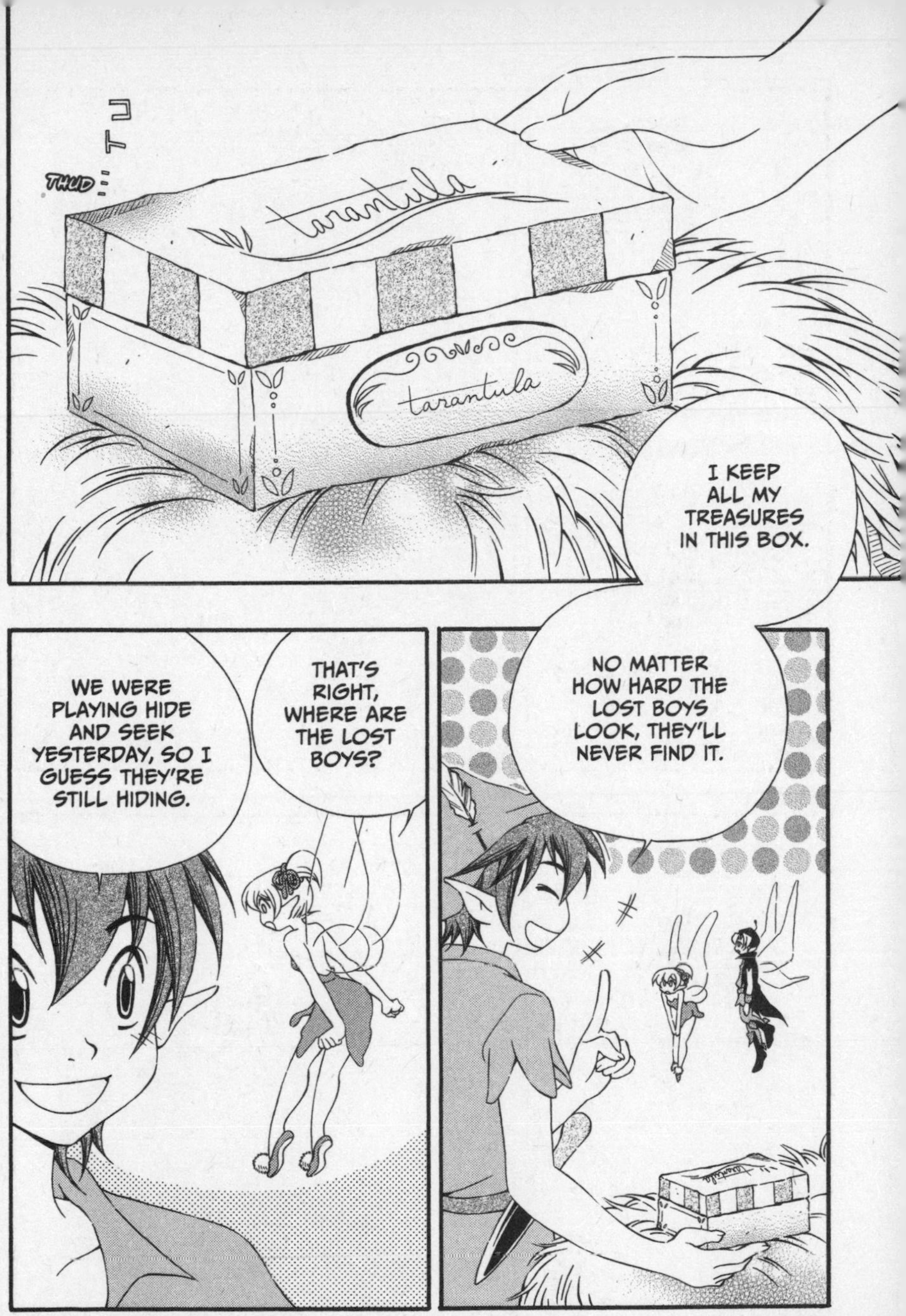
THUD
tarantula
tarantula
I KEEP ALL MY TREASURES IN THIS BOX.
NO MATTER HOW HARD THE LOST BOYS LOOK, THEY'LL NEVER FIND IT.
THAT'S RIGHT, WHERE ARE THE LOST BOYS?
WE WERE PLAYING HIDE AND SEEK YESTERDAY, SO I GUESS THEY'RE STILL HIDING.

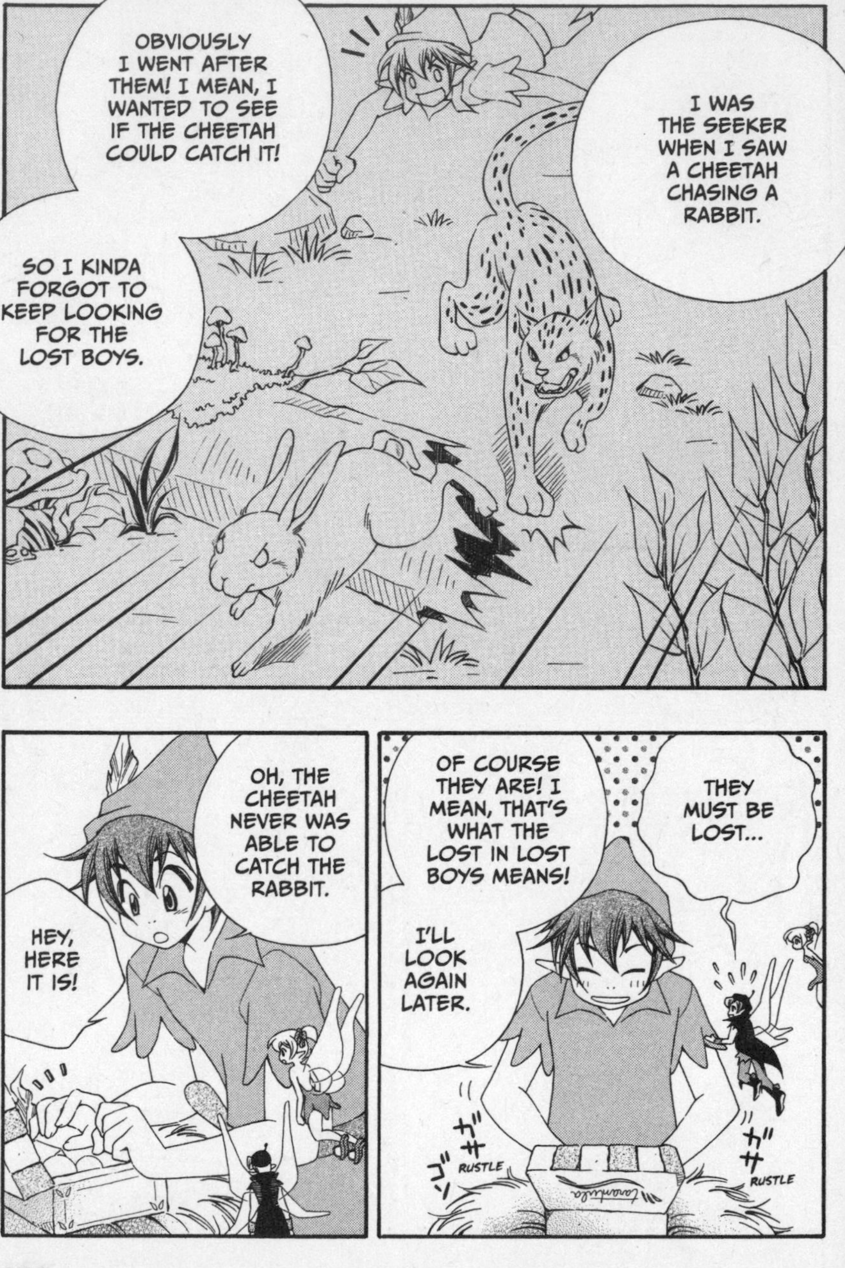
I WAS THE SEEKER WHEN I SAW A CHEETAH CHASING A RABBIT.
OBVIOUSLY I WENT AFTER THEM! I MEAN, I WANTED TO SEE IF THE CHEETAH COULD CATCH IT!
SO I KINDA FORGOT TO KEEP LOOKING FOR THE LOST BOYS.
THEY MUST BE LOST...
OF COURSE THEY ARE! I MEAN, THAT'S WHAT THE LOST IN LOST BOYS MEANS!
I'LL LOOK AGAIN LATER.
ガサ RUSTLE
ゴソ
ガサ RUSTLE
OH, THE CHEETAH NEVER WAS ABLE TO CATCH THE RABBIT.
HEY, HERE IT IS!

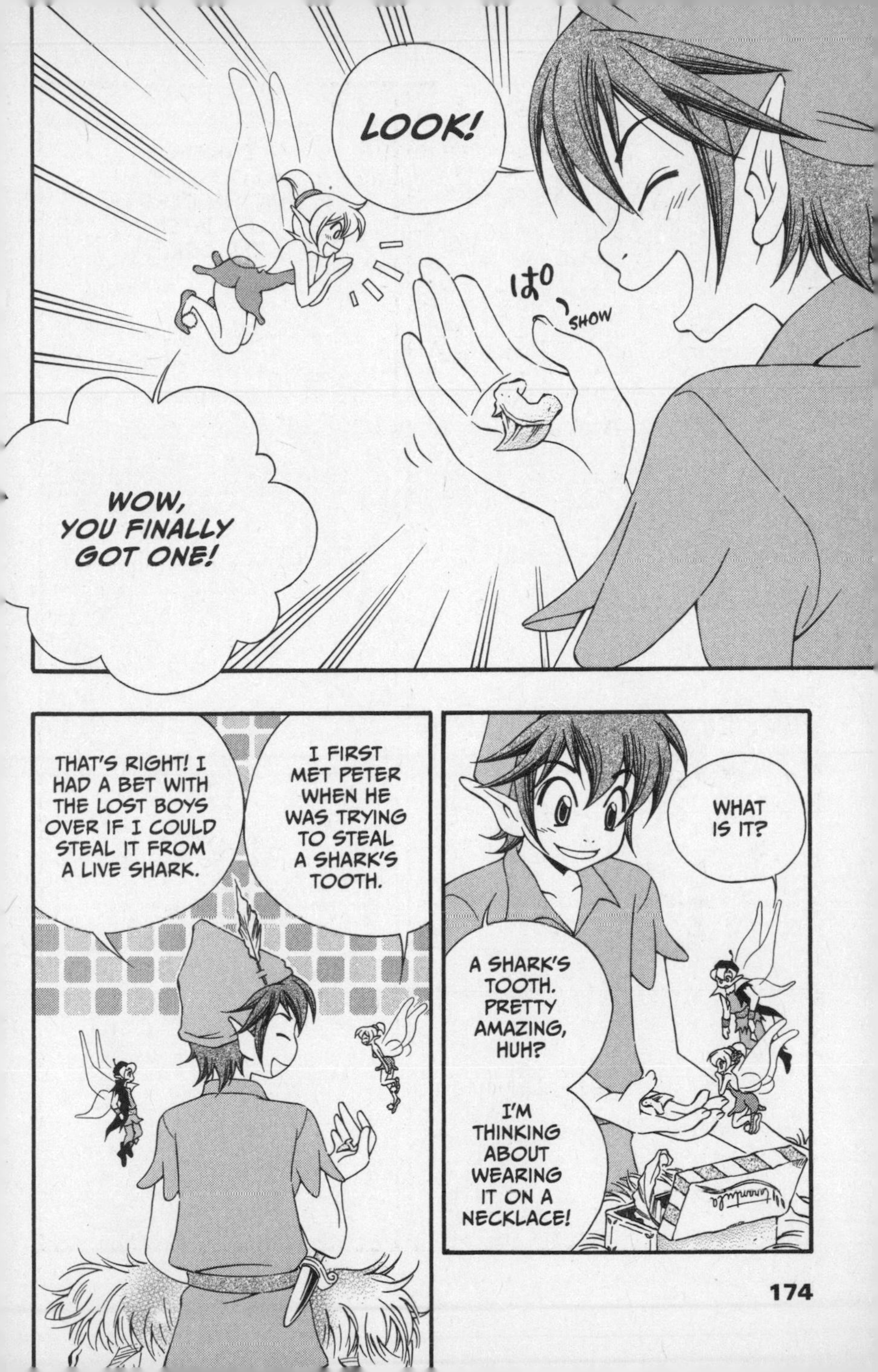
LOOK!
ぱっ SHOW
WOW, YOU FINALLY GOT ONE!
WHAT IS IT?
A SHARK'S TOOTH. PRETTY AMAZING, HUH?
I'M THINKING ABOUT WEARING IT ON A NECKLACE!
I FIRST MET PETER WHEN HE WAS TRYING TO STEAL A SHARK'S TOOTH.
THAT'S RIGHT! I HAD A BET WITH THE LOST BOYS OVER IF I COULD STEAL IT FROM A LIVE SHARK.

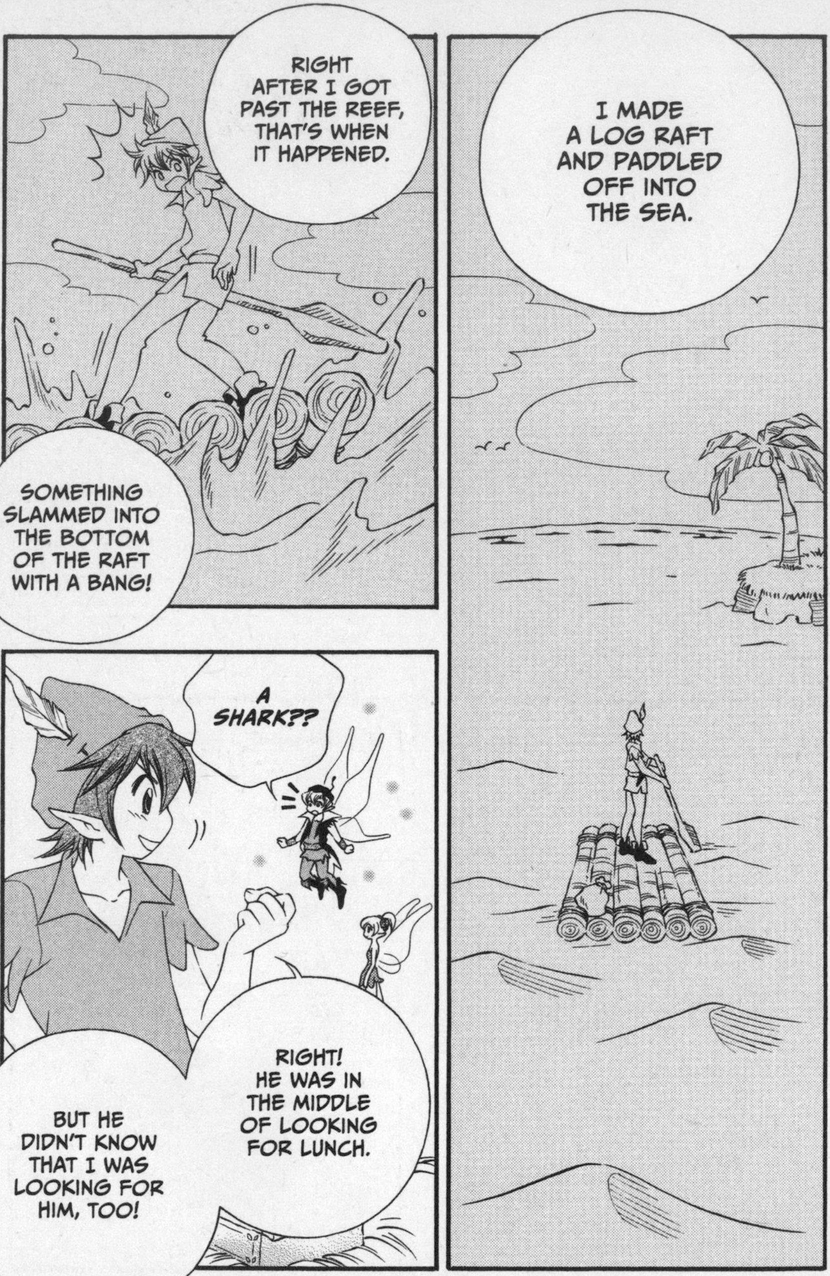
I MADE A LOG RAFT AND PADDLED OFF INTO THE SEA.
RIGHT AFTER I GOT PAST THE REEF, THAT'S WHEN IT HAPPENED.
SOMETHING SLAMMED INTO THE BOTTOM OF THE RAFT WITH A BANG!
A SHARK??
RIGHT! HE WAS IN THE MIDDLE OF LOOKING FOR LUNCH.
BUT HE DIDN'T KNOW THAT I WAS LOOKING FOR HIM, TOO!

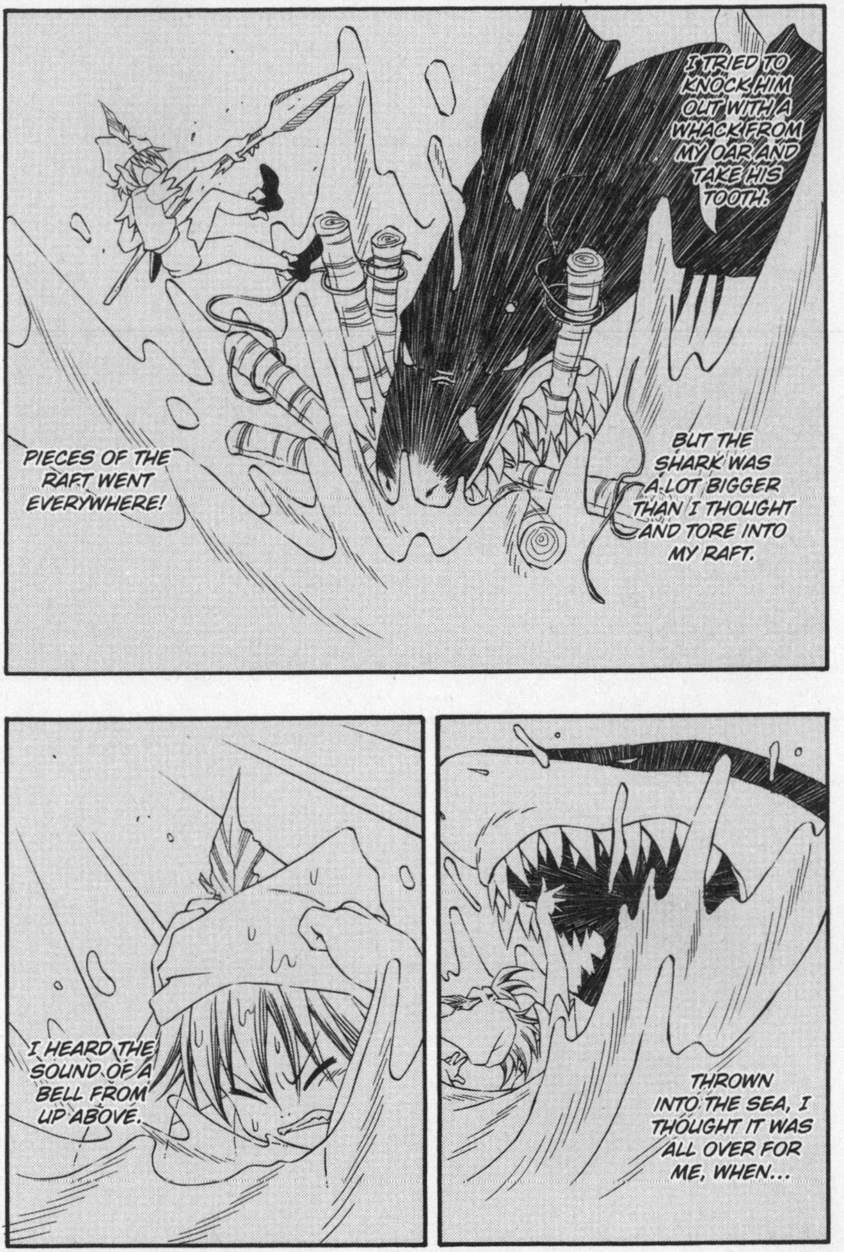
I TRIED TO KNOCK HIM OUT WITH A WHACK FROM MY OAR AND TAKE HIS TOOTH.
BUT THE SHARK WAS A LOT BIGGER THAN I THOUGHT AND TORE INTO MY RAFT.
PIECES OF THE RAFT WENT EVERYWHERE!
THROWN INTO THE SEA, I THOUGHT IT WAS ALL OVER FOR ME, WHEN...
I HEARD THE SOUND OF A BELL FROM UP ABOVE.

READ THIS WAY

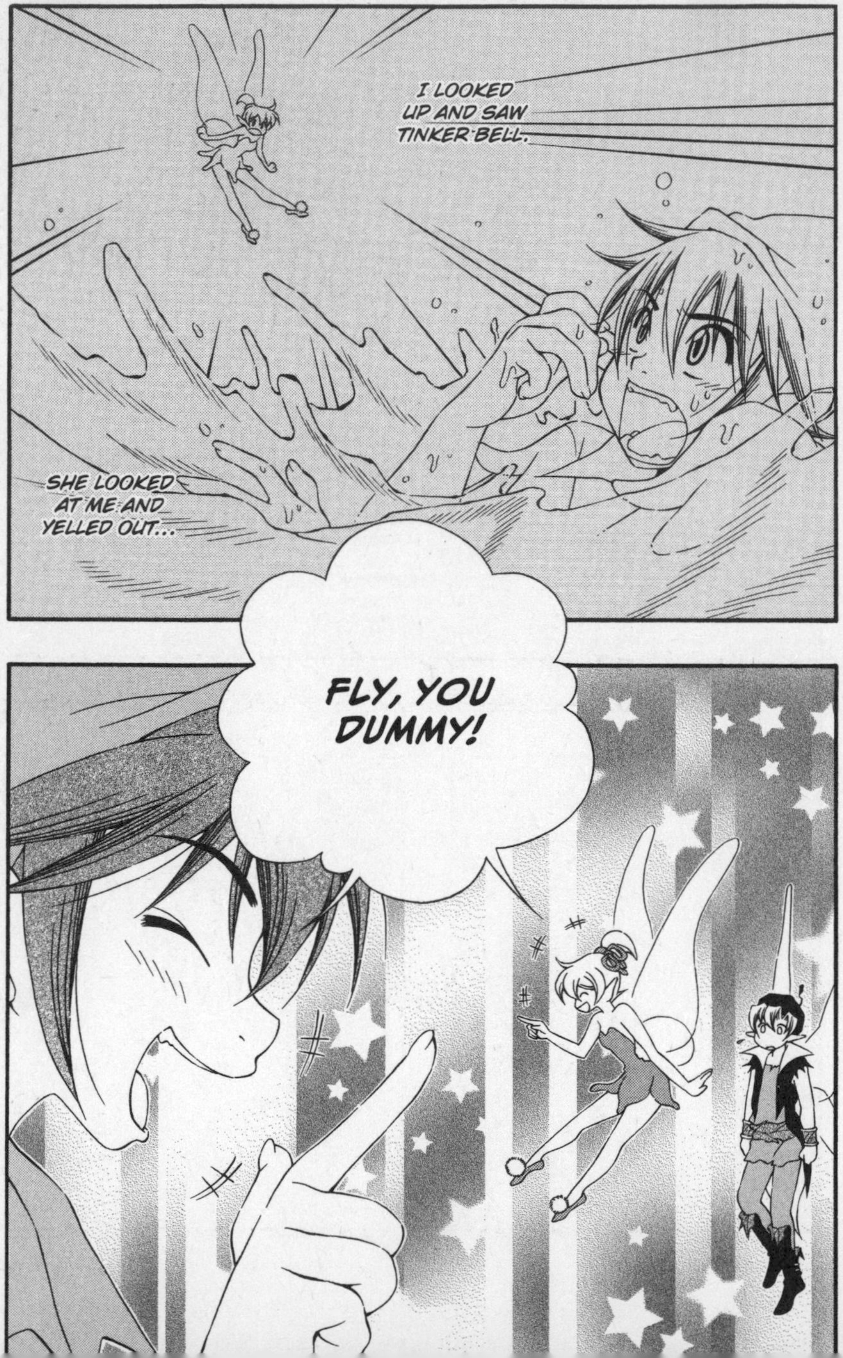
I LOOKED UP AND SAW TINKER BELL.
SHE LOOKED AT ME AND YELLED OUT...
FLY, YOU DUMMY!

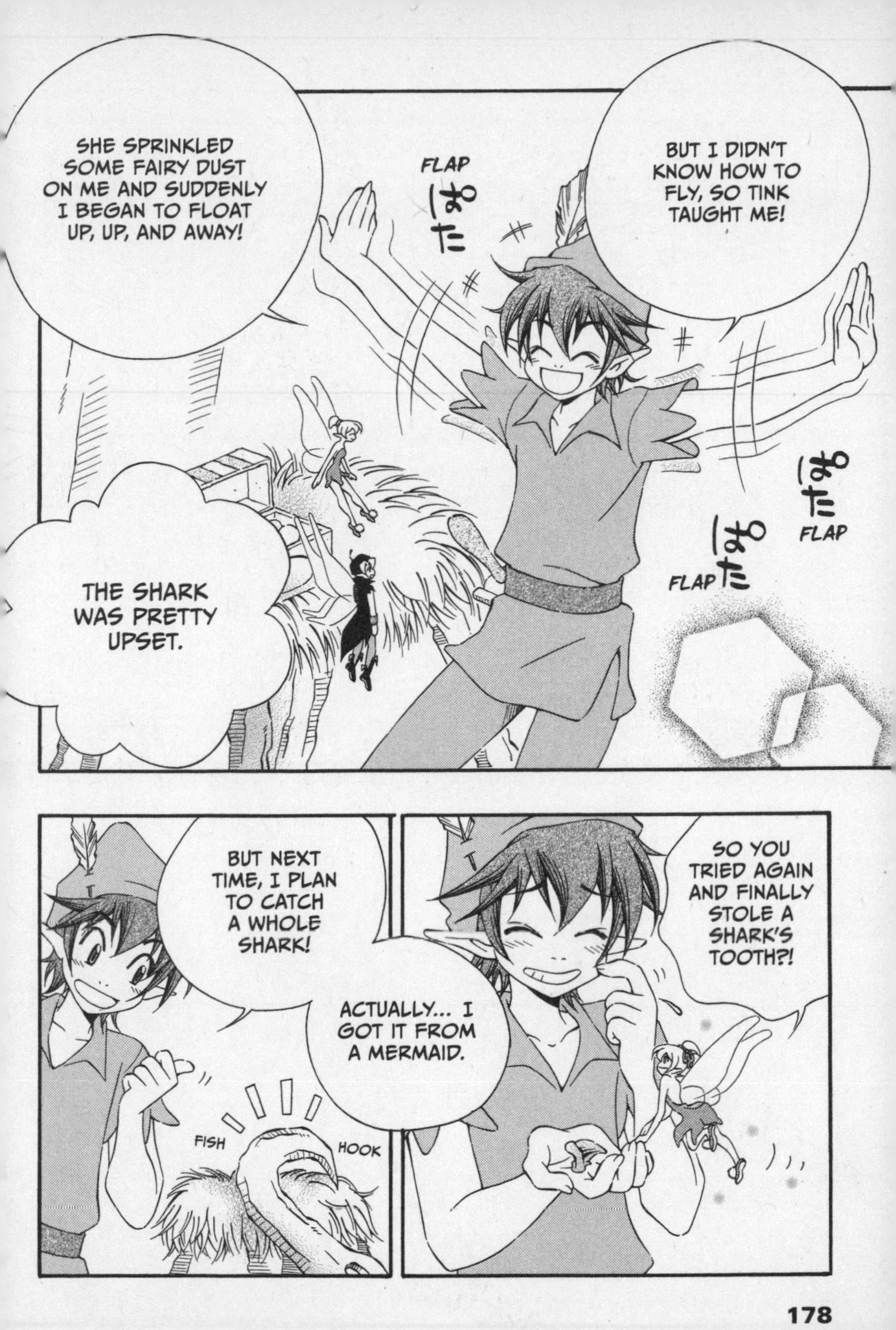
SHE SPRINKLED SOME FAIRY DUST ON ME AND SUDDENLY I BEGAN TO FLOAT UP, UP, AND AWAY!
BUT I DIDN'T KNOW HOW TO FLY, SO TINK TAUGHT ME!
ぱた FLAP
ぱた FLAP
ぱた FLAP
THE SHARK WAS PRETTY UPSET.
SO YOU TRIED AGAIN AND FINALLY STOLE A SHARK'S TOOTH?!
ACTUALLY... I GOT IT FROM A MERMAID.
BUT NEXT TIME, I PLAN TO CATCH A WHOLE SHARK!
FISH
HOOK

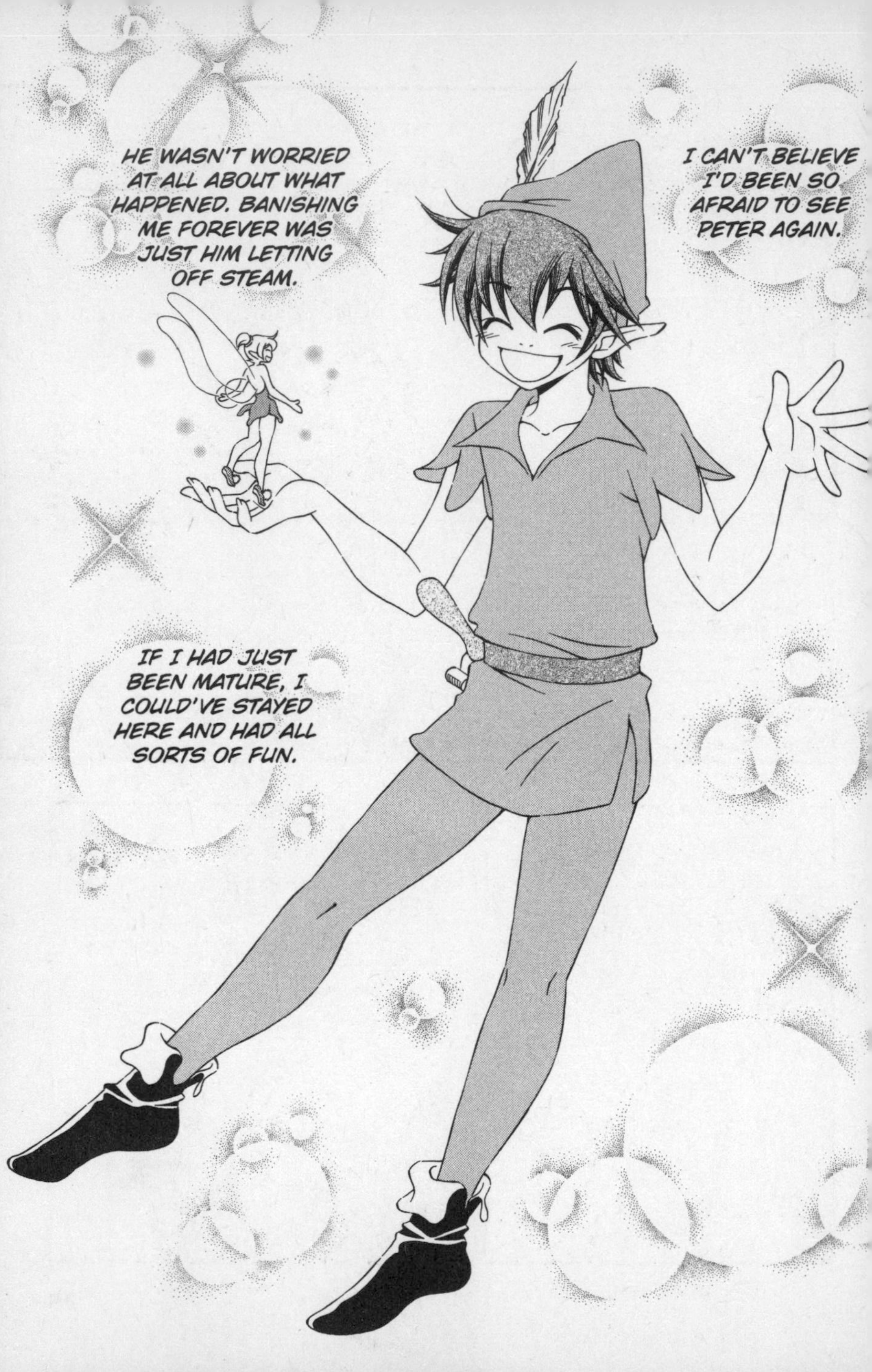
I CAN'T BELIEVE I'D BEEN SO AFRAID TO SEE PETER AGAIN.
HE WASN'T WORRIED AT ALL ABOUT WHAT HAPPENED. BANISHING ME FOREVER WAS JUST HIM LETTING OFF STEAM.
IF I HAD JUST BEEN MATURE, I COULD'VE STAYED HERE AND HAD ALL SORTS OF FUN.

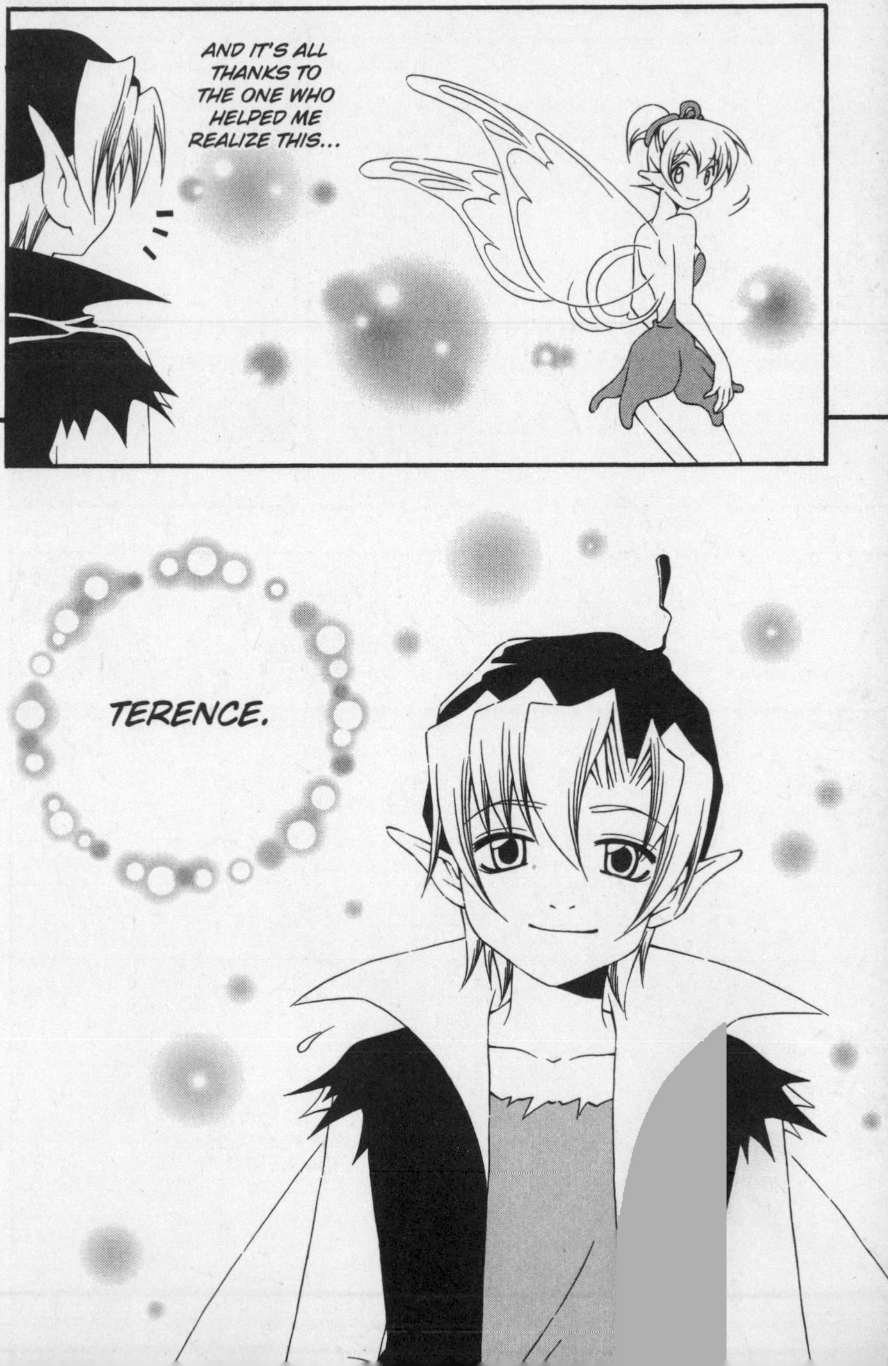
AND IT'S ALL THANKS TO THE ONE WHO HELPED ME REALIZE THIS...
TERENCE.

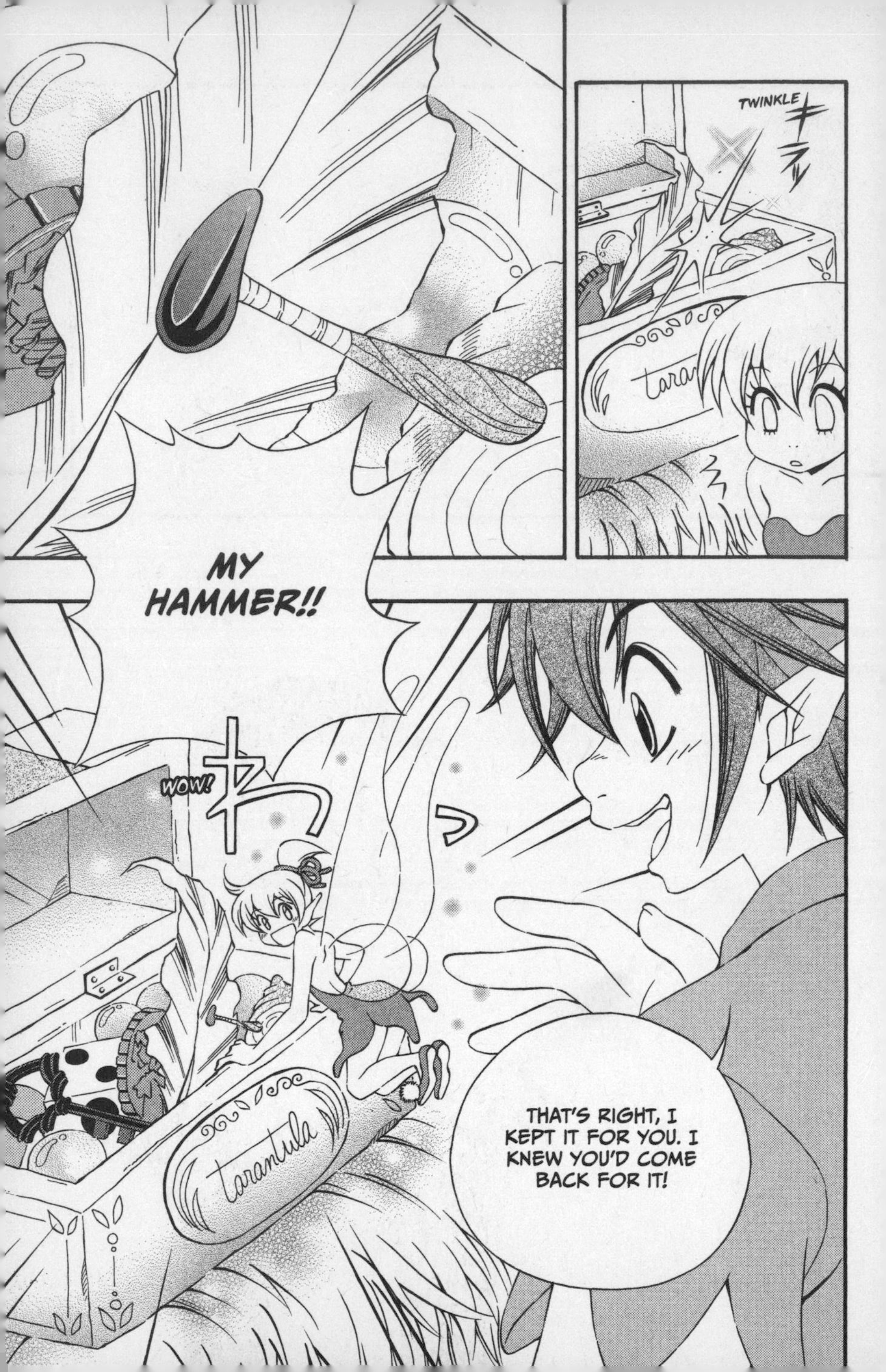
TWINKLE キラッ
MY HAMMER!!
WOW! わっ
tarantula
THAT'S RIGHT, I KEPT IT FOR YOU. I KNEW YOU'D COME BACK FOR IT!

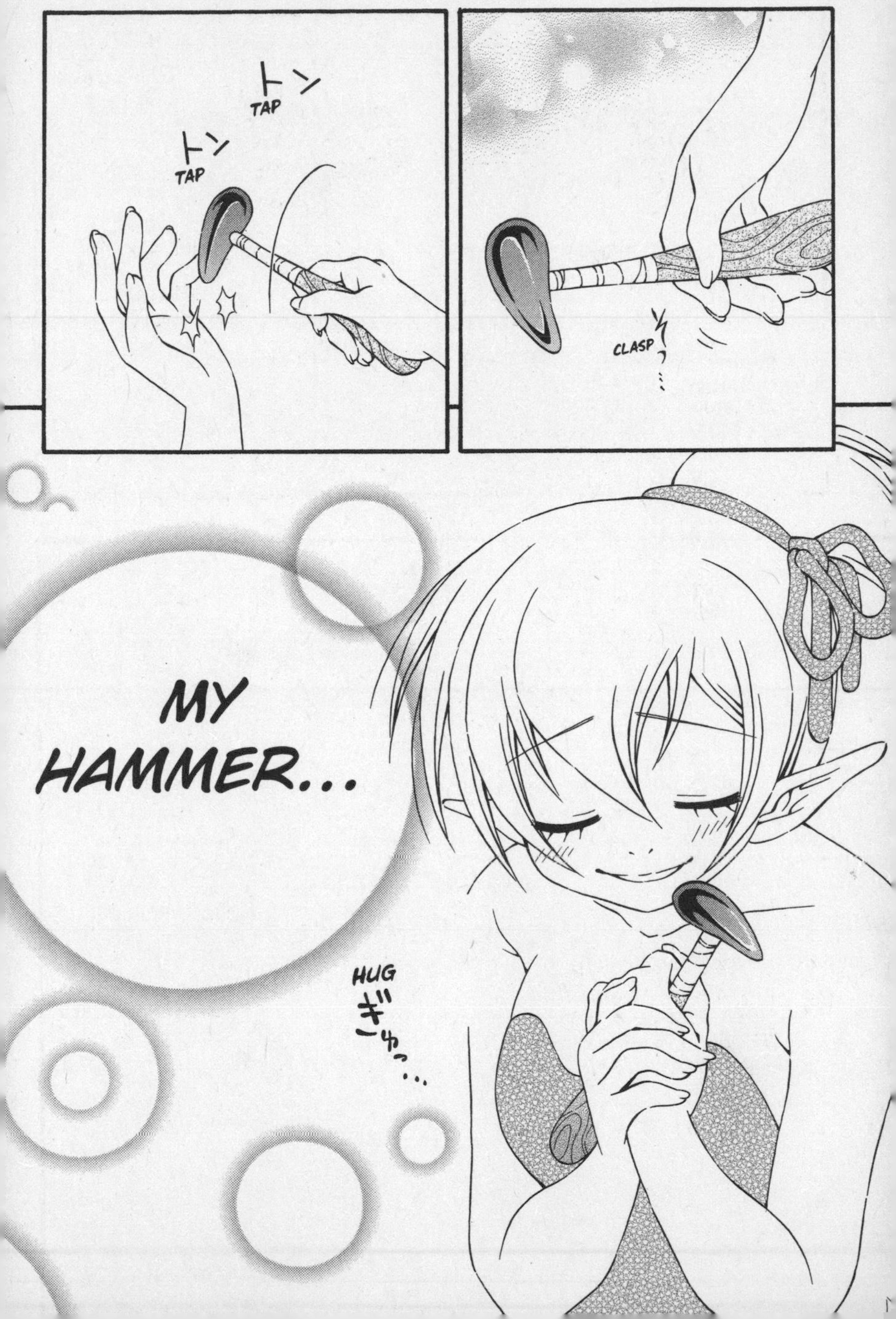
CLASP
トン
TAP
トン
TAP
MY HAMMER...
HUG
ぎゅっ...

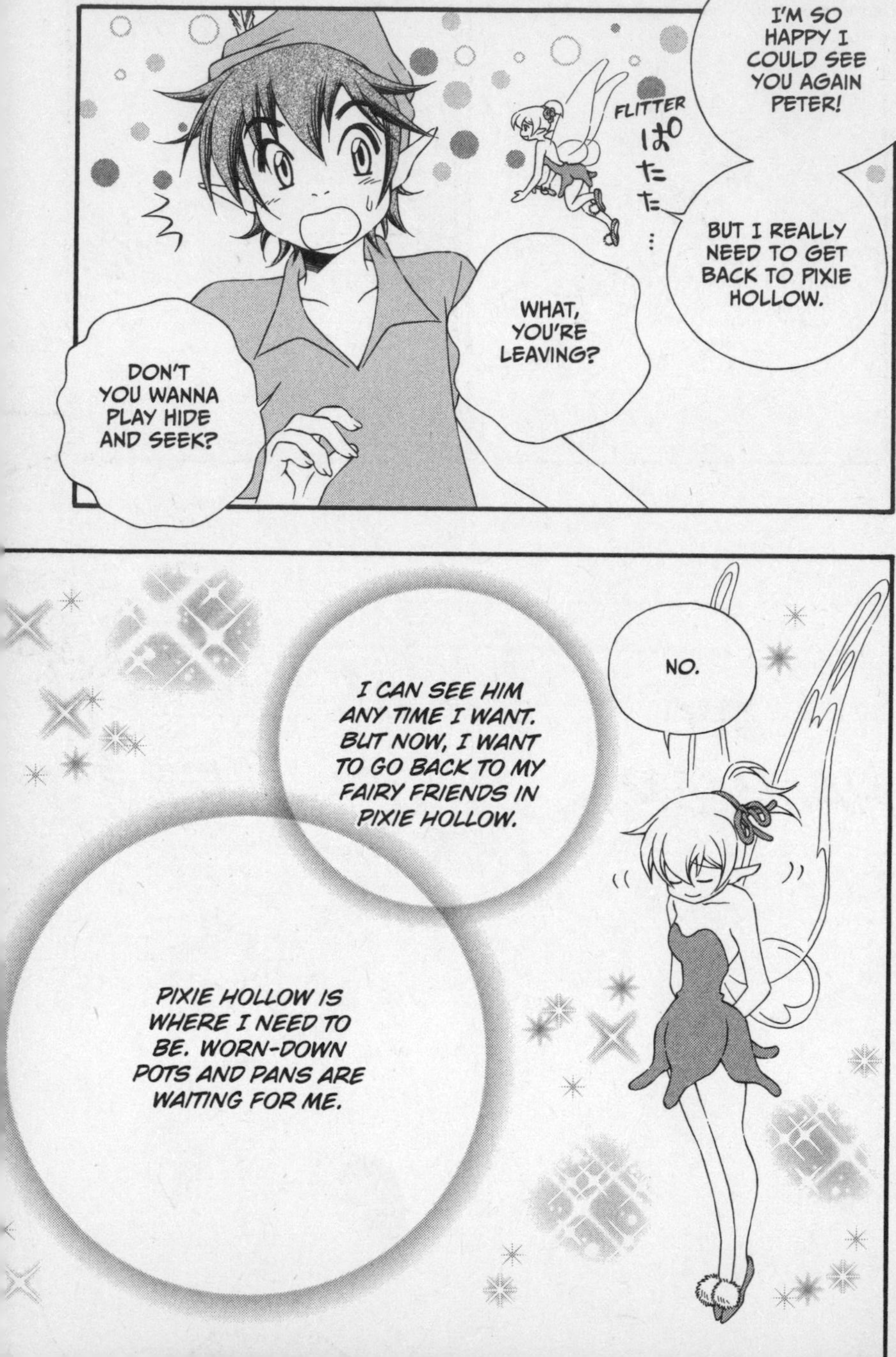
I'M SO HAPPY I COULD SEE YOU AGAIN PETER!
BUT I REALLY NEED TO GET BACK TO PIXIE HOLLOW.
FLITTER
ぱたた…
WHAT, YOU'RE LEAVING?
DON'T YOU WANNA PLAY HIDE AND SEEK?
NO.
I CAN SEE HIM ANY TIME I WANT. BUT NOW, I WANT TO GO BACK TO MY FAIRY FRIENDS IN PIXIE HOLLOW.
PIXIE HOLLOW IS WHERE I NEED TO BE. WORN-DOWN POTS AND PANS ARE WAITING FOR ME.

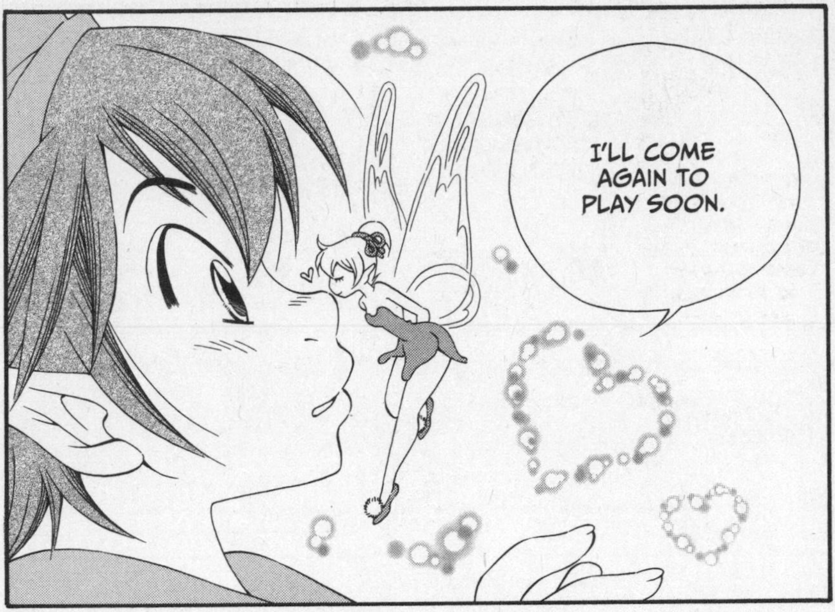
I'LL COME AGAIN TO PLAY SOON.

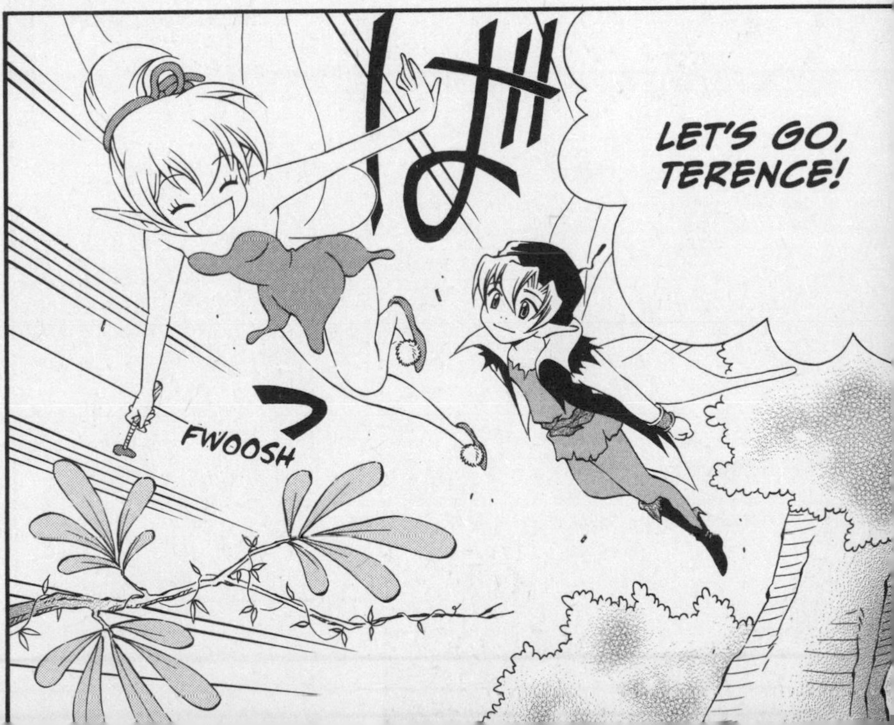
LET'S GO, TERENCE!
FWOOSH

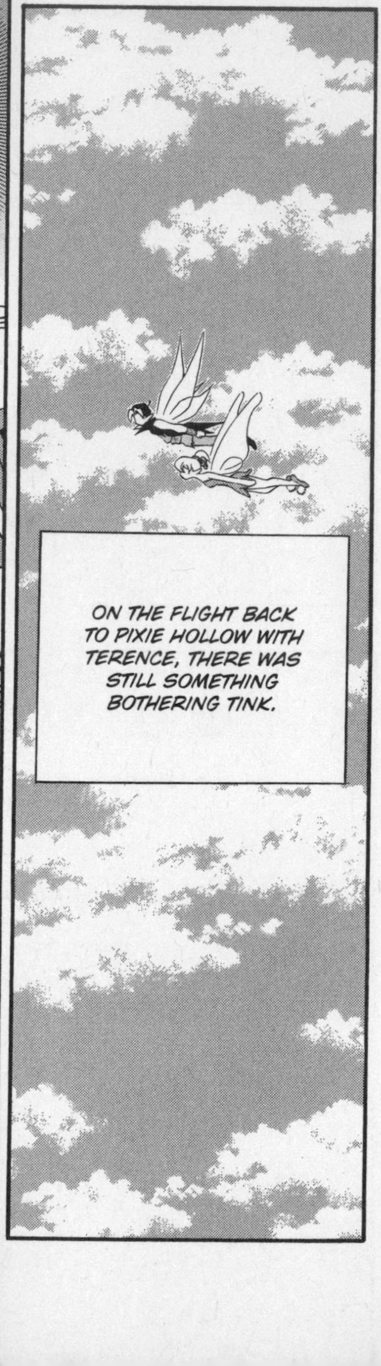
ON THE FLIGHT BACK TO PIXIE HOLLOW WITH TERENCE, THERE WAS STILL SOMETHING BOTHERING TINK.
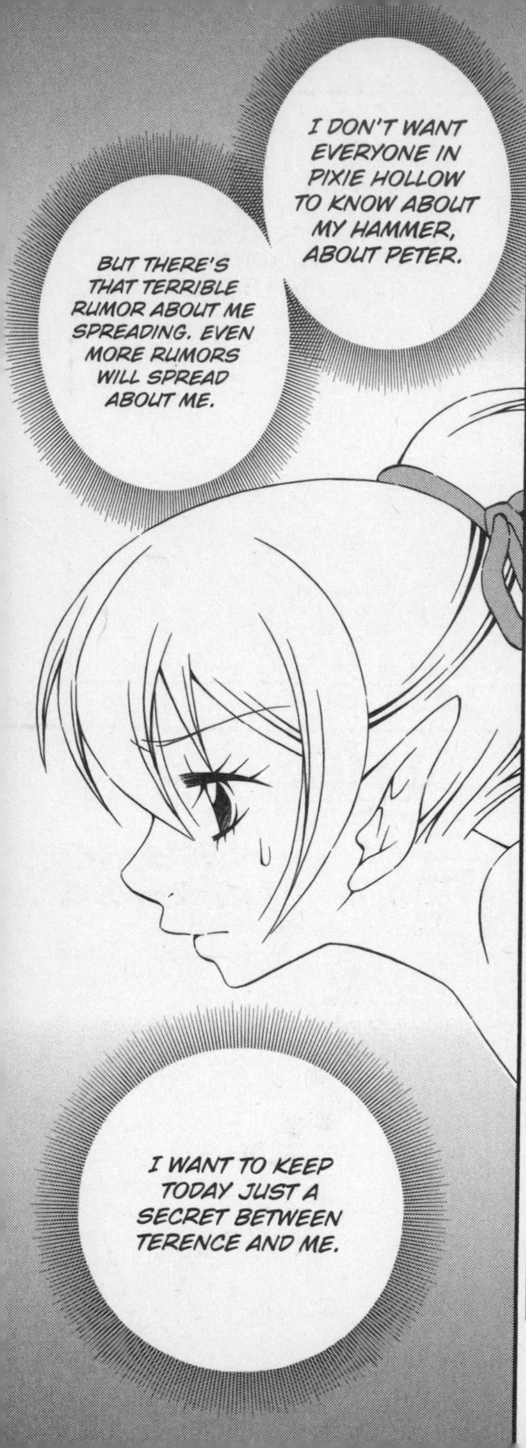
I DON'T WANT EVERYONE IN PIXIE HOLLOW TO KNOW ABOUT MY HAMMER, ABOUT PETER.
BUT THERE'S THAT TERRIBLE RUMOR ABOUT ME SPREADING. EVEN MORE RUMORS WILL SPREAD ABOUT ME.
I WANT TO KEEP TODAY JUST A SECRET BETWEEN TERENCE AND ME.

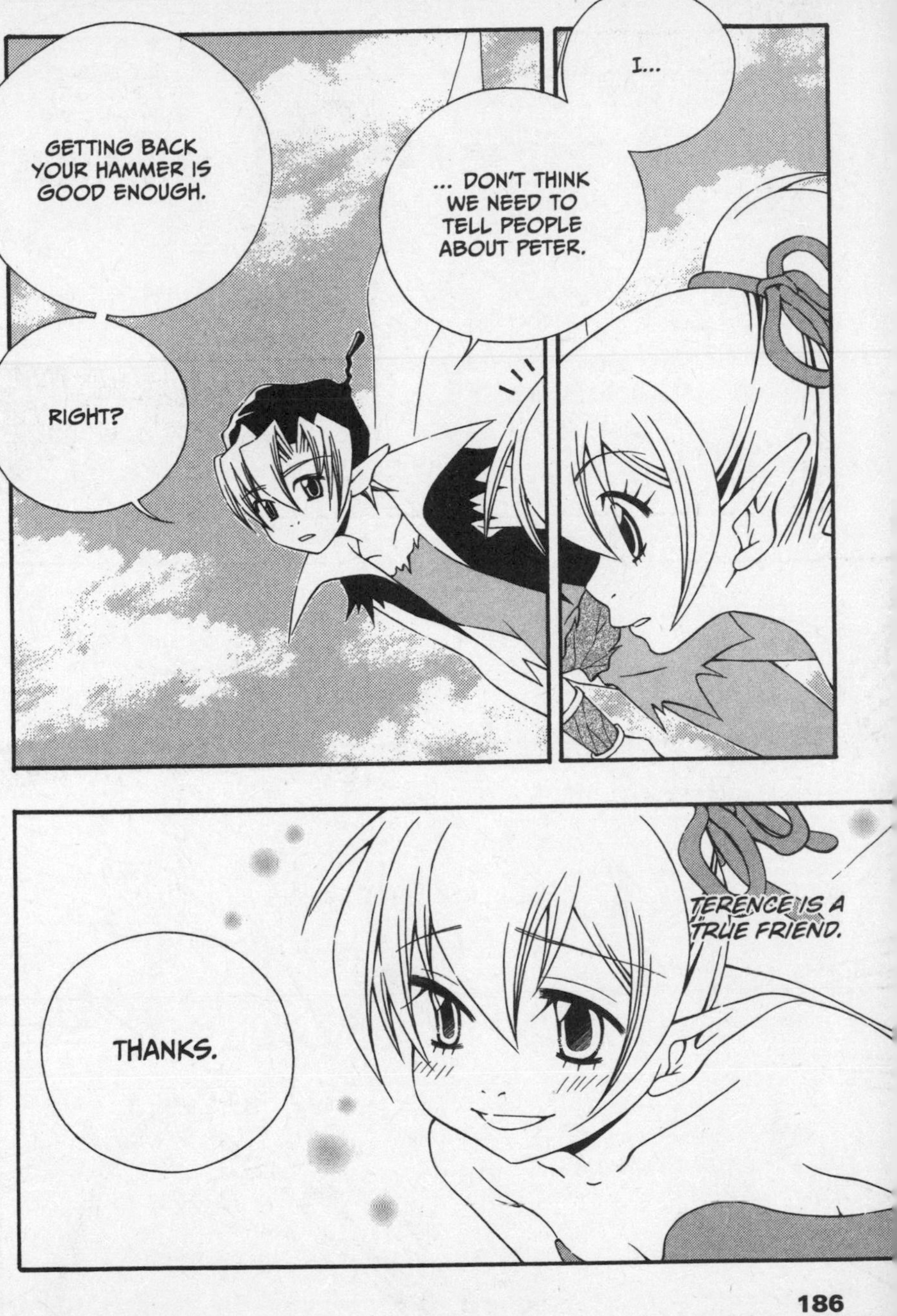
I...
... DON'T THINK WE NEED TO TELL PEOPLE ABOUT PETER.
GETTING BACK YOUR HAMMER IS GOOD ENOUGH.
RIGHT?
TERENCE IS A TRUE FRIEND.
THANKS.

READ THIS WAY

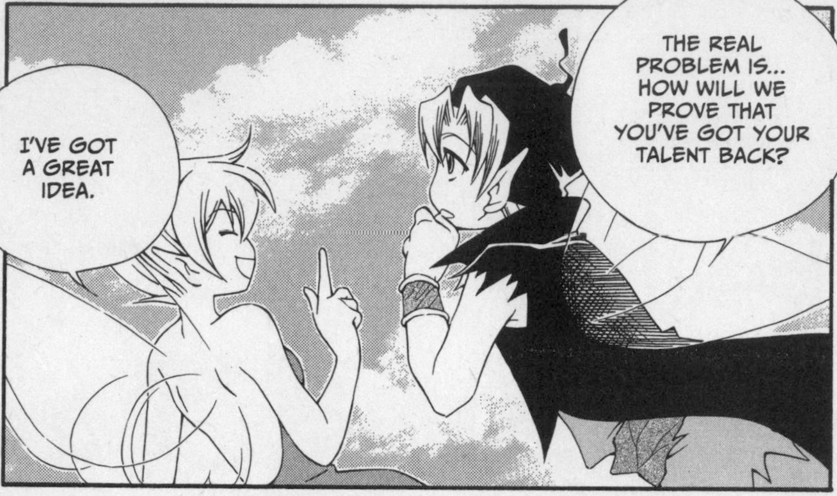
THE REAL PROBLEM IS... HOW WILL WE PROVE THAT YOU'VE GOT YOUR TALENT BACK?
I'VE GOT A GREAT IDEA.

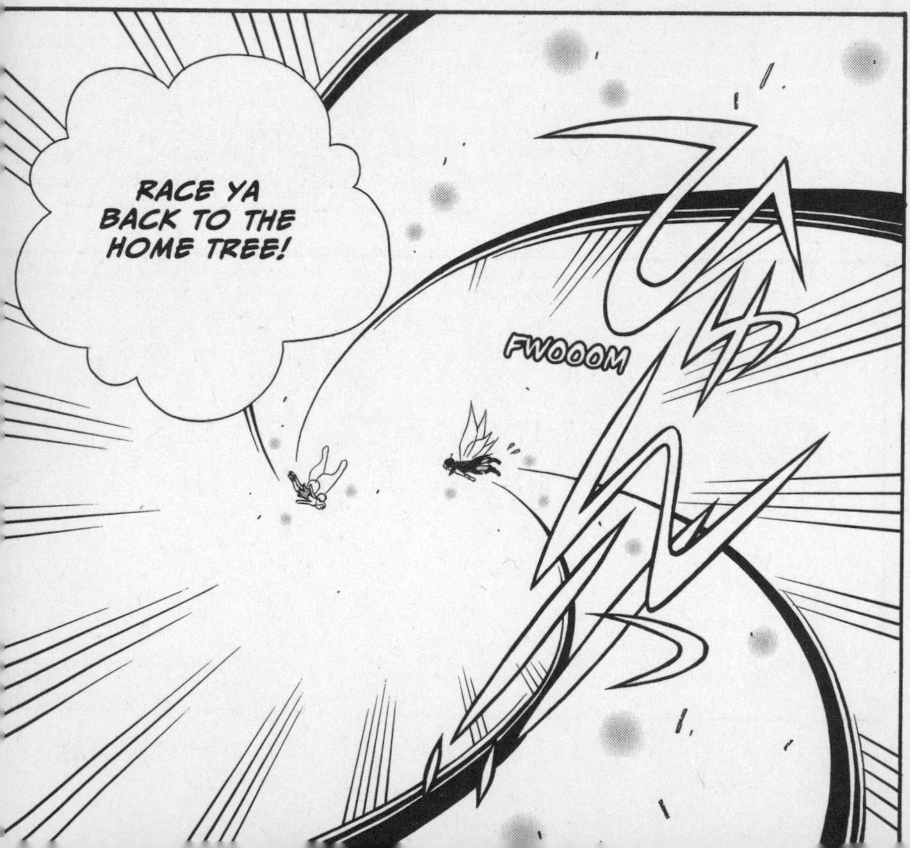
RACE YA BACK TO THE HOME TREE!
FWOOOM

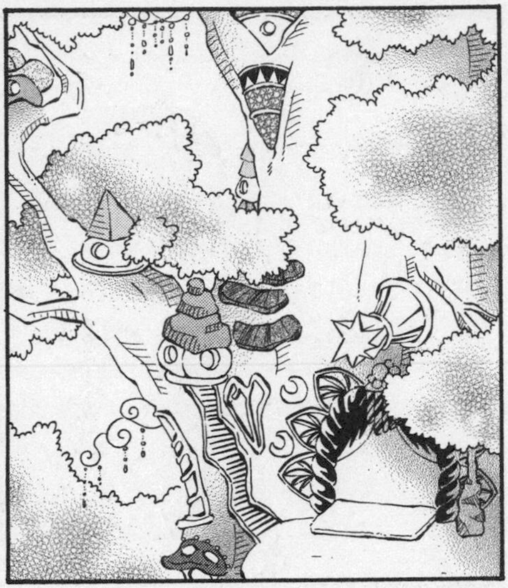

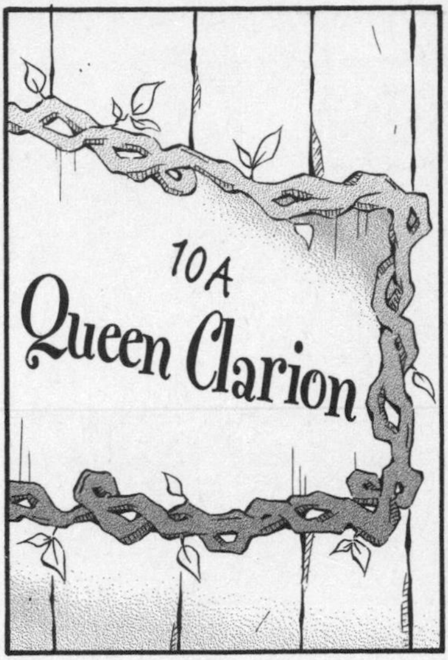
10A
Queen Clarion

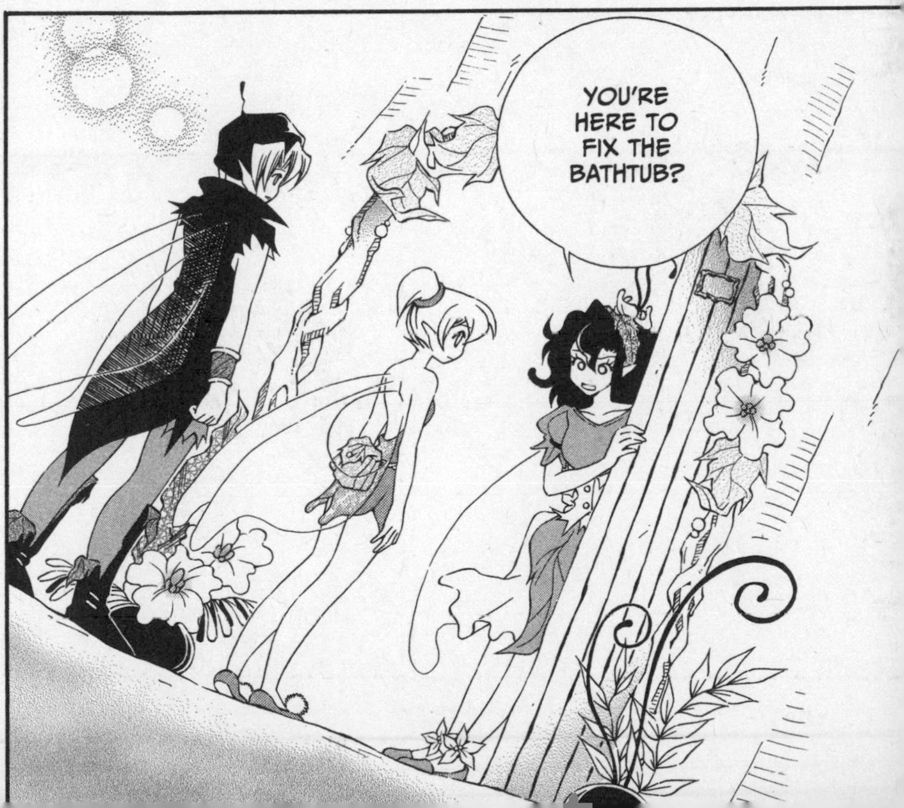
YOU'RE HERE TO FIX THE BATHTUB?

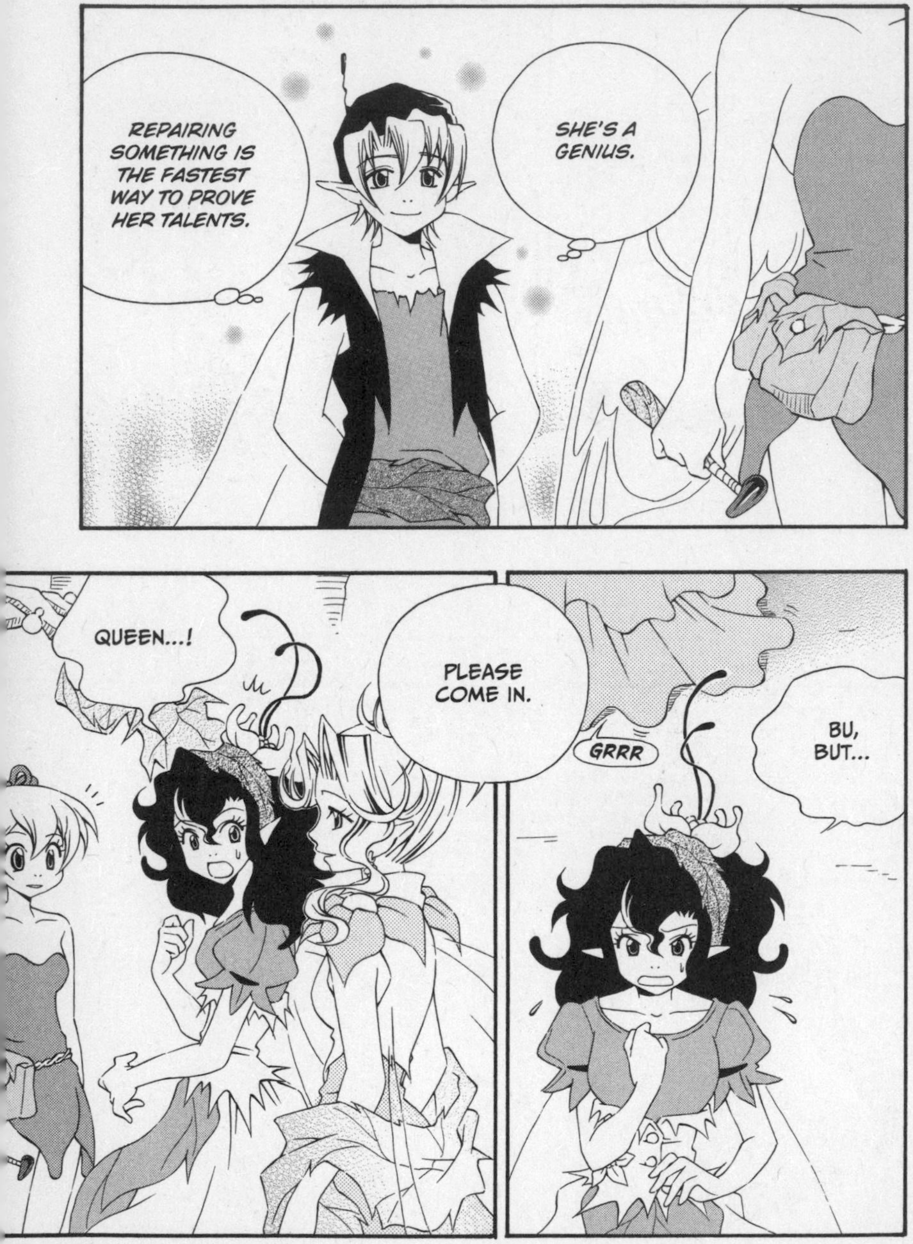
SHE'S A GENIUS.
REPAIRING SOMETHING IS THE FASTEST WAY TO PROVE HER TALENTS.
BU, BUT...
GRRR
PLEASE COME IN.
QUEEN...!

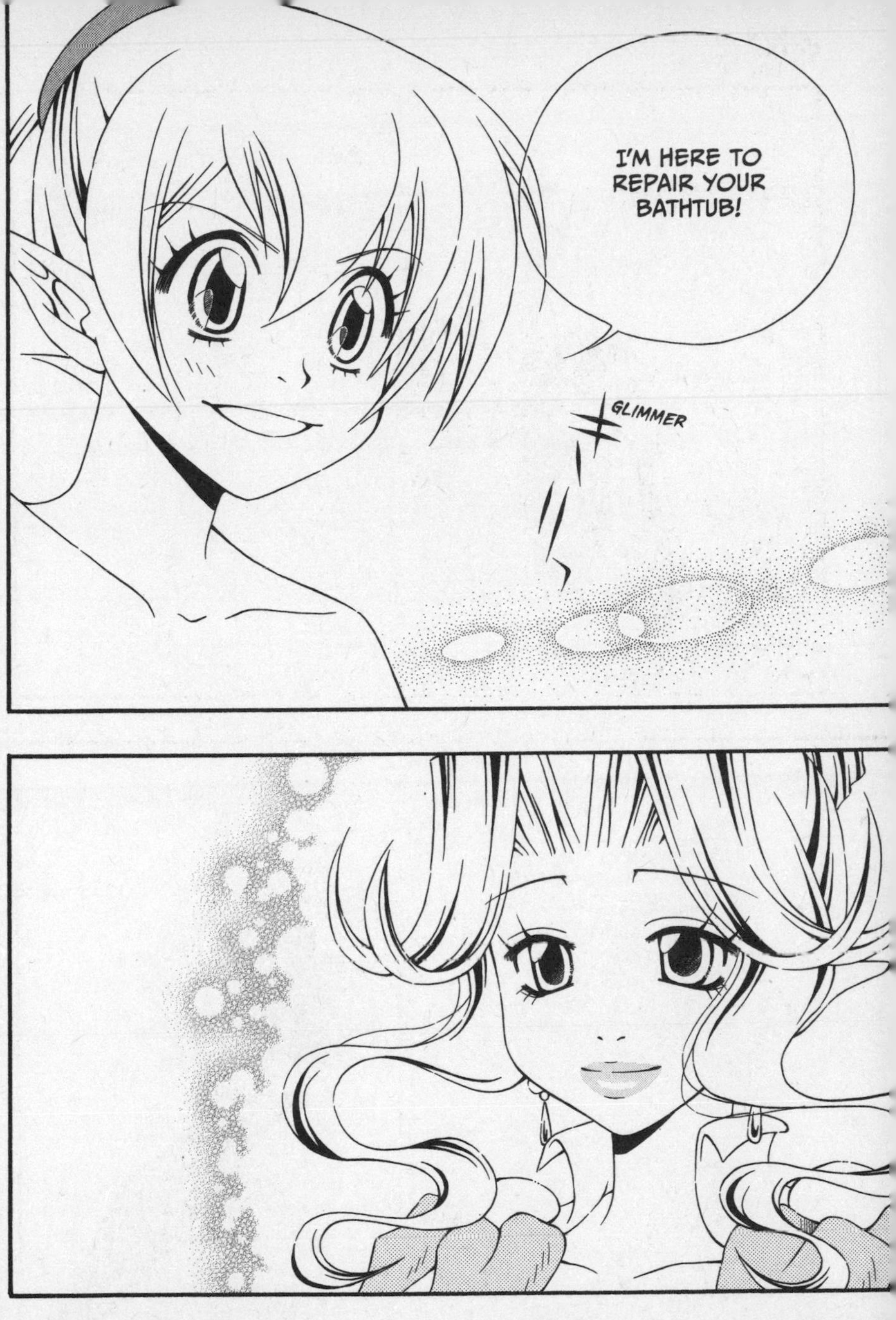
I'M HERE TO REPAIR YOUR BATHTUB!
GLIMMER

READ THIS WAY

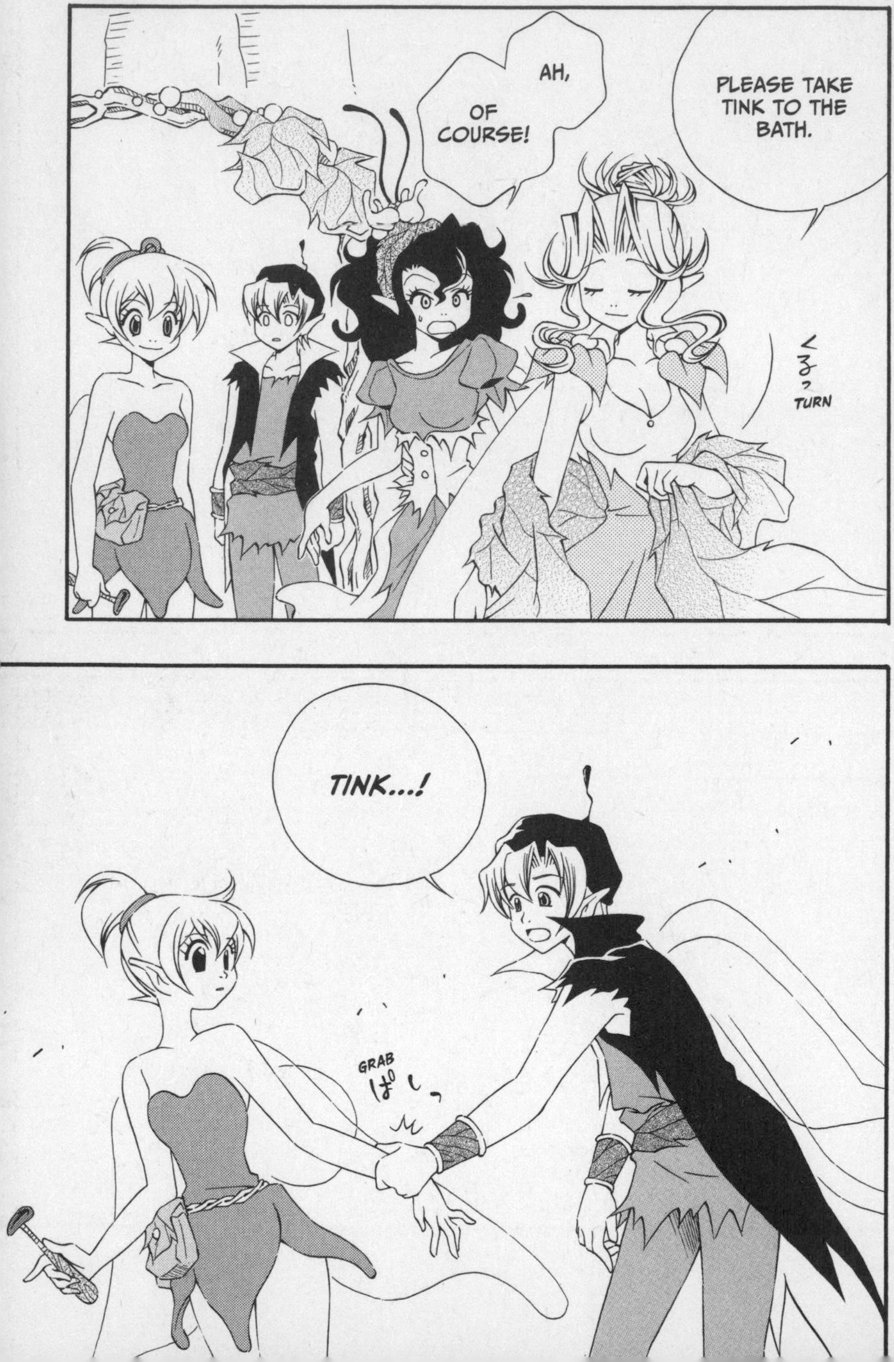
PLEASE TAKE TINK TO THE BATH.
くるっ
TURN
AH, OF COURSE!
TINK...!
GRAB
ぱしっ

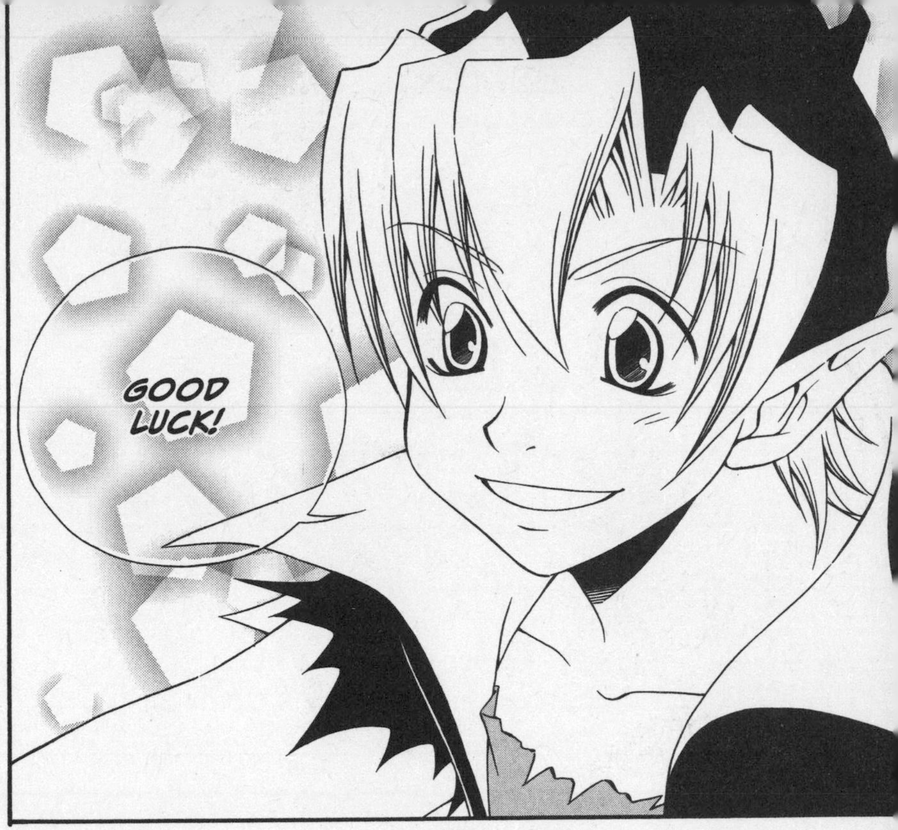
GOOD
LUCK!

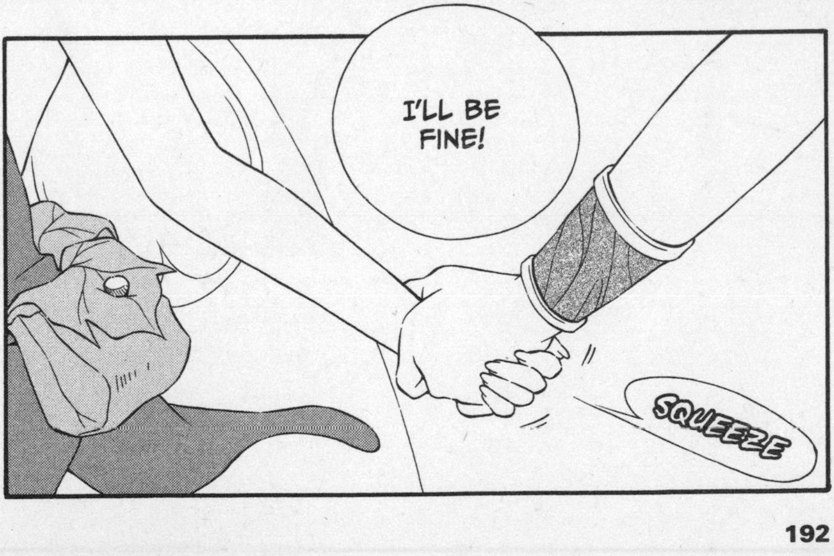
I'LL BE
FINE!
SQUEEZE

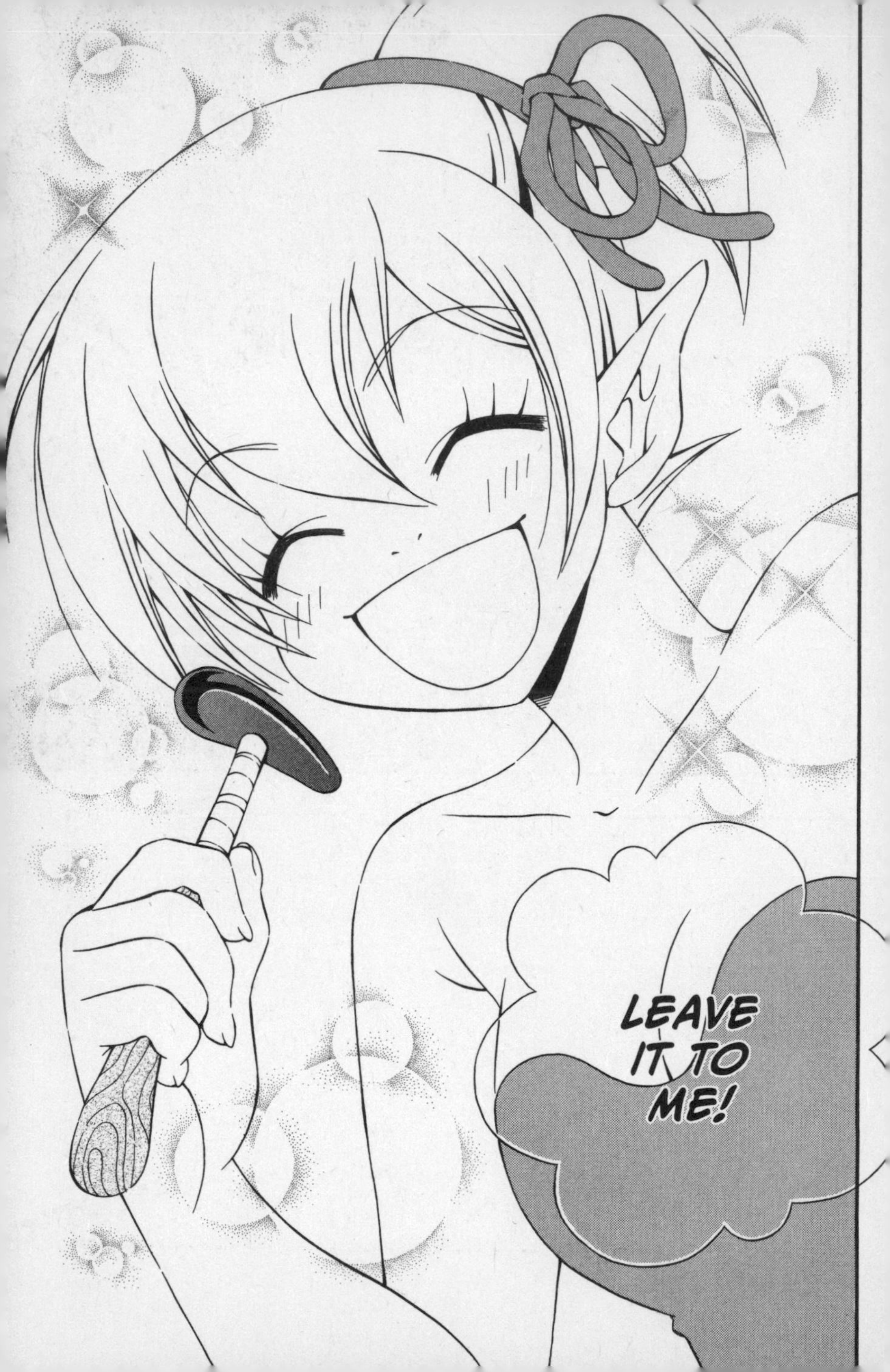
LEAVE IT TO ME!

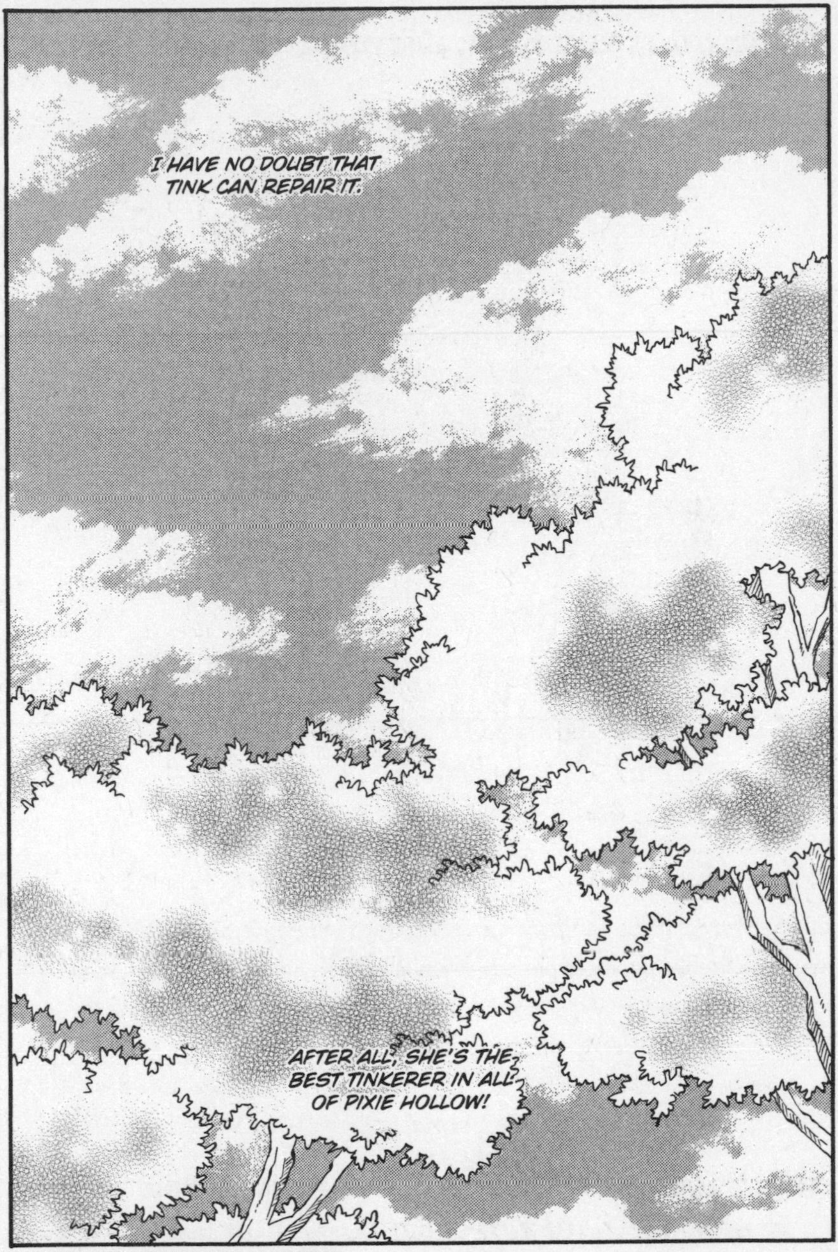
I HAVE NO DOUBT THAT TINK CAN REPAIR IT.
AFTER ALL, SHE'S THE BEST TINKERER IN ALL OF PIXIE HOLLOW!

THE END OF TINKER BELL'S SECRET

Check out the next Disney Fairies Manga!

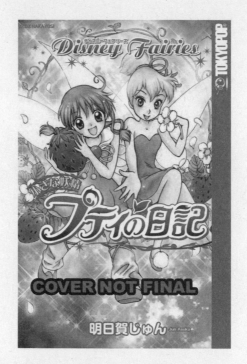

The Petite Fairy's Diary

Petite is the smallest -- and clumsiest -- fairy in all of Never land's Pixie Hollow. She's even smaller than a bug! With the Moon Ceremony coming up soon, the Fledgling Fairies are preparing to present their talents in order to graduate as Major Fairies, but Petite hasn't found hers yet! With Tinker Bell's help, can Petite discover her talent before the biggest celebration of her lifetime begins?

Join Petite and the rest of the Pixie Hollow fairies in another whimsical Disney Manga adventure filled with hijinks, romance and pixie dust!

Let's Count!

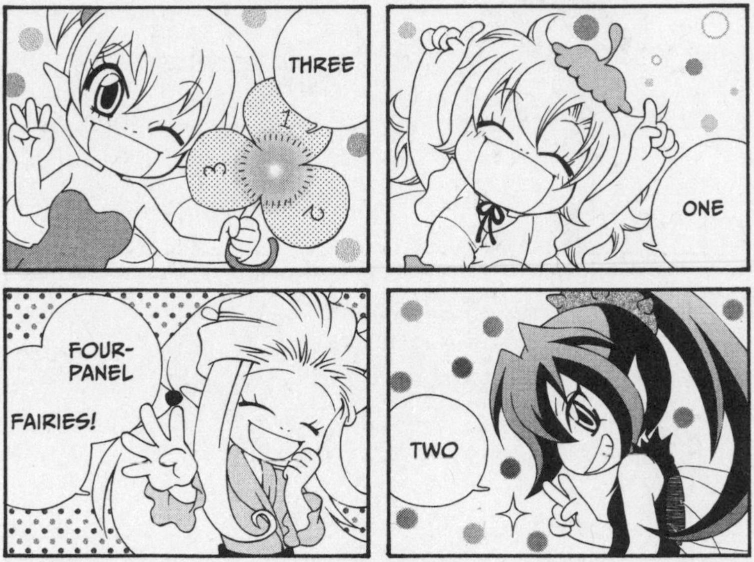
ONE
TWO
THREE
FOUR-PANEL FAIRIES!

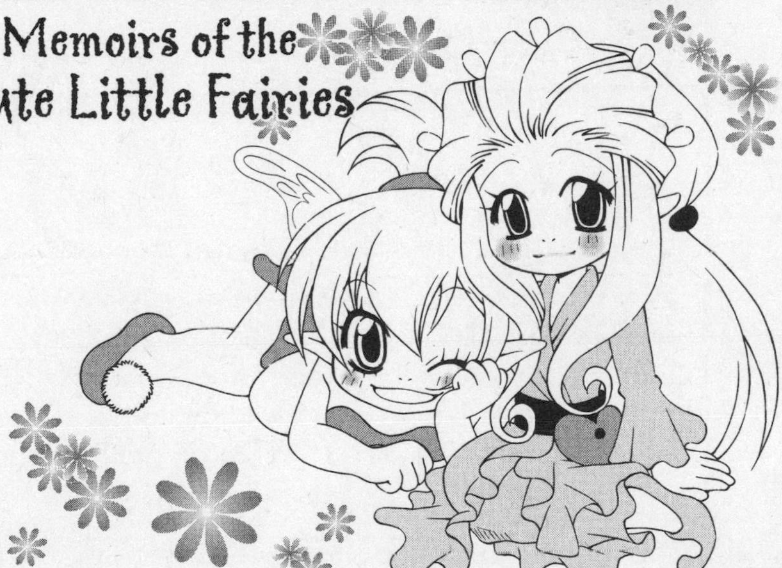
Memoirs of the Cute Little Fairies

Memoirs of the Cute Little Fairies

How many hearts are there?

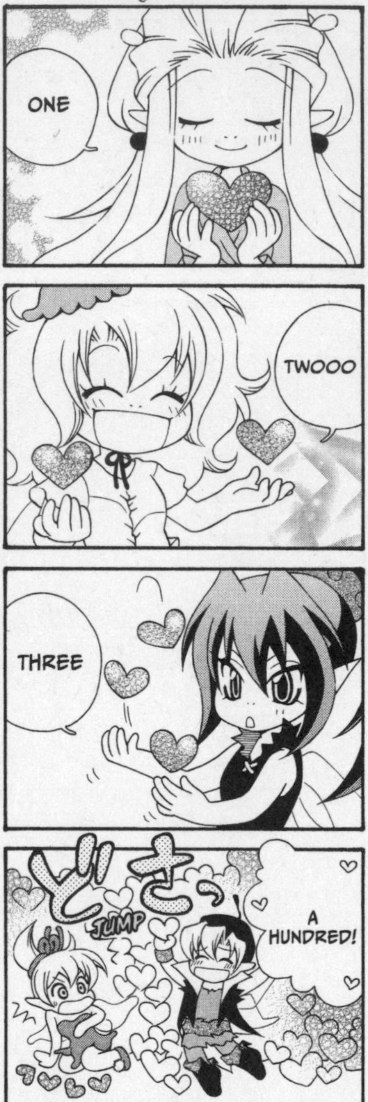
ONE
TWOOO
THREE
どさっ
A HUNDRED!
JUMP

Go for it, Terence!

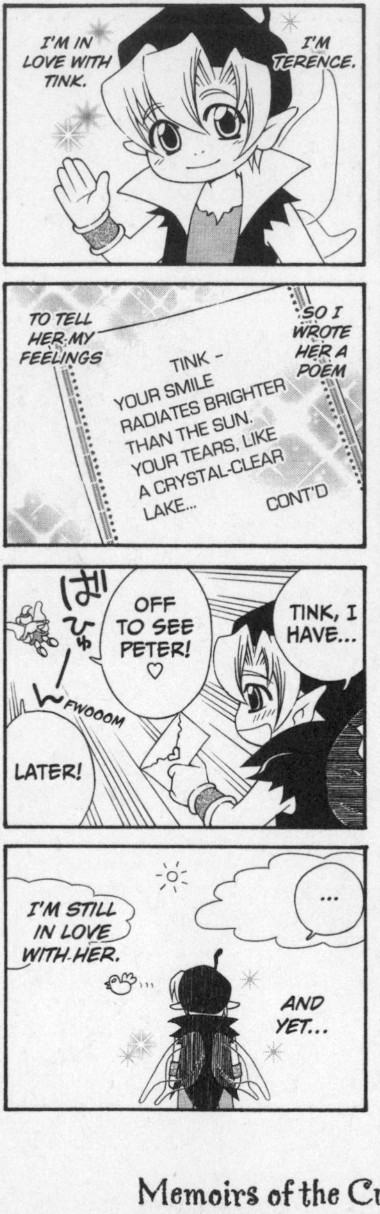
I'M TERENCE.
I'M IN LOVE WITH TINK.
SO I WROTE HER A POEM
TO TELL HER MY FEELINGS
TINK - YOUR SMILE RADIATES BRIGHTER THAN THE SUN. YOUR TEARS, LIKE A CRYSTAL-CLEAR LAKE...
CONT'D
TINK, I HAVE...
OFF TO SEE PETER! ♡
ぱひゅーん
FWOOOM
LATER!
...
I'M STILL IN LOVE WITH HER.
AND YET...

To be continued in volume 3... maybe.

Memoirs of the Cute Little Fairies

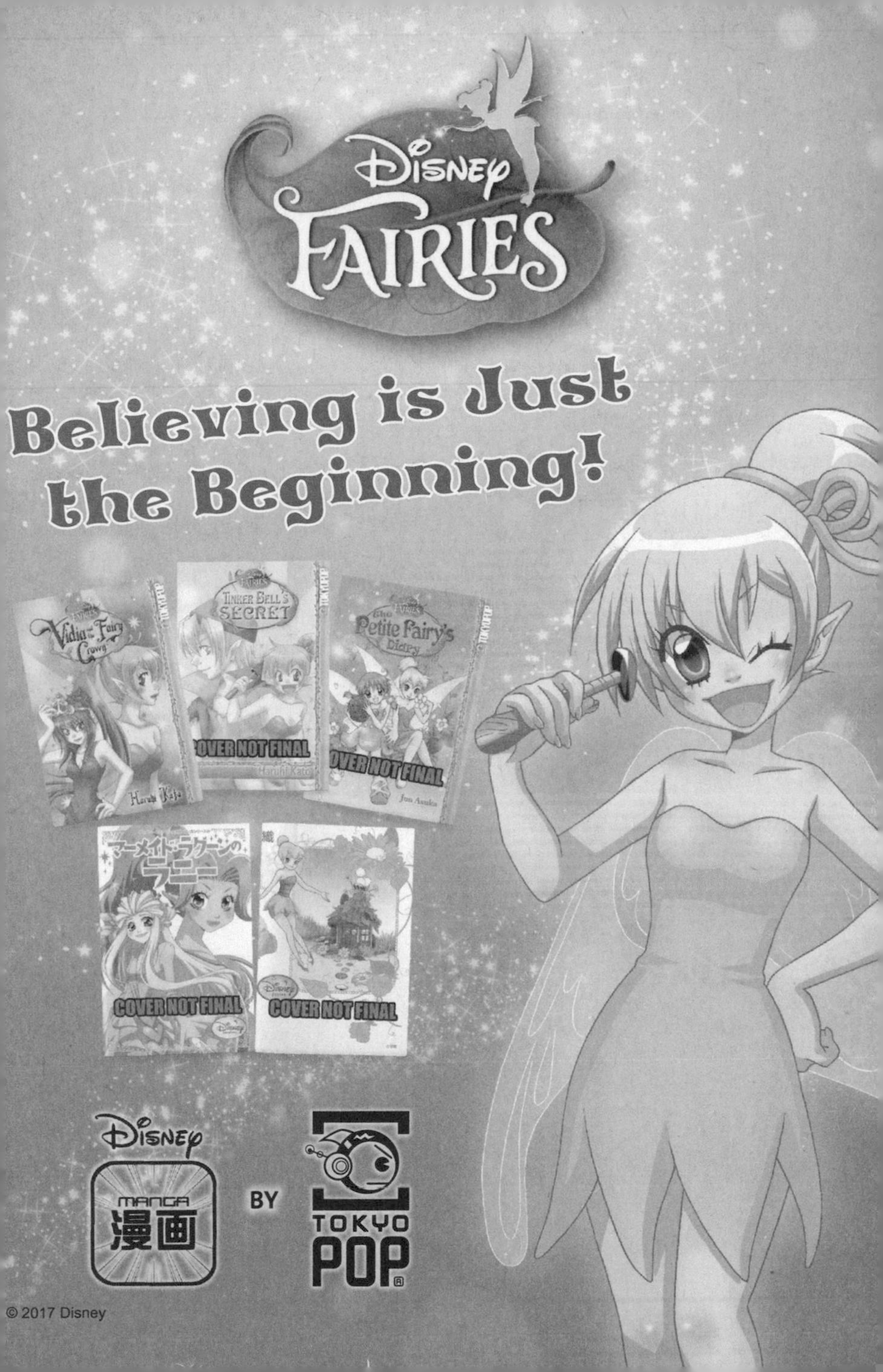
Disney
FAIRIES
Believing is Just the Beginning!
TINKER BELL'S SECRET
Petite Fairy's Diary
COVER NOT FINAL
Haruhi Kato
Jun Asuka
マーメイド・ラグーンの
ラニー
COVER NOT FINAL
COVER NOT FINAL
Disney
MANGA
漫画
BY
TOKYO
POP

MAGICAL ★ DANCE

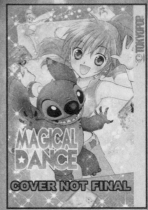

MAGICAL ★ DANCE

COVER NOT FINAL

Rin joins a troupe with her fellow students and soon realizes that she has two left feet. She practices day and night but is discouraged by the lack of results and almost gives up on her dreams. Impressed by her passion and dedication, Tinker Bell appears to give her a little encouragement in the form of Disney magic!

FROM THE CREATOR OF DISNEY KILALA PRINCESS!

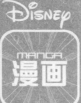

Disney

MANGA
漫画

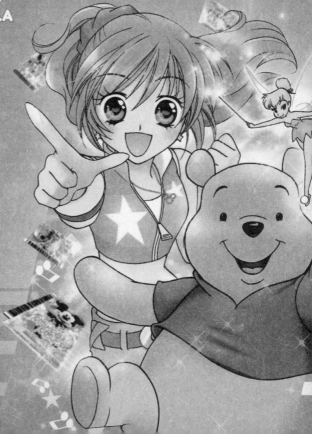

DESCENDANTS

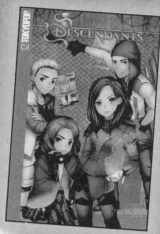

Full color manga trilogy based on the hit Disney Channel original movie

Inspired by the original stories of Disney's classic heroes and villains

Experience this spectacular movie in manga form!

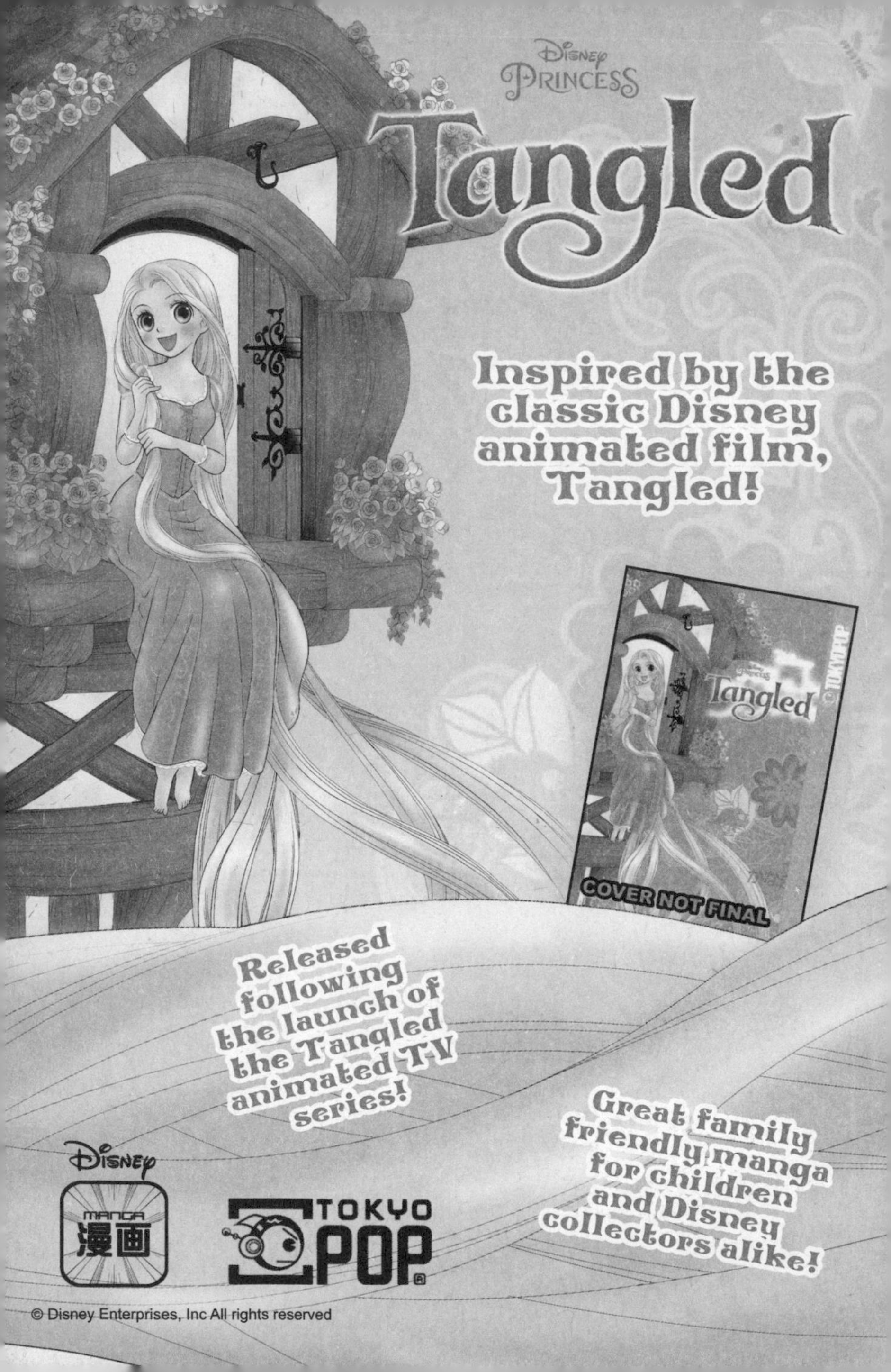
Disney Princess
Tangled
Inspired by the classic Disney animated film, Tangled!
Disney Princess Tangled TOKYOPOP
COVER NOT FINAL
Released following the launch of the Tangled the animated TV series!
Great family friendly manga for children and Disney collectors alike!
Disney
MANGA 漫画
TOKYO POP
© Disney Enterprises, Inc All rights reserved

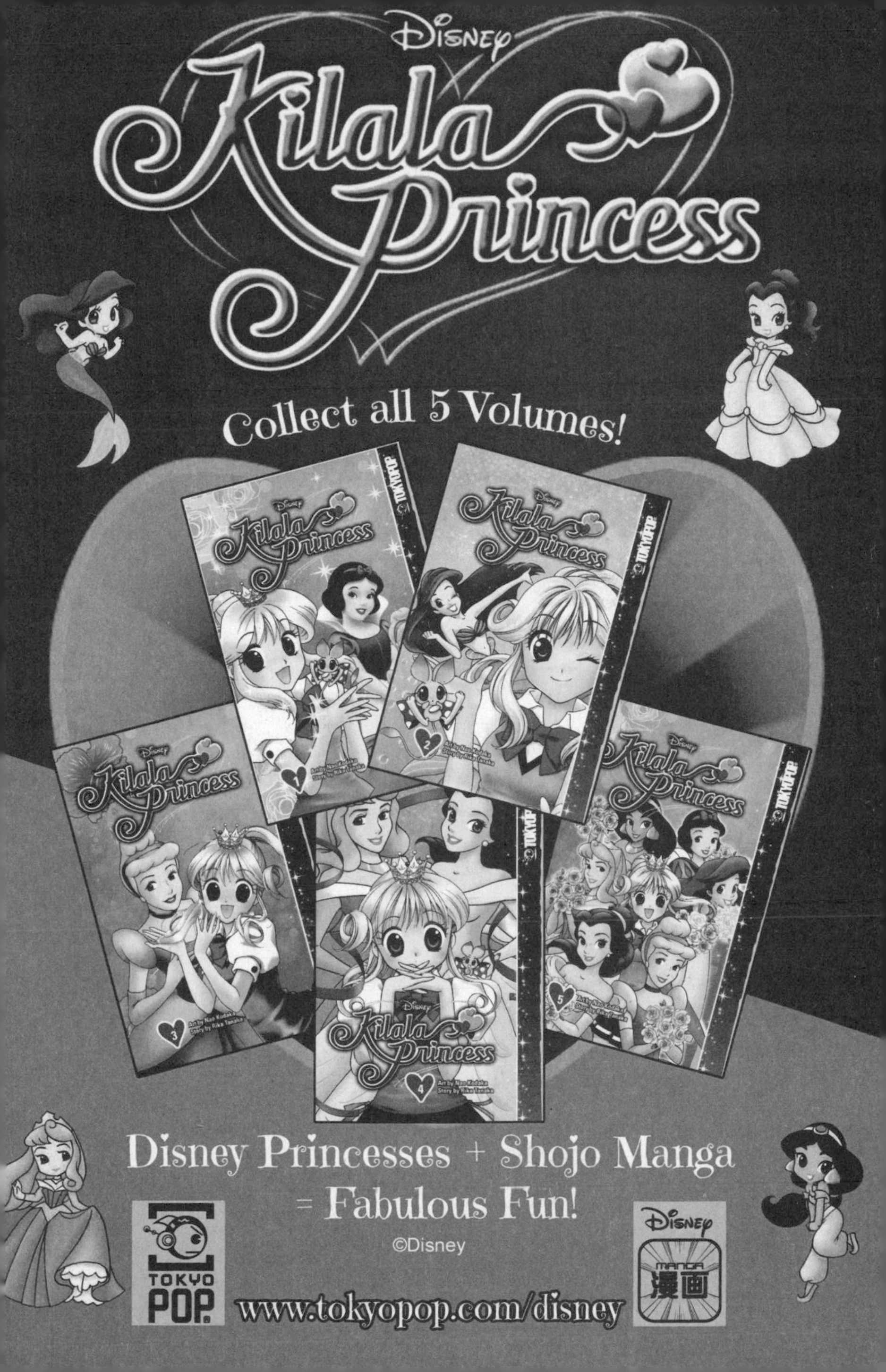
Disney
Kilala Princess
Collect all 5 Volumes!
Disney Princesses + Shojo Manga
= Fabulous Fun!
©Disney
TOKYO POP
www.tokyopop.com/disney
Disney
MANGA
漫画

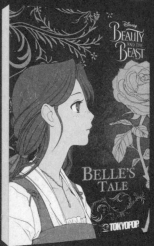
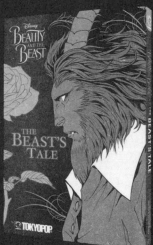

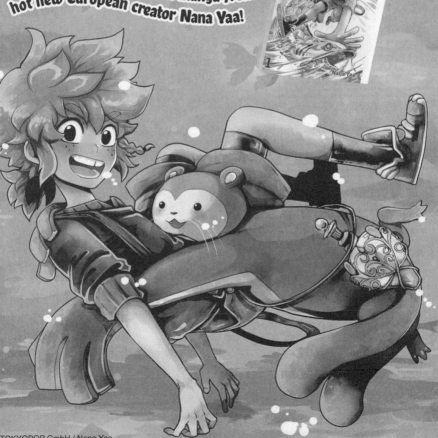

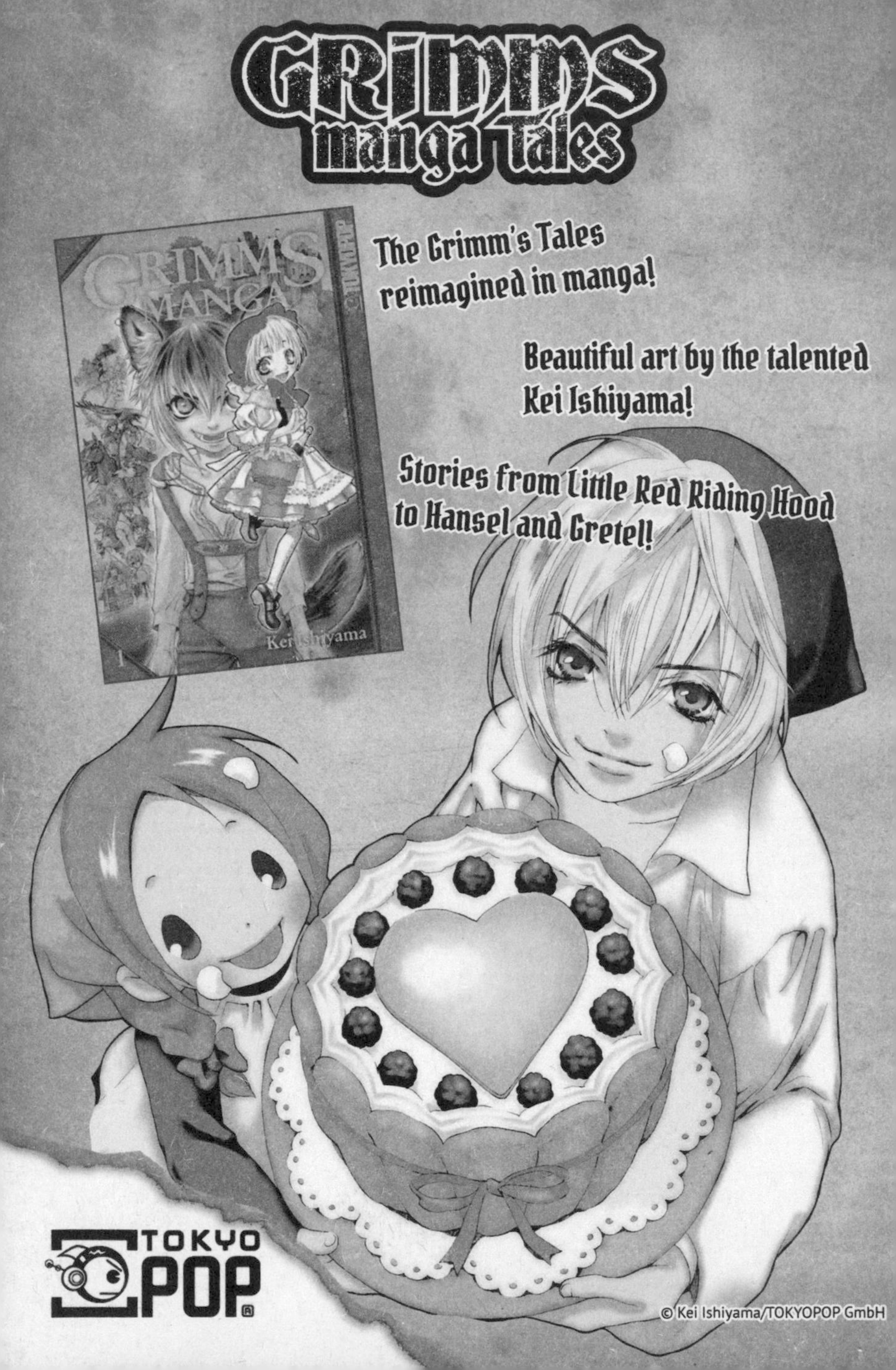
GRIMMS manga Tales
GRIMMS MANGA
TOKYOPOP
Kei Ishiyama
1
The Grimm's Tales reimagined in manga!
Beautiful art by the talented Kei Ishiyama!
Stories from Little Red Riding Hood to Hansel and Gretel!
TOKYO POP
© Kei Ishiyama/TOKYOPOP GmbH

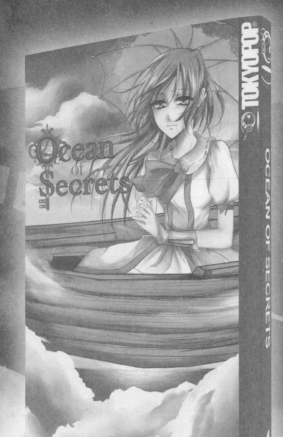

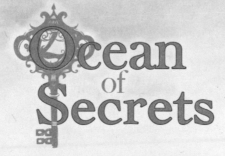

Disney Fairies: Tinker Bell's Secret
Manga by: Haruhi Kato

Publishing Assistant - Janae Young
Marketing Assistant - Kae Winters
Technology and Digital Media Assistant - Phillip Hong
Retouching and Lettering - Vibrraant Publishing Studio
Translations - Jason Muell
Graphic Designer - Phillip Hong
Copy Editor - M. Cara Carper
Editor-in-Chief & Publisher - Stu Levy

A 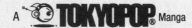 Manga

TOKYOPOP and 🐱 are trademarks or registered trademarks of TOKYOPOP Inc.

TOKYOPOP inc.
5200 W Century Blvd
Suite 705
Los Angeles, CA 90045 USA

E-mail: info@TOKYOPOP.com
Come visit us online at www.TOKYOPOP.com

f www.facebook.com/TOKYOPOP
🐦 www.twitter.com/TOKYOPOP
▶ www.youtube.com/TOKYOPOPTV
𝔭 www.pinterest.com/TOKYOPOP
📷 www.instagram.com/TOKYOPOP
t. TOKYOPOP.tumblr.com

ISBN: 978-1-4278-5700-2
First TOKYOPOP Printing: August 2017
10 9 8 7 6 5 4 3 2 1
Printed in CANADA

STOP

THIS IS THE

How do you re
just start in the top right panel and follow the numbers:

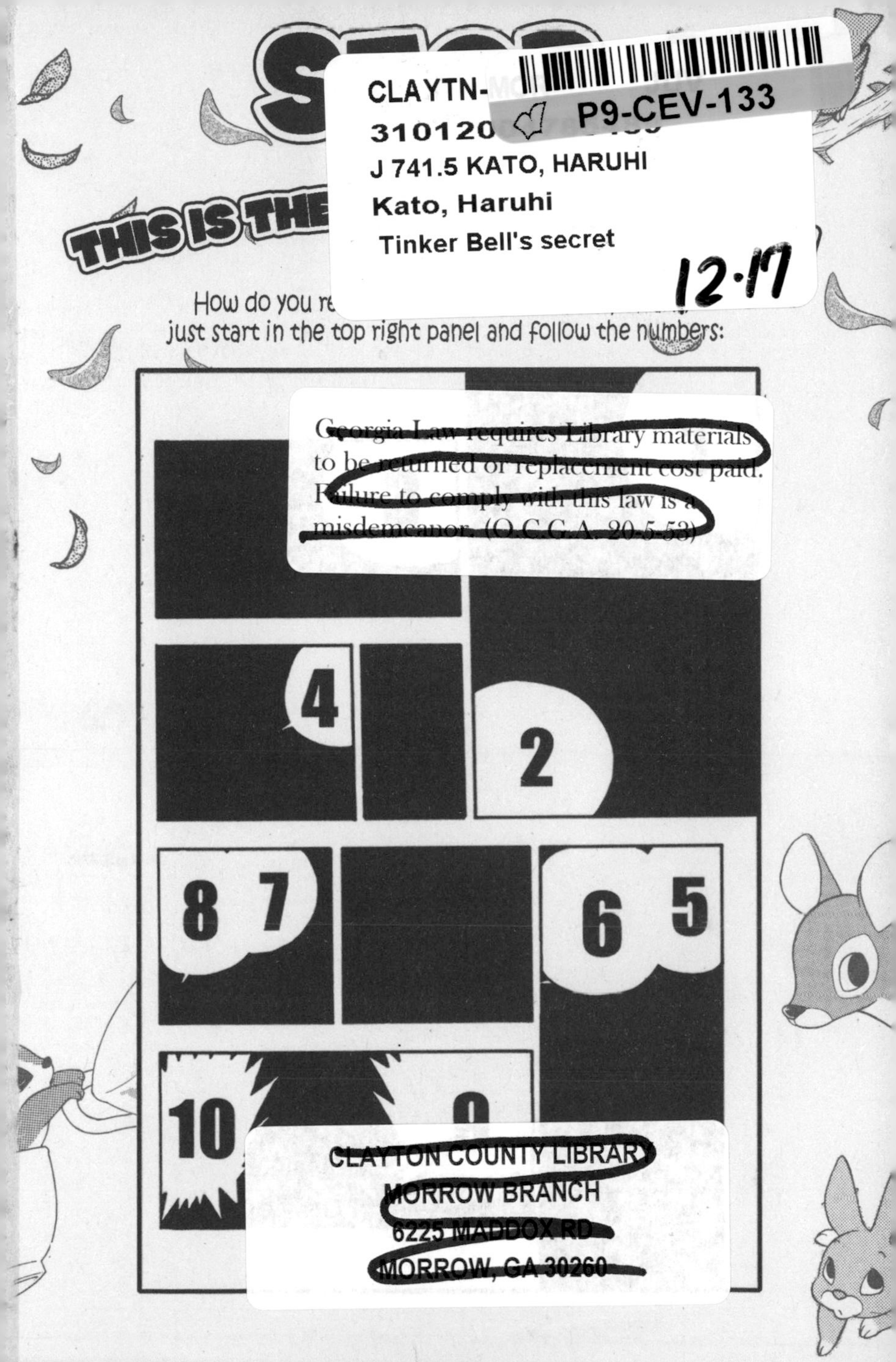
2
4
5
6
7
8
10